ABOUT THE AUTHOR

D0534067

Linguist, international businessman, BBC Television Producer/Director, impresario . . . Douglas Boyd's life took many turnings before he became a full-time author. None of them, he says, had such an impact as the time he served with the RAF in divided Berlin, where his military service as a Russian linguist ended with him behind the bars of an East German political prison, followed by the threat of further incarceration on his return to Britain. He has drawn on this experience in the writing of this book.

His three previous best-selling novels *The Eagle and the Snake*, *The Honour and the Glory* and *The Truth and the Lies* are available in Warner paperback and his fifth novel, *The Fiddler and The Ferret*, is published by Little, Brown and Company.

Douglas Boyd

THE

VIRGIN

AND THE

FOOL

WARNER BOOKS

A *Warner* Book

First published in Great Britain in 1996
by Little, Brown and Company

This edition published by Warner Books in 1997
Reprinted in 1998 (twice)

A CIP catalogue record for this book is
available from the British Library.

ISBN 0 7515 1922 7

Typeset in Sabon by M Rules
Printed and bound in Great Britain by
Clays Ltd, St Ives plc

Warner Books
A Division of
Little, Brown and Company (UK)
Brettenham House
Lancaster Place
London WC2E 7EN

For Jenny

PART I
August 1995

On the far side of the globe, Europe was still gasping its way through the hot dry summer of 1995 but on the peninsula of Kamchatka, jutting out into the Bering Sea far to the north of Japan, the last day of August was virtually the end of the brief Siberian summer.

On the way up Mount Tolbachik, the second highest volcano in Siberia, the half-track had had to plough its way through hub-deep snow in places. It had been stolen or illicitly sold from some Red Army depot and still had the painted star and serial number showing on both sides. Four years after the collapse of the Soviet Union, nobody in Siberia bothered even to try to conceal the theft of government property.

As the vehicle neared the crater at 16,000 feet above sea level, the snow thinned to sparse patches. Most of the flakes driven on the gale-force wind melted the moment they touched the smoking earth. From a thousand fumaroles and a million small cracks sulphurous fumes oozed; without the wind the smell would have been overpowering. Above the roof of the half-track the cloud base was so close that, at 5.30 p.m., it was already dusk.

The driver braked jerkily to a halt. He was a Koryak, with features most Westerners would have taken for Japanese. His people had roamed the forests and mountains of the region before the first Cossack trappers arrived from the west and long before the American whalers came from the east. His grandfather had worshipped the mountain and offered sacrifices every spring: living animals hurled into the fiery maw of the volcano to guarantee good hunting in the year ahead. The legends of his people spoke of other sacrifices in earlier times: a first-born son had been the best gift the tribe could offer. The Koryak was wondering – but without any particular expectations – whether the mountain god would be grateful for the offering of the living, breathing woman sitting behind him.

Through the windscreen of the half-track, for as far as the eye could see, was a monochrome panorama of lunar desolation in which man-size cinder excrescences were dotted across an ash-field the colour of breeze blocks, looking like a ghostly army of petrified soldiers on parade. The last few hundred feet of the mountain's mighty bulk were invisible except where a fiery glow pierced the murk overhead from time to time with a loud roar, as though a blast furnace fuelled by the fires of hell had been briefly tapped by its attendant demons.

As a vulcanologist of twenty years' experience, Karen McKenzie knew better than most people exactly how dangerous it was to be where they were. The roar of the unmuffled engine died as the Koryak turned the key in the ignition, leaving her to analyse the ambient noises, checking them out one by one from habit: the creaking and groaning of molten rock on the move, the hissing of gases escaping under pressure, and underlying both, a series of rumbling subterranean explosions like a drum-roll played by some infernal tympanist on the very skin of the planet.

'You took the wrong turn,' Karen told the driver. 'I told you before, where the track forked, we should have turned right for Atlasovo, not left. This way just leads to the crater. Right now, you can't even get that far.'

She pointed ahead to where a narrow stream of lava from a lateral vent cut the track. Couldn't the man see there was no way across it? Why was he just sitting there, doing nothing?

Taking his silence for indecision, she warned, 'For God's sake don't try and turn here. The cinder crust is very thin. Your tracks may be okay but once the front wheels go through, the tyres will melt in the hot ash beneath. Take my advice and reverse down the track as far as the fork.'

The man behind her on the rear seat was a Siberian with a broken nose and eyes hidden in rolls of fat that showed Eskimo blood somewhere in his line. When he launched into a torrent of Russian slang that Karen had no chance of following, she turned round. 'You're lost,' she insisted. 'This is not the way to the logging camp at Atlasovo.'

The Siberian jerked a dirty thumb at the Koryak. '*On radílsya zdyes*. He born here. He know mountain real good.'

Why are they both so pig-headed? she asked herself. It was obvious there was no way forward.

'Get out!' said the Siberian, speaking English for the first time, with a strong American accent. 'You get outta da car, okay?'

'You're joking,' Karen protested. 'Without an asbestos suit and a hard hat . . .'

A rock the size of a man's fist hit the half-track's corrugated metal roof and bounced off, reinforcing her point.

'Out!' he repeated.

She felt the muzzle of an automatic pistol pressed hard behind her left ear and in the rear-view mirror she saw the Siberian's eyes, dead and dispassionate. Another shower of small rocks landed off to their right. Lightning, generated by the electromagnetic energy of the volcano, crackled in the

clouds above their heads as she climbed out of the car backwards and stood facing the men, realising too late that they
had not lost the way but brought her to this desolate spot
quite deliberately, in order to kill her.

It was not the first time she had been at the wrong end of
a gun. Years before on Mount Nyiragongo, an active volcano
on the Zairean border, she had been kidnapped by a group of
armed rebels. 'Always look them in the face,' was the advice
of the nuns at the mission hospital where she had been locked
up for the night with several other whites. 'Whatever you
do – don't turn your back on them.'

That time she had stood her ground, refusing to cringe
like a victim in front of the giggling, excited teenage boys
nervously fingering their assault rifles and hyping each other
up to kill. She did the same now, unsure how much the trembling in her knees was due to the vibration of the ground on
which she stood and how much came from visceral fear of
the two hard-faced men who, she sensed, would end her life
with as little compunction as when they killed, skinned and
gutted a seal or a horse for food.

'This is all a mistake,' she stammered. '*Eto oshíbka. Ya
tólko geológ i nyé bogáta* – not rich, understand?'

The Koryak was pulling a sawn-off military shotgun from
beneath an old sack behind his seat. After cocking the ham-
mers, he kept the side-by-side barrels pointing at Karen's
face so that the muzzles resembled two baleful eyes glaring at
her. Like a flashbulb, a jagged line of lightning imprinted on
her retina the image of his broken, dirty nails. He was only a
boy, she saw, barely out of his teens. He had the small frame
and wiry build of someone who had known hunger throughout childhood. His hair was cut short as though he had
recently finished his military service. The Siberian thumbed
the safety catch of his automatic and she saw clearly in the
light of another lightning flash the name *Makarov* engraved
on the side of the weapon.

'Why?' she asked. '*Pochemú?*'

'*Ya nyé znáyu.*' The Koryak motioned her away from the half-track, neither knowing nor caring who had ordered this killing or why.

Another flash of lightning imprinted on Karen's memory the image of the Siberian's face. The only distinguishing mark on his slab-like features was a large brown wart by the left nostril. The collar of his shirt was threadbare, with holes that had been neatly darned, presumably by a wife. Did she know what her husband did for a living?

The two men separated and came towards her, one on either side of the track. Karen took one step and then another backwards, keeping a constant distance from them as they herded her towards the gully where the lava flowed. Each time she put down a booted foot, she felt the ground carefully, fearful of stumbling or provoking them to shoot by some sudden movement.

Panic prevented her brain from working. She clenched her hands, digging the nails into her palms, and tried to stop herself from hyperventilating by reciting under her breath a rhyme she had learned long ago in an Ontario schoolyard – an ocean and a continent away to the east: 'Women are dying, babies are crying. Concentrate!'

The two men kept their distance, taking one step for two of her paces. They were nervous of being so near the crater and wanted to get the job finished as soon as possible. They could have killed her where she stood, but that would mean carrying her corpse to the lava stream. So they chose the lazier alternative of making her walk to her own cremation. Within minutes of her body being thrown, alive or dead, into the molten lava, it would be reduced to a handful of carbon and a puff of water vapour.

Karen was dressed for the mountain in thick-soled boots, heavy jeans and a winter-weight anorak which blocked some of the heat but even so she could feel the skin on the back of her neck starting to burn as she neared the gully. Irrationally, she thought, If only I hadn't put my hair up this morning . . .

She risked a look behind and judged there were fewer than twenty paces to go.

Nineteen, she counted. Eighteen. Seventeen. Sixteen.

At fifteen, she felt icy calm. Her mind was made up. She told herself that Tolbachik was on her side, because she knew the volcano better than these men who might have spent their lives in its shadow yet were as ignorant of its workings as the Sicilian peasants who still believed Mount Etna to be a gigantic subterranean forge where the smith-god Vulcan made lightning for Jupiter, Zeus-Pateras, God the Father . . .

'*Davái chasy!*' the Siberian shouted. He transferred the Makarov to his left hand and beckoned to Karen, intending to snatch her watch before killing her.

As his fingers closed around her wrist another shower of cinder bombs came out of the cloud after a particularly loud explosion in the murk above them that had the ground quaking beneath their feet. A smoking boulder large enough to kill a man landed only a few metres away with a puff of grey dust, making both men flinch instinctively. Karen grabbed the chance to wrench her hand free and pulled the hood of her anorak over her head, leaving just a narrow gap to see through. Then she was running in a straight line for the lava wall behind which the yellow-red stream of molten rock was hissing, crackling and groaning its way downhill.

The men let her go. Why waste a bullet to kill a woman who was running towards certain death? They saw her outlined against the orange glare, the unzipped anorak flapping around her slim figure as she scrambled up the bank of solidified lava that edged the gully. At the top, Karen stopped, both arms wildly flailing as she fought for balance before toppling out of sight with a brief scream that reached them over all the other noises.

The Koryak zipped up his anorak and pulled the hood across his face to shield it from the worst of the heat. He handed the shotgun to the other man, then scrambled up onto the lip of the gully and stood exactly where Karen had been a moment before. In front of him the gully was nearly two metres wide. In places upstream and downstream it was considerably narrower because of a tendency for the sides of the channel to roof over and form a tunnel. But even there no sane person would try to jump across.

Half-blinded by the glare from below, he turned and squinted downstream into the flow of molten rock, looking for any sign of a human body. There was nothing to see.

He jumped down from the levee, hurrying after his companion who was already halfway back to the vehicle.

'*Oná myórtva!*' he cried: she's dead.

PART II
June 1982 onwards

.1.

Tom Fielding walked out of the bookshop at the top of Park Street. Below him lay the city and port of Bristol, fuzzy in the heat haze of the first really hot day that summer. He turned his back on the Victorian Gothic might of the Wills Memorial Building and strolled down the hill, leafing through the pages of the book he had just bought.

In a university city like Bristol he was immediately identifiable as gown, not town. At twenty-eight he looked younger than some of his own students. Above the thoughtful hazel eyes a shock of unruly fair hair looked as though it had never felt a brush or comb. His clothes were cheap and chosen for comfort: a light windcheater, faded blue jeans and Jesus sandals on his bare feet.

Passing a newspaper stand, he took in the felt-tipped headline out of the corner of his eye. *THE END IS NEAR!* referred not to the Second Coming but to the Falklands War between Britain and Argentina, now in its final stages.

At the bottom of the hill, too immersed in his book to

look where he was going, he stumbled on an uneven paving slab and stubbed his big toe. The pain made him look up and take an interest in his surroundings. The grass of College Green was covered with office workers eating their lunchtime sandwiches outside on this first day of summer. Among them was the unmistakable figure of the man Tom was hoping to see.

Seated on a wooden bench in front of the cathedral, bursting out of his crumpled red-and-cream striped seersucker suit, Professor Michael Ashmole was obviously suffering from the heat. Above the fleshy jowls, his forehead shone with perspiration which he mopped from time to time with a large red polka-dot handkerchief, replaced in his breast pocket after each use.

In contrast, the girl sitting beside him looked cool and alert. She was in her mid-twenties, wore no make-up and had mid-brown hair cut close to the head like a boy's. Lean and fit, she was unmistakably North American from the trainers on her feet to the designer jeans, Toronto University tee-shirt and heavy tortoiseshell frames of her spectacles.

Tom had been trying for two weeks to get confirmation from Ashmole that his short-term contract as a lecturer in the history department would be renewed next term, so he sat down on the next bench to wait for the conversation to end.

Whether from affectation or bad memory, the professor rarely used the correct name when addressing members of his staff.

'John,' he called, blinking over the top of his gold-rimmed half-moon glasses. 'You're the very person. Let me introduce you to a fellow Russian scholar, Miss . . .'

He waved a podgy paw at the girl on the bench beside him, who stretched out a hand. 'Karen,' she said. 'Karen McKenzie. Nice to meet you, John.'

Her grip was surprisingly strong for such a petite build. 'The name's Tom,' he corrected her. 'Tom Fielding.'

She looked baffled.

'John teaches a course in Russian history,' Ashmole was saying in his plummy voice. 'But his hobby is exploring local archives. If you're so interested in Bristol's exciting past, I couldn't leave you with a better man. Now, if you'll excuse me, I have another appointment.'

He moved with surprising speed for such an unathletic person and was fifty paces away before Tom saw the pile of books left on the bench and snatched them up, to run after Ashmole.

'Professor! You left these behind.'

Ashmole peered through his glasses at the topmost book. The lenses were so dirty and scratched that it must have been hard to see through them. There was a library reservation slip bearing his name stuck into the pocket pasted inside the front cover.

'So I did,' the professor muttered. '*Fossil Man in Spain* by Obermaier? Why ever did I reserve that, do you suppose?'

'I've been trying to talk to you for the last two weeks,' Tom said. 'About my lectures next term. I really do need to know . . .'

'Terribly busy just now, John.' Ashmole's podgy paw kneaded Tom's arm. 'Have a word with my secretary. She'll tell you when I'm free.'

Before Tom could stop him, he darted between the traffic coming down the hill and was gone. Angry at the brush-off, Tom made his way back to the bench, to find Karen laughing.

'He made my day,' she gasped. 'He really did. Less than twenty-four hours off the plane and I meet that legendary English phenomenon, the absent-minded professor.'

'It's an act,' Tom snapped. 'When Ashmole wants something, he's astute and quite ruthless.'

'Astute and ruthless?' The words did not fit the image of a bumbling academic that Ashmole had left in Karen's mind.

Tom nodded. 'He was given a personal chair here three

years ago. Within eighteen months he had managed to early-retire the previous head of department and grab his job. The prof is only incompetent when it comes to unimportant things like remembering people's names. He's also very well connected. The rumour is that he has powerful friends in Whitehall who enabled him to jump the queue.'

'How wrong can you be?' Karen wondered. 'I'm right about one thing, though. He doesn't like women much, does he?'

'Sitting on this bench was probably the nearest he's been to one in weeks.' Tom looked at his watch, about to make an excuse to go. 'So you're a Russian scholar?'

Karen shook her head. 'The professor got confused. My subject is geology. It was my great-grandmother who was Russian.'

'*Ty govorísh pa-rússki?*'

She answered fluently but with an old-fashioned accent.

'Got it,' Tom said. 'Doukhobors.'

Intrigued at meeting a descendant of the religious refugees who had fled to North America in the nineteenth century, he sat down beside her. 'Tell me about your family.'

'The Russian side?'

He nodded.

'Well, great-grandma Dudinskaya came over in 1899. I never knew her, but my grandma brought up me and my sister when Pop died and Mom took over the business – she's an architect. Doodie didn't learn to speak English properly until she was eighteen.'

'Doodie?'

Karen laughed. 'Grandma Dudinskaya. She taught my sister and me Russian as a sort of secret language which the three of us shared. I guess our accents would sound pretty weird to a Soviet.'

'They'd probably shoot you on sight as a White revanchist.'

'Don't joke,' she said. 'When I told Doodie that I was

coming to Europe, she made me promise never to go to Russia. For her, having grown up in the closed Doukhobor community, it's still the land of the devil.'

'So what were you and Ashmole talking about?' Tom asked.

'I was networking,' Karen grimaced. 'Ashmole's sister is married to my professor at the U of T, so I got an introduction to him, in case he could be any help – but he wasn't. I'm doing a doctorate on Mount Etna. Geologists are very possessive, and since it's a British volcano, any introduction I can get . . .'

'I thought Etna was in Sicily.'

'It is,' she agreed. 'But the British kind of own it scientifically, if you know what I mean. They're not so keen to share their mountain with a transatlantic competitor, so I'll have to edge my way in gently.'

'Don't you have enough volcanoes in North America you could study?'

'Sure we do. But volcanoes are very different than one another – and Etna's the one I want to study. I guess you don't have any connections in geology?'

'Sorry.'

'What's your status, Tom?'

'I teach a course of Soviet history, 1917 to 1939.'

'You're on Ashmole's staff?'

'The lowest of the low. My post is renewable every three years. Right now I don't know whether I'll have a job at the start of next term.'

'So tell me about Bristol.'

Tom laughed. 'That crap about exploring archives was just Ashmole's way of palming you off on me. Having had a conventionally specialised British education, I can't tell you very much about anywhere west of the Baltic, I'm afraid.'

They strolled up the hill towards a pub called The Prince's Bar which was hot, humid and noisy from the crush of students unwinding after exams. Tom fought his way through the crowd with two mugs of hand-pulled bitter held high above his head. Karen swallowed some of the beer, concealing her distaste; it was warm and unlike any drink she had known before but she could see from Tom's enjoyment that it was supposed to be special, so she took a couple more mouthfuls before pushing the glass away.

The clock above the bar showed 2.30 when she excused herself. 'I have to rush now. I have an appointment with the Dean at three p.m.'

'Dressed like that?' Tom queried.

'Oh no. I'll hurry back to my room and put on high heels and a skirt. A dab of lipstick. Perhaps some earrings.'

'The Dean's not gay,' he grinned. 'That would really turn him on.'

'Can I ask you a favour?' Karen sat down again and looked Tom in the eyes. 'I don't know another soul in this city and one of my hang-ups is walking into a restaurant all alone. If you're free this evening, can you fill me in on how the power structure works around the campus? In return, I'll buy you dinner someplace not too expensive, so it'll be a paid consultation.'

Tom finished his beer, to give himself time to think about it. 'There's a pizza parlour near my pad, in Regent Street, Clifton,' he offered. 'It's called Pizza Siciliana.'

'Sounds great. See you there at eight o'clock?'

He nodded.

'Who's the new woman?' the barman asked after Karen had gone.

Tom shrugged. 'Some transatlantic scholar, slumming in Bristol for a year.'

Although he had enjoyed talking to her, Karen McKenzie was not the type of woman he normally fancied. He could have made a list of what was wrong with her. She was too intense, too direct, too skinny. Her breasts were too small and her hips as slim as a boy's, whereas he always picked girls with curves.

He had suggested the pizza parlour because there was a pub next door. There he planned to have a pre-dinner drink, during which he could invent an excuse to wriggle out of the meal if necessary.

.2.

The prices were low and the portions generous. The customers crowded into the pew seats that separated the stripped pine tables were mostly students, noisy with end-of-term energy. The only lighting came from candles stuck into empty Chianti bottles.

'You spent a whole year in the Soviet Union?' Karen asked.

'There's an exchange programme between Bristol and Leningrad universities,' Tom explained. 'Since I'd done Russian for "A" level and spoke it reasonably well, it seemed like a bit of an adventure to spend a year in Russia after I graduated.'

'Like taking a vacation job, working for the Mafia.'

Tom looked puzzled. 'Is that a reference to the theory about the KGB hiring that Turkish gunman to kill the Pope?'

'I'm talking about the way Moscow frustrates the natural development of democracy in Poland.'

He laughed. 'Listen, I understand the émigré point of view of people like your grandmother, but I can tell you that the comrades don't have horns and tails. I lived in Leningrad for the best part of a year – among students, professors and lecturers. I like the Russians I know.'

Karen's great-grandmother had come from a little village near Tsarskoye Selo. It seemed strange to be talking to someone who had actually been *over there*, as the old folks still called it. She wanted to know what it was like. 'What's the first memory that comes to mind of your time in Leningrad, Tom?'

'Blacks.'

'Blacks?' She sounded surprised.

'The hostel where we stayed was full of African students.'

'Another memory?'

'Honesty,' he said. 'The first time I went on a tram, I couldn't believe that everyone voluntarily put their fare in a box. At rush-hours, people just pass you the money and you hand it on to someone else until it reaches the box.'

'And another?'

He thought for a moment. 'Two hundred people turning up at a poetry reading in a factory canteen. I heard Yevtushenko reading *Zima Junction* to a crowd of women track-layers and footplate men in a shunting yard once. It was mind-blowing.'

The picture conjured up by Tom's answers was so at odds with her preconceptions that Karen tried to cancel them out by asking, 'What about surveillance?'

'I never met a KGB man.'

'I'll bet they knew all about you.'

'If you want to be paranoid,' Tom said, 'there are tigers behind every bush in other countries too. Join one of the left-wing associations on the campus here and play spot-the-girl-from-MI5.'

Karen had finished her salad. While Tom ate the rest of his pizza, she poked through the sheaf of typewritten pages on the table beside him. 'This is so faint, I hadn't even realised it was written in Russian script until now.'

'Can you read it?'

'I guess, if I concentrated. They've changed a few letters. No hard signs, for example. But why's the quality so bad?'

'It's a *samizdat* manuscript,' he explained, swallowing the last mouthful of pizza. 'They're all like this. Probably the sixth or seventh carbon copy of a copy of a copy of the original.'

'Those guys could use a Xerox.'

'They're illegal over there,' Tom explained.

'What are?'

'Photocopiers, for the general public.'

'For God's sake, why?'

He laughed. 'The KGB make it as difficult as possible for *samizdat* authors.'

'And you like those people?'

'The girl who gave me this' – Tom tapped the sheaf of paper – 'was taking a risk for something she believed in.'

'She could have been a stooge for the KGB.'

'I know.' The risk had been part of the thrill.

'What's it like?' she asked, meaning the manuscript.

'Unreadably awful.' Tom grimaced. 'It's a badly written allegorical mishmash of half-baked political innocence in the setting of a Russian fairy story.'

'Then why did you take the risk of bringing it out?'

'I couldn't let the girl down. The guy who wrote it is her lover. He's in a camp, somewhere in the Gulag. I promised her I'd try to get it published in the West.'

She toyed with the bill, which had just arrived. 'Whatever did your folks think of the idea of going to live in Russia for a year?'

'My father disapproved.'

'And your mother?'

'She thinks what he tells her to.'

'What do they do?'

'Father's a vicar,' said Tom shortly. His tight mouth and tone of voice made Karen wary of more personal questions.

When he tried to take the bill from her, she held on. 'I invited you, remember?'

She counted the money onto the table coin by coin, until Tom took her purse, put down enough for the meal and a tip and pushed the purse back to her side of the table.

Karen ran a hand through her hair and took off the heavy spectacles, making Tom think how much more attractive she looked without them. Her face was lightly freckled and the only make-up she was wearing was a slight trace of lipstick.

In picking up her purse, her hand brushed Tom's lying on the table. She wondered what was in his mind; he had been friendly enough, but it was hard for her to read anything in his closed-in British features.

She stood up. 'Well, thanks for spending my first evening in Bristol with me.'

'Thank you for the meal.'

'Do we . . .? Oh no, I've taken up enough of your time.'

'Go on.'

'I was wondering whether we have half an hour for what Professor Ashmole would probably term a post-prandial peregrination, to take advantage of this balmy English evening?'

'Why not?'

Was that English enthusiasm? Karen wondered. Getting to read the faces and voices in this strange country was going to be more tricky than learning a new language.

*

They strolled through the streets of Clifton in the sunset light that tinted the facades of the Georgian terraces a delicate pink. Karen was drinking in the strange sights and sounds all around as they walked uphill and across the grass of what Tom had called Clifton Down.

'How can it be down, when it's up?' she wondered.

'According to Skeat . . .'

'Who he?'

'A reverend gent who compiled the *Oxford Etymological*

Dictionary. He says that "down" the substantive is right. It's cognate with "dune", meaning a hill. The adverbial and prepositional use is a corruption of "of-dune", meaning off the hill.'

'Thanks, professor.'

'I thought you wanted to know.'

'Oh my God!' Karen ran ahead to the edge of the gorge. 'That's what I wanted to see.'

'You like the suspension bridge?' Tom asked when he caught her up. 'There you have Isambard Kingdom Brunel's idea of how to use nineteenth-century technology to span the Avon gorge. The boy genius was only twenty-three when he designed it.'

'Not the bridge,' she said. 'The gorge. Just imagine the forces it took to carve a slot like that through those cliffs!'

'What did it, an earthquake?'

She shook her head. 'Erosion. About one million years BC, the South Wales ice cap blocked the normal outflow of the river, which backed up and eventually carved the gorge as a new way to the sea.'

'You really care, don't you?' Tom said.

'About?'

'Geology.'

'It's my job.'

'A lot of academics just drift into teaching a subject because they got good results in it when they were students.'

'Not me. I started out majoring in architecture. I was supposed to follow in Mom's footsteps. You know, junior partner in the family business. One day all this will be yours . . .'

'So why did you change?'

'You remember Mount St Helens, the volcano in Washington State?' She gave him another clue: 'Spring of 1980.'

'Oh, the mountain that blew itself to pieces?'

'Right.' Her hand touched his arm briefly. She wanted

Tom to feel what she had felt. 'The moment I saw those pictures on television, I just knew that I was meant to be a vulcanologist. Afterwards I rationalised it into a desire to find out how the planet works, etcetera, etcetera, but the decision was really here.'

Karen pressed a hand on her flat belly. 'I guess that's what they mean by a gut reaction, eh?' She laughed at herself. 'The next day, I was on a plane flying into Seattle. With a couple of introductions and a lot of fast talking, I managed to get myself on board a helicopter carrying seismographic recording equipment into the closed area. And when I saw that Plinian column . . .'

'Plinian, as in Pliny?' Tom queried.

'Right. Pliny the Younger first described the phenomenon.'

'When his uncle died in the eruption of Vesuvius?'

'Right. The column of steam and ash over Mount St Helens reached a height of twenty kilometres in less than ten minutes. Just imagine seeing that as I flew in, Tom! Picture the naked, terrifying power of it.'

'Your road to Damascus,' he said. 'You had a vocation.'

Karen's eyes searched his, to see whether he was mocking her. They walked on in silence for a while and stopped halfway across the bridge, looking down at the silvery ribbon of river in the gloom below.

'Is that how it was with you,' she asked, 'when you decided to become a historian?'

'No, I was always going to study history.'

'Why modern history?'

'I suppose because I was always fascinated by the mystery time just before I was born. I want to understand the forces that made people the way they are today.'

'People?' she queried. 'You mean your parents' generation?'

To change the subject, he told her how Bristol's disappointed lovers traditionally committed suicide by jumping to their deaths from the bridge exactly where they were standing.

'Sobbing with unrequited passion,' as he put it, 'they stick their last pathetic notes in the railing here before climbing over. There's a story that one Mary Ann Henley, after being crossed in love, survived the jump in 1885 because her crinoline served as a parachute. It doesn't seem likely, but it is documented.'

Karen leaned over the rail, eyeing the 300-foot drop to the bottom of the gorge, and shivered. 'Did you ever feel like that, Tom?'

He shook his head.

'You must have wondered why I came to Europe now – just before the vacation – instead of waiting for the beginning of the fall semester . . .'

Staring down into the void, Karen asked herself why she was opening up like this to a near-stranger; it was not her normal behaviour. She turned to Tom. 'I was supposed to get married this afternoon, would you believe?'

'Why do you wear those things?' he asked, taking off her spectacles. 'They're so ugly.'

'I thought they made me look studious.'

'You should have contact lenses.'

He was standing very close to her. In the last rays of the sun her hair glowed with red highlights.

Karen could feel that he wanted her. 'Where do you live, Tom?'

'Five minutes away, in Clifton village. Above the restaurant where we ate.'

'I think I'd like to spend the night with you,' she heard herself say.

Uncertain whether she was teasing, he played it as a joke: 'Your eyes are green,' he said. 'Your hair is almost red. Which signal do I believe?'

'Go for the windows of the soul, Tom. They never lie.'

*

Karen was sitting up in bed next morning, watching him make coffee after returning from a local bakery with two delicious-looking Danish pastries.

She pulled on her jeans and tee-shirt to pad across the floor of his attic studio and look out of the big picture window with its view across the roofs of Bristol. She blinked twice at the sight, but it was real. In the cloudless blue sky a hundred hot-air balloons, all of different colours, were sailing above the city.

They seemed like a symbol of her new freedom. For the second time in her life she had stepped off the path that other people wanted her to follow. The first was when she upset her mother by changing her major from architecture to geology. But not getting married to her brother's best friend was an even bigger step along her own path through life.

She was aware of Tom standing behind her.

'Isn't that beautiful?' she whispered, pointing. She felt so light that, if she could have taken a deep enough breath, she would have flown away with the balloons in a big, beautiful opalescent bubble named Freedom.

Karen felt Tom's hands slip inside her tee-shirt and girdle her waist. She shut her eyes and soaked up the feeling of his fingers on her skin. Slowly they moved up her ribs and cupped her breasts. Her body spasmed with a jolt of electricity as he took her nipples between his thumbs and forefingers.

A long, delicious while later she let him turn her round and felt his lips on hers. His fingers eased inside the waistband of her jeans, exploring the base of her spine. The other hand was between her shoulder blades, cold and firm on her warm skin as it pressed her urgently towards him. His lips found her ear lobes and then her neck. Somehow she managed to pull the tee-shirt off without interrupting his embrace. She dropped it to the floor and arched her head back, eyes still closed, enjoying the sensations of his lips and fingers on her skin.

'Don't hurry,' she murmured.

His fingers found the zip of her jeans. She eased them over her hips, let them drop to the floor and stepped free, eyes still closed and feeling Tom's lips on her breasts. When she could not bear it any more, she put both hands on his head to push him gently lower still until he was on his knees, burying his face in her luxuriant pubic hair, with one hand fondling her tight buttocks while the other reached upwards, seeking a nipple.

Head arched back, she saw a pink and white hot-air balloon vertically overhead, framed in the open skylight. There were two faces peering over the basketwork side of the gondola, no more than twenty feet above her. With a throaty roar from the burners, the balloon started to ascend, travelling straight up in the temporary absence of breeze and rapidly getting smaller and smaller until it was just a speck in the clear blue sky.

.3.

Dear Fran, Karen wrote to her sister . . .

I love this city. Bristol is so *old*! I spent yesterday
morning wandering through streets of Regency houses
where you could imagine Beau Brummel tipping his hat
to ladies in crinolines and couples driving past in
hansom cabs. Then I took in the docks where the slavers
tied up in the eighteenth century. I wandered around
with half-closed eyes, imagining creaking timbers and
the smell of tar and rope and casks of rum from the
West Indies stacked on the dockside. Maybe I've got my
dates wrong, but you know what I mean.

I kept going into shops, pretending I wanted to buy
things but actually just to hear the sales girls talk. They
have the cutest accent, called the West of England burr.
It should be spelled BURRRRR. I can't write it down for
you. You'll have to take a vacation here and hear it for
yourself . . .

I suppose I'm really writing already because I met the

most amazing guy on my first day in Bristol. The Scarlet
Pimpernel of Leningrad, no less! He's a Russian history
lecturer here who actually smuggles *samizdat*
manuscripts out of the USSR for fun, would you believe!
Don't ask me what we have in common because I
couldn't tell you.

I felt so free on my very first day in town, free from
Larry, free from Mom expecting me to do what she
knows is good for me and free from the guilt of not
doing it. I guess you could say I was high on freedom.
Was that why I told this guy I wanted to sleep with
him – and me a nice girl from Midland, Ontario who
had only known him for a few hours! I don't know why
I'm telling you all this – you'll think I'm crazy – but I
woke up next morning at his place feeling like a chick
that has broken out of its shell. Suddenly it seems that
everything I want in life is there just within reach. All I
have to do is stretch out a hand and grab it. Does that
sound crazy?

I had to play it cool with him afterwards but I hope he
wants to see me again. For God's sake don't tell anyone
about all this. Or maybe there is one person you should
tell, because I arrived here to find a long letter from
Larry waiting for me. He'd sent it by courier, so it got
here before I did. I only opened it and read it because I
thought he might be going to commit suicide or
something dramatic. I should have known Larry. He's as
dramatic as a postage stamp. The letter was so logical
and reasonable, yuk! He says he understands me wanting
to be free for quote a couple of years before settling
down to marriage and kids unquote. What's wrong with
a lifetime's freedom? Oh, and he intends to wait for me.
Big deal! He was so damned understanding about me
backing out at the last moment that I could puke. Why
did I let everything go that far before calling it off?

The phone just went. It was Tom. I didn't tell you

that was his name. He wants to meet this evening. He sounded very laid back about it. I was going to say I was busy. Then I thought, that was what the old me would have done. So I said yes just to prove that I've broken out of the shell. Now I'm frightened, Fran. Supposing yesterday was just a dream?

Write me. I miss you and Mom and Doodie. I miss everyone really – even Larry in a way. But I miss him like a big brother, that's the problem. D'you think I'm mad, loving you all and yet not being able to breathe when I'm with you? Don't answer.

Love, K

Later in the week, Karen wrote:

I've done it, Fran! The geology faculty has accepted me as a mature student. That gives me a good excuse not to come home for a year and by then I'll have sorted myself out, I hope. By then Larry will have found the nice girl he deserves. By then you'll be slimmer and I'll be an aunty . . . By the way, Tom was great. He sort of coached me in how to talk to the geology prof and it really worked.

I'd like to tell you about him – Tom, not the prof – but he's hard to describe. I could begin with all the things he's not, starting with tall, dark and handsome. Then there's rich, charming and successful! In fact just about everything we were taught to look for in a man, he's not. Would you believe, he doesn't own a car or even know how to drive one! But it doesn't seem to bother him. His pad is full of books – on the shelves, in the hallway, all over the bed. The hi-fi doesn't work and he doesn't have a television. He doesn't know the latest films or which group is top of the charts. Doesn't sound like I'm having a ball, but I am. When I'm with him, I feel so FREE. Tom never tries to pressure me. It sounds like some feminist crap but the result is, I see myself almost for the first time as a person, not as the object of someone else's emotions.

I try to work out whether all this is real or whether I'm making a fantasy. Do you know what I mean? Have I psyched myself into falling in love with the first guy I meet over here or would it have happened anyway, if Tom and I had met in Toronto or New York?

I don't really know what he feels. We don't have deep meaningful conversations. Most of the time we're together, if we're not in bed, he's got his nose stuck in a book, yet I feel so goddam good with him. 'And what does that crazy sister of mine mean by *good*?' I can hear you asking. It's hard to be specific. Try words like *peaceful, strong, independent*. I seem to have the space around me to think clearly about what I want in life. That can't be wrong, can it?

A hundred times I wanted to pick up a phone and talk for hours like we used to, but I have to get used to living in poverty, so letters it is. I could save money by moving in with Tom – his idea – but that seems too much of a commitment.

Write me, I miss you.

Tom sprawled across a corner seat in the Prince's Bar, immersed in a book, with a pint of hand-pulled Smiles' bitter in front of him, waiting for Karen. The students had been down for a week and the pub was empty and quiet. Outside, the weather was hot, cloying and heavy, with a thunderstorm hovering leadenly overhead, threatening to break like a monsoon.

'Hi!'

He looked up. Karen had been jogging and was dressed in brief dayglo green running shorts and a thin white cotton singlet that clung to her moist skin. A pair of Reebok trainers completed the image.

He stood. 'Can I get you a drink?'

'A humungous cup of iced Coke may just stave off terminal heatstroke.' She slumped onto the cushioned seat and leafed through Tom's book while he was at the counter. It was the one he had bought the day they met and was now full of notes he had scribbled in the margins. Most of them were frustratingly indecipherable.

She put it down and took the Coke from him with, 'Thanks!'

'So you bought the new spectacles. I like them.'

'It's no big deal,' Karen shrugged. 'I change them all the time.'

She thought he was going to take them off and recalled the moment on the bridge when the small intimacy of him removing her spectacles had been exactly the cue she needed to say the sentence that led to everything else.

Then Tom contented himself with saying, 'I prefer the new ones. They're kinder to your face.'

'So do I,' she brushed away the compliment.

'Have you made up your mind?' he asked.

'About coming to France with you?'

He nodded.

Karen tried to read in his eyes what he wanted her to do. There were moments when she wished Tom would pressure her; this was one. The invitation to stay at his family's holiday cottage in south-west France had been made like all his other suggestions – in such a way as to leave her free to choose.

She played for time: 'I'm still wondering whether your parents will want me around. After all, it's a family holiday home. I'd be an intruder.'

'They won't come down for a while,' he said. 'Father thinks it's immoral to begin a holiday before the first of August, and my brother Adrian's going on some fact-finding tour to the Falklands with a load of other MPs, so we'll be alone for at least a month.'

'You're sure you want me to come?'

He blinked. 'If I didn't, I wouldn't have asked you. Anyway, if you don't like my family, you can leave when they arrive.'

'Why shouldn't I like your folks?'

'Well, you'll get on fine with my sister Megs and my mother but my father's a very difficult man with strong likes and dislikes.'

'Such as?'

'Foreigners, for example. His clock stopped in 1940 when Britain stood alone against the foe.'

'And is a Canadian a foreigner in his book? I thought we fought on the same side?'

'Trouble is, once you get on the wrong side of him, you can't do a thing right. Then there's Adrian. He's pompous but harmless, but you'll have to watch out for his wife. She's very bright and totally opportunistic. I sometimes think she had the two kids simply to give her husband the right image for a Conservative political candidate. He's her glove puppet, you see. She's hoping to manipulate him into Maggie Thatcher's cabinet. I think she may manage it.'

'You're exaggerating . . .'

'Perhaps I am.'

'I think you are.' Karen smiled at the images he was conjuring up. 'I can't imagine someone like you growing up with these people you're describing. What do you do there, all summer? Sit around playing cards?'

'There's a farmer in the village who hires me by the day, to work on the vines. I earn enough for food and the wine's cheap. It's the only place I ever save money.'

'You work as a labourer?'

'Why not?'

'You're so out of condition.' Karen laughed at the idea. 'If you'd told me you were going to spend the summer doing manual work, I'd have got you working out in a gym to build up some muscles.'

'Sufficient unto the day is the evil thereof,' Tom yawned. 'Matthew VI, verse 34.'

The barman was busy stacking empties, with his back to them. Tom ran the back of his hand lightly up the front of Karen's singlet, brushing her nipples with his knuckles.

'Don't do that in public,' she murmured.

'I want you.' He leaned forward and nibbled her ear.

'What does that mean?' she asked.

'I want you to come to France.'

She took a deep breath. 'Then I'll come.'

.4.

'I'm afraid your lady friend has *rather* put her foot in it.'
Adrian Fielding, LLB, MP, was dressed for tennis in a
clean white shirt and shorts, with two rackets clasped in his
hand. His wife walked past Tom without speaking and
marched into the kitchen of the old house. They heard her
hectoring voice giving orders to the Swedish au pair girl who
was supervising the children's supper.

'What's Karen done?' Tom asked. He was tired and
sweaty after a day working in the fields under the hot sun.
His muscles ached and he wanted a shower and a drink.

Adrian blocked his way into the house. 'She took a siesta
in the garden.'

'That's not a crime.'

'The old man found her lying fast asleep under the cherry
tree, topless.'

Tom laughed and made to push past. 'Come on, Adrian.
We're living in the Year of Grace 1982. Newspapers and
magazines are full of pictures of topless girls.'

'Perhaps. Everything in its place. But this is not St Tropez,

Tom. It's our family garden. The old man was understand-ably shocked.'

'I'll talk to Karen,' Tom said tiredly. 'Now, if you don't mind, I need a wash and a drink.'

Before dinner he walked Karen into the village for an apéritif in the small bar. They sat chatting with the locals about the prospect for the grape harvest.

On the way back to the house, Tom said, 'Apparently my father discovered you sleeping topless in the garden this afternoon. He's a bit old-fashioned, so you'd better keep the top half of your bikini on in future.'

'I took it off because it was wet. I'd been swimming in the river.' Karen was puzzled. 'I thought I'd been most discreet, hiding myself away at the bottom of the garden in the shade. Did he come looking for me? And if I upset him, why didn't he say something to me?'

'That's not the way my family works.'

'Is that the reason Margaret never lies in the sun or goes swimming, because her father doesn't like it?'

'Megs is allergic to sunshine, comes out in a rash if she strips off.'

'Poor girl! She doesn't look to me like she has much fun.'

'She worries me,' Tom admitted. 'Megs doesn't have boyfriends. She comes home from college each weekend and when I ask her why, she says it's because Mother is lonely.'

'She's very close to her parents.'

'Too close. It's time she had a life of her own.'

'We should have invited her to come for a drink.'

'Oh, she'll be busy, helping Mother prepare dinner.'

'Like I said, she doesn't have much fun.'

The evening meal was set on a trestle table on the verandah where the children, aged four and six, were saying goodnight to their grandfather. The handsome, grey-haired man in the dog collar was asking them questions about what they had been doing that day and making it sound like an inquisition.

What happens if they get an answer wrong? Karen wondered. Is there a penalty to pay? She had noticed that Tom's father rarely ventured outdoors during the day, preferring to stay in the house for most of the time, poring over his books.

No one at the table took any notice of her arrival. By the time the main course was served, Tom realised that only he and his sister were talking to Karen. After her third remark to Kim had gone unanswered, she left the table and went up to her room. Tom hurried after her to apologise.

'That's okay,' Karen shrugged. 'I should have left before your family arrived, you did warn me. But I wanted them to like me.'

'It's a storm in a tea cup,' Tom said. 'It'll blow over. I'll talk to Father after the meal.'

'Talk all you like,' she said. 'I'm going.'

'Where to?' he asked.

'I'll buy an Interail ticket first thing tomorrow morning and head for Venice, Florence, Rome – places I've always wanted to see.' She took her holdall out of the wardrobe and began folding clothes.

Tom was leaning against the door jamb. He wanted to say, 'I'll come with you,' but he knew his father's anger. If he left and broke up the family holiday, his sister and mother would suffer for it. And that would not be fair.

He looked out of the dormer window. Below, the quiet conversation continued as Megs cleared away the dishes from the main course and brought the cheese platter. Nothing had happened.

'Every family has its rules,' he said, wondering why he was defending them all. 'You just broke one, that's all.'

'Trouble is, there are more rules than people here. I gave your niece and nephew a packet of chewing gum each this afternoon.'

'Kim mentioned that to me before dinner.'

'Another rule I broke,' Karen shrugged. 'The kids brought the gum back five minutes later, still in its wrapper. They told me that candy is bad for their teeth, so it's forbidden. I saw their mother watching from the house, to make sure they were handing it back. Those kids are scared of her, Tom.'

'Wouldn't you be scared of a mother with that Maggie Thatcher hairstyle and parade-ground voice?' he joked.

'I didn't mean to criticise your family.'

'You're only saying things that I sometimes think.' He put his arms around Karen, to stop her packing. 'It's my fault. I knew this wouldn't work out but I didn't want you to leave.'

'And that's another thing,' she said. 'All this creeping around in the night to get to each other's bedroom . . . At twenty-eight you're not supposed to have a carnal relationship or go skinny dipping by moonlight?'

'I know,' Tom said. 'But I'll miss you.'

Years later, when he was a very angry man in prison, the woman Tom called 'my favourite shrink' suggested writing it all down as a way of coming to terms with injustice and keeping at bay the psychological condition she referred to as 'terminal bitterness'.

'Treat it like a first-person novel,' was her advice. 'That way you can explore and come to terms with your own motives and feelings without having to guess at other people's.'

Of Karen's visit to France, Tom wrote:

I had known all along that my family wouldn't like her. She was too open and too honest to integrate with their coded, closed-in behaviour. So why did I expose her to their rejection?

It wasn't just that I wanted her body available. One of the untaxable benefits of being a university lecturer is that each academic year brings a new crop of young women students eager for a relationship with an older man, especially one they can respect because he knows more about their subject than they do. So I wasn't starved for sex.

With Karen, love-making was not a battle or a competition. If one time wasn't so good for her or for me, it didn't bother either of us, I think – perhaps because the essential arrogance of youth deluded us into thinking that today was better than yesterday and tomorrow would always be better still.

She had a public smile borrowed from some North American toothpaste commercial on television, but also a private one that I'd catch now and again when we were alone and I glanced up from a book and saw her watching me. We'd look at each other for a minute or two without saying a word and then go back to whatever we were doing. Or maybe one of us would stretch out a hand and we'd end in a tangle on the bed – or the floor if the bed wasn't near enough.

But it was more than that. The truth is that, from the very first night we spent together I felt better when she was near me. So, the reason why I took her to France was the most obvious of all: I didn't want us to be apart all summer in case by the time we met again she might have changed her mind about me.

With hindsight I should have said goodbye to the family that evening when they tacitly conspired to send Karen to Coventry like a naughty schoolgirl. But I knew how angry Father would be if I left prematurely and broke up the family holiday which had been a ritual for years. When it was too late I realised that I should have abandoned Mother and Megs to brave Father's anger on their own. I should have left them all to play the game called Family and gone away with the woman I loved. But I didn't.

Yet Fortune favours the cowardly too sometimes! A couple of days after the others had gone back to Britain at the end of August, leaving me alone in the old house by the

*river, I saw this backpacker trudging tiredly up the track
from the main road. It was early evening. I was sitting on
the verandah, wearing just shorts and sandals, enjoying a
can of cool beer from the fridge after working in the sun all
day. I hadn't had time to shower. I ran towards her and
said something stupid like, 'So you came back.'*

*Karen didn't say anything. She was too tired. She just
shrugged the backpack off, dumped it on the ground and
slumped in my arms. We fell to the ground, laughing. She
smelled of sweat and dust and I suppose I did the same. We
made love right there in the garden without another word
being said by either of us and I understood Napoleon's line
to Josephine: 'Don't wash, I'm coming home.'*

*There was no one to see, and if there had been, it
wouldn't have stopped us. Afterwards we swam naked in
the river and then made love again. At some point we ate a
meal and went to bed but I don't think we said more than a
dozen words to each other all night. It was long after dawn
when we fell asleep at last.*

*When we woke up I told her that I was not coming back
to Bristol – at least not to the University – because Ashmole
had sacked me on the last day of summer term. She wanted
to know why I hadn't told her earlier.*

'I didn't even tell my family,' I said.

'Why not?'

'From habit.'

*The way Ashmole had put it was that the faculty was
forced to make some financial cutbacks under Mrs
Thatcher's latest plan to abolish education in Britain.
Because I had only a temporary contract, I was the first
victim. I had reminded him of his vague promises about
renewing my contract but, since he had never actually said
anything binding, that didn't get me anywhere.*

*I told Karen how I had stood, numb and wordless,
looking out of the mullioned window of his study. Through
the diamond-paned leaded lights I could see the flagged*

courtyard where groups of students were walking past, wheeling bicycles, carrying books – all secure in a world of which I had thought myself a life member. But they were 'in' and I was 'out'.

Was it significant that Ashmole got my name right for the first time? He said how much he had enjoyed having me on the staff and that my students would miss me. And then, before I'd fully taken in that I'd been kicked out, he showed me a letter from the Institute of Slavonic Studies in London, offering me a one-year research fellowship. The money was nearly twice what Bristol had been paying me, plus expenses for travel and subsistence.

'Wow!' said Karen. 'That's fantastic.'

I wasn't so sure. I had had lunch with the Director of the Institute before coming out to France. It was on Friday, 13 July, a suitable day on which to meet Clive Ponsonby for the first time. I couldn't work him out. He was obviously no academic but he spoke idiomatic Russian with a Moscow accent and was very knowledgeable about current developments inside the USSR. He mentioned that he'd spent some time as a diplomat working in the Moscow embassy.

Karen's reaction, when I told her all this, was that he sounded like an intelligence officer. At the time it didn't bother me. Ashmole had told me that there would be more money available to the faculty for the following academic year. He had promised to have me back – this time on the permanent staff – so I was looking on Ponsonby and his Institute as no more than a source of money for the next few months.

.5.

Tom walked up the white donkey-stoned steps of the Regency house near the British Museum. Behind the glass of the ground-floor windows were folding metal grilles like lift doors. Iron bars protected the windows of the basement where a row of geraniums in pots was the only sign of human habitation. In the middle of the vivid splash of Mediterranean red a large ginger cat was sleeping in the morning sun.

By the bell-pull was a polished brass plaque on which was engraved:

London Institute of Slavonic Studies
Library hours: 10 a.m.–12 noon
on Mondays, Wednesdays and Fridays.

A handwritten postcard taped to the plaque added:

Please telephone for appointment.

*

Somewhere at the back of the house an old-fashioned servants' bell tinkled. Tom was about to ring a second time when he heard footsteps inside. The door was opened by a horse-faced woman in her mid-thirties, dressed in a fawn twinset over a matching knitted skirt. A single strand of pearls was her only jewellery.

'Mr Fielding?' she said, in a public school voice. 'I'm Pat Strong, the Director's secretary. Mr Ponsonby's expecting you. Please come in.'

Tom followed her along a corridor floored with institutional brown linoleum. There was a smell of fresh paint and floor polish that reminded him of boarding school. Inside the building it was quiet, the only noise being a muted rumble from the traffic in the street.

'If you'd like to wait in the library . . .'

He was shown into a room with walls completely covered by bookshelves. There was no window and the air was stuffy, as though the door were seldom opened. Tom glanced curiously at some of the titles in Latin and Cyrillic script. The section devoted to the Russian Civil War was extensive. He noted several titles that had not been there on his previous visit.

The woman returned, accompanied by a short, fat, bald man who looked about fifty. He was wearing a cheaply cut grey suit which matched the colour of his skin and would have been invisible in any crowd.

'Brodsky, Ivan,' he said in a thick Russian accent, seating himself at the large oval table which took up the centre of the room.

'Mr Brodsky is our librarian,' said the woman briskly, taking the next chair. 'Did Mr Ponsonby give you a copy of the questionnaire?'

'No.' Tom sat down opposite them.

'It's boring stuff, I'm afraid.' She smiled apologetically.

Tom filled in his date and place of birth, schools attended with dates, foreign countries visited, languages spoken, posts held.

She took the completed form from him and scanned it before extracting another piece of paper from the folder in front of her.

'This,' she said, 'is part of an ongoing survey. All fellows are asked to co-operate, but you don't have to.'

'Go ahead,' said Tom.

'Who rules the Soviet Union?'

'The General Secretary of the Communist Party is Leonid Brezhnev. Has been for the past eighteen years.'

'What's the motto of the KGB?'

'*Zashchita partii*: the shield of the party.'

'What do you know of Mikhail Gorbachev?' This from Brodsky.

'Not much. He's a liberal newcomer.'

'How high do you think he'll rise?'

'I'm a historian,' Tom answered. 'Not a prophet.'

'What's your opinion of the miners' strike?' the woman asked.

'I don't have one. If anything, I'm on their side. It's a sod of a life they have, after all. Would we want to go down a mine and do eight hours' hard labour in the dust and the wet, whatever the money?'

'Which nations boycotted the Olympic Games in Los Angeles?' she asked.

'The Soviet Union. But, anticipating your next question, I can't remember why.'

The questions rambled over history, current affairs and sport. At the end, when the woman closed her folder and left the room, Brodsky changed to Russian, grilling Tom about his trips to Russia, asking for names, descriptions of people and places. When talking about Moscow, he had the *moskóvski govór* – the accent and slang of the capital. When talking about Leningrad, Tom would have taken him for a native of Peter the Great's city.

After he too had left the room, Tom spent a quarter of an hour browsing through some of the books that covered the

Civil War, making a pile of half a dozen of the more interesting ones on the end of the table.

'Tea?'

He had not heard the door open. The woman was standing there with a tray, set with Royal Doulton china with two
cups and saucers. Holding the door open for her was a tall,
lean man of around forty. He exuded a coiled-spring physical
energy and had a blue chin that must have needed shaving
twice a day. Smartly dressed in a sober, dark blue pinstriped
suit with polished black leather shoes, he could have been a
Guards officer in mufti.

'Tom!' There was a smile of welcome on Ponsonby's face,
but the steel-grey eyes were cold and uninvolved. 'Sorry to
keep you waiting.'

His voice matched the clothes. It sounded far back, as
though he were perpetually balancing a boiled sweet on his
tongue and was scared of it slipping down his throat and
choking him.

'Pat tells me you were very tolerant during her interrogation,' Ponsonby grinned, showing perfect teeth. 'Load of
balls really, but we co-operate because they give us the
funds.'

'Who do?'

The cold grey eyes focused on Tom's for a second as
Ponsonby waved his secretary out of the room and poured
the tea, pushing one cup towards Tom.

'Classy filly, isn't she?' he said. 'Pity about the teeth but
her hindquarters move like silk, did you notice?'

Tom did not reply.

'I liked the outline of your research submission,'
Ponsonby continued smoothly. 'You called it *Clarifying
Confusion*. Can you fulfil the promise of the title?'

He sprawled back in the large easy chair at the head of the
table with both feet on its polished surface and sipped his tea,
listening as Tom began to elaborate on the outline of the
project that Ashmole had helped him put together at the

beginning of the vacation. It was to be an exhaustive survey of a largely unresearched area of Soviet history: the logistical functions of the Trans-Siberian railway in moving troops, munitions and supplies during the Russian Civil War.

Once or twice Ponsonby nodded but did not interrupt. At the end, he picked over the pile of books Tom had chosen, rejected three of them and chose several more from the bookshelves very rapidly, obviously familiar with their contents.

'If you don't want to carry all these,' he said, 'tell Pat to post them to you. She has bugger-all to do and needs exercise.'

'It's okay,' said Tom. 'I'll take them with me.'

'Keep in touch,' said Ponsonby. 'Anything you want, just ring and ask for me. If I'm mobile, leave a number where Pat can reach you. I'll get back to you within a day or so. I can feel in my bones that this is going to be a good paper. Has Ashmole told you that he thinks it will merit a doctorate?'

Tom nodded.

'"Dr Tom Fielding" sounds good, doesn't it?' Ponsonby stood up, shot his cuffs and consulted a gold half-hunter watch taken from his waistcoat pocket. Tom wondered how many of the Edwardian mannerisms were learned and what was the real man.

There was an unsealed envelope with his name on it, lying on the tea tray. When Ponsonby shook it, a cheque made out to T.W.C. Fielding, for the amount of £10,500, fell onto the table. Tom picked it up with murmured thanks.

'Six months in advance.' Ponsonby smiled. 'You don't have to declare it for tax, so it's all yours. And when you need travelling expenses, just call Pat. She'll send you a cheque by return.'

'You're very generous.'

Ponsonby was staring at Tom's hands. 'Been in a fight?' he asked.

'Grape-picking.' Tom looked at the cuts on his knuckles. 'Why? Are you a sportsman?'

'Rugger.' Ponsonby grinned. 'I play a pretty mean game.'

The moment of informal contact was gone. For the next fifteen minutes, he grilled Tom about contacts in Russia whom he intended to consult. 'Lot of travelling,' he commented. 'Are you happy about that? No commitments to get in the way?'

'Absolutely none,' said Tom.

Ponsonby nodded at the pile of books. 'How long will it take you to plough through all that bumf?'

'I'm a fast reader. About a week.'

'You'll see what the problem is. During the Civil War, both sides were working so hard slaughtering each other that few records were kept. If you keep in a bit of the blood-and-guts, the odds are that we can arrange a contract for a book. The Institute has friends at the university presses; it shouldn't be a problem.'

I came down those white steps and onto the pavement walking on air at the thought of unlimited travel, a doctorate and a book with my name on it. After living for three years on Ashmole's pittance, the cheque in my pocket was riches indeed.

When Karen said it all sounded too good to be true, I got angry. Looking back, I was angry because I knew she was right.

I used some of the money to lease a larger flat on the first floor of the same house in Bristol. There was central heating and room for Karen to move her things in. We spent so much time together, it seemed the logical thing to do.

My first research trip using Ponsonby's money was to Leningrad. The night before I was due to fly out, Karen was in a strange mood. Any mood would have been strange. That was one of the things I liked about her: she never sulked or acted up. Normally, if she didn't like something, she said so openly.

*I couldn't work out what was wrong. We'd eaten
downstairs in the pizza parlour where she had picked at her
food and been silent. Upstairs I asked a couple of times
what was bothering her.*

'Come on, out with it. Something's on your mind.'

'I had a letter from Doodie,' she said.

'So?'

'She had a dream that I was going to Russia and wrote
to warn me not to.'

'So what? You're not coming with me.'

'Doodie has premonitions. Mom always laughs at them,
but sometimes the old lady is right.'

'Tell me about the dream.'

'In it, some man was using me to do something wrong
over there. She wasn't sure what it was.'

'And did you get caught?'

'No, but I had . . . she called it "bolshóye neschástye" – a
great unhappiness.'

'She must be nuts,' I said.

.6.

Like many central London bars on a Saturday evening, the pub opposite the Institute was empty except for a few residents watching sport on the television. Without consulting Tom, Ponsonby bought two pints of low-calorie lager and dumped the glasses on the table in front of him. There was an unzipped holdall full of muddy sports gear on the floor by his feet.

'How was the game?' Tom asked, looking at Ponsonby's black eye.

'You should see the other guy trying to walk. I doubt he'll ever become a father now.' Ponsonby lifted his glass. 'Pat tells me your trip to Russia was a great success. Did you look up old chums in Leningrad?'

'I was too busy and anyway most of the students I used to know have moved on by now.'

'. . . which left you at a loose end for company in the evenings.'

'You're never alone with a good book.'

'Pick up a girl at the weekend, did you?'

'I wasn't there long enough to make friends.'

'But unlike when you lived in Leningrad as a student,' Ponsonby remarked, 'this time you had dollars in your pocket. You could have bought a nice girl to keep you warm for the night.'

Tom shook his head.

Ponsonby arched one of his dark eyebrows. 'Two girls, if you're that way inclined.'

'Paying for sex wouldn't interest me. I'm not that desperate.'

'Lucky you,' Ponsonby murmured. 'And how did they treat you at the university in Leningrad?'

'Everyone was very helpful after I'd mastered the current terminology.'

'There was no Civil War . . .'

'Exactly. It was the suppression of bourgeois-reactionary and interventionist counter-revolutionary forces.'

'We do the same,' Ponsonby chuckled. 'Britain invented the concentration camp during the Boer War, but we don't shout about it.'

'The Department of Soviet History couldn't have been nicer, once I slipped the professor fifty dollars, as you suggested. Their one and only photocopier was broken, so I offered to bring in a spare part on my next trip.'

'I'll bet that went down well. Meantime, how'd you manage?'

'Luckily I'd taken along a 35mm camera and tripod for copying documents.'

'Photography's your hobby. I remember you said that on the questionnaire.' Ponsonby was looking at the clock behind the bar, working out how to fit in a little diversion on his way home. 'How did you like Moscow, Tom?'

'It was bloody cold. My previous visits have been in summer.'

'Make any friends there?'

'One of the guides from the Intourist desk at the hotel tried very hard to get me into bed.'

'And did she succeed?'

'It was a bloke,' Tom laughed.

'And if it had been a girl, doing it for free?'

'Still no thanks.'

Ponsonby took a dozen sheets of foolscap paper covered in Tom's handwriting from his muddy holdall and passed them across the table. The margins were filled by notes in a spiky hand, full of anger. 'Your first essay was quite brilliant, Tom. But read my comments. I think you'll find them helpful.'

He took an envelope out of the holdall. 'You must be running short of funds, with all that gadding about.'

Tom counted ten fifties. 'You're very generous.'

'Brodsky told me that your spoken Russian is first class.' Ponsonby leaned forward and held Tom's gaze for a moment. 'Could you pass for a native, if need be?'

Tom laughed. 'A very stupid peasant in Vladivostok might think I had a Leningrad accent, if that's where I said I came from. But I wouldn't try to con a real Russian.'

'No,' said Ponsonby thoughtfully. 'Well, there's no reason why you should, is there? I must be going now. Got to get back to the little woman in suburbia, you know. Write everything up, Tom – whom you met, your impressions of them – that sort of thing.'

'What's that got to do with researching the Civil War?'

Ponsonby drained his glass. 'All grist to the mill, dear boy. And, by the way, call me Clive.'

He leaned down to pick up his holdall. 'You didn't mention to anyone your connection with us?'

'You told me not to. So far as my Russian contacts are concerned, I'm still just plain Tom Fielding of Bristol University.'

Ponsonby straightened up. 'It's bureaucracy unlimited over there. They cross-refer even the slightest incident. There was some trouble a couple of years back with an American student who went over on a bursary from us and was caught passing out bibles in the street. So, best not to mention the Institute at all.'

Ten minutes later, Tom was in Dillon's bookshop, browsing in the bargain books section to kill time until the next Bristol train.

'Dr Fielding?'

Tom had told Brodsky several times that he was not entitled to the honorific. 'What a coincidence,' he said.

'Not really.' Brodsky was talking Russian. 'I've been trying to get up my courage to ask you a favour, ever since Mr Ponsonby left.'

'What can I do for you?'

'Have you the time for a drink before you catch your train, Dr Fielding?'

'Can't we chat next time I come up to use the library?'

'I'd rather not.' Brodsky pulled Tom into a corner conspiratorially. 'You see, this is a family matter. Mr Ponsonby would not approve.'

There was something compelling about the man's tension: the darting eye movements and furtive manner. Tom walked with him two hundred yards to the Tavistock Hotel. In the long bar, full of Israeli tourists all talking noisily, he swallowed draught Guinness and listened to Brodsky's request.

'I have a sister who lives in Moscow, Dr Fielding. Conditions are not easy for her, so whenever I can I send some money. My salary does not permit me to be generous, but those few dollars make all the difference to a woman in her position.'

'I can imagine.'

'Yes. Well . . .' Brodsky's hesitation ended with a rush of words. 'I was wondering whether, on your next visit, you would be willing to look her up and give her a little present from me?'

'Can't you post it?'

Brodsky laughed sadly. 'Dr Fielding, I am a non-person in my own country. If Olga were to receive a letter containing money from me, it could have repercussions. Her husband is dying of cancer. She doesn't need any other problems.'

'Use another name.'

'Her mail is intercepted. They would know who had sent it.'

'And if a Westerner turns up at her apartment, won't that cause even more problems?'

'It will not be necessary to go to her home,' Brodsky said. Hearing some of the Israelis nearby speaking Russian, he switched to English and pulled his chair closer to Tom's. 'Olga works at a shoe counter in the GUM store. You could hand her the money there and nobody will realise that you are anything other than a customer paying for a purchase.'

'I'll think about it,' said Tom.

'Thank you.' Brodsky looked immensely relieved. 'But please, whatever you decide, say nothing to Mr Ponsonby. It could cost me my job.'

The State Universal Store – always known by its initials GUM which stood for *Gosudárstvenny Universálny Magazín* – claimed to be the biggest shopping mall in the world. The noise inside the three-level turn-of-the-century building was like the hubbub of a railway station without the train announcements. On the first floor, the long queue at the shoe counter was getting restive.

'I waited for four hours last week,' complained the fat woman standing next to Tom.

She was bundled up in a shapeless quilted winter coat and was wearing galoshes. When Tom did not reply, her elbow in his ribs made the point that she was talking to him. 'They said there was a delivery of children's winter shoes, and what was on sale when I got to the counter? Women's open sandals, in the middle of November! I swapped a pair for these gloves.'

'They look very nice,' Tom mumbled.

'Are you a foreigner?' Her voice was suddenly suspicious, not so much of his accent as his politeness.

'Student,' he said.

'Why don't you buy your shoes in the West?' She turned to her neighbour on the other side. 'As if we haven't got shortages enough without foreigners coming over here and complicating things.'

'I thought we were queueing for hats,' said Tom hastily, to give himself a reason to walk away. 'I need a fur hat for the winter. You can't buy a hat for a Russian winter in London.'

'Are you stupid?' a man asked behind him. 'The hat counter is next door.'

'What kind of a hat?' another man asked.

'*Shápka* – a fur cap.'

'You've come to the wrong place,' said the first man. 'Tourists always do that. The best place to buy a hat is at TsUM, not GUM. It's near the Bolshoi Theatre.'

'Come with me, Englishman. I can get you any hat cheaper than you will pay here.' The second man grabbed Tom's arm. He was an Azerbaijani, dark-skinned, with a thin face and black *bandido* moustache.

Now that he was not a competitor in the struggle for shoes, Tom was suddenly surrounded by people advising him what to look for in a hat and how much to pay. It was a Russian conversation: everyone talking at once.

'Don't trust that black bastard,' the fat woman warned. 'Outside the store, Englishman, he'll grab your money and scarper.'

'. . . leaving you looking for a new hat and a new wallet,' someone laughed.

For two tense hours after escaping from the queue, Tom wandered around the store on all three levels, trying to work out how to get near the woman serving at the shoe counter without standing in the queue again. His chance came just before closing time as she pushed a large empty fibre-board container on castors back to the stockroom. Tom bumped into her and apologised.

'You dropped this.' He stooped as though picking up from the floor the handkerchief inside which he had wrapped Brodsky's fifty dollars.

'Not mine, comrade,' she said. She was dressed in a worn brown overall and headscarf and looked tired.

'It's a present to Olga from Ivan.'

She looked at Tom for a long moment before the package was slipped into the pocket of her overall and she continued shoving the container along the narrow walkway. Tom's heart was hammering inside his chest. At the end of the walkway stood a militiaman who was staring in his direction. Tom walked out onto one of the wrought-iron bridges that spanned the store from side to side, to get back his breath. Looking down at the crowds of shoppers below he saw two other militiamen staring up at him. The fat woman from the shoe queue was talking to them. Tom grinned and waved at her, pointing to his new fur hat. She blew him a kiss.

The risk was trivial, compared with what I was to do afterwards, but the thrill was a sustained high that lasted the whole two hours. The nearest I had come to it before was in my first year at university when I joined a mountaineering club and did some really hairy climbs in the Alps during the summer vac. Before I fell and broke several ribs and my shoulder while instructing in a slate quarry near Snowdon, I couldn't get enough of the high that climbers know when they're on a sheer face with only finger- and toe-holds and a drop of hundreds of feet below them. It's an adrenaline rush that continues the whole time on the mountain.

Post-operative complications with my shoulder kept me

out of serious climbing after that. I wouldn't settle for second best, so I sold my gear and tried to forget the call of the hills. That day in GUM, I realised that the kicks I had got in the past from smuggling samizdat manuscripts and taking messages were mere fell walking, so to speak. Because they were unplanned, there had been too little time to be really nervous hour after hour, day after day. This time the high went on and on: I was back on a rock face with no rope and only my own nerve to keep me from falling.

As I hurried out of the store, trying not to look over my shoulder all the way back to the hotel, I had taken the first step on the path to addiction – as surely as someone injecting a hard drug for the first time, or indulging a big sexual kink, or sitting at a gambling table or placing a bet on a horse. I was, quite simply, hooked on that most ancient of all addictions: my own adrenaline.

I didn't sleep that night, but lay awake sweating, alternately promising myself never to do anything so risky again and knowing that I would . . . as soon and as often as I could.

.7.

'I'm *extremely* pissed-off with Brodsky. He had no business embroiling you in his sordid schemes.' Ponsonby's face was dark with anger as he paced round the library at the Institute. 'The fat little turd has confessed that he asked you to take something with you on your last trip. Has this happened before?'

'Twice,' confessed Tom. 'I took in $50 the first time and $500 the second time.'

'And on your last trip?'

'He gave me a large package of some painkiller drugs you can't buy in the Soviet Union. They're for his brother-in-law who's dying of cancer.'

'Brodsky doesn't have a brother-in-law,' Ponsonby spat. 'His sort don't even have fathers.'

'I've met his sister, the man's wife.'

'He doesn't have a sister either, dear boy.'

Ponsonby calmed down and sat at the table opposite Tom. 'I'm afraid he's been using you in a low-grade smug-

gling racket. It seems to me a pity that you put your personal liberty at risk just for that little creep to make some
cash. You'd have got ten years in a labour camp if you'd
been caught. Maybe more.'

'I really believed his story.' Tom took a deep breath of the
stale air in the library and flushed with anger and confusion.
'I could smash his face in for this.'

'Don't bother,' Ponsonby said. 'Disciplinary action has
been taken. The main thing is that you carried off these little
missions quite brilliantly. So let's channel your justifiable
indignation into a more useful purpose than mere Brodsky-
bashing.'

There was a slow-speed Tandberg reel-to-reel tape
recorder on the table, connected to an omnidirectional
microphone. Ponsonby pressed the start button. 'I'm going to
ask you a lot of questions, Tom. And I want you to tell me
everything that happened, each time. Understood?'

After two hours he stopped the machine and compli-
mented Tom on having excellent recall.

'Thanks, but I still feel angry.'

'With Brodsky?'

'With myself. I behaved like a real prick. I was within an
ace of cocking everything up the first time, with all that
attention I attracted in the queue at GUM.'

Ponsonby disagreed. 'I would call that brilliant improvi-
sation, dear boy. Most amateurs overcomplicate, whereas
you kept your cover story masterfully simple. It must have
taken considerable sang-froid to stand there, waving at the
fat lady when you thought she was denouncing you to the
two militiamen.'

'Self-preservation was the name of the game.'

'Then you're obviously a First Division player.' Ponsonby
smiled. 'Supposing I were to ask you to help with something
more deserving of your talents, would you have the bottle to
do it?'

'Depends what was involved.'

'Say I asked you to collect something for us on your next trip.'

'Us?'

'The Institute.'

'Like what?'

'How do you think we get our current research material out of Russia and the satellite countries? There are lots of things one cannot just put in the post.'

'Such as?'

Ponsonby stood up and stretched. '*Samizdat* manuscripts, letters to the Press from dissidents under house arrest, an occasional roll of film. Will you get involved?'

'I'd have to know more about it first.'

Ponsonby consulted his pocket watch. 'If you're free for lunch, be my guest and I'll fill you in.'

Upstairs at Wheeler's Restaurant in Charlotte Street, Ponsonby ordered for them both: *bisque de homard*, followed by *sole meunière* and a pastry for dessert, all washed down with two bottles of the house Chablis.

Afterwards, swilling a large Armagnac in a balloon glass, he said, 'I've been thinking while we were chatting, Tom. You're a natural at this game, one of those rare people who are better off without training.'

'Training in what exactly?'

'Tradecraft. How to spot when you're being tailed. How to lose a follower by changing trains in the Metro or leaving a shop by a different exit. That sort of thing.'

'Isn't it useful, Clive?'

'Can be, dear boy. But it has one colossal disadvantage. If your watchers are good, it tells them that you've been trained, and that makes them wonder why – which in turn makes you a priority target.'

'You think I've been watched?'

'Bound to have been,' Ponsonby shrugged. 'Not necessarily all the time, of course. And probably only by trainees who'll never make it into the first team. This identity you've created for yourself is a good cover: the innocent pro-Soviet academic with a perfectly bona fide reason to travel frequently to and within Russia. Stick to it. That way, if you do slip up, they'll probably take you for a deluded Western liberal, rather than anything more menacing. On reflection, I think we should let innocence rather than tradecraft be your shield.'

They chatted about Tom's work for a few minutes, then Ponsonby asked, 'Can you rustle up a girlfriend to take on the next trip? In my opinion, there's nothing like having his arm around a pretty girl's waist to make a chap seem really innocent.'

Dear Fran,

Don't tell Doodie or let her see the stamp on the envelope: I'm writing this on my way to Russia!

Tom has to do some research in Leningrad and I'm going along for the trip. I got fed up with the warm damp winter in Bristol and I'm looking forward to a good Canadian freeze, you know what I mean? I have this picture of myself riding with Tom in a horse-drawn troika, skimming across the snowy wastes together to the sound of sleigh bells. But it's more complicated than that. You'll understand the real reason I wanted to go: we were brought up to think of Russia as a never-never land and I have to take this chance to see what it's really like where our ancestors lived.

Perhaps when I see the country for myself, I'll understand what made Doodie's parents flee from their home, leaving everything behind except a couple of icons. They must have hated the place, yet if they did, why did they go on speaking the language and huddle together in the Doukhobor community, exactly like immigrants in Little Italy who dream of going home one day and buying a vineyard in which to end their days? Maybe that's the connection that made me accept Tom's invitation: going home . . .

But I nearly didn't make it. There was a problem with my visa. It looked like it wasn't going to come through on time for me to catch the flight. Tom didn't know why. If those guys in the Kremlin are afraid of letting a second-generation Canadian woman into their country just because her great-grandparents once lived there, maybe Doodie was right after all?

And then, only a couple of hours before check-in time, we heard that my visa was waiting to be collected at the Embassy. After picking it up, we jumped out of a taxi at Heathrow as the flight was being called for the last time and ran along miles of glassed-in corridors to the gate where we were scowled at for our late arrival by the Aeroflot ground staff. I couldn't believe it, they were scolding us as though we were kids! But Tom said it was normal Soviet behaviour. And you should see the flight attendants. They look like a ladies' wrestling team. The food they served for lunch would have been rejected by the old winos and bag ladies who used to come to that soup kitchen in Toronto where we helped out one winter . . .

Why did I fall for Ponsonby's pitch? You can't con an honest man. In all seductions, the victim must be willing. I agreed to that mission for one reason only: because it promised to be the highest and longest adrenaline trip of my life so far. Until then I had been putting only myself at risk, but this time Karen was involved. I told myself – like a Victorian husband selling his wife's jewels to pay a gambling debt – that I would make it all up to her in some undefined way afterwards.

When the visa didn't come through I felt immense relief that Karen would not be able to accompany me. It was as though a burden of guilt had been lifted from my shoulders by fortuitous bureaucracy. And then the gods tested me. The visa arrived, we sat in the taxi heading for Heathrow and I could have said to her, 'Don't come. It's a trap.' But I didn't. I wanted what was going to happen so badly that even putting her at risk seemed an acceptable price to pay.

In Leningrad I gave Karen a survival course in everyday living, Soviet-style: vital instructions like not leaving valuables such as soap or her contraceptive pills in the bathroom, and carrying the bath plug which I had brought from England everywhere in her shoulder bag. She treated it all like a joke. I knew that I should warn her that it wasn't, but I didn't, so I was to blame for everything that happened.

The tension made me exceptionally sexy that week. We came back to the room more than once a day to make love and ended each evening gasping and sweating in a tangle of sheets on the floor – like two equally matched wrestlers pausing between rounds. All the love-making and the crisp, cold, dry weather brought a bloom to Karen's cheeks. She had never looked so beautiful.

I couldn't sleep. In the early hours, I lay awake feeling like a cross between James Bond and Judas Iscariot.

Karen was both literally and figuratively wearing rose-coloured lenses that week. Instead of the cruel land, full of menace, about which her grandmother had told her so many stories as a child, she found herself in a city so beautiful that, like many of the older inhabitants, she insisted on calling it by its old name of Sankt Peterborg. The modern, functional sound of Leningrad did not do justice to the vistas of rococo architecture wherever she looked: churches and cathedrals, canals and bridges, the important buildings all painted in pastel colours.

The days were short but the weather was ideal for sight-seeing: cold and crisp with a hard, bright light that showed off the colours of the buildings to advantage. Using the hours of daylight to the maximum, Tom took her to all the tourist sights: the Admiralty, the Peter and Paul fortress and the

Hermitage Museum in the Winter Palace. They strolled along the snow-covered Neva embankment and ate *pirozhki* – little meat pies bought from open-air stalls. With them, Tom drank *kumiss* and *kvass* – rough rye beer and fermented mare's milk, neither of which Karen could stomach.

At Petrodvorets, Peter the Great's look-alike Versailles, built as a self-indulgence after his victory over the Swedes at Poltava in 1709, she was literally breathless at the sight of the huge cascade with the palace hovering at the top and the double stairway coming all the way down the hill with its profusion of gilded gods and goddesses dancing with satyrs and fauns, leaping, wrestling with each other and with serpents and lions, seducing maidens and being seduced, even groping each other in the grottoes.

'You must come back and see it in summer,' Tom said. 'When all the fountains are playing, it's an unbelievable sight. There are more than a thousand jets of water spilling down the hill and clothing all the statues in rainbows.'

He felt like a native showing off his home town. After days of sightseeing, he took her to eat in cheap restaurants where foreigners seldom found their way. There she drank Russian beer and ate *pelmeny* and *blini*, surrounded by friendly students who were very different from the frigid, hostile Slavs she had imagined. Fascinated by her accent, they took her to heart like a long-lost relative in a spontaneous effusion of emotion that could never have happened in the West.

Canadians and Russians were kin of a sort, they told her: people from the vast frozen north with ideas as big as their countries. In Leningrad, as they pointed out, Karen was on latitude 60 degrees north, level with the northernmost tip of Newfoundland or Anchorage in Alaska.

For the last day of the visit Tom had bought her a ticket at the Intourist desk in the foyer for a trip to Tsárskoye Seló on her own, making the excuse that he had to meet some contacts at the university.

'I'd rather stay in town with you,' Karen protested. 'I'm OD'ing on Russian rococo palaces.'

'No,' Tom insisted. 'You go. It's a must.'

She felt warm and trusting. They had made love twice that morning, once before getting up and again after breakfast. 'Okay,' she kissed Tom goodbye. 'I'll miss you. Have a nice day.'

She drifted through the trip, half-listening to the guide's commentary in English and German, getting out of the coach at the Pulkovo observatory to hear about the ferocious fighting that took place there during the 900-day siege of Leningrad in World War II that cost around one and a half million lives. There were some elderly German tourists on the trip who took photographs and talked soberly among themselves. Karen wondered whether any of the men had been there before, during the fighting to which the guide had referred.

Twenty-five kilometres to the south of the city lay the fantasy wonderland of the Tsar's Village. Built to outshine Versailles, Tsárskoye Seló made Disneyland look cheap. Frozen lakes, gardens, palaces, gilded cupolas all glistened in the winter sunlight.

Karen wondered whether her great-grandmother had walked along the paths she walked and seen the sights she was looking at. When she hung back to be alone with her thoughts, the bossy Intourist guide rounded her up like a sheepdog harrying a straggler from the flock, her hard voice barking statistics to frighten the dawdler back into the fold: Tsárskoye Seló was the first township in Russia to be lit by electricity . . . the first railway on Russian soil had run from there to downtown St Petersburg . . . the restoration after the Great Patriotic War had cost so many billions of roubles . . .

Big deal, Karen thought dreamily. It was odd being without Tom after spending six whole days and nights with him. You're in love, Karen McKenzie, she whispered to the frozen landscape as the coach sped back to the city. But that was okay; Tom seemed equally involved. She just wished he would talk about his emotions sometimes.

She blocked out the guide's commentary detailing the weight of girders in a bridge and the number of rivets joining them together by sinking into a delicious reverie, recalling things that Tom had said and done during the night. She had not the slightest premonition of the nightmare into which he was leading her.

.8.

Tom was sitting on the bed when she returned to the hotel room.

'I had a wonderful time!' Karen threw off her bulky white skiing anorak and put her arms around his neck, rolling onto the bed with him on top. 'How was your day?'

'Fine.'

'You sound uptight.' She pushed him away, the better to see his pale, tense face. 'Something go wrong at the university?'

He made a small joke: 'I've been waiting for the bath plug.'

He went into the *en suite* bathroom. The door swung open behind him because the lock was broken. Karen heard water running. The bedroom was hot and stuffy after being outdoors for most of the day. She tried to open the window to let some fresh air in, before remembering that it was screwed shut for the winter.

A couple of taxis waited by the rampart of re-frozen snow that had been cleared from the parking area in front of the hotel. Past them, down at the landing stage, an ancient flat-decked car ferry was just casting off on its last trip of the day to Kronstadt and the other islands. The reflection of its feeble yellow deck lights on the flat black surface of the water made it look as though the vessel was joined at the keel to a Siamese twin.

The phone rang. Before Karen could pick it up, Tom ran out of the bathroom with a towel round his waist, dripping water on the floor.

'Who's that?' she asked after he had put the phone down.

'Nobody there.' He did not look at her. 'Must have been a wrong number. Come on, it's time we were leaving.'

'I haven't had time to change yet, Tom.'

'You'll have to come as you are.' Without properly drying himself, he was pulling on his clothes.

'What's the hurry?' Karen wanted to know.

'Just shut up and get ready.'

The Pribaltiskaya Hotel was seven kilometres from the city centre. Tom ignored the licensed taxis and hailed a black Volga that was cruising past: some functionary's official transport in which the driver was moonlighting. From him Tom bought a paper-wrapped 200-gram bottle of vodka which he began drinking before the end of the journey.

The food in the Hungarian restaurant near the Finland station was watered-down borscht, followed by goulash that tasted as though it had been prepared from a Siberian mammoth which had spent several millennia in the permafrost. To get a bottle of Bull's Blood wine, Tom had to pay in dollars that went straight into the waiter's pocket. Two gypsy fiddlers played between the tables. One of them was so drunk that he backed into the table and knocked over Karen's glass, spilling wine on her white ski pants.

'How to ruin a perfect holiday on the last night,' she commented, trying to soak it up with a wad of paper handkerchiefs. 'You still haven't told me why we had to rush out early to eat in a dump like this, Tom.'

He had drunk most of the vodka and more than half of the wine. Outside the restaurant, he picked up another unlicensed taxi, asking to be dropped off on the other side of town, in front of the Baltic station from where trains left for Estonia, Latvia and Lithuania.

Inside the main entrance, he told her to wait. The dimly lit waiting hall was full of soldiers on leave and peasant families, some of three generations, who looked as though they were planning to spend the night sleeping on their bundles of baggage. There was nowhere else to sit or lie down.

'Where are you going?' Karen asked Tom. His white face alarmed her as much as the amount he had drunk.

'I'll be back in five minutes,' he said. 'Don't move from here, whatever happens.'

Once he had gone, Karen felt that everyone was staring at her. A thin gypsy woman with long, straggling dark hair and a small baby in her arms came and stood in front of her, begging for money. Even with a couple of roubles thrust into her dirty hand, the woman would not go away but continued whining for more money.

To get rid of her, Karen walked purposefully towards the exit that Tom had used and left the building. On this side of the station the only street lighting came from a couple of ordinary domestic light bulbs swinging in the wind a hundred metres away outside a shed in the marshalling yard. By their feeble light she could see a crowd of men standing around in the gloom. Between them, on the piles of dirty snow cleared from the streets, lay boxes and packages of all sizes. In low voices everyone seemed to be haggling over the merchandise that was being inspected by the light of pocket torches. Karen realised that she had stumbled into some kind of black market.

When several shots rang out nearby she did not immediately realise what the noise was. Then the echoes were drowned by the noise of pounding feet and Karen found herself caught up in a stampede of men, each holding his bundle or box, and all intent on fighting their way into the station. From nowhere Tom appeared, forcing a passage through the crush towards her.

'I told you to stay in the station,' he panted, eyes staring. 'Here, shove these in an inside pocket.'

Pulling her close, he thrust into Karen's hands a pair of 35mm film cassettes and hissed, 'Take the Metro to the Nevsky Prospekt and pick up a taxi there, to get yourself back to the hotel. I'll see you back there.'

'Where are you going, Tom?'

'Just do it.' His grip on her arm was painful.

'Don't leave me!'

Panicking, she reached for him but he ignored the plea on her face and broke her grip so that she was swept away on the flood of jostling, shouting men clawing their way into the vast entrance hall of the station.

Outside, Tom stood still. Someone had turned off or shot out the lights in the marshalling yard. Men shouted and dogs barked. There were flashing lights and several canvas-covered trucks braked noisily to a halt, their tailboards slamming down as soldiers in greatcoats carrying rifles jumped out and ran right and left to form a cordon around the whole area. A searchlight stabbed through the darkness until a hoarse voice ordered it turned off with the all-purpose Russian expletive: '*Yob tvóyu mat!*'

A black car skidded on a patch of ice as its driver gunned the engine to get away before the two horns of the cordon could close. With no lights on, it nearly ran Tom down. As it fish-tailed past he grabbed the twin radio aerials on the rear wings and somehow got his feet onto the solid, old-fashioned rear bumper, clinging there as the car swung round the corner of the station, crossed a red light and accelerated along the poorly lit streets.

Two blocks later, the driver braked savagely to a halt after spotting his unwanted passenger in the rear-view mirror. Tom fell sprawling to the ground. Before he could stand up, two men leaped out of the car and dragged him upright, pinning him against the brick wall of a factory, hitting him and shouting in *blátny yazyk* – thieves' slang. Realising that they had taken him for a police informer, Tom exaggerated his English accent and begged for mercy. With a fist in his solar plexus and a shove that sent him reeling into a brick wall, they got back in the car and drove off.

In the crowded Metro carriage, Karen clutched the films, thrust deep into a pocket. It seemed that everyone was staring at her, including two militiamen in uniform.

When they followed her off the train at the Nevsky Prospekt station and stopped her on the platform to ask for her papers, she was so flustered that she nearly took out the films by mistake, instead of her passport. Unable to read the Roman script, they took their time asking questions: why was she alone, where was the travel group to which she belonged, in what hotel was she staying?

Karen put on an exaggerated North American accent and tried to look irritated, as a bona fide tourist might, replying over and over again, 'Ya ne govoryú pa-rússki.'

At last they let her go and she walked off, worrying that her legs were going to give way under her. She felt sick at the way Tom had used her – was using her still. How could you? she asked. *How could you do this to me?*

Once in the street, it would have been tempting to throw the films into a rubbish bin if she had not seen how often people immediately went to pick over everything that was thrown away in Russia; she had no option but to keep the films on her.

Tom cursed himself for not keeping the films and brazening it out, back at the station. Blaming the panic on Karen's face for making him lose his cool and run, he determined never again to work with anyone else, whatever Ponsonby advised.

The immediate problem was that he had lost his bearings, never having been in this part of Leningrad before.

Under Soviet law it was a crime for a foreigner to spend the night elsewhere than in the hotel where he was registered, so somehow he had to find his way back across several kilometres of St Petersburg to the Pribaltiskaya Hotel before morning, without attracting attention.

Back in the hotel room, Karen was kneeling on the floor of the bathroom, vomiting weakly into the toilet. When the spasm passed, she stayed there, staring at the two films which had rolled across the floor when she pulled off her anorak to be sick. How could she get rid of them? She could not flush them down the toilet; nor could she throw them out of the window.

Anger replaced fear. Damn Tom! she thought. How could he use her like this? If he were caught, she would also be facing fifteen years in a labour camp.

What hurt most was not the knowledge of the risk he had placed her in, nor even the deception involved in bringing her to Leningrad as window-dressing for whatever crazy game he was playing. It was the bitter thought that he had not been turned on by her that week so much as by the thrill of what he was doing. She had been merely the vessel for his lust, not its object.

There was a knock on the door. Thinking it was him, she shouted out, 'Go away and leave me alone!'

The knocking persisted until she opened the door, to find the night key-lady outside. Ignoring Karen's tear-stained face, the woman asked in broken English for any spare clothes she had to sell, '. . . becoss tomorrow you go *domói*. I pay *dólary*.'

She would not go away until Karen handed over Tom's best pair of jeans, for which she kept trying to pay until the door was slammed in her face.

The next knock came two hours later. By then, Karen had control of herself and opened the door to find Tom leaning against the wall, grinning at her stupidly. He stank of spirits and beer, had a cut on his face and looked as if he had been dragged through a sewer.

Behind him the key-lady was smiling, displaying a mouth full of steel crowns. She placed a finger on her lips to indicate that she would keep her mouth shut. 'No trabble,' she said to Karen. '*On pyán*. Ees tronk, yuur man.'

'I let you in,' Karen said coldly, after closing the door, 'only because to keep you locked out all night would draw attention to us both. I've put a blanket on the bathroom floor. You can sleep there.'

'What is this?' I hissed. 'Some kind of joke?'

I tried to get close enough to whisper in her ear, but she pushed me away with, 'You stink of alcohol. I don't want you near me.'

I told her to keep her voice down, that I hadn't been drinking but had just poured beer and vodka down the front of my shirt and swallowed a bit, to account for coming back to the hotel alone and so late.

'Then you're high,' she accused me, not knowing that I was tripping on my own adrenaline. 'You've either been smoking or boozing.'

'The films?' I whispered. 'Where are they?'

'That's all you're worried about, isn't it?' She pushed me away. 'Don't worry, they're safe.'

I could see that she was in a turmoil: hurt at the way I had used her, angry at me and frightened at what could have happened to us both. So I told her everything about my own impromptu adventures and the escalation when first Brodsky and then Ponsonby gave me real missions to carry out.

Karen's reaction took me by surprise. 'You sound as though you're in love,' she said. 'In love with this Ponsonby. You've shown more emotion talking about spying for him than you ever showed me.'

Much later, when my favourite shrink discussed how handling emotions is a learned process, I realised that I had

*never told Karen how deeply I felt for her. Coming from a
family where repression of feelings was the normal mode of
behaviour, where voices were never raised and arguments
never vented conflict, I couldn't say the things she needed
to hear. I just didn't have the vocabulary with which to do
it. What should have been a declaration of love turned into
a plea for her co-operation along the lines of: 'You're the
only person I could trust, don't you see? For God's sake,
don't let me down now.'*

*'Don't worry,' she said coldly. 'I shan't give you away,
Tom. Ponsonby will get his films even if I have to stuff
them up my cunt to get them through customs for you.'*

*I ignored the danger signal. The word was in common
enough usage, but Karen had never used it in my hearing,
nor employed any swear-word more forceful than the
occasional 'goddam'.*

*Why didn't I tear the damned films up or, better still,
burn them and flush them down the lavatory? I don't
know. Instead of saying, 'I don't care about the films, I
don't care about Ponsonby, I care about you,' I accepted
her offer and weakly promised myself that I would sort
everything else out when we got back to Britain.*

*I stripped off in the bathroom and took a shower. When
I made to come out, Karen said, 'You can spend what's left
of the night in there. I don't want you beside me.'*

*Suddenly crashing down from my week-long high, I fell
asleep in minutes, wrapped in the blanket on the bathroom
floor – while Karen, I suppose, lay awake till dawn,
planning what she could possibly do to hurt me where I
had hurt her.*

*In the morning we hardly spoke. I stopped off in London
to deliver the films. When I got back to Bristol, Karen was
subdued. For the rest of that week she slept on the bed and
I slept on the sofa. In the daytime we led our separate lives.
In the evenings she tried in a thousand different ways to
persuade me to stop working for Ponsonby.*

Her final attempt was made dry-eyed in the pizzeria downstairs where we had eaten the first evening: 'If you won't stop this, I'm ending our relationship, Tom. Here and now.'

I tried to bargain with her, promised that I would never again involve her.

'You fool,' she said. 'I'm not worried about me. In the end you'll make a mistake and they'll catch you. Well, I'm not the girl to sit around weeping for a lover who's been stupid enough to be sent to the Gulag for twenty years' hard labour. If you prefer the thrill of whatever you're doing for Ponsonby to being with me, that's your decision.'

Next day, while I was out, she removed all her things from the flat. I obtained her new address from the Students' Union accommodation bureau and left messages on the shared phone which she never returned. On the few occasions when we met on the campus, all she would say was an unsmiling, 'Hi, Tom.'

Ponsonby would have made a good drug-pusher. I'll never know how much he was aware of what was going on between Karen and me. Certainly he had at least one pair of ears and eyes in Bristol, keeping him informed. For the rest of that term, he fed my habit by giving me a succession of little jobs in Russia. On one, a sixth sense made me abort the rendezvous at the last moment. I watched in a shop window as my contact grew bored with waiting. When he left, I followed him into a shop, at the rear of which he spoke to two men sitting in a black Volga. It was as close as that. The other jobs were so innocuous that I wondered at the time whether some of them were just training exercises.

Whatever, each time I landed in Russia I was riding on an adrenaline high until the moment when the plane took off again heading for the West. It was a clever way of distracting me from Karen. I thought about her a lot, but never made the decision she was waiting for. And then, at the end of term, I learned from Ashmole that she had gone back to Canada. I realised that I had said goodbye to the best thing in my life – not for the money or Ponsonby's praise but for the cheap thrill of adrenaline.

Now my favourite shrink tells me they have a word for it in her business: dice-throwing.

'You don't know,' she says, 'how much you value something – until you've lost it.'

Why didn't I follow Karen to Canada? Even then it might not have been too late. The answer is that I didn't want to miss even one of those sordid little jobs, leaving packets of money in dead drops and collecting even smaller packets to bring home. Put coldly in black and white, I chose to be Ponsonby's retriever rather than Karen's lover.

And then, out of the blue came the air ticket in a letter that read:

> *Dear Tom,*
>
> *I won this in a competition. I'd like to see you again, so I hope you'll use it. Only problem is, it's an APEX ticket so you can't change the flight. I just hope you can make it.*
>
> *Love (I think),*
> *Karen*
>
> *P.S. Don't tell my folks I sent the ticket. All will be explained.*

.9.

The black Saab 900 convertible glided down the ramp of the multi-storey car park at Toronto's Lester Pearson Airport. Above, the sky was a perfect cloudless cerulean blue, except low to the east where a grey haze of pollution hung over the city stewing in its own juices. According to a local news station to which the car radio was tuned: 'The air temperature downtown this sultry July afternoon is 38 degrees Centigrade with 95 per cent humidity.'

The Saab accelerated onto Highway 400, heading north. Karen's brother was at the wheel: a powerfully built man of thirty-five whose muscular frame and tanned face contrasted with the smart and expensive lightweight suit and handmade shoes. With his expansive manner and flamboyant gestures, there was no physical resemblance to his sister, as far as Tom could see.

'It doesn't bother you, the roof being down?' he asked. It was a cue for his passenger to ask about the car, which had less than 500 kilometres on the clock. The leather seats still gleamed with showroom wax.

'No, that's fine, Mike,' Tom said, unaware that the Saab was a status symbol.

'So this is your first visit to Canada? It's a hell of a coincidence, you flying in today of all days.'

'It is?'

'When we heard, we postponed the wedding by two hours so that you could be there.'

'I didn't even know there was a wedding.'

Tom had been expecting Karen to be at the airport to greet him. Even though he could guess the answer without being told, he had to ask, 'Who's getting married?'

'Karen, of course.'

Tom stared to his right, across the flat countryside rolling past. He would have liked to stop the car and get out.

'She was kind of engaged when she went to Europe,' her brother continued. 'Maybe she told you? They had even set the date for the wedding but Karen called it off at the last moment. I thought it was all over between her and Larry – he's my closest friend and the lucky guy. But it seems she just wanted time to make up her mind.'

The landscape blurred. Tom heard Mike McKenzie describe the Canadian Shield, across which they were driving, as the oldest rock on the surface of the planet. The longitudinal furrows gouged out of it by Ice Age glaciers had become a myriad lakes great and small, making an obstacle that the early settlers had found impassable, except for a few trappers and traders who had to travel and live like the Indians to survive there.

The Saab skimmed across lake and swamp on a new highway with Tom saying, 'How interesting,' from time to time.

At the church a hundred smiling faces introduced themselves to him on the lawn outside the freshly painted white wooden building, so different from the ancient stone-built parish churches of England that he knew. Karen's grandmother Dudinskaya – a shrivelled little woman called Doodie by everyone – crossed herself whenever he came near.

Normally he would have been fascinated to talk to someone who had grown up in a Doukhobor community and run away at the age of eighteen to marry a man from another culture, with whom at the time she had no more than a few dozen words in common. But that day he did not feel like talking to anyone.

The most disturbing person present was Karen's twin sister, Fran. The two women were so similar in looks that Tom found it hard not to stare at her. And when she spoke, it was with Karen's voice. Her husband and her brother Michael were partners owning a chain of furniture stores together with Larry, the bridegroom. She seemed to be a happily married woman whose husband and two small daughters constituted her whole world.

'How interesting . . .' Tom heard himself repeating the same words, like a record stuck in a groove.

Inside the church, filled with light pouring through the tall windows of clear glass, there was a harmonium being played not very well by a friend of the family. Tom was shown to a pew near the front, just behind Karen's family. A hush among the congregation announced the bride's entrance on her father's arm. As she drew level with where Tom was sitting, the green eyes he knew so well locked onto his for a moment through the white lace veil. The service seemed to last a long time, the priest's homily on love and duty going on and on while Karen's slim figure in white stood beside the groom, her back to the congregation. Two pre-teen girls in yellow satin dresses were holding posies of freshly picked garden flowers just behind her, whispering together until the bride turned and shushed them gently.

And after the words: 'Do you, Karen Evdokia McKenzie, take this man . . .?' Tom held the back of the seat in front of him for support.

Karen turned and looked back down the church at him for a long moment before saying clearly, 'I do.'

Afterwards, in the garden of her parents' home, the groom

proposed a toast tō 'our guest of honour who has come so far to share our happiness today'.

Later he thrust a glass of champagne into Tom's hand and said, 'I'm truly proud to meet you. Karen's told me how helpful you were when she first came to Britain.'

And Karen lifted the veil and offered a cheek as cold as death for Tom to kiss, saying, 'I'm so glad you could be here.'

All he could think of to say was: 'No spectacles? At least you took my advice about contact lenses.'

'Oh, I learned a great deal from you,' she said levelly. 'In so many ways.'

After the ceremony, I wandered away from the party in the garden of the family home and found myself following some rusty railway tracks to the lakeshore where there was a deserted landing stage and some derelict warehouses. I thought it a bleak scene for a summer evening, until I realised that the bleakness was inside myself.

I heard a car drive up, the wheels crunching the cinders beside the tracks. A door slammed and a familiar voice said, 'Tom?'

For a moment I thought Karen had followed me. My heart leaped. I turned round to see her sister standing there. In her yellow satin dress and matching shoes, Fran looked as out of place as I had been feeling since I arrived at the wedding.

'I saw you leave the party,' she smiled, walking towards me. 'Please forgive us all for neglecting you. At a family event, an outsider can feel real . . .'

'Outside,' I said.

'That's right.' She smiled Karen's smile and came closer.

'Don't worry about it,' I said. 'I just wanted to be alone for a while.'

'It's the time-difference that upsets the body clock. Karen was really weird for several days after she came home.'

She stood beside me watching the sun's reflection on the lake and flights of water-fowl taking off in the still air. I could smell Fran's perfume. It was the same one that Karen used.

'You should have stopped her,' she said.

'How could I?'

'That's why she turned around before taking the vow.'

'You're telling me that I should have run up the aisle and interrupted the service?'

'That's exactly what you should have done, Tom.'

'It was Karen's decision.'

'She doesn't love Larry. She loves you.'

'Then why did she marry him?'

'To hurt you. Whatever did you do to her?' Fran asked. 'Did you sleep with someone else?'

'No.'

'Well, you sure as hell hurt her some way or other. I've never known my sister like this before. We always shared secrets since we were kids – not that I ever really had any – and now she won't tell me a goddam thing that's on her mind.'

'She didn't talk about Leningrad?'

'No. She hasn't even talked to Doodie about anything.'

I heard Fran's feet crunching the cinders back to her car. She opened the door and said, 'There's going to be a great unhappiness, Tom. And it's all your fault.'

There is just one other image of the wedding which comes to mind. I was standing by the car as the happy couple drove off on their honeymoon. Karen's window slid down and she said something. It was already dusk and she was wearing dark glasses, so I couldn't see her eyes. I leaned forward to ask whether she had been speaking to me and she said, 'Goodbye, Tom.'

I don't remember anything else. I must have spent the night there and someone must have driven me back to Toronto the next day. I found a room in a shabby motel down by the shore of Lake Ontario where most of the rooms were rented by the hour. There I got drunk and stayed that way. Twice I paid a woman to come up to my room but nothing happened either time.

'It's no big deal,' one of them said as she was getting dressed. 'Stay off the booze for a few weeks and you'll be okay.' But I knew it wouldn't be that easy.

I took the ferry one afternoon to Toronto Island and walked the breeze-swept boardwalk, trying to clear my head of the alcohol fumes. There was a strange time-slipped community dwelling on the island only a few minutes from the skyscrapers across the water: quiet, car-free people who had chosen to live without contributing to or suffering from the hustle, noise and pollution of modern life. In a tea-house run by several elderly ladies I wallowed in an ancient wicker chair and ate buttered scones and drank strong tea, leafing through a pile of old magazines.

The two women in flower-power dresses at the next table were residents, by the look of them. One was reading the Tarot for the other. A card dropped face down on the floor between the tables. Neither of them noticed. I'd never taken any interest in fortune telling but as the minutes ticked by I became convinced that there was some message for me in that card.

I bent down and picked it up. The picture showed a rather simple youth dancing among wild animals.

'What does it mean?' I asked the woman who had dropped it.

She looked at the card and then at me. 'It's the running man,' she said. 'He's the Fool.'

PART III
Summer 1983

.1.

The reception was being held in Professor Ashmole's study, overlooking the courtyard of the Faculty of History. Tom was still wearing the cap and gown in which he had received his doctorate. There was a photographer from a Bristol newspaper and another from an agency who was taking a picture of Tom's parents, posing with him for their local paper in the Lake District. In the centre of the group, Dr Thomas Winston Churchill Fielding was holding a bound copy of *Clarifying Confusion*. The printing and binding costs had been paid by the Institute, and the result in morocco leather with gold-blocked title was handsome and not too slim.

Ponsonby, smart as a shark on Saturday night in a new three-piece dark blue pinstripe suit and a good inch of cuff showing below his sleeves, was chatting with a rather dumpy woman from one of the university presses who wore her greying hair in a bun. Next to him, the Dean was sipping a dry sherry with Ashmole. Tom's sister Margaret was talking with his brother Adrian, whose wife Kim was networking with the Dean's wife. Most of the other people present, Tom had never even seen before.

After the photographers left, strangers kept shaking his hand and offering congratulations. Ponsonby's eyes looked almost warm for a moment as he crushed Tom's hand in his and observed, 'I see your proud parents looking suitably impressed over there, listening to the prof singing your praises. So what's your next move? Will you be starting work on the book version straight away?'

'I haven't decided.' Tom's head was spinning from Ashmole's disclosure minutes before that the departmental budget had not been increased, so there would be no post for him to return to in the coming academic year.

'I was sorry to hear from the prof that you'd had a spot of bother with your lady friend,' Ponsonby murmured.

'I didn't even know he knew.'

'That old pussy knows everything that goes on, on and off the campus.' Ponsonby took two glasses of sherry from a passing waitress and handed one to Tom. 'I might just be able to help take your mind off things. There's a job I'd like to talk over with you. Are you free this afternoon?'

Tom shook his head. 'I promised to take my parents on a tour of the town. Mother's never been here before and my father's last visit was when he did aircrew training somewhere near here during World War Two.'

'Is that how Pater got the limp?'

'He baled out over Berlin early in 1945. He was lucky to be taken prisoner by a *Heimwehr* detachment. His best buddy – the navigator – was lynched by some civilians when he came down just half a mile away. Ask him about it. He'd love to tell you.'

Ponsonby chuckled, 'That sounds bitter. Don't you get along with the old man?'

'He's still fighting what he persists in calling the last war.'

'Even so, you can't abandon your aged parents on a day like this, dear boy. And certainly not just to get boozed up with a rugby-playing reprobate like me. So how about us meeting for a chat this evening?'

'I said I'd have dinner with Ma and Pa at their hotel.'

Ashmole homed in on the woman from the university press. Temporarily abandoned, Tom's parents were looking uncomfortable. Behind their backs, Margaret was making tentative signs that it was time to go. Her father's game leg hurt when he stood for too long; he was leaning heavily on his stout walking stick, his lips a thin line of self-control. Tom held up five fingers.

Ponsonby caught Tom's sleeve to regain his attention. 'Suppose we meet tonight after the family meal? I'm dining in with Ashmole. I'll leave as early as I can, so shall we say ten-thirty p.m.? I've got your address in Clifton.'

The taxi pulled up in front of the pizza parlour five minutes early. Tom was waiting across the street, outside a pub with a glass in his hand.

'Lovely evening,' Ponsonby greeted him.

'Can I get you a pint?'

Ponsonby checked out the crowd of drinkers spilling across the pavement. 'Rather not, dear boy. Too many ears, you know.'

His eyes flicked over Tom's face. 'Unless you need a quick refill first, I'd prefer to do our talking far from the madding crowd.'

On the Down it seemed to Tom that the mild summer evening was filled with couples holding hands, laughing together or walking quietly side by side. He half-listened to Ponsonby's account of dinner with Ashmole, impatient to know what was on offer this time.

'It's more than just another mission.' Ponsonby had been tense ever since leaving Tom after the little ceremony in Ashmole's rooms. In hooking either a man or a fish, judging the pull-in was equally crucial. Ashmole's bad news had been a carefully timed blow from the gaff but during the hours

Tom had spent with his parents he might have recovered from it.

'This is the big one, Tom,' he began. 'A job that could change the course of history.'

'Bringing something out?'

'And how.'

'When?'

'Now.'

'Aren't your professional whores better for a big job than enthusiastic amateurs like me?'

'The trouble with the pros,' – Ponsonby managed to inject a sneer into the word, implying that gentlemen like Tom and himself were in another league from the players who did it for money – 'is that the other side never take their eyes off them. The poor bastards are watched forever. Even Philby and Burgess were never trusted off the leash.'

'And you think it would be any different for me?'

'By becoming a member of the privileged academic layer of Soviet society, you've enjoyed an unusual freedom of movement for a foreigner, Tom. Not many foreigners get into closed cities like Sebastopol, where the Black Sea fleet is protected from prying eyes like a virgin in a harem. But you did it. That's better than any pro could have achieved. And don't forget, the amateurs in this game include the likes of T.E. Lawrence, who was no slouch at intelligence. He used his professional activities as historian and archaeologist to cover for skulking all over the Turkish domains in the Middle East before the First World War.'

The flattery was oblique, but the glow of pride Tom felt at being compared with such a historic figure as Lawrence momentarily lifted the depression that had been hanging over him like a cloud since coming back from Canada.

Ponsonby was monitoring his body-language. Go easy, he warned himself, you're not dealing with some gung-ho businessman who spends every weekend running around playing soldiers with the TA. Softly, softly catchee Fielding . . .

'If you can manage to ensconce yourself permanently over there and continue your civil war research,' he said, 'I think you'll be that rarity in Russia: a person who can come and go more or less where he pleases. Mobility will make all the difference between the success and failure of my big one.'

Tom was not convinced. 'You underestimate the xenophobia of the Russian mind, Clive. However much I've been tolerated so far, they won't allow me to quote ensconce myself permanently unquote anywhere. I'll always be on sufferance.'

'Not necessarily,' Ponsonby chuckled. 'Not if the KGB is your sponsor.'

'And why would the Committee sponsor me?'

'Because you'll buy your way in, dear boy, by spilling the beans about the Institute being used as a cover for espionage.'

'I tell them about you?'

'Oh, not about me,' Ponsonby said.

'So what do I tell them?'

'More or less the truth. Just make Brodsky the director and leave me out of the picture. You can do it.'

Tom could feel adrenaline coursing through his body. To hide the excitement, he leaned over the parapet and gazed into the darkness below. A man jogged past them, breathing easily. *Pat-pat-pat*, the sound of his trainers on the asphalt surface faded into the distance. He was wearing a dark blue tracksuit with a light rucksack on his back. Tom recollected seeing him standing outside the pub – not with anyone but just watching the crowd. His busy eyes had made Tom think: either a crook or a copper.

The jogger stopped at the end of the bridge to take another look at the ill-assorted pair talking so quietly in the middle of the span: one man in waistcoat and tie, carrying his jacket neatly folded over one arm, and another in tee-shirt and jeans beside him.

'Let's move on,' said Ponsonby.

Tom waited until they were well out of the jogger's earshot before responding, 'You're offering me a one-way ticket, Clive. If anything goes wrong, I'll be spending the rest of my life in Russia.'

'You'll be back before the year's out,' Ponsonby promised. 'It could be even sooner.'

'And how exactly do I get back?' Tom queried. 'They're hardly going to let me buy a plane ticket for the next flight to London when I've had enough.'

'You'd be surprised, dear boy,' Ponsonby said airily. 'Defectors of no further consequence are usually allowed to walk, if they're prepared to face the music when they get home. Take Lee Harvey Oswald. Disillusioned with Russia, he went back to the States and took his Russian wife with him. And there was Anthony Wraight, an RAF officer who defected in 1956, changed his mind after three years and was back in the UK for Christmas of 1959.'

'That makes two. How many others are still there, rotting in Perm or Sverdlovsk, refused permission even to visit Moscow, let alone walk into the Embassy and read the cricket scores in *The Times*?'

'Did you know that, of the twenty-one American service-men who chose to stay in China after the Korean war, all but three came home eventually? So did the only Briton.'

'I need a pee,' said Tom. 'I had quite a few jars before you arrived.'

They walked into a public toilet and stood side by side at the urinals. When Tom was about to say something, Ponsonby shut him up with a nod at the closed door of one of the cubicles.

They had just finished when there was a squawk of electronic noise and a distorted man's voice said, 'Do them, Charlie. I'm coming in.'

The cubicle door burst open at the same time as the jogger walked in, holding his rucksack in one hand and a walkie-talkie in the other.

'Let's go, gents,' he said, flashing an identity card so fast that no one could have read it. 'The charge is: act of gross indecency in a public place. Make no trouble and we'll have this sorted in an hour or two and you'll be on your way home, nice and quiet, no bother with the neighbours.'

'Fuck off,' said Ponsonby calmly. 'You're getting on my tits, young man.'

'We are police officers. I must warn you that if you give us a hard time, the publicity . . .'

Taking care that Tom should not see it, Ponsonby thrust his own ID card into the plain-clothes man's face. 'Ever seen one of these before?'

The jogger stepped back and lowered his walkie-talkie. 'Hold it, Charlie. We've made a mistake.'

'You can say that again,' Ponsonby snarled. He handed his jacket to Tom before swinging round and head-butting the jogger viciously hard. As his victim collapsed moaning into the urinals with blood streaming from his broken nose, Ponsonby grabbed the radio from his hand and threw it onto the tiled floor, where it shattered, pieces skidding into the reddening, urine-filled gutter which was blocked with cigarette ends. He turned to the second plain-clothes man, who was gaping open-mouthed in surprise, kneed him in the groin with a simultaneous punch in the solar plexus, grabbed his radio and smashed it likewise.

He walked out of the gents' with a huge smile on his face. 'I haven't had more fun since we last played against the Australians,' he said gleefully, taking his jacket from Tom. 'Those fucking perjurers will have to pay for the radios out of their salaries. Serves 'em right.'

He slipped his jacket on, smoothed his hair back, then led the way back across the bridge to the Clifton side of the gorge.

'Supposing Moscow doesn't want to let me come home when I've done this job of yours?' Tom said. 'What then?'

Ponsonby tapped the side of his nose. 'We have our methods. We'll get you out.'

'Even if I'm under surveillance?'

'It's been done many times, via Prague or Budapest to Vienna – sometimes over the Finnish border.'

'I'd have to trust you.'

'We'll be putting a lot of trust in you too, Tom. People's lives will depend on you – and it's no exaggeration to say that my whole career hangs in the balance. But I know you can pull it off, although not many other people could.'

Tom was staring down at the steely gleam of the river at the bottom of the gorge. In his head was an echo of Karen's voice saying, 'I think I'd like to spend the night with you.'

It would be good to get away from all the places that reminded him of her.

Taking his silence as an expression of reserve, Ponsonby said quietly, 'You'd be put on salary, of course. The exact grade will have to be worked out by Establishment, but I'd guess it'll work out to around twenty grand for the year, paid straight into your bank account. Since you won't be touching it whilst you're over there, that will have increased with interest by the time you come back. Oh, and there'll be a bonus on completion of fifty per cent. How does that sound?'

Tom looked up. 'And what do I do when I come back, Clive? Do you expect me to spend the rest of my life working for you people?'

'No way, dear boy,' Ponsonby guffawed. He felt a surge of elation at how easy hooking this fish was turning out to be.

'As a field man,' he continued more soberly, 'you'll be blown sky-high. And desk work calls for altogether different talents. So our gratitude will manifest itself in the usual appropriate way. We don't want you feeling discontented, for obvious reasons, so we'll arrange for your reinsertion into the academic circuit.'

'Thanks to Ashmole?'

'Or another friend in the groves of academe. You'd be surprised how many there are.'

'I'll have lost two years of seniority by then.'

'According to what Ashmole tells me, that sort of thing never worried you up till now, did it?'

'No,' Tom had to admit.

'Well, then?'

'I'll do it,' said Tom.

Ponsonby put an arm around his shoulders and gave him a rugby man's victory hug. 'I need a drink. Several drinks.'

'The pub'll be shut by now.'

Ponsonby nodded at the chic Avon Gorge Hotel and bent his steps towards it. 'They'll serve us in the residents' lounge.'

'Are you staying there?'

'There are times, dear boy,' said Ponsonby grandly, 'when the cost of a hotel room is a small price to pay for getting monumentally pissed. Tonight is one of them.'

.2.

The elegant town house near the northern end of Harley Street was divided into consulting rooms hired by the hour because the prestigious address impressed patients.

Tom arrived early and sat in the waiting room, reading the glossy magazines: *The Field*, *Tatler*, *Vogue* and *Marie-France*. An elderly blue-rinsed secretary sat at a desk in the corner, typing notes and keeping an appointments list for several consultants. All the patients waiting were from the Middle East. Next to Tom a woman veiled in a floor-length black chador with her hands concealed in white cotton gloves was talking animatedly in Arabic to another woman dressed in high heels and a short skirt, wearing make-up and jewellery. Their two undisciplined little boys ran around the room, making a nuisance of themselves and taking no notice of their mothers' pleas to sit still.

A buzzer sounded on the secretary's desk. 'Dr Nathan will see you now,' she smiled at Tom.

He walked along the carpeted corridor to a doorway at the end. A visiting card was stuck into a small brass frame

screwed to the wall beside it, reading *A.T. Nathan, MD*.
There was a string of other letters after the name, none of
which Tom recognised. He knocked and waited.

'Come.'

The décor was off-white paint over wood-chip paper.
There was a sink in one corner with a medical faucet of the
type that can be turned on and off with the elbows. Behind a
screen Tom could see an examining couch. The only other
furniture was a couple of comfortable chairs in front of a
glass and metal desk and an executive swivel chair behind it.

The woman seated there was dressed in a man's grey
waistcoat over an open-necked grey cotton shirt. A pair of
nondescript dark grey trousers and low-heeled black shoes
completed the androgynous image. Her dark brown hair was
cut short. She was thin, pale and wore no make-up or jewellery except a wrist-watch. She could have been any age
between thirty and fifty.

'Tom Fielding?' she said, standing up and holding out her
hand.

Her skin was cold and there was no return pressure. It
was like shaking hands with royalty.

They sat and looked at each other for a moment across
the desk.

'Do you mind if I call you Tom?'

'Go ahead.'

'My name's Tessa.'

Her voice was a low contralto, pleasant and well modu-
lated. In the background there was the sound of a Bach
oratorio coming out of the wall-speakers at very low level.
Tom imagined clients lying on the couch behind the screen
with closed eyes, listening to the music and letting Dr Tessa
Nathan's oh-so-balanced voice probe into their problems.

'I'm sorry to keep you waiting,' she said. 'It wasn't inten-
tional. I have a client who is suicidal. One can't just tell her
that the time is up or she might throw herself under a tube
train on the way home.'

'I understand,' said Tom.

'Mind if I smoke?'

There was a large red-on-white NO SMOKING notice on the wall. 'Someone else does,' he suggested.

There was a small aluminium foil dish on the desk, already containing several stubs. Dr Nathan lit a king-size low tar cigarette, inhaled and confided, 'I'm trying to cut down but not doing very well. You don't smoke?'

Tom shook his head. She reached into a briefcase standing on the floor beside her chair and lifted out a manila folder two inches thick. It was marked SECRET and CONFIDEN-TIAL with Tom's name on the top right-hand corner.

'Defection,' she said, 'is a fascinating area. If you add an "a", you get *defecation*. Essentially, that's what it is: shitting on a country or an organisation to which loyalty is owed. It's the act of an immature person subject to the delusion that his or her true worth has never been recognised the way it should have been.'

'I suppose so,' Tom agreed.

'You being an intellectual,' she continued, 'it's as well to have the motivation clear in your own mind.'

'Like an actor preparing for a role?'

She slipped on a pair of heavy-framed reading glasses that reminded Tom of Karen when he had first met her, and started to leaf through the file in front of her. Occasionally she scribbled a word in a shorthand note pad with her gold propelling pencil. It took a smoker's acquired dexterity to juggle her glasses, the cigarette, the pencil and the file.

As she turned its pages, Tom saw several photographs of himself. The most recent showed him standing beside his parents at the awards ceremony. Others were of the family house near Keswick and various relatives. There was a glossy 10 × 8 of his brother. Taken just after his election as Conservative Member of Parliament, it showed him standing side by side with the Prime Minister on the terrace of the

House of Commons. The rest of the file was filled with sheet upon sheet of double-spaced typing.

'D'you know much about treachery?' asked Dr Nathan.

'Nothing,' said Tom.

'Social class isn't very important. The famous Cambridge spies were well-heeled, of course, but Leo Long was a working-class boy, Bettany came from a terraced house in the Potteries and Geoffrey Prime was also from the bottom of the ladder. Most American traitors come from middle-class homes, although Michael Straight was very upper-crust. So what does that tell us?'

Ponsonby had said, 'We find Dr Nathan very helpful.' Tom wondered where the monologue was leading.

'Family strife is far more important than class,' she murmured. 'You never got on very well with your dad?'

'We're very different people. My father's finest hour was flying around Europe dropping bombs on civilians. It must be a disappointment to him that I have no ambition to kill people.'

She made a note. 'Would you have been a conscientious objector, in time of war?'

'How can I say?' Tom asked. 'In an emergency, you do what you have to do. But you don't need to go through life telling people about it for ever afterwards.'

'Did he ever use physical force with you?'

'No.'

'Never?' There was a hint of surprise in her voice.

'Oh, a few times,' Tom admitted. 'Pain from his leg gives him a short temper. I learned young to keep out of the way when the weather put him in a bad mood.'

'Thomas Winston Churchill Fielding. The middle names were his idea?'

'Winnie was his great hero.'

'Do you mind – the name, I mean?'

'It was a good way of ensuring that I vote for the Left.'

'How far left?'

'Actually, I don't bother to vote,' said Tom. 'It was just a figure of speech.'

Dr Nathan nodded, scribbling. 'George Blake hated his bullying, bombastic father. Treachery was his revenge. Vassall and Prime also came from unhappy homes. Philby, too.'

She looked up with a conspiratorial smile. 'Well, who'd want a father like that horrendous old man of the sands with his succession of nubile young Arab wives, forever threatening his son's masculinity?'

'I don't feel threatened,' Tom protested. 'We just don't get on together.'

'We're trying to build a legend,' she said. 'This is all grist to the mill. What about your uncle who committed suicide?'

Tom shifted in his chair and immediately had the feeling that the movement had been noted, assessed, analysed.

'Uncle Brian was gay,' he said. 'He had a lot of other problems too, or so my mother told me.'

'He hanged himself in your parents' garage, I see – with the tow-rope taken from your father's car. That seems rather a pointed statement, doesn't it? And he was wearing female clothing at the time.'

'I never knew the details,' Tom said. 'I was three years old when it happened and Father doesn't allow his brother's name to be mentioned in the house. I didn't know I'd had an uncle until Mother let it slip one day when I was fourteen.'

Dr Nathan made another note. 'Both Alger Hiss and Whittaker Chambers were affected by family suicides. Have you had any relationships with men?'

'No.'

'Nothing more than adolescent experiments at school: mutual masturbation with other boys, that sort of thing?'

'Not even that,' said Tom.

'Religion?'

'None.'

'Shall I put C of E?'

'Put agnostic, if anything.'

'It's quite a stroke of luck,' she said, 'your father being a priest.'

'He's a vicar who should have been a biblical scholar. He has no feeling for pastoral work.'

She was talking as she read through the pages of notes. 'Quisling's father was a Lutheran pastor. Fuchs was the son of a Quaker preacher and doctor of theology. Vassall's father was an Anglican priest and Blunt's daddy was the vicar of St John's, Paddington. Then there's Herbert Norman . . . He came from a zealous missionary family. Sir Roger Hollis – who may or may not have been working for the KGB when head of MI5 and MI6 – was the son of the Bishop of Taunton and related to both a canon of Wells Cathedral and the Dean of Salisbury.'

Juggling the spectacles, the pencil and a fresh cigarette, Dr Nathan lost her place in the file.

'Oh, sod it,' she said. 'Any ideas why so many priests' sons become traitors and espouse atheistic political philosophies?'

'You tell me, Tessa.'

'Hypocrisy?' she wondered. 'Perhaps they're fed up with all the hypocrisy and want to strike a blow for a different truth?'

Tom remembered an old Irish beggar-woman being turned away from the door of the vicarage when he was eleven years old. It was only two days after his father had preached a sermon on the First Letter to the Corinthians.

'Though I speak with the tongues of men and of angels, and have not charity . . . I am nothing!' The boy had screamed St Paul's words at the man in the dog collar. 'You sit in your study translating Greek and Hebrew and Aramaic, but you don't understand the meaning of the words.'

'Charity begins at home,' had been the icy reply. 'Sir Thomas Browne, 1605–82, an English Christian philosopher.'

The boy had run after the old woman and given her his week's pocket money, for which he was later beaten, because: 'You must learn to respect my wishes, Tom. By giving to mendicants, you encourage their fecklessness.'

Dr Nathan had found her place in the file again. 'For a host of reasons, universities are said to breed traitors.' She looked up at Tom. 'Perhaps that's because educated young people despise patriotism and see it as a source of evil?'

'More likely it reflects a high priority to recruit graduates because they are more likely to get into influential positions or have access to classified information.'

'Very sane.' She lit another cigarette from the stub of the previous one. 'Resentment, now . . . Being sacked must have come as a shock.'

'It did.'

'You could work on being sacked because of Mrs Thatcher's cutbacks.'

'It's the truth.'

'Then use it. What about drugs, Tom?' Dr Nathan put down her pencil. 'This is in confidence, you understand.'

'I thought it was all in confidence?'

'No ciggies, but you smoke pot?'

'In Bristol, you just walk or drive through St Paul's at night and stick out your hand with a tenner in it. It's easier to buy an eighth of resin than a bottle of Coke.'

'And you've experimented with other substances?'

'No.'

'Alcohol?'

'My intake is limited by budget. Otherwise I'd get pissed every night.'

Dr Nathan smiled as though she had been taught how to. 'I'm getting on your nerves, aren't I? You've been very patient, Tom. Frankly, I'd like to have done this in a more leisurely fashion, but those people are always in a hurry.'

She waited until they were standing up and shaking hands to ask about the break-up with Karen. Tom's first reaction was to walk out of the room. Then one word led to another until he found he couldn't stop talking. Twenty minutes later he stood up for the second time.

Dr Nathan was tipping her travelling ashtray into a plastic freezer bag and stowing it away in her briefcase. Without looking up, she said, 'You were pretty deeply in love with this girl?'

'I suppose I was.' Tom paused. 'But I hadn't realised how much, until that moment at the church when it was too late.'

.3.

Working up Tom's legend took two intensive days and nights, locked up with Ponsonby and his secretary in the Institute. After grabbing a few hours' sleep in a bedroom on the top floor, Tom bumped into his mentor coming upstairs unshaven, tieless and with his shoes in his hand.

'Morning, Tom,' was the greeting. 'Just keeping Pat in training. Think nothing of it.'

For meals they ate take-out Chinese and Indian food heated in a microwave oven by the secretary, who seemed to have few other duties; the telephone never rang and there were no visitors.

'So I just wander into KGB headquarters, Clive?' Tom said. 'I tell them that I've had a burst of idealism, seen the light and refuse to be a tool of Western imperialism any longer?'

'More or less.' Ponsonby was lounging in a chair with his hands clasped behind his head. He had taken off his jacket to reveal a satin-backed waistcoat and fancy red-and-black sleeve garters. 'You're an overgrown student of twenty-nine.

You've spent all your adult life in the rarefied atmosphere of university. You're not political, but you're an idealist and you don't want to be tangled up with me and the Institute any more.'

'Does that sound plausible?'

'It's in character, but they'll spend weeks, maybe months, taking your story to pieces in order to find the real reasons for your defection. And remember, interrogators always look for dirt, so you begin noble and then reveal the seamier side of your character bit by bit as they pry deeper.'

'Such as?'

'There are eight main factors in treachery, Tom.' Ponsonby uncoiled himself and moved to the blackboard which had been set up in the library. His chalk squeaked across the surface, writing a list of characteristics in bold capitals.

'In no particular order,' – he spoke over the noise of the chalk – 'except that the first one has to be access to secret information, they are flawed character, money, sex, resentment, blackmail, self-satisfaction and ideology.'

He stood back, looking like Einstein after writing $E = mc^2$ for the first time. 'Nobody has them all. You score quite well.'

'It's not how I see myself.'

Ponsonby ticked ACCESS TO INFORMATION. 'You've got information to sell – about me and the Institute and the jobs you've done in Russia. It's not exactly the NATO order of battle, but it's genuine. Too big-time and you'd attract too much attention.'

He ticked FLAWED CHARACTER on the board. 'You don't have the psychological profile of a traitor or defector but you do have the sort of family background that could produce an embittered dropout, jealous of his successful brother, the MP.'

'I wouldn't want to be Adrian, if you paid me!'

'I didn't say you would, dear boy. But you could credibly

pretend to be jealous of him, resentful of his success in the world and the fact that your father always preferred him and held him up as an example. And so on.'

'Continue.'

'Money . . .' Ponsonby erased MONEY. 'It doesn't really come into this because they're not paying you anything. And I wouldn't advise you to say that we paid you very much. Imply that you felt used and abused – and only made a few quid out of us by falsifying your expenses claims. If we had been stingy with you, it's an added reason to drop us in the shit.'

'Right.'

The chalk shrieked a large tick against SEX as Ponsonby continued, 'In traitors, sex often means gay or other black-mailable behaviour. Gays want to betray their government because they associate it with a father-image. The cousins believe there's a sexual element of some kind in any treach-ery – and so do the comrades. In your case we have this Canadian femme fatale who screwed your balls off and then married another bloke.'

Tom winced. 'But how will walking into the KGB and betraying my country be construed as taking revenge on Karen?'

'You can't damage her, so you hit someone else. It's normal human behaviour. Dr Nathan thinks it quite credible that your resentment about the way Ms McKenzie treated you could fuse with a wider resentment at the way life has shat on you, making you turn on your father-figure.'

'It'll certainly upset my father.'

'I think she means a composite Freudian father-figure, which includes the Rev. Fielding, your elder brother who was always held up as an example to you . . . the government whose policies offend you . . . even Professor Ashmole.'

'And Brodsky?'

'Now you're getting it.' Ponsonby grinned. 'Brodsky's the villain of the piece. He's the bastard who embroiled you in this sordid business. He forced you to go on when you wanted to stop. Etcetera. The important thing is not to be glib or too clear about anything, but to let bits and pieces of resentment surface in no logical order. Be confused and confusing.'

'I'm confused all right.'

'Stay that way. Let's work on this.' The chalk made a treble circle around RESENTMENT. 'This is the key to the majority of traitors' motivation. In your case, Ashmole cheated you out of your job in Bristol. People have killed for less.'

'Nutters, maybe.'

'Don't be so logical, Tom,' Ponsonby growled. 'Resentment is the fire of hell that burns the soul and warps the intellect. Get into your head that you merited the job, had been promised it and want to revenge yourself on the society which Ashmole represents.'

'It all sounds so bloody feeble.'

'Traitors are feeble people, Tom.' Ponsonby paused to let that thought sink in. 'You have to think yourself into a frame of mind where all the slights and injustices of life – real or imagined – add up to an intolerable burden. Use some imagination, dear boy.'

The duster erased BLACKMAIL, SELF-SATISFACTION and IDEOLOGY.

'Will my story stand up under examination?' Tom wondered.

Ponsonby gave a short laugh. 'Whether a prick stands up when it's put to the test, depends on how much lead there is in the pencil. It's up to you, whether or not they buy it. But frankly, I've heard many less plausible stories. As you can see, yours has most of the right ingredients. The best legends are always close to the truth, Tom. I think we can pull this off.'

'We?' Tom snorted.

Ponsonby wiped the board clean and sat down at the head of the table. He leaned forward and looked Tom in the eyes. 'It's my neck on the block too, dear boy. In these cost-conscious days with the Treasury breathing down our necks, I'm only as good as my last success. And I can assure you that I have no desire to be out of a job. In my line of work, there's only one employer. If I get the sack, I'm professionally dead. So get it into your head that if I didn't think this was worth investing several years' work in, you wouldn't be sitting here now. I'm a survivor, Tom. I don't back losers.'

'But am I a survivor?' Tom wondered. 'That's the sixty-four thousand dollar question.'

'Frankly, I wasn't sure at the start.' Ponsonby broke eye contact and leaned back, hands clasped behind his head. 'I'll be frank. You were very much a low-cost try-out in the squad, to begin with. Now you're in the first team and I'm passing you the ball. I've got a feeling we're going to score.'

'This will make the third postman you've put in place over the years for Viktor, Clive,' the D-G objected.

'Number Two is cracking,' Ponsonby said. 'She's drinking so heavily now that she's no longer reliable. I want to bring her home pdq.'

'After only three years?' The old man raised a spiky eyebrow. 'This will make two people walking around the streets of London who know something.'

'Neither of them knows a damned thing,' Ponsonby disagreed. 'Any more than Tom does. Like him, the others were paid to live in Moscow, but have no idea why. In each case I used false flags, so they don't even know for whom they were working. They never even heard Viktor's code name.'

'How d'you know the new boy won't crack up like the others?'

The D-G's voice was so quiet that Ponsonby had to lean forward to hear what he said. One apocryphal anecdote had a sacked senior officer of the Firm coming out of the old man's office misunderstanding the muttered decision and believing that he had just been promoted.

'Because Dr Nathan thinks he's right for the job.'

Ponsonby wondered whether that was the right thing to say. If there was one species the D-G disliked more than amateurs, it was psychologists. Yet because of the restrictions placed on the movements of Western diplomats in the USSR, it was only in the immediate vicinity of Moscow and a few other cities that Embassy staff could make brush passes and service dead letter drops. Elsewhere, it was always tourists, businessmen or students who acted as couriers. They had the advantages of being cheap, deniable and replaceable. Using and losing amateurs had been a fact of life in intelligence since Biblical times. Having them vetted for psychological defects was a new fashion.

There was silence in the room while the D-G toyed with the carnation in his buttonhole – a sign to his personal entourage that he was visiting Downing Street later that day. He disliked the man standing in front of his desk, thought him lazy and slipshod. It was common knowledge in the Firm that, but for the fluke of a walk-in, Ponsonby would have been sacked years before.

His personal file held more hostile comments than favourable ones. Typical were '. . . an officer with the temperament of a field man, but lacking the circumspection', '. . . resentful of discipline', . . . 'and far too inclined to act before seeking authority'.

Even Ponsonby's psychological profile, written by a predecessor of Dr Nathan, was marginal: 'Under stress this officer could become physically violent.'

'What's the time-scale for the new boy?' was the next question.

'Luckily, Fielding is a natural. He's currently all chewed up over this Canadian girlfriend of his giving him the push. If I keep him hanging around, he'll come to his senses and wake up to the grim reality of going to live in Russia with no return ticket. Then he'll tell me to piss off. Anybody in their right mind would. So I want to send him in right away – literally within a few days.'

'What motivates the man, Clive?'

'I think it's the kick,' Ponsonby said. 'Dr Nathan agrees with me. Somewhere behind Tom Fielding's bland and dreamy academic front is a man of action he has been sub-consciously denying all his life because he doesn't want to be like his patriotic father. Now that he's discovered the thrill of running with the ball under his arm and the pack behind him, baying for his blood, he can't get enough of it.'

'I'll give you one more postman,' the old man decided. 'But if this one cracks up before Viktor comes on-line, we write off the whole operation. Understood?'

PART IV
1950–1974

.1.

At the end of World War II, the terms of the Yalta agreement obliged Allied commanders in occupied Germany and Austria to hand over to the nearest Russian forces any citizens of the Soviet Union found in the western zones of occupation. Particularly targeted were the hundreds of thousands of men who had fought in German uniform under the renegade General Vlasov and in the various SS Ausland divisions. Russian liaison officers investigating war crimes – the majority of which had taken place in Eastern Europe – demanded wholesale repatriation of units like the Latvian SS, the Lithuanian police battalions and the Ukrainian SS Galizien Division who, they said, were guilty of some of the worst atrocities that had taken place.

The stories which the men who had worn those uniforms told to their American and British captors were radically different. They maintained that they had fought not for Hitler so much as against Stalin. If they had exploited the German invasion of their countries, to fight alongside the *Wehrmacht* against men who spoke their own language, it was because this represented their only hope of driving the Russian invader from their native lands.

British soldiers under Field Marshal Alexander wept openly as they rounded up their charges to hand them back to the Russians, wartime allies whose firing squads could be heard at work in some cases only a few metres away on the other side of the zonal borders. In one incident at Judenburg when 33,000 Ukrainian Cossack cavalrymen were to be handed back to the Red Army, men hurled their wives, their children and themselves into the swollen River Drau to drown, rather than face repatriation.

In an administrative sleight of hand, 10,000 Ukrainians of the SS Galizien Division were mysteriously transferred across the Alps to a British POW camp at Rimini where they destroyed their papers and claimed to be from the formerly Polish areas of Ukraine, which made them ineligible for return to the Russians. Among them was a sensitive foreign-language teacher called Roman Kravchuk.

The Rimini camp's Ukrainian Orthodox church, lovingly created from a converted Nissen hut crowned with a home-made cupola and cross, echoed with a convincing show of religious and patriotic fervour when Archbishop Ivan Buchko paid a visit and blessed the men who still wore their Waffen-SS uniforms, with only the Swastika badges removed. Shortly afterwards, Buchko's lobbying of the British government paid off: the men who had sung so lustily for him were removed from the lists of suspected war criminals liable to repatriation, and their status as POWs was amended to that of EVWs.

It was as a European Volunteer Worker that Roman Kravchuk and several thousand former comrades-in-arms travelled to Britain, whose government offered them work permits in an effort to make good the post-war labour deficit in textile mills and factories. The Ukrainians settled in well, being generally preferred both as employees and neighbours to the first West Indian immigrants who were just arriving.

In a Bradford cotton mill Kravchuk found himself working alongside men from Lithuania, Latvia, Estonia, Poland, Albania and Georgia. Before fate had made soldiers of them, they too had been teachers, lawyers, doctors and business-men. Like him, they found it hard to adjust to the frustrations and monotony of factory life. They missed their families, their homes, their way of life – and they shared a passionate hatred of Russia and Communism which had deprived them of all these precious things.

In the summer of 1950, the Cold War turned hot in Korea, at the cost of many thousands of casualties and millions of refugees. To the west and south – in Indonesia, Malaya and Vietnam – terrorism was the weapon used by Communist insurgents to drive out the Dutch, British and French colonial powers.

In Washington, National Security Council directive NSC 68 was construed by Allen Dulles and officers of the newly constituted OSO and OPC as permission to emulate the Communist guerilla tactics and take the war into the new enemy's camp. Across the Atlantic in London, Sir Stewart Menzies, head of MI6, was forbidden by the Socialist gov-ernment of the day to conduct covert operations on Russian soil. However, his masters' outdated concept of political geography enabled the more hawkish officers in MI6 to con-vince Menzies that the veto did not apply to the satellite countries from the Baltic to the Balkans whose populations, they claimed, were seething with discontent.

It was music to their ears when ambitious revanchist politicians like Stefan Bandera from Ukraine – later to die in Munich at the hands of a KGB Smersh assassin – approached them and promised that the first sign of support from London or Washington would be the spark to ignite a bush-fire of nationalism and redraw the borders of Europe along the lines of the old status quo pre-1938. On both sides of the Atlantic plans were drawn up for covert operations – for which there was no shortage of embittered men like Roman

Kravchuk who spoke the necessary languages, had military experience and little to lose by volunteering for a desperate venture.

In rented Victorian family houses in fashionable Chelsea, the volunteers were taught how to operate clandestine radio sets, how to use codes and one-time pads. They were trained in tradecraft, silent killing and what to do in the event of capture. In an indoor firing range nearby refresher courses were given in the use of captured German weaponry with which most of the trainees were already familiar.

Instructors of the MI6 training school at Fort Monckton near Gosport on the south coast gave instruction in unarmed combat and living off the land. Lessons in the use of small boats and combat swimming took place in Portsmouth harbour at night. Survival exercises on Dartmoor, in Snowdonia and the Scottish Highlands taught Kravchuk and the others how to live rough, avoiding police and army patrols as they collected mock intelligence and transmitted messages back to their handlers in London under conditions as near as possible to the real thing.

After high-speed dashes across the Baltic aboard the reconditioned German E-boat No. S208, small parties of Lithuanians, Estonians and Latvians landed on lonely seashores to find themselves betrayed in advance. Georgians and Albanians were dropped from unmarked aircraft into remote and mountainous areas of the homelands they had left several years before, often to the same reception. Only in western Ukraine did a few bands of armed men survive long enough in the Carpathian mountains to form pockets of resistance which were large enough to engage the Russian occupation forces in pitched battle.

Directing the campaign against them was Moscow's satrap, Nikita Khrushchev. As First Secretary of the Ukrainian Communist Party, he was eager to curry favour with Stalin by ruthlessly exterminating the partisans to the last man. To hasten the job, he called in ground-attack aircraft and armour, including columns of huge T34 tanks, some of them veterans of the great battle at Kursk eight years previously when Soviet armour had brewed up 2,000 German tanks in four days during the long, hot summer of 1943.

Starvation, scorched earth, massive deportations — there was no weapon Khrushchev would not use, no cost in lives too great, for the advancement of his political career. No one criticised his actions, for if the mass of Ukrainians resented being once again under Moscow's yoke, few flocked to the banner of independence being forlornly waved by a few partisans holed up in the mountains. Having suffered four long years of war, famine and destruction, most of the population wanted an intact roof over their heads, warm clothing and proper food far more than any hypothetical abstraction like political freedom.

When it became apparent to Menzies and Dulles that the promised national uprising was never going to take place, the Ukrainian partisans were written off, as all the others had been. Overnight, Kravchuk and his comrades who had thought themselves heroes discovered that they were discarded pawns in a game whose rules nobody had explained to them.

.2.

'What's the kid's name?' asked the soldier at the road-block.

A raw-boned six-foot Siberian who looked as though he had never had a square meal in his life, he towered over the thin, grey-faced woman in front of him. Wearing an old *Wehrmacht* greatcoat and with a bundle of belongings slung on her back, she had appeared seemingly out of nowhere in this landscape of corpses and burned homes.

The boy beside her had spindly legs and a gaunt face from which oversized dark eyes stared hauntingly. He was dressed in cast-off clothes several sizes too large for him. Bone-weary, neither he nor his mother had seen the barrier across the road until they were within a few paces of it. The soldier did not bother to unsling his rifle to cover their approach.

After handing over her papers, the woman dropped her bundle to the ground and stood upright. When the soldier repeated his question, she could not get the name out, but stammered, 'It's . . . it's . . .'

The boy looked boldly up at the face of the man in uniform. He was more interested in the piece of bread in the soldier's left hand, but his father had said, 'Always look them in the eyes.' So he did.

'It's Viktor,' he said.

His mother's face was frozen with fear. He squeezed her hand as though to say, 'It's all right, leave this to me.'

'Viktor,' she repeated, watching the soldier slowly decipher her own new name letter by letter in the internal passport which she had soaked in rainwater and deliberately rubbed with a fingernail to degrade the black-and-white image until it was possible to think that the blurry face in the scratched photograph could have been hers.

Behind the first soldier she could see another man in uniform lounging in the doorway of the cottage, doing up his trouser buttons. An illiterate Uzbek tribesman, he could see no point in coming out into the rain in order to stare at a meaningless piece of paper, so he stayed where he was, shivering and blowing into his cupped hands to get them warm. His rifle was leaning against the wall, two paces away from him. When the woman got her wits back, she considered grabbing the weapon and shooting both of the men in uniform, and then decided that the noise risked bringing other soldiers to the scene long before she and the boy could make their getaway.

The moment of opportunity was gone as the Siberian looked up and caught her eye. 'It says on your passport, "Place of work: Tractor Factory Number Thirteen in Odessa". What are you doing so far from home?'

'I needed food.' The woman got back her tongue and tried to make her voice sound whining and common. 'Food for the boy. He's sick, you can see. Bandits or no bandits, a child has to eat. I was told we might be able to buy food from the peasants, if we got far enough from a town.'

The Siberian nodded understandingly. 'All the same,' he said, pocketing her papers, 'I have to arrest you. Those are the orders. No one is to be allowed through the cordon – not even a dog.'

'We're not bandits,' said the boy.

'This is a forbidden zone,' the soldier told him. 'The inhabitants have gone. We have been told to shoot on sight because the only people here are the counter-revolutionary bandits, hiding in the hills and the forest.'

They could hear the sound of a firefight less than a mile away: sporadic rifle shots from the partisans – or bandits as Moscow called them – overlaid by automatic fire from the troops that were flushing them out. The weapons that the partisans were using had mostly been left behind by the *Wehrmacht*: Walther and Luger pistols, Schmeisser machine-pistols and the famous MG42 heavy machine gun. Even the radios on which they were calling for the promised airdrops of ammunition were German.

The lanky Siberian turned his head, listening to the cough of a cannon on one of the T34 tanks that had been brought up for the final assault on the log bunkers of the partisans' forest HQ.

A faint cheer went up from the beleaguered men as a lucky shot from a British Boyes anti-tank rifle cut the tread on a T34. The cheer was almost immediately drowned by a metallic scream which made everyone at the roadblock hit the ground instinctively as the pilot of an IL-2 *shturmovík* spotted a smoke grenade marking the target of the partisans' bunker complex hidden beneath the forest canopy and dived vertically, flattening out just above the tree-tops for his attack. In World War II, Russian infantrymen had nicknamed the IL-2 *letyáyushchi tank* – the flying tank – but the retreating *Wehrmacht* soldiers who had seen it from the front and underneath had a more expressive name for it: *der schwarze Tod* – the Black Death.

Firing nearly horizontally, the pilot swathed a path of total death through the trees just over a mile away from the roadblock. In addition to the .50 calibre machine guns, the twin P-37 cannon were firing armour-piercing rounds. A salvo of 28 mm rockets whooshed away from the wing-mounts and impacted right on the marker smoke. As the *shturmovík* pulled up into a steep climb, a package of 200 2½kg hollow-charge anti-tank bombs fell away from its belly and cleared half a hectare of trees, the dull crumps of the explosions and the crashing of forest giants in their death throes echoing back from the distant hills. In a tactic known as *krug smérti* – the circle of death – a second IL-2 entered its ground-attack run as a third took up position above and behind it.

'What have you done to your hands?' the Siberian asked, helping the woman to her feet.

She steeled herself to show him. Digging a grave with bare hands and a bayonet had left them raw, with septic cuts and the nails broken and filthy. 'I was searching for potatoes,' she said. 'We haven't eaten for two whole days.'

Hearing the word *kartófel*, the Uzbek left his shelter and braved the rain. He had to shout his question over the noise of machine guns as the second *shturmovík* commenced its strafing run. His accent was almost incomprehensible as he offered, 'Show us where you found the potatoes and we'll let you go.'

The woman pointed back the way they had come, along the dirt road that led through the forests westwards to the Polish border, its surface chewed up by tank tracks and the imprints of booted feet. 'In an abandoned garden, behind a cottage destroyed in the fighting. But the frost had got to the potatoes. They were all rotten. Believe me, I looked. I dug for hours, you can see.'

'Viktor what?' the soldier snapped, turning on the boy suddenly.

'Viktor . . . Ivanovich . . . Nosarenko.' The child spoke slowly and clearly, as though to an idiot.

The rain was turning to sleet, cutting down visibility too late to save the maimed and burned men at the receiving end of the *shturmovík* attack. As the planes wheeled away to return to base, the tall Siberian looked at the stale rye bread in his hand from which the boy could not drag his eyes away. The Uzbek and he had only this one piece between them, saved from the morning rations. It would be hours before they would enjoy a hot meal. He broke the bread in two and gave one half to the boy, saying to his glowering comrade, 'He can have my share.'

'*Spasíbo, továrisch*,' Viktor said solemnly. 'I hope you get the bandits.'

'So do I. Then we can all go home.' The soldier patted the boy's head, wondering when he would see his own son, 2,000 kilometres away in Novosibirsk.

'My papers,' said the woman.

He handed them back. 'Go quickly before anyone comes.'

They were well out of earshot when the boy asked, 'Is it all right to eat the Communists' bread, Mummy?'

'Eat it,' she said. 'Even if Stalin himself cooked it, your belly won't know the difference.'

Even so, the boy hesitated. 'Were those the men who killed Daddy?'

'No.'

'They looked like them.'

'They're all the same,' she said bitterly. 'Uzbeks, Chechens, Siberians, Tartars – all stooges for the Russians.'

'But the soldiers talk our language,' said the boy. 'Are we Russians too?'

'They all talk bad Russian,' she told him. 'We can understand them because the language is so like our own. But we are different: we are Ukrainians. Your father was a Cossack, never forget that.'

'Which father?' the boy asked, confused. 'Kravchuk or Nosarenko?'

'Forget Kravchuk,' she said tiredly. 'He's dead.'

It was hard enough to keep putting one foot in front of the other, without having to think as well. 'From now on, your father was a brave Communist who died fighting the fascist invaders of our land during the Great Patriotic War. Ivan Nikolaievich Nosarenko was his name.'

They stopped walking just before nightfall. In a shell-shattered *izbá* where three generations of corpses lay decomposing on the small vegetable plot behind the remains of the miserable hovel they had called home, the woman found some melted hailstones in a metal bowl, half-full of mouldy grain, which had been used for feeding the chickens. With no way of making fire even if they could have risked the smoke, they ate the uncooked mess by scooping it up with their fingers before crawling beneath a door which had been torn off its hinges by the explosion of a grenade.

By hunting through the ruins, the woman had found a second treasure. A ragged old horse blanket had been trapped beneath the decomposing corpse of the worn-out nag in what had been the stable. Using all her strength, she managed to pull it free. The blanket was bloodstained and stank of dung but it might stop them freezing to death. Beneath the inadequate shelter of the door, she pulled the blanket over the boy and herself, after enveloping him in her old greatcoat so that he could share her body heat. His legs were cold – as cold as the corpse she had buried that morning.

It seemed so unnecessarily cruel of fate to trick her into mourning the same man twice: once when Kravchuk was posted missing during the turmoil of the *Wehrmacht*'s retreat in 1943, and again when he died in her arms that morning. She wished that she had never received the clandestine message telling her that he was hiding in the mountains with the partisans. The few days they had spent together were memorable only for hunger and cold and danger. The tears she shed now were born of hopelessness more than grief.

Her sobs woke the boy. With the bread and half the chicken feed in his stomach, he felt warm. He could not remember when he had last felt so warm. He snuggled closer to her and whispered drowsily, 'It's funny to have another name. Did I do it well when the soldier asked me his questions?'

'You did it perfectly,' she said, holding him tight. 'You are the cleverest boy in all the world.'

Like his father, Viktor's mother had been a teacher. Condemned by her new identity to unremitting manual labour in a factory that built heavy agricultural machinery, she sublimated her bitterness by putting all her learning at her son's disposal, coaching him at night and weekends so that he was always top of his class in Odessa's Junior School No. 57.

Each day he scanned the copy of *Konsomolskaya Pravda* in the school library and memorised a chunk of First Secretary Khrushchev's turgid speeches to the Ukrainian Parliament or Comrade Stalin's latest *ukaz* from Moscow, which he then recited to the class despite his chronic shortness of breath. Smitten by asthma, he had to stop and rest several times each day on his way to school as he climbed the Richelieu steps, known to film buffs all over the world from the shot of the baby in the pram in *Battleship Potemkin*.

Reciting Party big shots' speeches was a sure way of endearing himself to the teaching staff. In every way, Viktor seemed the ideal pupil: a chubby, dark-haired boy with his red Young Pioneer scarf always clean and neatly knotted around his neck. Excused physical training and games because of his asthma, Viktor developed a startling aptitude in mathematics that stood him in good stead when he moved to the local secondary school. Greedy for the rewards this brilliant pupil could bring him, Viktor's new principal entered him for the Odessa junior regional mathematics Olympiad, which he won.

Soviet society produced the athletes and sportsmen who stunned the world and won so many medals in the Fifties, Sixties and Seventies by pitting talented children from an early age against their peers on a ladder of increasingly tough competitions known as Olympiads, up which the candidates fought their way against all comers from regional to national and eventually all-Union levels. The winners were rewarded with substantial privileges for themselves and their families. Their reflected glory made life a lot more comfortable also for the trainers and coaches who nurtured the youthful talent. The system produced remarkable results by comparison with the hit-and-miss conditions under which amateur sports talent was spotted and developed in the West.

Impressed by its success, the men in the Kremlin decided to use similar methods to distil from the 300 million inhabitants of the USSR the large numbers of top-level mathematicians, chemists and physicists they needed to beat the West in the arms race and the race into space. Hence the academic Olympiads.

Two days after the telemetry *beep-beep-beep* of the dog Laika's heartbeat was first picked up by shortwave radio hams all over the world in November 1957, Viktor won the Ukrainian Republic Mathematics Olympiad for under-sixteens, which qualified him to enter the all-Union Olympiad the following year. His school maths teacher, Alla Borisovna Timonenko, who travelled with him to Moscow the following summer, was disappointed by the result. The spotty-faced adolescent with the shock of thick black hair and dark eyes to match made a couple of uncharacteristic errors, which she put down to nerves, and then suffered an untimely attack of asthma that did not settle down until they were flying back home to Odessa.

Nevertheless she had had the privilege of going with Viktor and the other young prodigies to the Kremlin, there to meet a beamingly avuncular Nikita Khrushchev, now First Secretary of the Communist Party of the USSR and ruler of all the Russias. It was a moment to remember.

'Next year,' Ms Timonenko shouted over the noise of the motors in the rattling old prop-driven Ilyushin, 'you won't be frightened by Moscow – all the people and all the noise. Next year, you'll win, Viktor Ivanovich.'

She owed her upgraded three-room apartment to Viktor; even the clothes she was wearing could never have been afforded on a teacher's salary without the enhancements that came from being the coach of a prodigy, so she spoke as much to reassure herself as to rebuild his confidence.

The boy in the window seat beside her smiled apologetically. 'I let you down, Alla Borisovna,' he said in his usual measured delivery. 'I let my mother down too – and the school.'

'You did your best.' She sighed and patted his hand.

Viktor looked out of the plane window and wiped the smile off his face. His mistakes in the Olympiad had been quite deliberate and carefully calculated. Although he enjoyed the travel and other privileges, he had no intention of coming within the top ten in the all-Union Olympiad, for that would lead automatically to studying some scientific discipline – which would conflict with the promise to his dying father, one day to lead Ukraine to freedom from the Russian yoke.

The countryside below the Ilyushin, as it lurched its way south through the turbulence of a building thunderstorm, appeared completely flat from the air as they overflew the vast, featureless fields of the collective farms, devoid of hedges or even a single tree. On the western horizon lay a smudge of mountains which marked the border with Roumania and Poland where Roman Kravchuk lay buried in a shallow grave known only to his wife and son.

. . . and where, thought Viktor, I passed the first test in the Olympiad of deceit when I was eight years old.

After winning the Republic Olympiad, he and his mother had been allocated a two-room apartment. She insisted that he sleep in the tiny bedroom; each evening she made up a bed for herself on the settee in the combined living room and kitchen. That evening, Viktor pleaded his asthma as a reason to go early to bed. From the slit in his mattress where another boy of his age might have kept childish treasures or maybe pictures of girls, he took out his most precious possession.

The sheaf of handwritten paper consisted entirely of love poems – not for a girl, but for a country. In rather flowery Ukrainian, they told of the Cossack heritage of liberty from serfdom and independence from all foreign overlords. Written by Viktor's father in the humid and dusty air of a Bradford cotton-spinning mill, they had been handed to the boy as their author lay dying from splinters of a shell fired by one of Khrushchev's T34s.

One poem called the fertility of the Ukrainian soil: 'that cursèd gift of God, that fatal beauty which draws German, Russian, Pole, Tartar and Turk alike to rape our land'. Others recalled the valour of Yermak Alenin and Stenka Razin, the Volga pirates, and of Viktor Khmelnitsky, who defeated the invading Polish army in 1648, and Matvei Platov, whose Cossacks chased Napoleon all the way to Paris and who might have driven the British from India if the Tsar he served had not been insane.

Viktor found the familiar words soothing. With his photographic memory, he had no need to reread the poems, but he liked the feeling of handling the creased paper with its faded writing. Best of all, he liked to gaze at the photograph of a man in British battledress with the same Slavic features and thick dark hair as himself. It was inscribed 'To my Son, who one day will right a people's wrongs'.

The other photograph showed the same man in civilian clothes – in the centre of a group of uniformed instructors at Fort Monckton whose names were written underneath their faces: Major Kiernan, Sgt-Major Bates, 'Dusty' Miller and 'Spoofy' Hayward. The officer in the centre of the picture was identified as Captain Trevor Barton.

'Where were you,' Viktor wondered, 'when my father called you on the radio?'

It had never occurred to Roman Kravchuk or the other

ill-fated partisans that they had been cold-bloodedly abandoned to their fate by both their British and their American handlers – nor that their last desperate appeals for arms drops and medical supplies were never heard. They were automatically recorded in the antenna-festooned villa outside Munich where the mission had started, but never listened to because Captain Barton and the other handlers had all gone home.

Clinging to a belief in the men who had trained him, Viktor's father had wrongly blamed only the Americans. 'We should never have trusted them,' he had told his son, just after he was wounded. 'Captain Barton would never have let us down like this. You can trust the British. An Englishman's word is his bond.'

.3.

In September 1961 Viktor entered KGB training school No. 104 in Puscha-Voditsa, a suburb of Kiev which had been completely rebuilt after the fierce fighting of November 1943. The main building of the school was a restored elegant Tsarist hunting lodge, surrounded by ugly modern buildings. The whole complex was set in, but fenced off from, the largest public park in Ukraine.

The previous month, Francis Gary Powers, the shot-down U2 pilot, had been sentenced by a Moscow court to ten years' detention for espionage activities. Instructors and trainees discussed the case endlessly, seeing the overflight as an expression of the aggressive intentions of *glávny vrag* – Russia's main enemy, America. Viktor's personal opinion was that the CIA was the KGB's best friend – and vice versa.

At the training school he again reversed tactics; from now on it was essential to come first in every test because only the first three cadets in each intake could choose to which

Directorate they would be posted at the end of the initial six months' training course. When the results went up on the notice board during the first term, his name was always at the top of the list.

His mother had moved to Kiev in order to be near enough to see him each Saturday afternoon and evening – the cadets' only free time. Years of heavy manual work had broken her health. No longer strong enough to continue at the tractor factory, she had lost her entitlement to accommodation in Odessa, so had little to lose by the move.

Viktor had wangled for her a cramped one-room apartment that was allocated to the widowed aunt of a fellow cadet, who no longer lived there. It was on the ninth floor of a tower-block with inadequate communal cooking facilities and stinking toilets, each shared by forty or fifty people. There was no lift and the staircase was used as storage space by residents, making it hazardous by day and downright dangerous at night, for all the light bulbs had been stolen.

The shortcomings were nothing to Viktor's mother; proximity to her adored son was the only thing that counted for her, although she was wary of making emotional demands on him. She blamed herself for not marrying again so that he could have had a substitute father on which to model himself. Worried by his lack of interest in girls, she listened with great relief when Viktor told her that he had met a girlfriend at the end-of-term dance in Puscha-Voditsa.

'Tell me about her,' she said eagerly. 'Is she pretty?'
'Not at all.'
'You have a photograph?'
He shook his head.
'But she has a nice nature?'
He shrugged.
His mother put both hands on Viktor's shoulders and searched his black button eyes in which no one – not even she – had ever been able to read anything.

'Then why?' she asked.

'Her father's a general.'

His mother buried her face against his chest. 'Kravchuk would be proud of you,' she murmured.

Marina Kirova was not the sort of girl to give a picture of herself to her boyfriend. In the flesh she looked overweight, plain and unhappy; in photographs she looked frightened as well. She was not very bright and was ten years older than Viktor. However, to his eyes her shortcomings were more than compensated for by the beauty of her father's rank. General Alexei Kirov was in charge of all KGB training in the Ukrainian Republic.

An overbearing bully, the general had made his daughter's life a misery from birth. At first it was because she was a girl, not the son he wanted. Once she started school, his silent disapproval changed to angry shouting when every test placed her at or near the bottom of the class. And when puberty removed the last traces of girlhood sweetness and left her, in his words 'as attractive as a horse's arse', his rages at her unmarriageability drove Marina to secret eating and later drinking too, until obesity was added to her problems.

Perversely, General Kirov guarded her virginity jealously. Suitors for a general's daughter were not hard to find in the USSR, whatever her looks, but each time a young man appeared in Marina's unhappy life, the general frightened him away. He was determined that his daughter was going to marry a future member of the Politburo. In the brilliant cadet, Viktor Nosarenko, he saw at last an acceptable son-in-law.

Thanks to the billiard-ball haircut that was regulation for all cadets at Puscha-Voditsa, Viktor was bald for the duration of the course. Without hair, his pudgy face, snub nose and button eyes were distinctly lacking in sex appeal. His flabby out-of-condition body looked better in a uniform than bathing trunks, but the same could be said about Marina. The two young people made a physically unattractive couple.

Invitations to eat with the Kirovs each Saturday compelled Viktor to shorten his weekly visits to his mother. Sometimes he had only a few minutes to spend with her, drinking a cup of tea in some cheap downtown café en route to the general's luxury apartment off Bessarabskaya Square, which was among the most prestigious addresses in the city.

The smart restaurants he now frequented with the Kirovs were eye-openers to Viktor. Raised on his mother's budget cooking, of which the high spots were occasional luxuries such as the long, thick circular sausages called *kolbása* and *bítki* – meat balls in sauce – he found himself having to eat five-course meals and drink vodka glass for glass with the general. Each Saturday meal ended with Viktor watching Marina and her mother stuff themselves with *medívnyki* – spiced cakes dripping with honey – or *varénki*, which are little dumplings stuffed with sugared sour cream.

'There are two good things about fat women,' General Kirov confided in his gravelly voice to his star cadet as they strolled along Kiev's Champs Elysées – the Kreshchatik – one Saturday night near the end of Viktor's last term at Puscha-Voditsa. They had eaten an expensive dinner at the Dnieper restaurant on Lenkonsomol Square.

'Tell me.' Viktor always showed a polite interest in what the general had to say. He felt uncomfortably full after eating all the tidbits that Madame Kirov had thrust onto his plate throughout the meal and wished that alcohol did not go to his head so quickly.

'The first is that they make sure you eat well,' the general laughed. 'The second is that they're very comfortable in bed.'

Viktor blushed and stammered, 'I hope you don't think, comrade general, that I and Marina have . . .' Embarrassed, he stopped under a streetlamp, making Kirov turn and look at him.

The general clapped him on the shoulder and belched vodka fumes in Viktor's face. He had no intention of letting

his star cadet leave his jurisdiction before marrying Marina.
'It's time,' he belched, 'that some randy young bastard like
you showed my daughter that her mouth's not the only ori-
fice which can give a woman pleasure.'

He came even closer and winked. 'Next Saturday, I'm
taking her mother to visit family friends in Kharkov. You
two young love birds will be alone all night in the Kirov
family nest.'

'Next Saturday,' said Viktor uncertainly, 'there is a com-
pulsory film show at Puscha-Voditsa. All cadets must
attend.'

'I'll have a word with the commandant.' The general
undid his uniform jacket, hitched his belly up above his belt
and farted richly into the night air.

His chauffeur-driven black Zil was kerb-crawling along,
keeping pace with the two men on the pavement. There
were few other cars about. From the rear window his wife
stuck out her head and called, 'Alyosha, darling, when you
men have finished talking . . . we need to use the little girls'
room.'

'Don't forget . . .' The general released Viktor. 'Next
Saturday, take Marina out for a meal – you can use my car
and driver – buy a couple of bottles of Livadia wine and get
her drunk. And then get stuck in there, eh?'

'General . . .' Viktor caught the older man's sleeve; he
might never have another moment as propitious as this for
his next question. 'There is just one thing I wanted to ask
you.'

'Go ahead, my boy.' Another fart fouled the air.

'My instructors tell me that I should pass out top next
month . . .'

'I'm counting on it.'

'Well, naturally I hope not to disappoint you,' Viktor hurried on. 'But there's a rumour that I have been earmarked for
the First Directorate.'

'My doing,' smirked the general. 'First Directorate has

the best jobs with the highest salaries, trips to the West, access to the *beriózkhka* shops, rapid promotion. Marina will enjoy the travel.'

'I know all that,' Viktor interrupted. 'But I want to join Second Directorate.'

'Counter-espionage?' Kirov sneered. 'It's dull, plodding, poorly paid work. There's no kudos and a brain like yours will be wasted there.'

'I think that's how I can serve my country most effectively, general. So that's where I want to go.'

With a copy of the final exam results in his pocket, Viktor climbed the stairs to his mother's room and found her sitting up in a chair, wearing her best dress to greet him. The room was entirely taken up with a table, two chairs, a cheap cupboard – one half for food and the other for clothes – and her bed. Black fungus grew on the cracked plaster of the wall above the bed, which was wet from a perpetually leaking toilet on the floor above.

Since coming to live in Kiev, his mother had developed a deep, racking cough that left her thin frame breathless and exhausted after each paroxysm. She concealed the blood on her handkerchiefs from him, anxious not to distract him from his studies.

'How are you, Mother?' he asked gently, worried by her thinness and the bright spots of colour in her cheeks.

She lied, as always, and told him she was feeling better.

To get rid of the sour smell of cabbage and nappies which seeped into the room from the corridor, Viktor opened the small window that looked out into a light-well, only to find that he had let in the sound of a baby crying, the screams of a couple arguing at the tops of their voices, and the noise of several radio sets tuned to different channels, all mixed and amplified by the acoustics of the light-well. The noise was worse than the smell, so he shut the window again.

His mother cried with joy when he showed her the examination results, repeating again and again, 'You were always the cleverest boy. Kravchuk would be so proud.'

'And I have some other good news,' said Viktor. 'I'm going to marry General Kirov's daughter.'

She remembered the day he had talked them through the roadblock. '*Moi syn*,' she said, 'keep on like this and one day you will be the President of Ukraine.'

Half-laughing and half-crying, she put her thin arms around his waist for a moment until a coughing fit made her sit down on the bed, to get back her breath.

Seven days later, Viktor lay snoring on General Kirov's bed while the restored clock on St Andrew's church struck midnight. On the other side of the large red stain in the middle of the sheet Marina lay unhappily awake, a hand pressed to her belly to still the pain.

On the way to Bessarabskaya Square from his mother's apartment Viktor had picked up a whore on the Kreshchatik and paid her to show him ten techniques which, she said, made women wild with desire. Tried one after another exactly in the order the whore had said was most effective, the various tricks of tongue and fingers had both horrified and hurt Marina. Lacking any kind of sex education, she had assumed that his crude attempts to arouse her were for his own pleasure.

When he penetrated her, still dry, she whimpered, 'That hurts, Viktor!'

'*Molchi!*' he growled, pinning her arms down. 'Shut up!'

When he rolled off her, she thought, so that's what they call love. She wondered if all men fell asleep immediately after sex or whether the booze was to blame, for Viktor had taken the general's advice and ordered a bottle of Georgian brandy before the meal and two bottles of Livadia wine with it. For once he had drunk more than his share.

In the pocket of his uniform trousers, neatly folded over the chair by the dressing table, was his posting to the training school of Second Directorate in Minsk, effective September

1st. The marriage was scheduled for mid-July, followed by a honeymoon on the Black Sea coast in a rented dacha. Everything, so far as Viktor could see, was going according to plan. As a KGB general's son-in-law, all doors in Minsk would be open to him. And after Minsk would come Moscow . . .

.4.

On 9 August 1974 most Western diplomats in Moscow were discussing the implications of President Nixon's resignation the previous day in order to avoid impeachment by Congress over his involvement in the Watergate break-in. Clive Ponsonby had more pressing matters on his mind.

Cruising like a shark beneath the smooth diplomatic waters of the Fourth of July reception in the US Embassy ballroom, his well-tuned nostrils had picked up the scent of sexual frustration emanating from the wife of one of his CIA colleagues. She was a tall, willowy blonde from Texas, a former Miss El Paso. Only three weeks after joining her husband, she was already bored with the claustrophobic living conditions of a junior secretary's wife in the Soviet capital.

She had heard the gossip about Ponsonby during meetings of the Embassy wives' club. The smouldering fire of lust in his eyes as they devoured her cleavage that night kindled a response in her more violent than any she had known with her husband. Helping his prey to a dry Martini from a passing drinks tray, Ponsonby had managed to brush the back of his hand against her breast while handing her the glass. Instead of apologising, he had said, 'I'd like to do that again.'

'Where and when?' she asked over her second Martini. Like a kiss of fire, the tip of his middle finger stroked her bare forearm from elbow to wrist, but she did not care who was looking.

'I'll work on it,' Ponsonby promised. 'Stay wet.'

For a confirmed womaniser like him, the difficulties of avoiding surveillance both by the KGB and his own security colleagues simply added spice to the pleasures of philandering. Five frustrating weeks later, he had found the ideal place for an assignation and made a brief phone call to the former Miss El Paso to give her the rendezvous, emphasising before he hung up that she was not to give any sign of recognising him until he had first satisfied himself that there were no watchers. Ponsonby always exaggerated the danger of surveillance, having found that most women were turned on by the fear of being discovered in the act.

He spent a couple of hours that afternoon checking out the safe apartment near the Kropotinskaya Metro station. It had been used for an agent meeting the previous week and, in conformity with the standing rules inside the Soviet Union, would not be used a second time for any clandestine purpose. Since the rent had been paid up to the end of the year, it seemed the obvious place in Ponsonby's mind to use for a fast fuck.

Satisfied that there were no microphones or cameras in the apartment, he looked at his watch and found that it was time to walk the three hundred metres to the Metro station and make sure no one was following the lady from El Paso. His hand was already on the door leading into the corridor, when he heard the sound of a key turning in the lock. He stepped back into the small kitchen and pulled the communicating door closed behind him, leaving just a narrow slit to see through. A man wearing the dirty grey overalls of a maintenance engineer was standing outside in the hall doorway with his head turned away. At his feet was a well-worn cloth tool-bag. He pulled a woman's thick lisle stocking over his head before picking up the tool-bag and slipping inside the apartment.

'You can come out, Mr Ponsonby,' he said quietly in an excellent English accent, after closing the door.

'Who are you?' Ponsonby asked.

'Call me Viktor. It means the winner, doesn't it?' By using his real name, Viktor was defying all the rules of the game, which dictated random, computer-chosen code names for every operation and agent.

'And am I the loser?' Ponsonby asked.

Viktor laughed. 'On the contrary, you're a very lucky man. During the next half-hour, I'm going to change your professional prospects greatly for the better.'

'There's some misunderstanding,' said Ponsonby. 'I'm a diplomat, not a businessman.'

'You're listed as a junior consular attaché. In fact, you're an officer of British Intelligence. For the last eighteen months I have been checking out your colleagues in Moscow to find the one I can deal with. You are that man.'

Ponsonby was mildly amused at what looked like the beginning of a clumsy attempt to blackmail him. He opened the bottle of Johnny Walker Black Label he had brought to drink in bed with Miss El Paso, and slopped some into two glasses.

'I'm honoured,' he said, raising his glass.

Viktor ignored the other one. 'Firstly, you're British. I don't trust the Americans. Secondly, your age. Someone younger would be too junior in your hierarchy, while someone much older might be retired before my plan comes to fruition.'

'Go on.'

'Thirdly, you're ambitious but lazy. Since being posted here, you've spent more energy in seducing our women than stealing our secrets.' A more industrious man, Viktor had reasoned, would grow bored with the long years' wait ahead and ask to be assigned to other duties.

'What would be the biggest coup you can imagine?' he asked.

Ponsonby thought for a moment. 'Getting a copy of the Kremlin telephone directory?'

'How would you like to be known as the officer who brought home the real, as distinct from the published, specifications of every new Soviet ICBM – before it even enters service?'

Like a camera, Ponsonby's eyes were taking close-ups of every visible detail of the man opposite him. They did not amount to much. Viktor's hands were concealed in white cotton gloves. His shoes were brown leather, clean, polished and expensive. His height was around five-eight and he weighed about 95 kilos. The voice was calm, dispassionate and showed no signs of nervousness. The black hair could be a wig, it was so thick. The facial features, distorted and hidden by the stocking, were totally unrecognisable.

Ponsonby listened with increasing respect to the plan being outlined, which ended with Viktor offering a freebie as proof of the meeting for Ponsonby's masters in London: 'In a few months they will learn that the number of ABM-1Bs deployed around Moscow under the 1972 Anti-Ballistic Missile Treaty – the system known as Galosh – will be reduced. Instead of one hundred, there will be only sixteen. The permitted total will be made up by eighty-four Gazelle ABMs which have a shorter range and higher speed. The intention is for the Gazelles to pick off any incoming warheads which are not destroyed outside the atmosphere by the Galoshes. How's that for an appetiser?'

'I'd be more impressed by some information that I can check for myself, here and now.'

Viktor passed across the table a sheet of paper on which was typed a complete list of intelligence officers in the British Embassy, with a list of sexual preferences. Against

Ponsonby's name was the note: *married, hetero, v. active.*
Asterisked in the line below were the names of five of his colleagues' wives with whom Ponsonby had had sexual
relations.

Viktor flicked a cigarette lighter and watched the piece of
paper turn to carbon which he crushed to dust on the table.
Then he drained his glass and stood up.

'My first instruction to you is to leave Moscow and find
yourself a niche in London where I can reach you.'

Ponsonby explained that it was normal for an MI6 officer
to spend fifteen years abroad before being posted back to
London.

'Do it,' Viktor ordered curtly. 'Sleeping around the way
you do, you're bound to be the target of an entrapment operation if you stay in Moscow.'

'And when will you start to deliver?'

'It might be one year. It might be ten.'

'Why so long?'

'I'm aiming for the top, Mr Ponsonby. There's no point in
risking being caught sending you dribs and drabs on the way
up.'

'Then why make contact with me now?'

'Too many thieves fall foul of the law because they only
think of disposing of the loot after they have it. They panic
and are caught red-handed. The more intelligent approach is
to find one's customer first and then steal what he wants.'

'I can't fault your logic,' Ponsonby admitted. 'But I doubt
that my masters will be prepared to keep me on the back
burner for so long on the strength of this one conversation.'

'Mr Ponsonby . . .' Viktor paused for emphasis. 'You'll
have to convince them that I will not deal with anyone but
you. It might be in a year's time or it might be in ten, but
when I make contact, you will be handed on a plate one of
the greatest coups in the history of the Cold War.'

Seats had been booked on the British Airways flight to

London next morning. Ponsonby was lying on the bed, watching his wife pack her dresses into a large suitcase with the help of one of the Embassy security women, when the phone rang just before midnight. He recognised the American accent immediately.

'You bastard,' said the former Miss El Paso. 'I stood around on that fucking station for two hours, feeling like a whore with no takers on Saturday night.'

'Go fuck yourself,' he said, putting down the phone.

'Who was that, Clive?' his wife asked.

'No one.'

She leaned over the bed, putting her arms around his neck. 'D'you know what'll be so nice about going home to London, darling?'

'Tell me.' The other woman's voice had turned Ponsonby on. His hands kneaded his wife's buttocks and his nostrils flared, scenting her perfume.

'Knowing that when you pick up the phone and there's no one there, it's just a burglar checking up,' she said. 'It'll seem so safe after living here.'

'I know what you mean.' Ponsonby pulled her onto the bed. Over her shoulder, he saw the security officer's eyes riveted on his right hand, which was exploring the cleft between the buttocks of the woman in his arms.

'You don't have to go,' he murmured to her. 'The bed's a king size.'

She walked out of the room, giving him the finger.

'Up yours too,' he grinned.

In the living room she turned on the television to cover the noises coming from the bedroom. Her first encounter with Ponsonby had been when he came into her office shortly after her arrival in Moscow. Without any preamble, he had casually but deliberately felt her buttocks.

He was usually referred to by her female colleagues as 'that cocksure chauvinist bastard in Consular', so the move had not come as a total surprise. She had kept her cool, removed his hand and said, 'That constitutes sexual harassment.'

With that infuriating smile of his, Ponsonby had replied, 'So does having a pretty little bum like yours and wearing a tight skirt which shows your panty line.'

'I'm going to report you,' she said. Yet, despite all her convictions, she had done nothing about it.

After watching the television for a few minutes, she heard Ponsonby's wife cry out. She tiptoed to the bedroom door and stood listening. Half an hour later she was still standing there, angry at herself but unable to walk away.

PART V
Autumn 1983

. 1 .

I remember the fat lady so clearly because she was the first person who didn't work for the KGB to whom I had got close in two and a half months.

She lay without a stitch of clothing, face down on the broken beach lounger in the rest area by the Moskva river, just outside the Moscow city limit. The other loungers were all locked away for the winter with the deck chairs and awnings. By the marks in the sand, she must have found this one dumped behind some bushes and dragged it out to expose her flabby white body to the open air for the last time that year. Each time she shifted position, the lounger wobbled on its damaged leg and shock waves ran through her ample buttocks. With her thin greying hair pulled back off a face that had given up smiling long ago, she could have been any age between forty-five and sixty-five.

The sun was almost completely hidden by a leaden overcast. The air temperature was eleven degrees Centigrade and plummeting. Only a Russian, I thought, would be lying there, trying to soak up the last few units of *ultra-violet light on a day at the end of September when the wind was blowing from Siberia, bullying the leaves off the trees with whispered threats that its big brother winter was on the way.*

I pulled the collar of my anorak higher and lengthened my stride as I passed the woman on the second tour of the rest area. Just beyond her was a crudely lettered notice on the bank which reminded bathers that 'swimming in an unsober condition is dangerous'. How Russian can you get?

The naked woman, the wording of the notice and the empty rest area were my first taste of freedom after the ten-week debriefing, locked away in a KGB dacha which was lost in the forests somewhere to the south of the city. I had had plenty of time to reflect on my actions. What stopped me from admitting to myself how crazy I had been and telling my interrogators that I had changed my mind and wanted to go home? After all, they hadn't arrested me, so presumably I should simply have been put on a plane back to the West.

I suppose it was the vague idea of competing with my father, a bemedalled war hero ten years younger than I was when he made his first escape as a POW from a Luftwaffe hospital with his leg still in plaster. He had gone on doing his duty, trying to escape, right up to the grim end in Colditz castle. He hadn't given up, so how could I?

There was an unreal air to the whole debriefing which made a rational decision harder. The unreality began when I walked into the old Lubyanka building on Dzherzhinksy Square only to be told by two bored militiamen on the main entrance to take a taxi to the new prestige headquarters on the ring road, known in the intelligence community as Langley East.

There I had met for the first time the man whose neatly piled civilian clothes lay on the river bank of the rest area, just beyond the fat lady on her broken lounger. The pink blob in the middle of the steel-grey river was my case officer – a major in the KGB who was swimming diagonally against the strong current with a powerful crawl stroke.

I stood by Major Ivan Petrovich Ivanov's clothes, wondering what was going to happen to me next, uncertain what to make of his announcement when he arrived at the dacha that morning: 'You're free, Feldink. It's all over.' His pudgy, Khrushchev-like face had a button nose and eyes almost hidden in folds of fat. I couldn't tell if he was joking or serious.

As a reminder that my freedom was conditional, if not an illusion, there was a uniformed and armed driver sitting on the wing of the black Volga in which Ivanov and I had been driven back towards the capital. He had ignored my sporadic attempts at conversation but the dark eyes in his inexpressive Tartar face were alert and watchful.

I wondered whether Ivanov was showing off – overdoing the cold-water swim for my benefit. Russians love showing foreigners how tough they are. He was having trouble fighting the current in mid-river and was being swept sideways. He looked pretty shot as he finally made it through the eddies to the bank. When his feet touched bottom he stood up, spluttering water all over me. I stretched out a hand to help him ashore, but he ignored it, preferring to slide and scramble up the muddy bank where he stood in his dripping undershorts, chest heaving from the exertion. Then he lay down on the sparse grass to do fifty press-ups and grunted one sentence of advice at the top of each lift.

'You should take up cold-water swimming, Feldink.'

Like hell, I thought.

'There's no other exercise like it.'

'I believe you,' I said.

'You're flabby after sitting in the dacha all those weeks, answering questions. You need toning up.'

I nodded, wondering how much longer I was going to have to stand in the biting wind while he fought the flab.

'It's not just the exercise,' he said. 'It's the cold. It tones up the skin and muscles – even the vital organs. Look at me. I'm forty-nine years old. I drink, fuck and smoke more than most men of thirty – and I'm in better condition than the majority of non-smoking teetotallers half my age.'

Although carrying at least thirty pounds more weight than a Western doctor would advise, Ivanov's short and stocky form exuded crude physical energy.

'I'll think about it,' I promised.

I thought my torture by cold was over when he stood up, but had to endure watching him do fifty knee-squats before rubbing himself down briskly with a small towel taken from his worn brown leather briefcase. By then the dim disc of the sun had vanished completely behind the overcast. Even the fat lady capitulated to the wind. She sat up and began pulling on her baggy underwear without any pretence of modesty. When Ivanov dropped his wet shorts to the ground and kicked them off there was a sexless intimacy in the scene that was disarming. By coincidence, both Ponsonby and his Russian opposite number were fitness freaks. Of the two men, I felt a sneaking warmth for Ivanov whereas I had never found anything likeable in Ponsonby. Yet Ivanov was supposed to be my enemy. It was confusing.

Throughout the interrogation I had been treated more like a guest of honour than a prisoner. Although the estate on which the dacha stood was guarded by armed and uniformed KGB troops, there were no locks on the doors and windows, and each afternoon I had been escorted for a walk in the surrounding birch forests by one of the interrogators. Twice a week, Ivanov had appeared like Father Christmas, loaded with vodka and caviare which he shared with me as we went through the transcripts together.

'You're wanting to know what happens next.' Ivanov wrapped the wet shorts in his towel and shoved them into *the briefcase, which was otherwise empty. 'You've heard of the Serbsky Institute?'*

I didn't like what I had heard, and protested, 'I thought you said I was free?'

He put an arm around my shoulders and led me back to the car. 'Kant said that freedom is the insight into need, whatever the hell that means. In our society freedom is comparative, not absolute. So let's say that today you are more free than yesterday. That's good, isn't it?'

'Very good,' I agreed, wondering what was coming next.

Moscow's Institute for Forensic and General Psychiatry was a dingy-looking complex of outdated buildings on Kropotinskaya Ulitsa, the street named after Pyotr Alexeyevich Kropotkin, an exiled anarchist prince who committed suicide when he returned to Moscow in 1921 and saw the reality of what the October Revolution had achieved.

The Institute was founded that same year by Vladimir Serbsky, a psychiatrist whose theory that mental illness was caused by the social conditions in pre-Revolutionary Russia had more than once got him into trouble with the Tsar's secret police. How he accounted for post-Revolutionary madness is not on record.

Known informally as the Serbsky Institute, the hospital achieved worldwide infamy in the Seventies and Eighties as the place where the Soviet government incarcerated dissidents after Western media attention made their exile to the Gulag politically undesirable. It was estimated that as many as 50,000 sane people were sent there for psychiatric assessment during those years after they had been accused of anti-Soviet activities which ranged from complaining about food shortages to distributing *samizdat* publications or seeking permission to emigrate. Locking such undesirables within the Institute's grim Victorian walls had a secondary advantage for the KGB, since it was the ideal place for a dissident, once officially labelled mad, to be drugged and shocked out of such unacceptable behaviour.

'There was a certain logic to it all,' Ivanov said as his car pulled up in front of the main door. 'After all, if Communism had created the perfect society, then those who sought to change the status quo were obviously crazy, so it was right to lock them up as madmen.'

'How long am I going to be locked up in there?' Tom asked, getting out of the car.

'That depends,' Ivanov grinned, 'on how you make out.'

Tom feared that he had been brought to the Serbsky for some kind of truth test – whether by drugs or whatever passed for a lie detector in Russia. It was already dusk outside. In the gloomy, high-ceilinged entrance hall which was painted dark green and brown, the main light was not working. A dim glow came from one underpowered bulb above a grille behind which sat a uniformed woman receptionist. The major gave his name, and the name of the doctor who was expecting him. Unfazed by the proffered KGB identity card, she glared at him with all the officiousness of the Soviet petty bureaucrat.

Dotted about the hall, people were waiting in small groups, conversing in whispers as though not wishing to disturb the ghosts of Russia's most famous dissidents who had passed this way, some of them never to return. It was like a set from a modern play, Tom thought. Scene One: the anteroom to hell.

There was only one door leading inside the building: a huge wooden portal, guarded by a uniformed militiaman. When Ivanov's name was called out, he walked forward with Tom, their footsteps echoing on the bare floorboards. The door creaked slowly open after Ivanov had identified himself for a second time, allowing them to walk through into a sort of airlock. Only after the first door had closed did the second one open. They found themselves in a floodlit courtyard around which were grouped the wards. An air of hopeless

neglect hung over the whole complex. Disused medical apparatus stood in corners, some of it so rusted that it was
impossible to guess what function it had ever served. Many
windows were barred like prison cells; others had been
whitewashed on the inside, which was somehow more menacing. A group of militiamen lounged on chairs at the far
end, smoking and chatting beneath a television camera on a
bracket which surveyed the area. In its blind spot a pile of
crates was stacked against one of the exterior walls, reaching
nearly to the top. A fit man could have run up them and
leaped over the wall to freedom.

Ivanov seemed to know where he was going and crossed
the courtyard to a building which looked like all the others.
Inside they tramped up two flights of steps. The stairwell
was wired-over to prevent patients throwing themselves over
the banister. According to a notice on the wall, inmates were
entitled to thirty minutes' sports activity every afternoon but
there was no indication of how or where it could be carried
out. Men with prison-pallid faces, wearing identical grey
pyjamas, shuffled along the corridors soundlessly in identical
grey felt slippers, instinctively crowding the wall to get out of
the way of Ivanov and Tom. Others sat on beds packed into
small wards with only inches between them and not even a
bedside locker for personal belongings. The majority of these
were as still as statues, heads down, seeing only the floor
between their feet. A few looked up at the sound of shoes in
the corridor. Their eyes had the blank unfocused stare of the
heavily sedated, the pin-point pupils an indication of how
long the treatment had been going on.

Ivanov left Tom in the care of a harassed-looking woman
of about fifty who wore a white coat, a starched white linen
hat like a chef's and a white overall. She introduced herself as
Dr Anna Maximova and asked a few questions, looking at
her watch repeatedly, before excusing herself '*do zavtra*' –
until tomorrow.

There was a strong scent of salami in the room where

Tom was locked up for the night. Since the supper which was brought to him on a tray consisted of cabbage soup followed by a very small overcooked hamburger drowning in a sea of watery gravy, he wondered whether the sausage smell was to cover up some kind of tranquilliser which was being sprayed into the air. The window did not open, so there was nothing he could do about it.

The food was so awful that he ate little. It seemed a good sign that the tray was removed without comment; if the meal had been drugged, Tom thought, surely they would have made a fuss that he had left most of it. Shortly afterwards one of the inmates unlocked the door and stuck his head inside the room. With a finger across his lips, he hissed, 'Don't drink the water. They put things in it.'

Just as quickly, he was gone, slamming the door and turning the key in the lock. By the time Tom had crossed the room to peer out of the wired glass panel in the door, there was no one in sight. Was the man paranoid, Tom wondered, or perfectly sane and simply giving a warning to a newcomer? There was no way of telling.

There were no sheets on the bed, just a urine-stained mattress and a single blanket. The central heating was turned up so high that even in vest and shorts, lying on top of the blanket, Tom sweated all night long. Locked up in the place where so many writers, poets and playwrights had been assessed as mad and held prisoner, in some cases for years, he had no need of nightmares. He dozed uneasily from time to time until, unable to stand the thirst any longer, he washed his face under the tap, drinking a few handfuls of water at the same time.

In the approved practice of hospitals everywhere, he was awoken at 5 a.m. so that he would be ready for his breakfast which arrived two hours later. Four hours after that, Dr Maximova reappeared in her white coat and chef's hat, to administer a Rorschach test. Wanting to appear co-operative, Tom suggested clouds and sheep and puddles; in fact, the shapeless blobs reminded him most strongly of other ink blots. The next test was of TAT pictures, about which he had to write a short story.

As though to encourage a rather backward child, the doctor kept repeating, 'Kharashó, eto óchen kharashó.' Good, that's very good. At the end, she added smugly, 'All these tests are used in the West, you know, Comrade Feldink.'

She produced a number of coloured cards which Tom had to arrange in order of his personal preference. Other medical staff came and went, openly discussing with Dr Maximova the patients who were with them, making no pretence of privacy. It was with immense relief that Tom heard Ivanov's voice in the corridor, calling his name. Until then he had only seen the major in civilian clothes. Not knowing of the KGB ruling that all officers must wear uniform for one day each week, he wondered what was the significance of Ivanov's being in uniform.

As they walked back across the courtyard to the exit, Tom's relief turned to aggression, mixed with uncertainty: 'I mean, picking coloured cards from a pack, major. What the hell does that test?'

'Blame Oswald,' Ivanov guffawed. 'A lot of people in Washington thought he had been brainwashed to kill Kennedy while he was living in Russia. My opinion is, he must have been nuts to come here in the first place – but nobody asked me. Anyway, the word went out that future defectors should be assessed on the way in to see if they were likely to do anything embarrassing – and if so, shipped immediately back to the West.'

As they stepped outside into the street and got into the waiting car, Ivanov said to Tom, 'Pushkin wrote one hundred and seventy years ago that the motto which should be inscribed above the gates of Moscow was "Abandon reason all ye who enter." Now you know what he was talking about.'

.2.

Ivanov's driver was the same beady-eyed young Tartar who had been at the wheel the previous day. Without being told, he headed for the Crimea Bridge across the Moskva River and pulled up in Gorky Park where teams of workmen were setting up banners and bleacher seating in preparation for some military reunion.

After spending the night in his over-heated hospital room, Tom shivered as he got out of the car and zipped up his anorak. The wind was keen and the sky grey and lowering in what he would come to know as Moscow's normal winter weather. Wearing just his thin gabardine uniform, Ivanov set a fast pace through the park and along the river bank. There were few other pedestrians about and the traffic that Tom could see on the bridge was sparse. Compared with the centre of any Western capital, the emptiness and sense of desolation were depressing.

Ivanov stopped by one of the concrete benches and set down his battered old briefcase. From it he took a *propiska* – a residence permit – which he opened and held in front of

Tom's eyes. The photograph pasted inside had been taken at the dacha by a KGB girl photographer who had spent five minutes taking the picture and half a day flirting with one of Tom's interrogators.

Tom studied the photo. His face looked thinner than before; he had lost weight despite the lack of exercise and the stodgy food at the dacha.

The second line below his name was headed *mésto rabóty* – place of work. Whoever had filled in the form, had written: Moscow University. Ivanov's thumb indicated a stamp on the page opposite the photograph. 'Three hundred million people would pay a lot of money to have that Moscow residence entitlement. Take good care you don't lose it.'

'What's the catch?' Tom asked.

'There's a code built into the number.' Above the passport, Ivanov's eyes were watching Tom's. 'Every militiaman, GAI traffic policeman or other functionary who checks your papers will automatically feed back to Moscow when and where he saw you. That way, we'll always know where to find you. Otherwise you're free as a bird.'

'To go wherever I want in the USSR?'

Ivanov grunted. 'Russian birds ask for permission before they fly too high or too far from their allocated nesting area.'

Tom took the *propíska* and put it in his inside pocket. 'Thanks. You've been very . . . very decent.'

Ivanov laughed at the choice of word. 'We're flexible nowadays: rubber truncheons and sandbags when appropriate, kid gloves likewise. But why should we lean on a walk-in like you? You chose to make us a present of some useful intelligence. What would be the point of kicking your balls in and tearing off your toenails?'

He tapped the side of his nose. 'Keep our new image to yourself though, Comrade Feldink. We find that a healthy fear of the Committee is very useful when it comes to keeping the restless masses in their place.'

'Whatever you say.' Tom was finding the major's sardonic Russian sense of humour hard to handle.

'Sit down,' Ivanov ordered. 'I've got some things to show you.'

He lit a *papirós* – a long cigarette with a hollow tube instead of a filter tip – and inhaled deeply. From the battered old briefcase he pulled a large brown envelope which bore in the top left-hand corner the bold legend: *Komityét Gosudárstvenny Bezopástnosti.*

The first picture that spilled out into Tom's lap was of his parents getting into a black Rover saloon parked in front of their house. There was a shot of his brother Adrian's face on an election poster, another of the boarding school Tom had attended and several of the house in Bristol where he had lived. The most impressive was a telephoto two-shot of Karen and her husband walking hand in hand through the Eaton centre shopping mall in Toronto.

'We check up on things,' said Ivanov. 'You'd be amazed what we've found out about you, Feldink. You never told us about your uncle, for example.'

Tom flushed. 'How did you dig that up?'

'There are peace-loving people everywhere who help us. But why didn't you tell me? Because he was gay?'

'His name was never mentioned at home. I'd almost forgotten about him.'

'The black sheep, eh?' Ivanov laughed. 'Well, now there are two: him and you.'

The next 10 × 8 black-and-white enlargement was a close-up of Brodsky. 'Real name: Ivan Kuchinsky,' said Ivanov. 'A shabby little revanchist who claims descent from the Romanov line. We had him on our files.'

There was a photograph of Ponsonby's secretary coming out of the front door of the Institute, and another of Brodsky standing in the same place, watching a team of men carry furniture out of the building and into a couple of anonymous removal vans parked on the yellow line. The last print in this sequence was of a For Sale notice, fixed to the area railings.

'You really dropped them in the shit,' said Ivanov. 'They appear to have shut up shop for good.'

Tom handed back the pictures and was given another envelope. It hurt to look at the faces of the man he had briefly glimpsed outside the Baltic station in Leningrad and the others he had betrayed. He felt a small glow of pride that he had kept his mouth shut about the woman at the shoe counter in GUM, despite Ponsonby's injunction to spill everything he knew.

'What'll happen to these people?' he asked.

Ivanov shrugged. 'Labour camps,' he said. 'Five to fifteen years, depending on how co-operative they are.'

'That seems harsh.'

'They're traitors.' A wave of Ivanov's pudgy hand dismissed as unimportant the fate of a few deviants in a federation that numbered 300 million inhabitants. 'The USSR is a young and vigorous society, so we punish traitors harshly – like a healthy young body rejecting alien bacteria. It's a symptom of the sickness of Western society that you people forgive and pardon criminals so easily.'

'I don't agree.' Tom wondered whether it was prescience or just the cold wind making him shiver.

Ivanov grinned. 'Between you and me, Feldink, I think we overdo it. The great days of the Gulag are past forever, thank God, but there are still upwards of a million people in the camps. Think about it. When they're all let out – which will be soon, the way that upstart Gorbachev is talking about *glásnost* and *perestróika* – we're going to find that we've created a criminal class which may just turn out to be the most virile and adaptive element in our transparent and restructured society.'

The faces of his contacts would not go away even after Tom had handed back the photographs. Ponsonby had made it seem inevitable that pawns should be sacrificed in any game, but had those people realised that it was a game and they were only pawns? Had they been doing it for money or idealism? And would the pawn called Fielding or Feldink one day be written off in the same cold-blooded way?

Ivanov noticed him shiver. 'You're out of condition,' he said. 'Me, I never feel the cold.'

'It wasn't that,' Tom muttered. 'I was feeling guilty for shopping those people.'

'They knew the risks.'

'Maybe.'

'Supposing you were a sleeper,' Ivanov hypothesised, 'sent over here for some future job. Do you think that Brodsky-Kuchinsky would lose any sleep if I start grilling your tender body over hot coals in a couple of years' time?'

'He's a pro. I'm not. That's the difference.'

'Keep it that way,' Ivanov warned. He pulled Tom round to face him and kept him there, literally chest to chest.

'It may happen,' he boomed, 'that one day you see a face you know in a crowd – or hear a familiar voice asking you to do a favour for old times' sake. Take my advice, don't fall for it, Feldink. Just remember that paranoia is endemic in Russia, my friend. We watch everyone, everywhere, all the time. In the Soviet Union there are three-quarters of a million informers working for the Third Directorate, off and on – which makes one and a half million eyes watching you. Never forget!'

Ivanov lit another *papirós* and inhaled deeply. 'You want to know where I'm taking you now?'

'More tests?' Tom guessed.

Ivanov shook his head.

'That's all finished?'

'You sound surprised. Is there something we've forgotten to ask you? If so, don't worry. We'll always know where to find you.'

'So where are we going?'

'To the apartment of Professor Sibirsky of Mosuniv.'

Tom recognised the name; they had met a couple of times. 'Sibirsky was very helpful with my research,' he said.

'He's also very interested in the result: your thesis, *Clarifying Confusion.*'

'How did he get hold of that?'

Ivanov grinned. 'I had to be sure you were really the scholar you claim to be. So I asked Sibirsky to evaluate your work.'

'And why are we going to see him now?'

'You saw that "Place of work: Moscow University" in the *propíska*? You have been given a lecturer post in the Department of Soviet History. Sibirsky is the prof.'

The news did not sink in properly until they were getting back into the car. Tom stood for a moment filling his lungs with the cold air. I've done it! he thought.

In his pocket was a document which made him almost as free as anyone else in the USSR. To have landed a job at Mosuniv was better than he could have hoped . . . It could be a trick, of course, to put him off his guard, but he could not see the point of that.

Be a grey man, Ponsonby had said. It had not been easy to pretend for twenty-four hours a day to be someone else – a defector fuelled by bitterness and resentment. Tom was not sure how much longer he could have gone on doing it. As the black Volga accelerated away from the kerb, he felt welling up within him an almost irresistible urge to laugh with relief.

Waved on by grey-coated GAI traffic police at each junction, they sped past an encyclopaedic variety of Russian architecture, from substantial log houses to classical palazzi, interspersed with churches and street markets, stopping near the north end of Pyatnitskaya Ulitsa, just before the road swung left to cross the river heading for the Kremlin and Red Square.

Sibirsky had a large apartment on the first floor of what had been a nobleman's residence, near the seventeenth-century church of Sts Mikhail and Fyodor. Well-built, elegant and spacious, it was the antithesis of the Stalin- and Brezhnev-era tower-blocks in which most of his compatriots lived. That this was Party-approved luxury was testified by the guarded entrance hall which did not smell of stale urine, a lift that was in working order and clean hallways with no piles of rubbish swept into the corners and left there.

Tom stood with Ivanov on the first-floor landing, listening to a baritone voice, accompanied by a piano, with the intermittent sound of a woman's voice talking the singer through an old Russian music hall song.

'*Lévaya, právaya. Gdyé storoná? Ulitsa, úlitsa, ty brat pyaná.*'

The music stopped when Ivanov rang the bell and Sibirsky erupted onto the landing to embrace the major: 'Ivan Petrovich, *kak éto pryátno!*' How nice to see you . . .

Over the top of Ivanov's crew-cut head, the lean, grey-haired professor greeted Tom. 'Mr Fielding! It's good to see you again. I hope this Chekist bastard didn't give you a hard time?'

'Say yes,' ordered Ivanov with a wink at Tom.

'Come in. Come in.' Sibirsky pulled them both inside the apartment.

The interior of the professor's apartment was in another league from any private accommodation Tom had ever seen in Russia. Crystal chandeliers hung from the elaborate plasterwork of the ceiling. Above an elegant silk-wound ormulu French clock on the marble overmantel was a huge gilt-framed mirror in which were reflected the dozens of antique icons that decorated the walls, their colours glowing softly against the dark wooden panelling. Showcases held collections of snuffboxes and perfume bottles. The polished oak parquet floors were covered in priceless old rugs. Only the furniture was new: Finnish and expensive.

The piano which Tom had heard was a black Yamaha concert grand in showroom condition. Seated at it was a petite, dark-haired woman of around thirty, collecting her music and putting it into a briefcase.

'Don't go, Levitskaya,' Ivanov ordered. 'Play that tune again. I haven't had a good singsong for ages.'

She played the song twice through for Ivanov to add his bass to Sibirsky's baritone. Then came a medley of Russian folk songs, from 'Stenka Razin' through the Volga boatmen's song and ending with some Cossack lullabies.

'*Spi mladényetz, moi prekrásny, báyushki-bayú.*' Go to sleep, my beautiful child . . . Ivanov winked at Tom as though appreciating the ludicrous spectacle of a man in the uniform of a KGB major crooning a cradle song.

'*Tíkho smótrit mésyatz yásny v'kálybel tvoyú,*' he sang: The moon looks gently down on your cradle . . .

Tom shook his head at an invitation to join in and wandered over to the window. Outside, Ivanov's chauffeur was polishing the windscreen. He was a conscript – young, smart and keen to keep his cushy job as the major's driver. Across the wide river lay the massively ugly Stalinist bulk of the giant Rossiya Hotel and beyond that, just visible in the murk, the golden domes of the Kremlin.

Behind Tom's back the two men's voices were singing, '*Zlói chechén polzyót na béreg, tóchit svói kinzhál.*'

The Cossack mother was warning her child still in the cradle to beware the vicious Chechen who wanted to slit Russian babies' throats. The last time Tom had heard the lullaby was in the Sixth Form at school when a new Russian teacher had made all the pupils learn traditional songs to build up their vocabulary. The words were like the men singing it, he thought: a mixture of sentimentality and violence – unpredictable as the bear who was the totem of their race.

'You must learn to beware of anti-social elements like Levitskaya!' Ivanov's deep voice cut into Tom's thoughts. 'She hasn't a good word to say for our society. Have you, Levitskaya?'

The woman avoided eye contact and carried on putting her music away.

'She can't wait to get her emigration certificate,' Ivanov said, with his hand on her shoulder.

'*Molchí!*' Sibirsky growled at him. 'Stop baiting the girl, Ivan Petrovich. She's my singing teacher, this is my home and I don't need to listen to your racist shit within these walls.'

'She says she wants to go to Israel.' Ivanov winked at Tom. 'But when she gets out, she'll find her Promised Land in New York or California.'

'Shut up, you Chekist oaf!' Sibirsky shouted.

He took a roll of US dollar notes from his hip pocket and peeled off several which he handed to the woman. 'Thank you, Levitskaya,' he said in a more normal voice. 'This is for your escape fund. Same time next week?'

After the woman had gone, the major brought a bottle of vodka out of his briefcase and insisted that the three of them consume most of it, drinking toasts to Gorbachev and Reagan and Mrs Thatcher and anyone else who came into his mind. The round-bottomed glasses had to be drained each time before they could be put down. Tom had avoided alcohol during his interrogation; after two months without a drink and with little food in his stomach, his head was spinning by the tenth toast: 'To the KGB's disinterested patronage of international scholarship!'

Back in his office after leaving Tom with Professor Sibirsky, Ivanov re-read his final report on the debriefing:

The investigation of the defector Fielding (Feldink) has revealed no evidence that he was sent here for the purpose of espionage. The indications are that this man is just another politically naïve academic, defecting on the spur of the moment after an emotional disappointment. His psychological profile (see attached report by Dr Maximova) is similar to that of many other British defectors.

I requested Professor Arkady Sergeyevich Sibirsky, of Moscow University's Department of Soviet History, to read Fielding's treatise *Clarifying Confusion*. Sibirsky informed me that the research is thorough, the analysis sound, the style lucid. So Fielding had adequate grounds for resentment when he was sacked. I have further arranged with Professor Sibirsky to find a suitable post in his department at Mosuniv where Fielding can be employed and where I can personally continue to be his case officer. Sibirsky, a loyal Party member who has carried out numerous missions for the Committee while travelling in the West, has co-operated accordingly.

Feldink has been given a vacant post of Assistant Lecturer in the Department of Soviet History. Routine surveillance will be the responsibility of Third Directorate.

Ivanov signed the report and rang for a messenger. In the Russian system, the sheet of paper would be initialled by all his departmental superiors before being sealed into Tom's file in the central *referentura*.

.3.

On the first and third Wednesdays of each month Tom had to report to Ivanov. On his first visit to the KGB sector office on the Kusneztky Most, he felt like a delinquent going to see his probation officer when asked how he was settling in.

'Fine,' he replied. 'Arkady Sergeyevich has wangled me a studio apartment in an old house just off the Arbat.'

Ivanov was pouring two glasses of tea from a samovar on a shelf by the window. He turned and raised an eyebrow as though this were news to him and commented, 'Most foreigners are given accommodation way out in the suburbs. You're a lucky guy. Are you okay for money?'

'I have a salary of sorts. It's not much but with public transport costing pennies and my rent fixed at only five roubles a week . . .'

'Or £20 a month at the official rate of exchange,' Ivanov interrupted. 'Where could you find an apartment in the West at that price?'

'I know,' Tom agreed. 'I'm not complaining.'

The tea was scalding hot, very dark and strong. Ivanov held a lump of sugar between his teeth and sucked the tea through noisily. 'Food okay?' he asked.

That, Tom admitted, was a problem. He ate two meals a day in student canteens – but the diet was mainly beans, cabbage and potatoes, which he found hard to digest. Ivanov advised him to live like the natives by eating cheaply in canteens during the day and stocking up at the Arbat *gastronom* – one of the best in Moscow – for his evening meal. Then he asked about the job Tom had been given.

'I haven't found out yet,' Tom said. 'Arkady Sergeyevich is not around much and no one else seems to know what I'm supposed to be doing. So I'm more or less left alone to pursue my own research.'

'Don't worry about it,' was Ivanov's advice. 'You'll find that the level of staffing here is enormous by Western standards, but don't sneer at the idea of two or three people doing one job. It guarantees that we have no unemployment throughout the entire Soviet Union – and that's a record any Western country would be proud of.'

'It's a valid way of looking at things.'

'So what other problems do you have?'

'Makarova,' Tom said. 'With Sibirsky always jet-setting to or from some conference or other, the department is actually run by his deputy, an officious bureaucrat of a middle-aged spinster who obviously regards me as a dangerous foreign agent. I can't do a thing right for her.'

Ivanov looked at his watch. 'Beware of *les tricoteuses* like Makarova.'

'You know her?'

'I know the type. Stay on the right side of this woman. If you can work out how to get what you want from her sort, you'll have no problems in Russia.'

Six days a week, Tom commuted by Metro to the university. On the spotless, litter-free platforms and in the graffiti-less trains nobody talked or even looked at their neighbour. Sometimes he fantasised about shocking all the stolid Muscovites in his carriage with their empty shopping bags and tatty briefcases by shouting aloud, 'I'm a British spy!' But most of the time, he tried not to think about the double life he was living. Tom Fielding of Bristol was filed away in limbo; he had become Tomas Mikhailovich Feldink.

If weekday Moscow was somewhat drab, at the weekend the Soviet capital was about as lively as the dark side of the moon. After 9 p.m. the wide streets were deserted by traffic and pedestrians, most restaurants were closed and the only places where night life flourished were around the hard-currency bars of the larger hotels where whores, pimps and black market hustlers of all kinds clustered in search of the mighty dollar.

And the weather! At my meetings with Ivanov, the little major boasted like the good Muscovite he was how he loved the forty-below temperatures when blizzards blew in from Siberia and armies of headscarfed grandmothers were mobilised and equipped with wooden shovels to clear snow from the pavements. I found the cold and the snow inconvenient and physically uncomfortable. By December, the sunless greyness was wearing me down. There were moments when it seemed unbelievable folly to have signed away a year of my life to live in such a grim place because of what seemed now a temporary depression. It made a pleasant change when Sibirsky invited me to lunch one Saturday at the beginning of January.

I used to wonder why he had taken the risk of accepting a foreigner on his staff. The ostensible justification was my usefulness as a researcher, due to the access I had enjoyed to émigré sources in the West – people who would never have talked to anyone from Moscow. As so often in Russia, the real reason was quite different, but I was not to discover that until more than a year had gone by. In retrospect, that Saturday invitation was very significant: it

*was the first time Sibirsky talked to me about icons. I of
course had no idea what he was leading up to.*

Tom was waiting in the entrance hall of the Tretyakov
gallery, Moscow's finest museum of art, when Sibirsky
strode in and took him straight to the head of the queue,
waving aside the officious guides who were shepherding both
Russian and foreign visitors into groups for their escorted
tours. Sibirsky led the way at a brisk walk past the canvases
by Ilya Repin and Surikov, past the world-famous eleventh-
century mosaics and the halls of socialist realist and
contemporary art to the most important collection of icons in
the world.

'Do you know much about our national art form, Tom?'
he began.

'Not a thing.'

Sibirsky's eyes were caressing a fourteenth-century work
by perhaps the most famous of all icon painters, Andrei
Rublyov. 'The first thing to appreciate is that – since virgins
have little value in the Slav mind until they are impregnated –
Mary is always referred to as *bogoróditsa* or the mother of
God. From Byzantium we inherited two totally different con-
ventions of depicting her. In the *hodegétria* she is the aloof
queen of heaven and the child is a miniature adult male; in
the *eleoúsa* tradition the child is a swaddled infant, chubby
and loving as he presses himself to his mother's breast, while
she has a face of suffering and sorrowful tenderness. It's the
second tradition that Russians love better, perhaps because it
plucks at the half-remembered image of the earth goddess
who ruled our nomadic ancestors' lives as they followed their
herds across the steppes, long before Christianity was
invented.'

The lecture ended two hours later with them standing
together in front of the twelfth-century Virgin of Vladimir,
carried off as loot to Moscow's kremlin as early as the four-
teenth century. Beside it was Theophanes' Virgin of the Don,

which had been borne aloft into battle by the Tsar nick-named Dmitri Donskoi, who had used it to invoke God's support for his victory over the Mongols at Kulikovo.

Until that afternoon, Tom had mentally categorised Sibirsky as a frigid *aparátchik*. He was a figure of mystery at the university, seen occasionally at a distance hurrying from meeting to meeting attended by an entourage which inevitably included his deputy, Makarova. Now he was showing another face: the passionate lover of art. Tom wondered what it was all leading up to.

The floor attendant was shouting at some English tourists for using flashguns. Sibirsky took advantage of the moment to step forward and kiss the Virgin of Vladimir.

'You never know,' he said to Tom with a thin smile.

As they walked away through the echoing marble-floored galleries, Sibirsky waxed philosophical. 'We're a nation of believers, Tom. What other people could still believe in Communism after it had claimed a hundred million victims – in the purges, the famines and the Gulag – and so patently will never succeed in bringing about the Kingdom of Heaven on earth? Believers and iconophiles, that's us.

'I don't have to tell you what the people did, after Lenin banned the portraits of saints and the mother of God from the *krásny ugól* – the blessed corner of every cottage in Russia. They replaced their Christian icons with images of the Communist pantheon: Lenin, Stalin and the rest – but chiefly Lenin, the new godhead. What an impoverishment of our national soul! Give me the worst-painted virgin in the world, rather than that mean-faced, bald-headed old coot who glares down at us from the walls of every public build-ing throughout the land.'

They walked back to the apartment in the Pyatnitskaya Ulitsa, leaning into the sub-zero wind that was blowing in their faces. The professor's elderly Tartar housekeeper had prepared lunch. She was a good cook and the cellar was an oenophile's dream. After a week of eating student canteen food, Tom gorged himself on *bliny* – pancakes stuffed with salmon and caviare, laced with sour cream and washed down with an excellent Georgian champagne.

Sibirsky's conversation was disjointed, repeatedly giving the impression that he was leading up to something, only to stop himself at the last moment. Tom left just before dusk, planning to walk back to his room the long way round, crossing the Moskvoretsky Bridge and the empty vastness of Red Square to catch a glimpse of the woman at the shoe counter in GUM on the way. Her continued liberty was, or so he told himself, some kind of proof that he had not been drugged either at the dacha or in the Serbsky Institute.

And after a stroll round GUM, he would drop into the largest bookshop in the Soviet Union, the Dom Knigi on Kalinin Prospekt. Inside the shelves were replete with tens of thousands of volumes, guarded by assistants who appeared to have been on the Intourist combat course for repelling possible purchasers. Every book Tom had ever requested was, they informed him smugly, out of print.

'How do you know?' he had asked the first few times. 'You haven't even consulted the catalogue.'

'It's our job to know,' was the answer.

He had discovered that the best way to find a book he wanted was not actually to go into the store but to ask a young Armenian student who hung out among the crowd of touts in the side doorway. Any book that Tom wanted, the Armenian seemed to be able to track down within the week and supply for only a few copecks more than the official price.

The other way of finding a particular volume in Moscow was through the second-hand bookshops where, instead of a price, a ticket would be stuck inside each volume specifying another title for which the owner would part with it. After finding a book he wanted, Tom would hurry to every other second-hand shop he knew, hunting for the required title, and then race back with it to claim the original book. At first it seemed a waste of time but eventually he came to enjoy the spirit of the chase which was such a large part of the pleasure of shopping in Soviet Russia.

The Saturday afternoon round always finished with a visit to the *banya*. Communal bathhouses predated Communism by a long time and were for many Russians a regular habit – like going to the pub on Friday evening might be in Britain. The one Tom frequented was just off Arbat Square, only a few minutes' walk from his studio apartment.

The bath water looked as though it had not been changed since the Revolution. It made a dark green pool in the centre of the dimly lit and echoing tiled hall. Neo-classical busts of Tsarist generals stared out from their wall niches at the steam-filled expanse of the tepidarium in which dozens of pale-skinned men with bull necks and huge ponderous bodies lumbered around, some naked, some clad in towels. Among those lying inert on the stone benches between the columns which held up the domed ceiling, several were being beaten with 'véniki' – broom-like bunches of birch twigs – while others lay still because they were too drunk to move.

Russian beer halls are sordid places of bare walls and wooden floors where watered-down 'pivo' is sold in paper cups by coin-operated machines. So most boozers except the very hard-up prefer to do their drinking in the warmth and comparative comfort of the nearest baths, where the unisexual bonhomie makes it quite normal for strangers to share a drink or an impromptu picnic, or to ask each other to administer the beating with birch twigs which is a central part of the ritual. Some take it bent over, touching their toes like Victorian schoolboys suffering six of the best. Others lie flat on the stone benches to be beaten clean, then soap themselves from head to foot and throw basins of cold water over each other.

I had been in the sauna room and was dozing in a

*cubicle with the curtain drawn, trying to rehydrate my
quick-fried brain with a beer while skimming through a
book that the Armenian student had found for me, when a
hand holding a glass of beer poked through the gap in the
curtain. I took it with a word of thanks and found myself
staring at the leanest and hairiest man in the baths. Above
the furry legs, an oversized penis emerged from a forest of
black pubic hair. Above that, thick belly hair swirled in
patterns to a hairy chest and arms. Even the man's face was
hirsute, with much of it concealed by a dark, neatly
trimmed moustache and beard. Steamed-up pink-tinted
spectacles concealed a pair of cold grey eyes.*

'Beat me,' Ponsonby said.

*I was too surprised to be frightened. Back in London he
had told me to make a habit of using this particular
bathhouse on Saturday afternoons but I had never expected
him to turn up there.*

*He lay face down on one of the benches where I beat
him with a birch switch until he held up a hand, 'Not so
hard, dear boy. It's years since I've enjoyed this peculiar
pleasure, so take it easy.'*

*I assumed that the point of my mission was about to be
disclosed. With the hissing of steam, the slap, slap, slap of
the twigs on bare flesh and the echoes of a hundred
conversations, it was a good place to talk without being
overheard. Instead, we talked of my settling in. Ponsonby
knew a lot already and warned me that I was followed on
Tuesdays and Thursdays by a pair of thin-faced men in
leather coats.*

*'You've done brilliantly,' he said. 'Not well, but
brilliantly.'*

*His hand opened and dropped a crumpled piece of paper
on the bench. He sat up with a loud, 'Spasibo, tovarisch,'
and vanished in the steam.*

*Back in the cubicle, I smoothed out the soggy paper. It
was a deposit account statement in my name from Lloyds*

Bank, Cox and Kings branch, which showed regular monthly payments of £1,666 and a total of over £8,000 to my credit including interest. I tore the bank statement into small pieces and flushed them down a lavatory before leaving the bathhouse.

That night I lay awake for a long time, wondering what Ponsonby would eventually want in return for those regular payments. I was surprised at myself for not having asked him how much longer I was going to have to stay in Russia. It seemed obvious that the mission was going to last longer than a year, but in a way I didn't mind. It wasn't as if I had a job or a relationship to go back to, in the West. In Moscow my research facilities were wonderful and I had become more and more engrossed in the work, so I hadn't protested when he set me an odd task.

'The comrades are obsessed by sex, as you'll be aware by now, Tom. In this oddly puritan society of theirs, they think a man will do anything for a really juicy piece of pussy, except walk away from it. So get hitched, dear boy, if you want to give the image of someone who intends to settle down permanently in the socialist paradise.'

I knew that getting hitched, as he had so glibly put it, would not be simple. People were always coming up to me in the street or at the university, asking to buy Western clothes, toothpaste or a Walkman. Yet every time I tried to chat up a girl, the conversation petered out with a polite or embarrassed refusal of my invitations. I came eventually to accept that the average Soviet citizen had learned the hard way not to have anything much to do with foreigners. The loneliness this causes is, I think, the main reason why so many defectors opted to go home and face the music.

It was Sibirsky who provided a solution to my problem.

.4.

The clientele of the crowded, smoky café just off Gorky Street comprised almost twice as many women as men. After three generations, Russia had still not replaced all the soldiers slaughtered in World War II. According to the last census, the population numbered twenty million more females than males; the imbalance was a feature of everyday life that Tom now took for granted.

The only music in the café was a military band on Radio Moscow, coming from a small transistor set on a shelf behind the bar. The bare tables were all taken. The coffee was ersatz, sweet and tasted of plastic although the cups in which it was served were of chipped and unmatched china. Outside the closed door, a couple of dozen people were queueing in the street.

In the Soviet Union everything not expressly permitted was assumed by the law-abiding majority to be forbidden. Tired of being asked by militiamen, passers-by and those ubiquitous busybodies, the old *bábushki* sitting in doorways,

'Where is your permit to take pictures?' each time he indulged in some candid photography, Tom had adapted a second-hand briefcase to conceal one of the two Pentax MXs he had brought with him from the West.

Since almost every Russian male from factory worker to general carried a briefcase everywhere, the battered old case bought from a trader in the Arbat street market drew no attention. The hole which Tom had made for the lens passed unnoticed as just another split seam. With a cable release fitted into the handle, the case made an ideal camera hide. In a café, the muted whirr of the motor drive was usually hidden beneath the noise of conversation. Developing the films himself in the department's darkroom at the university, Tom was building up a library of pictures of Soviet life more as a hobby to fill the lonely weekends than for any specific purpose.

He placed the case on the chair beside his, facing a couple of eighteen-year-old girls who were seated at the next table with their heads close together, telling each other's fortunes from coffee grains which they had poured into their saucers. Exposing a couple of frames, Tom caught snatches of their whispered revelations to each other; they seemed to be more about job prospects and friendships at work than what a Western girl would call romance.

Sibirsky was at a conference in Kiev that weekend and had set up the rendezvous in the café before he left town earlier in the week.

'There's a post-grad student who wants to compare notes with you, Tom,' he had said. 'Her name's Rada Mikhailova. She's seen some of your work and likes it. You'll find her interesting. She's just come back from a year at the university in Irkutsk where she's been researching incidents along the Trans-Sib during the Civil War, so I think you should meet.'

Tom had agreed, partly as a way of relieving the boredom of a Saturday afternoon and partly out of curiosity at the knowing smile on Sibirsky's face when he made the proposal.

But the girl had not shown up. After waiting for more than an hour, he was trying to get the waiter to show enough interest to make out a bill so that he could leave. The weather that May weekend was relatively mild: a flat calm and temperatures that hovered around 10 degrees above zero. On the last two Saturdays, the woman to whom he had given Brodsky's money had been absent from the shoe counter in GUM. Maybe she was ill, but maybe the explanation was more serious. By leaving now, he could amble through the store before closing time and reassure himself that all was well.

The girls at the next table had exhausted their coffee grains and were now poring over a pack of Tarot cards, arguing over the meanings hidden behind the pictures. The mystic terms they were using meant nothing to Tom. He noticed that, like so many things in Russia, the pack was improvised, the hand-traced image on each card being crudely coloured with several shades of ink.

'Tom? You are Tom Fielding?'

He gave up trying to attract the waiter's attention and looked round to see the most attractive girl he had been near since arriving in Moscow. Unmistakably Russian with her high Tartar cheekbones and slightly slanted eyes, she seemed at first glance to be wearing more make-up than all the other women in the café put together – but that was largely the effect of her natural colouring and the sparkle in her clear hazel eyes. Her shoulder-length ash-blonde hair merged with the collar of her sable coat. Tom caught a whiff of perfume as she sat down. Although he did not recognise Miss Dior, it was obvious that the fragrance had not come from the perfume counter at GUM.

She sat down and crossed her long legs, encased in shiny black leather boots that reached nearly to the knees. Unzipping her fur coat, she let it fall open to reveal a red mini skirt which had also not been purchased in any Russian store.

Tom put out a hand. 'Rada Mikhailova?' It was unfashionable among young people to use the *ótchestvo* or patronymic; in any event Sibirsky had not told him her middle name.

Her handshake was firm. She brushed away the waiter who had followed her across the café with a curt: 'Nothing to drink.'

'Then you must leave,' the man said. 'People are queueing outside.'

'Let them queue,' she said, unworried. 'It cost me two roubles to get past your crooked pal on the door without waiting, so I'll stay just as long as I want.'

He departed, muttering to himself.

Rada turned her face to Tom, seemingly unaware of the effect she was having on him. 'I thought your paper *Clarifying Confusion* was great,' she said.

'You read it in English?'

She laughed and brushed her hair back from her wide, intelligent brow. 'I'm so lazy, I didn't even try. Arkady Sergeyevich showed me a copy he's had translated into Russian. Did he tell you that the State publishing house Gosizdat wants to publish an expanded version?'

'No,' said Tom. 'He didn't say a word about that.'

'Perhaps he wanted me to arrive as a messenger with good tidings? Or perhaps he intends stealing your book and having it published in his name? Our government never signed the Copyright Convention, so these things can happen in Russia, you know.'

With her bright scarlet lipstick and matching nail varnish, Rada Mikhailova stood out among the soberly dressed girls in the café like a shaft of sexual sunshine on a grey and neuter day. The girls on the next table had abandoned the cards for the moment and were sitting silent, fascinated by the woman with whom Tom was talking. Her fur coat had fallen open wider to reveal a red silk blouse, beneath which she seemed to be wearing no bra.

Rada's next question caught him off guard: 'How old are you, Mr Tom?'

'Thirty. How old are you?'

'I'm as old as the winter and as young as the spring.'

She stood up and, without asking permission, took two cards from the top of the Tarot pack on the next table, handing one to Tom and keeping one for herself. He turned his over. Despite the different design and the amateurish execution, it was unmistakably the twin of the card that had fallen to the floor on Toronto Island.

'The Fool,' said Rada. 'Is that you, Mr Tom?'

'What's your card?' he asked.

She laughed and tossed hers onto the table. 'You call her the High Priestess in English. In Russian, we say the Virgin. In either language, she's not me. The Virgin and The Fool? Today both the cards must be wrong.'

Tom returned them to the girls, who were more interested in Rada's clothes than in him. Neither of them said anything as her hand reached across their table to pluck a third card from the pack and turn it face up. A naked man and woman, looking like Adam and Eve, stood apart with their hands just touching. Above them Raphael, the Angel of Air, bestowed his blessing on their union. Between them, in the far distance was what looked like a volcano.

'The Lovers.' Rada's smile mocked Tom's lust.

He followed her out of the café, with an ache in his groin that reminded him just how long it had been since he had had a woman. There were no taxis in sight.

'It was a bad pack,' said Rada.

'Does that make a difference?'

'Oh yes.' She sounded quite serious. 'Everyone has their favourite pack which works best for them. Maybe that cheap deck is okay for those girls, but not for me. My father has a very ancient Tarot which came from Egypt. It belonged to one of the Romanovs before the Revolution. The cards are beautiful and they live in a case of tortoiseshell and gold made by Fabergé. When I use them for a reading, everything comes true.'

'You really believe in all this?'

'Of course. It's not so simple as you might think. For example the Lovers . . .' She hailed a black car cruising past, which screeched to a halt in front of them.

'What about them?' Tom asked as they got in.

'Of course they can mean romance. But on my father's pack that card is different. It shows a man choosing between two women, so it can mean an important decision as well.'

While Tom was paying off the driver at their destination, Rada disappeared down a flight of steps leading to a basement from which the sound of heavy rock music was coming. Tom caught up with her in the process of kissing a muscle-bound bouncer on the lips. Inside the club a couple of hundred members of Moscow's golden youth were flaunting designer jeans and black leather jackets, drinking Budweiser beer and listening to a pirated Stones' tape on a bass-boosted Bose PA system.

Strobe lighting on some sound-to-light system showed the crocodile emblem of the satirical weekly magazine repeated endlessly around the walls – with a difference. A girl croco- dile was on all fours performing fellatio on a prodigiously endowed boy crocodile who was standing up and laughing his scaly head off while his friend took her from behind. The air was almost unbreathably thick with a pungent smoke; at least half the clientele was smoking Caucasian hash. From somewhere in the gloom, Rada produced a cigarette and put it between Tom's lips. He pushed the roach away.

'You don't smoke?' she shouted over the music, taking a hit herself and handing the cigarette back to a man at the next table.

'Not here,' he shouted back.

He had developed a sixth sense about surveillance and the atmosphere in the club was making him uneasy. He was halfway up the stairs to street level, when Rada caught up with him.

'I thought the Krokodil Club would amuse you,' she said.

'Oh, I really need to get picked up by the militia.'

'There's no danger of that,' Rada laughed. 'They're paid to keep away from places like this.'

She moved up to his level, her breasts brushing against his arm. 'But I know somewhere you'll like better. Come on.'

'Where are we going now?' he asked as they emerged into the street and Rada hailed an unlicensed taxi.

'D'you like ballet, Mr Tom?'

'I don't know much about it.'

She tutted, mocking him again. 'You should be ashamed, Englishman. You're like all those other Westerners who bad-mouth my country. No wonder you have a poor impression of it, spending your weekend in boring, dirty cafés when you could be watching the best ballet company in the world.'

In the rather tatty foyer of the Bolshoi, Rada announced that she had two tickets which were a present from someone who was out of town and could not use them. It crossed Tom's mind that the disturbing young woman beside him could be Sibirsky's mistress.

'Why do you carry that awful old briefcase around with you?' she asked. 'Is it to make yourself look like a Russian? If so, I can tell you it doesn't work. You could have the hammer-and-sickle tattooed all over your body, but you'd still be English.'

When Tom explained that the case was his way of carrying a camera unnoticed, she exclaimed delightedly, '*Ty spión!* You're a real spy!'

People nearby turned and stared at them.

'Do you always talk so loudly?' he asked.

'Why not? Of whom should I be afraid? *A seryózno –*' Rada lowered her voice conspiratorially – 'you should be careful, Mr Tom. It's a criminal offence under the penal code of the USSR to photograph any strategic object: military installations, railway stations, even telephone cables and tramlines – I don't know why.'

The instant transition from insouciant exuberance to paranoid whispering was Russia in a nutshell, Tom thought.

The ballet was *Swan Lake*. He assumed that the dancing was good, although the costumes and sets looked old and well-used. Once the performance had begun, Rada seemed unaware of his presence in the next seat. In the spill of light from the stage – they were sitting in the twelfth row of the stalls – he surreptitiously watched her weeping at the music and the dancing and the tragedy being enacted onstage.

At the end of the ballet, Rada stood up moist-eyed to applaud all the curtain calls. After the curtain had fallen for the last time, she sat down and accused the British of being frigid and having no souls.

'Every Russian in the theatre was moved,' she claimed.

'I didn't see anyone else crying.'

'You can't always see Russian tears. We have learned to cry within.'

'Well, maybe I was crying internally too.'

'*Ne právda*,' Rada said. 'You don't know how, Mr Tom. It takes centuries of suffering to learn that trick.' Her eyes were laughing at him again.

'Is it the first time you've seen *Swan Lake*?'

'The hundredth, more like.'

'And you can still weep? The plot's banal. And was the dancing really so good as all that?'

'I'm hungry,' she said, not listening. Most of the audience had already left. 'Ballet always gives me an appetite. All that energy the dancers are using up on the stage . . . Did I tell you that I wanted to dance? I even went to ballet school for two years. I had to give it up when I grew too big.'

'Too tall?' he queried.

'And too large here for a dancer.' She touched her bust. 'You know, if you sit there any longer, staring at my tits, we'll end up locked in for the night.'

'I've got a better idea: let me buy you dinner.'

'If I can choose where.'

'Of course.'

Nearly deafened by the music of an amplified all-girl balalaika orchestra, they dined on French cuisine aboard the *Aleksander Blok*, a decommissioned cruiser moored near the Mezhdunarodnaya Hotel. From there they walked along the embankment of the Moskva River and ended the night in the basement disco of the giant hotel Rossiya, dancing in a sweaty crush of visiting businessmen, Western expats and diplomats.

After saying goodnight, Tom walked back through the empty streets and lay awake till dawn, trying to make sense of what little he knew of Rada Mikhailova. She had a better wardrobe than most women in Russia. She had money and was obviously used to getting what she wanted in life. She had the confidence of someone who had grown up in the privileged layer, possibly in the *nomenklatura*.

The word meant 'people with names' and owed its origins to the paranoid Georgian who had treated the Russian empire as his personal fief from 1922 until his death in 1953. Pathologically unable to trust strangers, Josef Vissarionovich Dzhugashvili had ruled like a medieval monarch – or maybe, as an ex-seminarist, he had inherited his style from the Renaissance popes. Whatever the explanation, he ran the military and civil services of the greatest twentieth-century empire by dividing the key appointments among a few hundred men whose names he knew. Hence the term. Over three generations those appointees and their families accumulated wealth rapidly in the absence of death or estate duties, for a state that had officially abolished private property could not admit its existence by taxing it. Thus the *nomenklatura* became a hereditary post-revolutionary aristocracy.

Did Rada come from this kind of background? Tom had never got a straight answer from her all evening. As much as she turned him on physically, she puzzled him intellectually.

In talking about work she showed a keen intelligence but none of the dogged temperament that would motivate someone to spend a year poring over dusty documents from the Civil War, three thousand kilometres from Moscow. When Tom asked her why she had chosen to specialise in this area of research, she laughed and said, 'To please Arkady Sergeyevich. He was my tutor.'

.5.

It was a measure of Tom's obsession with Rada that he had hardly thought about the woman in GUM all week, but it was still a relief to see her back at her post behind the shoe counter on the following Saturday.

After leaving the shopping mall, he wandered across Red Square past the Lenin Mausoleum with its perennially patient queue and spent an hour in the bathhouse near Arbat Square before going home to find an invitation in Rada's extravagant scrawl pinned to the door of his room. They ate in the very fashionable Aragvi restaurant in Gorky Street. The well-seasoned Georgian food was excellent, starting with *lóbio* – butter beans in a spicy sauce – followed by *tsi-plyáta tabáka*, which was a roasted spring chicken crushed between hot bricks. With a bottle of wine from the Caucasus and vodka, the cost was only 12 roubles each, or roughly £12 a head at the current rate of exchange.

Tom did not taste a thing. During the meal, each gesture Rada made and each look she gave him was like a knife turning in the open wound of his desire. When they left the restaurant, there was a queue of people standing behind them on the pavement, still waiting to eat although the Aragvi was due to close in thirty minutes.

A ripple of disapproval ran through the queue as Rada planted a long and lingering kiss on Tom's lips.

'It's not the price of the meal,' he said, 'but I want you.'

'I thought you'd never get around to saying that. You must be the only man in Moscow who wouldn't have tried to get my knickers off, the first evening we met.'

'You should be ashamed,' someone called from the queue.

An unlicensed taxi swerved across two lines of traffic and pulled up by them. '*Kudá?*' the driver shouted through his open window: where to?

Tom was feeling Rada's buttocks with his hands; her breasts were soft against his chest. She kissed him hungrily again and again.

'Are you going to get in my car or do it on the sidewalk?' the driver demanded.

After pulling out into the traffic, he adjusted the rear-view mirror to watch them embracing on the rear seat. After two violent decelerations with screaming tyres, Tom took his lips away from Rada's to find they were heading the wrong way. He shouted at the driver to concentrate on the road and counted the seconds until they arrived in the old Arbat and Rada was running up the stairs hand in hand with him, laughing. In his room he hurriedly locked the door, put on the desk lamp and switched off the ceiling light.

She looked around, taking in the books, the few personal possessions and the clothes hanging from a metal bar across one corner of the room. 'It's like a monk's cell,' she said. 'So tidy and so poor. Is this how you lived in England?'

She could have been asking about a previous incarnation. Tom grunted a reply and pulled her close, inhaling her perfume, exploring her body from the neck to below the panty line with fingers that could not stay still.

'You'll tear something,' she protested, pulling free to drape her coat over the back of the single chair.

Tom stopped her undoing the buttons on her blouse. 'Let me help.'

He stood behind her and cupped his hands over her breasts, feeling their weight through the heavy silk fabric. She was not wearing a bra. As the blouse slid away from the creamy skin of her shoulders he saw in the wall mirror the nipples that had been disturbing him all evening. They were brown and swollen, like breasts upon breasts. His hands enclosed them, as when plucking succulent ripe fruit.

Rada dropped her skirt to the floor and Tom saw that she was completely naked. Fur coat and no knickers, he thought.

She was watching his eyes in the mirror, turned on by the intentness of his gaze as they flicked from her breasts to her triangle of pubic hair. 'Do you like my body, Tom?'

The answer was obvious; she reached behind to grasp it and felt his moistness on the small of her back. Pulling free, she jumped into the bed, and pulled the sheets over herself to watch Tom dropping his clothes on the floor, kicking off his shoes and tearing his socks off.

Turned on by the sight of him naked and erect with desire for her, she reached out with both hands to grasp his hips and slowly pull him close, taking his flesh into her mouth, licking and sucking the essence that spilled from him so freely.

She woke up still engorged and with her breasts still sensitive from his caresses. Beside her, Tom seemed asleep, so she touched herself drowsily. After climaxing with her eyes closed, she opened them to find him watching her. When his finger replaced hers, pleasure became pain. She tried to stop him but he was too strong. He held her down, using his tongue and teeth on the skin of her neck and breasts, his fingers inside her, stretching and stretching. Pain turned back to pleasure as he pounded her rhythmically until her back arched and her head pressed back into the pillow with a cry, 'I'm drowning!'

Not drowning but flying, she thought dimly. There was nothing she could do about it, either way, for Tom was totally in control. Her muscles spasmed on his hand in a climax that went on and on. How strange, she thought, that such a gentle-looking man can be such a violent lover.

We spent all of Sunday in bed making love but when I saw her in the student canteen at lunch-time on Monday I wanted Rada again with the painful urgency of a horny hermit seeing a voluptuous woman for the first time in ten years.

I wanted to drag her away somewhere private and tear her clothes off there and then – to reveal her, touch her, feel her, explore her and lose myself in her. The need to plunge my flesh into her body hurt like an iron hand squeezing my balls.

She was standing in the queue at the counter, holding a tray and talking to a girlfriend, when she must have felt my eyes on her. Her spin-turn was as fast as a dancer's pirouette, the long unbuttoned raincoat swirling loosely around her legs. The knife and fork flew off her tray. She let them fall to the floor and met my gaze. We seemed to be alone in the room. It was as though I was looking through a long-focus lens: her hazel eyes, her smile, her scarlet lips were the only things I saw. Her nostrils flared as though she could smell my desire for her across the tables and all the other people, above the typically Russian mélange of odours: food, damp clothes, cheap eau de cologne and cigarette smoke.

She had buried her face in my armpit at 2 a.m. after licking the sweat from my chest. Eyes closed, she had murmured, 'It is the smell of you I love, Tom. What means "drozhzhi" in English?'

'Yeast,' I said.

'Yeast?' She pulled her head away and looked at me.

'Yeast?' She played with the sound of the word on her tongue: 'I yearn for your yeasty smell.'

She pushed her way through the crowd of students at the counter as fast as only Russians know how, to kiss me on the lips, pressing herself against me with a little whimper of desire.

'People are staring,' I said.

'I don't care,' she whispered, nibbling my ear. 'I need you. Where can we go?'

'To your place or mine, whichever's nearer.' I had no idea where she lived.

'It would take too long.'

'I've got the key to the darkroom.'

In the red glow of the safe light we tore off each other's clothes and coupled on the floor violently. Rada was half-dressed when I took her again, bending her over the enlarging table and rutting like a stag in the forest. I was aware of someone knocking on the door as I came. A voice was complaining about the noises Rada had been making. A fist banged on the door and a voice that I recognised as belonging to Sibirsky's busybody deputy, Makarova, demanded to know what was happening.

'Go away,' Rada called back breathlessly. 'Have you no imagination?'

She subsided onto a castored stool and pulled her blouse closed to sit, head down and chest heaving while she got back her breath. The movement of her breasts with each inhalation obsessed me. I wanted her more than I had ever wanted a woman before and she obviously felt pretty much the same. Her red hand reached out for my red body. Her fingers closed around my shaft and pulled me roughly towards her.

'Do it again,' she ordered huskily. 'And again and again and again.'

On the first really hot day in the summer of 1984, the green of the new leaves on the trees seemed impossibly vivid after the long greyness of Moscow's winter. Tom was in shirt-sleeves and lightweight trousers; Rada had on a sleeveless white cotton dress and matching high-heeled sandals.

They were sitting under the lime trees on a bench outside the offices of Gosizdat, the State Publishing Company. Tom was examining the contract they had just signed. It specified a print run of half a million copies of the expanded version of *Clarifying Confusion*, to be published as a book the following year.

'What will they do with 500,000 copies?' he wondered.

'Don't ask,' Rada laughed. 'The important thing is, they pay us a royalty for every copy printed, not sold. Remember, they printed three million copies of Brezhnev's seven-volume memoirs and nobody could read more than ten pages of that stuff without dying of boredom.'

'It's a crazy system.'

She disagreed: 'Not if you're on the inside, Tom. In the West you only hear the dissidents whining about injustice. For a writer who is prepared to produce what the government wants, it's a very nice life here. Take us. We're going to get the equivalent of five years' salary for this book. In addition we're now automatically members of the Writers' Union, entitled to use the subsidised restaurant and the library facilities of the club in Herzen Street. We may even qualify for a low-rent dacha out at Peredelkino, where we can spend weekends. How about that?'

Tom was looking at the bottom of the last page. For the first time he saw Rada's name in full: Rada Arkadeyevna Mikhailova. The middle name meant daughter-of-Arkady.

He looked up. In half-profile, there was a certain family resemblance. If it had still been the fashion among young people to use the patronymic, he might have guessed earlier.

'You're Sibirsky's daughter,' he accused her.

She grinned as though it was a joke.

'Why didn't you tell me?'

The grin faded. 'I thought it might change the way you thought about me.'

'It might have,' Tom admitted. 'But why don't you use the name Sibirskaya anyway?'

She shrugged. 'I grew up with my mother, so I've always used her name.'

'And why did Arkady Sergeyevich never tell me you were his daughter?'

'Secrecy comes naturally to us Russians, Tom.'

'But what's the point?'

'There doesn't have to be one.'

'Do people at the university know, like Makarova?'

'That witch knows everything.'

'Then why didn't anyone ever tell me?'

'There's a story of the Tsar and Lenin arriving on the same train at the spa in Karlovy Vary. The stationmaster meets them and asks what the weather was like when they left St Petersburg. It was sunny and dry but they both tell him, "Oh, it was cold and raining." '

'So?'

'Even Russians who hate each other will still conspire against a foreigner.'

'And how long will it take until I'm no longer a foreigner?'

'Maybe two generations, if you're lucky.'

The spontaneity which had fascinated him the first evening took Tom by surprise again now. As though a gesture wiped out the weeks of deception, Rada kissed him on the lips and announced her intention of inviting Arkady Sergeyevich on a river trip to celebrate the contract for the book. She went back into the Gosizdat building to use the receptionist's phone, returning a couple of minutes later to announce, 'That's fixed. He'll meet us in half an hour at the Kiev terminal.'

Tom was curious. 'What did he say when you told him that I knew?'

Rada laughed. 'He said, "It makes life simpler."'

They strolled down to the river, talking about the work still to be done on the book. A propos of nothing Rada stopped, put her arms around Tom's neck and looked him in the face. 'Most men treat me as though I am not really a person, just something to look at, to touch, to use.'

'And don't I look at you that way?' he teased her.

'Sometimes,' she admitted. 'But from you, I like it. The important thing is that when we are working you treat me like a respected colleague. You ask my opinion and you listen when I give it.'

Her tongue explored his mouth. In the sleeveless thin cotton dress, her muskiness floated up to his nostrils, making him want her with a painful immediacy.

'Let's go back to my place,' he said.

'Uh-huh.' Rada's tongue was caressing his.

'This is going to get embarrassing,' Tom muttered.

'I can feel it.' She was enjoying the effect she was having on him. 'But just for once, I should like to make something nice for my father.'

'What's that mean: just for once?'

'I caused him pain,' Rada said. 'Now I should like to make him happy.'

She refused to explain any more. Waiting for Sibirsky at the landing stage they watched the parties of foreign tourists embarking on the ancient tour boats. Out of the blue, Rada asked, 'Do you trust me?'

'Why shouldn't I? Because you lied to me about your identity?'

She shook her head. 'It wasn't a lie. I just didn't tell you the truth. But other people may lie to you about me. Russians can be very jealous of a girl in my position.'

'Envious,' he corrected her. 'But why should they tell me lies?'

The conversation was interrupted by Sibirsky's arrival. Like Tom, he was dressed in casual trousers and an open-necked shirt. He was carrying a picnic hamper which had been packed by his housekeeper: sliced salami, pickled cucumbers, rye bread and beer. They sat on the open deck eating it and enjoying the sun as the boat chugged its way asthmatically past the Novedevichy Convent. After the gloom and cold of the long winter, the light and warmth made Tom feel as though he was breathing pure oxygen.

A group of North American tourists were taking snap-shots of each other by the rail with the convent in the background. Tom persuaded Rada and her father to stand by them and framed a shot of a happy father with his arm around his daughter's waist. Then he put the camera away in his briefcase. Rada had persuaded him to buy a less decrepit one, but it was still the best way of walking around Moscow with a camera for anyone who did not want to attract atten-tion.

When Rada walked along to what she called the pointed end of the boat, Sibirsky watched Tom's face follow her every movement. The warm soporific breeze riffled Rada's blonde hair and blew the skirt of her dress up, revealing her long slim legs.

The professor put an arm around Tom's shoulders and hugged him briefly. 'I never thought a year ago that I'd ever again enjoy the simple pleasure of eating ice cream on a sunny day with my daughter.'

'Why not?'

'We'd lost contact,' Sibirsky said. 'Now, thanks to you, I see Rada most days when I'm in Moscow. An outing like this is a great joy for me. I have a lot to thank you for.'

Winston Churchill once wrote, 'Russia is a riddle wrapped in a mystery inside an enigma.' Tom was begin-ning to think that Rada was all those things. The longer he knew her, the more certain he felt that there were whole areas of her past life which were kept secret from him.

Drowsy with warmth and the beer he had drunk, he gave up trying to work it out. They drifted past the Lenin sta-dium, eating ice cream. Rada sat between the two men. Her own ice cream finished, she held hands with both of them.

With the contract in his pocket and her hand in his it was,

Tom felt, rather a good life. His mood of pleasant reverie was interrupted as a Canadian woman from the tour group came close, pointing out the sights to her friend. The familiar Ontario accent was like a finger from the past accusing Tom of deceit. He wondered what had happened to Karen and what she was doing.

'What's the matter?' Rada called when he stood up abruptly and walked away from her to stand by the rail.

'*Nichevó*,' he said. 'Nothing at all.'

.6.

'I'm sorry, Larry.'
'Don't say that.' He stood back to let Karen get in the elevator first. As the doors closed he would have liked to put his arm around her for comfort but that was not the way couples were supposed to behave right after visiting a lawyer's office to initiate divorce proceedings, so he stood away from her and watched the floor numbers change from twenty down to one and into the minuses.

In the basement car park beneath the BCE Tower they both got out and Karen thought, Why am I down here? It's *his* car now, not *ours*.

'Can I buy you a cup of coffee in the food court?' Larry asked.

She shook her head.

'Then can I drop you someplace?'

'No thanks.'

'I wish you'd tell me what you plan to do,' he said. 'I don't want to interfere, but I'd just like to know.'

'I'm going back to my first love, volcanoes. I told you.'

'Have they come up with a position for you, back at the university?'

'They offered me back my old job, but I want a better one now. I'm a PhD, remember? I've applied for an opening at the Smithsonian. I don't know if it'll come off.'

'You're not planning to go to Europe?'

'Why should I?'

He shifted his weight from one foot to the other. 'I thought maybe you'd be going back to Tom.'

'Poor Larry . . .' She squeezed his hand.

'The number of times I've heard you talking in your sleep . . .'

She took her hand from his. 'I'll never go back to Tom, don't worry about that.'

'Never's a long time,' Larry said softly. 'But then, you're a stubborn woman. If you hadn't been, you'd have left me much earlier.'

'I tried to make it work.'

'I know you did. And I'm grateful for it. If you ever need any help – I don't just mean money – you've only got to call, you know that. I hope you'll always see me as a friend.'

'And I hope you find the girl you deserve.' Karen turned her face away so that he could not kiss her and placed her cheek against his chest, feeling the reassuring strength of him and clutching his arms tight to feel the muscles through the cloth. Larry had bought new clothes for the visit to the lawyer's office. She wondered what was the significance of that.

Upstairs on street level Karen hailed a cab to take her to the CN Tower where she rode the elevator to the restaurant. She had never been up there before. It was something tourists did, not residents – but it seemed a symbolic beginning. For a while, she thought, I'll do things I never did before – and have a symbolic rebirth.

Sitting alone, picking at a meal she did not want, she watched the city of Toronto turning slowly below, asked the waiter for some paper and started to write a letter to her sister.

> Dear Fran,
>   I've done it – or rather, we have. Larry fixed everything. I almost wish he hadn't been so damned helpful – but you know Larry. I'm sitting here at the top of the CN Tower, remembering the last time I walked out on him and went to Bristol. I felt so free and young then. Now I feel centuries older, even though only a couple of years have passed. Is it guilt that makes me feel so heavy and old?
>   Larry asked me whether I was going back to Tom and I said no. I have no idea where he is or what's happened to him, but I could see Larry didn't entirely believe me. How awful for him to have lived with me all these months, thinking I was in love with another man. Oh, shit! Look after him. I don't need to ask, do I? That's what a family's for.
>   I think what finally decided me to break up was Doodie's funeral. I looked at Larry, so caring to Mom at the graveside, and I thought, there's a man who needs to be needed. It's not fair to make him waste any more time living with someone he doesn't even know.
>   Please don't give him my new address. He's got to stop thinking I'm his responsibility and start looking for someone new. If you can drop by sometime and bring my things, that would save me going back to the house.
>   Love to everyone, K

It was almost exactly twelve months to the day since Ivanov had taken Tom to Sibirsky's apartment for the first time. Most of the men standing in the production-line queue outside the Wedding Palace were looking uncomfortable and embarrassed in their best clothes, with their hair slicked back. The brides in white dresses looked rather wistful, as did their mothers – as though they would have liked to make more of the occasion. Many of the couples were getting married because it was the vital first step in qualifying for accommodation on the housing list – providing they were still together when their names reached the top of the list five years later, which was statistically unlikely.

Rada had chosen to wear the clothes she had worn when she first met Tom. The high-heeled boots and fur coat attracted glances of disapproval and envy from all sides, to which she seemed oblivious. Sibirsky was wearing a new suit he had just bought in Paris and Ivanov had put on his best uniform, with a chestful of medals that made him look as though he had taken Berlin single-handed. Even Tom had been persuaded by Rada to buy a suit for the occasion.

'There's nothing like having a KGB uniform in the party to get priority in the wedding queue,' Ivanov joked when they were called to the head of the line.

He was the only member of the wedding party who was behaving normally. Sibirsky seemed to have something on his mind and Tom was feeling guilty: it was one thing to have an affair with Rada but getting married to her as a way of improving his cover seemed somehow immoral.

She had been reading the Tarot the previous evening, as was her habit before any important event or if a decision had to be made. Hating all superstition, he usually refused to get involved or ask her what the cards foretold, even to humour her. But that night he had noticed that the Fool turned up yet again in her spread.

Casually, he had asked her what the card meant.

'Lots of things,' she had said. 'That's the mystery of the Tarot. It depends on whether you're reading for yourself or someone else, looking at the past or the future, whether the card is right way up or reversed. But essentially the Fool in this reading means taking a risk, ignoring dangers. There are no major arcana present in the spread, so the choice is mine to make. But the card was reversed.'

'What's that mean?'

'It could mean I'll regret the decision.'

She seemed to be regretting it still, looking straight ahead and not at Tom as they waited in the Wedding Palace. A concierge in a brown overall motioned Ivanov forward. The others followed him into a long gallery where a poor-quality tape recording of Mozart's Jupiter Symphony was playing. Behind a desk which occupied the centre of the vast open space, looking rather like an altar in a church, stood a short fat woman in a grey skirt and jacket. On the wall, instead of a crucifix was a large portrait of Lenin. The overall impression was of pomp and gloom.

I couldn't help contrasting the ceremony with Karen's wedding and wondering for the thousandth time what would have happened if I had run up the aisle that day in Canada and stopped her wedding. Would we have lived happily ever after? Or would I have dragged Karen into all this, one way or another? Of one thing I was certain: she was better off without me. It seemed the height of infidelity to be thinking of her at the precise moment I was getting married to Rada.

The official pointed out to us that it was the duty of women to bear children for the Soviet Socialist Motherland and enjoined us both 'to respect the socially useful institution of marriage' before pronouncing us man and wife according to Soviet law. A couple of minutes later we were ushered out again into the cold, grey September morning.

I could not work out Sibirsky's mood. He had been the prime mover in setting up the wedding and I had gone along with his plan because marriage represented the only way that I could see of getting a Russian internal passport, which Ponsonby had said was vital for my freedom of movement.

There had been a typically Soviet Catch 22: the way for

me to get the passport was by marrying a Soviet citizen, but Rada could only marry me once I had it. Ivanov's intervention with the Ministry of the Interior solved that problem.

Uncle Vanya, as she called him, had also made most of the arrangements for the celebration, which included hiring the white Volga limousine in which we were all driven to the Lenin hills, to pose in a formal cluster among the other wedding groups, leaning against the stone balustrade that overlooks the city.

I recognised the photographer as the KGB girl who had taken my ID picture at the dacha. She was moonlighting for cash, using her own cameras this time: a pair of Nikons that were worth a fortune in Russia. While she was taking close-ups of Rada alone, I grabbed the chance to buttonhole Sibirsky and accused him of behaving like a miserable sod on our wedding day.

He pulled the marriage certificate from his inside pocket and pointed to his signature on it. 'It's not wise for a Russian to have his name on the same piece of paper as a foreigner's, Tom,' he said. 'This document ties you not only to Rada, but also to me.'

I pointed out that he was the one who had wanted us to get married. He grunted something incomprehensible in reply, so I told him to cheer up because Beria was dead.

'What was that saying?' Sibirsky said gloomily. 'The king is dead, long live the king. We will always have our Berias in Russia, believe me.'

I put the certificate away in my wallet. 'Just when I think I'm getting to know you people, you show me how little I understand of the Slav mind.'

Sibirsky shrugged. 'It's not personal, you know that.'

Ivanov paid the photographer in dollars and we headed in the white Volga to the Aragvi restaurant where a private room had been reserved.

*

After *kharcho*, a spicy meat soup, the main course was *osterina na vertelye* – a whole sturgeon roasted on a spit. There were a few friends of Sibirsky's from the university and a couple of girlfriends invited by Rada, with their partners. They were friendly enough but Tom had the feeling which had been bothering him for the last few weeks at the university: that there was a conspiracy going on around him.

He tried to convince himself that this unease was no more than a symptom of the paranoia to which a foreigner could so easily fall victim in Russia, but when he recounted to Ivanov what Sibirsky had said about the marriage certificate, the major sobered up a little. Even by his own prodigious standards he had consumed an enormous quantity of vodka already that day.

He grabbed Tom's arm for support and said, 'He has reasons not to want to attract attention, Feldink. Don't take it personally.'

'What kind of reasons? Attention by whom?'

'How long have you lived in Russia?' Ivanov retorted. 'Haven't you learned not to ask questions yet?'

Tom had noticed that the line-up of icons on the wall of Sibirsky's apartment changed from time to time. At first he assumed that Rada's father swapped or maybe dealt in icons with other collectors, but lately he had come to suspect that Ivanov's habit of escorting Sibirsky to the airport on his trips abroad might have something to do with a racket in exported icons . . . which could explain both Ivanov's and Sibirsky's different but expensive lifestyles. Like a good Soviet citizen, he had decided that it was none of his business.

The meal was interrupted, as all Russian celebrations are, by repeated toasts. Everyone consumed a lot of alcohol. In the men's room afterwards, Tom saw Sibirsky and Ivanov arguing as they stood side by side at the urinals. Assuming that the row was private, he waited in the corridor discreetly out of earshot until they had finished. Ivanov pushed past him looking unhappy.

Through the open door leading into the private dining room, Tom saw Rada watching as Sibirsky took his elbow and led him along the corridor for a private chat. He did not seem to know how to begin, and muttered something about wanting Rada to be happy.

'So do I,' said Tom.

'. . . but there are many things you don't know about her yet.'

'Such as?'

'When her mother remarried, Rada was fifteen and too wild for her stepfather to cope with. They sent her to live with me for a couple of years. I'm a busy man and I travel a great deal. As a result, my daughter had too much liberty and money – and too little parental discipline – at a crucial stage of her growing up.'

A moustachioed Georgian waiter looking like the young Joe Stalin pushed past them carrying a laden tray, muttering about people getting in his way.

'Sometimes wealth can be a disadvantage for a young person,' Sibirsky muttered. 'It can attract a certain kind of parasite.'

'You mean drug-pushers?'

Sibirsky sounded surprised. 'Did she tell you about this?'

'We smoke a bit of hash from time to time.'

Sibirsky's pale blue eyes searched Tom's. 'Rada never talked about why she went to live with her aunt in Irkutsk for a year?'

'You told me it was to research military operations on the Trans-Sib for you.'

'And did you honestly believe that? Didn't you think there might be another explanation?'

'Not being a Russian,' Tom said, 'I don't always suspect everyone of lying to me.'

'I'm talking of the old Tsarist tradition of internal exile.'

'For what crime?'

'Ivan Petrovich is a good friend. He arranged for Rada to

be legally exiled from Moscow for one year, during which she had to live with my sister in Irkutsk. It was the only way to prevent her coming back here.'

Tom was mystified. 'Why shouldn't she come back to Moscow?'

Arkady Sergeyevich's grip on Tom's arm was almost painful. 'Because, Mr Tom – as she calls you – your wife was legally registered for the two previous years as a heroin addict and we wanted to keep her well away from her suppliers.'

I was numb. The pain in Sibirsky's eyes told me that what I had just heard was the truth.

'It started when Rada was eighteen,' he continued. 'She got tangled up with a lot of rich kids who hung out at a club called Krokodil.'

I don't know how most bridegrooms would have reacted. I'd had a bit to drink and heard myself saying, 'She took me there, the first Saturday we met. The club's expensive but harmless: loud music, Azeri hash and American beer.'

'Maybe it's harmless now,' Sibirsky agreed. 'But that's thanks to Ivan Petrovich. He arranged to have the place closed down for six months after everything that happened to Rada.'

The Stalin lookalike and another waiter came into the corridor for a smoke. Sibirsky lowered his voice and changed to English so they could not overhear. For an educated man, he had a peculiar habit of muddling tenses. 'When first I discover that Rada is addict, I ask Ivanov's advice. We are knowing each other for years and he has seen my daughter grow up. He was like cross-father . . .'

'Godfather,' I corrected.

'Ivanov says, "Keep her short of money, so these pushers leave her alone." It seems good idea – until I find out she is selling her body to get the cash for her habit.'

I couldn't believe what I was hearing. The door to the private dining room swung open behind a waiter. My eyes met Rada's for a moment. She looked about to cry. Feeling sick and angry, I pulled free from her father's grip and shouted, 'Why didn't someone tell me all this before?'

Sibirsky changed back to Russian but kept his voice low. 'Ivan Petrovich and I thought you'd run a mile,' he said gloomily.

'I'd have been right to do so,' I snarled.

Sibirsky caught at my sleeve to prevent me walking away. He told me that he loved his daughter and that was why he had worked on the idea of us getting married. Rada, he said, was a different person since I had come into her life — like the girl she used to be before getting mixed up with drugs. He ended up saying something about her needing me far more than I'd ever realise.

'Why tell me all this today, of all days?' I asked.

Sibirsky spread his hands helplessly. 'If I'd told you earlier, you might have called the whole thing off. But you had to know sometime because looking after Rada is your responsibility now — and you must know what to look out for.'

I couldn't breathe. I had to get outside, so I broke free from his grasp and pushed past the waiters. As I ran out of the restaurant, I heard Sibirsky calling after me, 'Don't be too hard on her, Tom. She loves you.'

Some wedding! I thought bitterly. Shivering in that damned suit and no overcoat, I walked aimlessly through the cold, empty streets, trying to find a way out of the maze I had got myself into. There was no way out. I had been feeling guilty about the way I was using Rada . . . and yet, as it turned out, I was the one being used!

Remembering the Tarot card on which the Fool had been walking on the edge of a precipice and not looking where he was going, I thought: That's me. I'm the Fool. And I've just fallen over the edge.

.7.

Through *blat* – the use of bribery and connections – Sibirsky had wangled a sub-lease of a redecorated three-room apartment which belonged to a cultural attaché in the Washington embassy. The brand-new red Lada Export parked beneath its windows was his wedding present.

Once inside the apartment, Tom shrugged Rada off and stood looking out of the window at the tower-block oppo-site. If he had had anywhere to go, he would have walked out there and then. But after wandering aimlessly through the streets for more than an hour, he had returned to the restau-rant because there was nowhere else to go. Scandalised when Tom wanted to hand back the keys to his room, both Rada and her father had insisted that he illicitly sublet it at a profit; the new tenant had already moved in.

'Can't you believe me when I say that all that drug scene is over and done with?' Rada sniffed. 'Can't you trust me?'

'Lies,' he said bitterly. 'So many lies.'

'But we have to trust you,' she pointed out. 'Suppose you

should turn out to be a spy, Tom? Both my father and I will be guilty by association. We'll end up in a camp for fifteen or twenty years. That's the way it is in Russia.'

'If I was a spy,' he asked rhetorically, 'would Ivan Petrovich have come along to the ceremony in his best uniform?'

'Perhaps it's Vanya's way of watching you,' Rada suggested. 'Had you thought about that, Mr Tom Fielding? I've known him since I was a kid. He pretends to be a bluff and simple man, but no major in the KGB is ever quite what he seems. He couldn't survive in their jungle if he were.'

'I can tell you this,' Tom said to the lights of the next tower-block. 'The only crime I have committed since coming to Russia is thanks to you and your father. I've become a landlord for the first time in my life – in a country where it's illegal.'

'Everyone does that.'

He heard her stockinged feet shuffle across the parquet floor and felt her hands creeping around his waist.

'I was so unhappy before you came into my life,' she whispered.

'You didn't look unhappy.' He was talking to their joint reflection in the window.

'How do you know what I was feeling inside?' she asked. 'Men think that if a girl wears make-up and pretty dresses, she must be happy. Inside, I can tell you that I was crying every day.'

Tom turned and faced her. Mascara was smudged around Rada's eyes and her cheeks were puffy. She seemed smaller, weaker, younger and in need of his protection. He put his arms around her and felt her cling tighter. Then the moment of tenderness was ruined: she raised her face to his and an image came into Tom's mind of her kissing the bouncer on the mouth at the Krokodil Club. Had he been one of the men who . . . ?

He shut his eyes and pressed his mouth hard on her soft

lips, hurting her deliberately. He heard a muffled, 'Please, Tom. Please.' But he did not let her go, forcing her down onto the carpet, where he tore at her clothes until she was half-naked.

'You're a fucking whore,' he snarled, kneeling astride her and pinning her wrists to the floor. 'You got a kick out of picking men up and doing it for money.'

'No,' she pleaded. 'You don't understand.'

'Then tell me. Tell me what it was like. I want to know.' His face contorted with anger and pain, he slapped her face – right, left, right, left – again and again, going on and on until she spat at him through split and bleeding lips, 'All right, I'll tell you – if you really want to know.'

And so he learned about the blurred succession of faceless bodies in bedrooms, in cars, in doorways, on her knees in the snowy streets . . . She tried to convey the desperation of grabbing each man's money and counting it, knowing she had to turn another so many tricks that night before she could buy what she needed.

'And do you know why?' she said through the tears. 'Because no one ever gave me what you do. The only time I felt like a real person was when that warm comforting rush in my brain drove reality away for a while.'

'And what about the men that used you?'

'I never even saw their faces,' she protested. 'I wouldn't recognise one if I met him tomorrow.'

'And the ones who sold you the drugs?'

'Thanks to Vanya's contacts in the militia, they're all in the east.' The expression was a euphemism for the labour camps. 'Their sentences are followed by periods of exile, so they won't ever be coming back to Moscow.'

Tom released her wrists, rolled off her and lay on the carpet beside her. Her skin was cold against his arm, despite the central heating. She sat up. Her cheeks were puffy from crying, her lips were rimmed with dried blood and one eye was swollen, nearly closed.

'You'll have a black eye tomorrow,' he said, wondering at himself. 'How could I do that to you?'

Rada sat up and looked at her face in the wall mirror. 'In Russia, it's not so uncommon for wives to let their husbands beat them.'

'You could hardly have stopped me. That's what makes me ashamed.'

'I could have stopped you.' Rada stood and pulled the torn blouse around herself. 'I was attacked in the street when I was sixteen. A boy from Kazan grabbed my handbag as I came out of the Metro. When my father heard about it, he arranged for me to take karate lessons. I was quite good. I could have stopped you any time I wanted.'

'Then why didn't you?'

'I thought it might make you feel better.'

Looking back, it's incredible how selfish I was. After all, I was deceiving Rada the whole time. Whatever she had done wrong was long before I came into her life, so why did I treat her so badly? To conceal my own guilt, is one reason. Another was the anger I felt at myself for getting into this situation. I was so mixed up that I put out a distress call to Ponsonby: a chalk mark on a wall near the Arbat bathhouse.

Dehydrated by the heat during his session in the sauna, Tom sat slumped on the slatted seat in his cubicle, wrapped in a towel. He had almost given up when there was a tap on the wooden upright and he pulled back the curtain to see Ponsonby standing there naked. He handed Tom a *vénik* of birch twigs and lay down on one of the benches.

'I want out,' were Tom's first words. 'You promised to ship me out of here if it all went wrong – and it has.'

Between the echoing tiled walls men were moving about naked or swathed in towels, appearing and disappearing in the clouds of steam. The conversation was sporadic, interrupted each time anyone came near. There was a mild satisfaction for Tom in the fact that, the longer it took him to bring Ponsonby up to date, the more of a thrashing the man on the bench had to put up with.

After a particularly painful slash from the *vénik*, Ponsonby sat up and warded off the next stroke. 'You've got some domestic problems, Tom. That's all. I'm sorry to hear about them but they're nothing to do with the reason you're here.'

'They're absolutely to do with it,' Tom contradicted him. 'So I repeat: get me out of here or I'll blow the whistle.'

'You can't drop us in the shit,' was the calm rejoinder. 'You know bugger-all about anything, so what would you tell them?'

'I could start by turning you in.'

Ponsonby wiped sweat from his forehead. 'I'm a minnow, Tom. The sharks in this game don't tell me what they're up to. I know very little more than you. And if you did betray me, I'd be handed back in a swap sooner or later, whereas you'd spend the rest of your life in a camp.'

Tom sat down on the bench beside Ponsonby with his head in his hands. 'Oh God,' he groaned. 'It's all such a bloody mess.'

'I'd like to help, but we've got problems at the moment.' In terse sentences Ponsonby brought Tom up to date. The previous summer Oleg Gordievsky, the KGB *rezident* in London, had been recalled to Moscow under suspicion of being a British double agent. After eleven years of working for MI6, Gordievsky decided to leave his wife and two daughters behind and make a break for the West.

Aggressively positive under Prime Minister Margaret Thatcher, his handlers decided to get their man out before he was arrested, interrogated, tortured and shot. Against them, the British ambassador in Moscow argued that it would be a breach of the Vienna convention on diplomatic behaviour to aid and abet the escape of a wanted Soviet citizen and that helping him over the border would 'constitute altogether a most undiplomatic act'.

On 19 July, only hours before he was due to be arrested, Gordievsky went jogging and eluded his watchers while clad only in running vest and shorts. Somehow, somewhere he picked up clothes and false papers, which enabled him to make his way by local transport to a location near the Finnish border where he was bundled into the boot of a car with CD plates and driven to freedom.

The international repercussions had still not died down. As Ponsonby put it, 'The border's been screwed up so hard since then that the pips are squeaking. It will be a few months before we can get you out, Tom. So, remember that I'm not deaf to your problems, I just can't do anything for the time being. And by the way, you've been promoted.'

He dropped a crumpled piece of paper on the bench, heaved himself upright with a muttered, '*Spasíbo, továrisch*,' and disappeared into the steam.

Back in his cubicle, Tom smoothed out the piece of soggy paper. According to the miniaturised bank statement, his balance stood at over £30,000 and the two latest monthly payments had been increased to £2,500 each.

Driving a red Morgan two-seater, Ponsonby cut a red light and braked sharply to collect Dr Nathan who was waiting outside the house in Harley Street. After three circuits of Regent's Park, he finished his résumé of the situation: 'It's a fuck-up. Tom's in place. Perfect job. Marvellous connections. And what does he do? Falls for this damned nympho and gets so damned uptight that he wants out, would you believe.'

'It might take the pressure off him,' she suggested, 'if you could find a way to bring our boy home for a brief holiday.'

'He might refuse to go back.'

'So what do you propose to do?'

'We've upped his money. It's the usual way to make an agent feel appreciated.'

'The real problem is inaction. Tom needs adrenaline.' Dr Nathan studied the 10 × 8 colour enlargement from a negative that had been taken by a woman in the group of tourists on the tour boat. It showed Tom standing beside Rada in the white cotton dress with Sibirsky smiling indulgently in the background.

'We just have to hope that Fielding was really in love with the girl,' she murmured.

A taxi horn blared beside the Morgan and Ponsonby had to ask her to repeat what she had just said.

'So what?' he asked.

'If he was, then once he's over the shock he'll forgive her for whatever she did in the past.' Dr Nathan could see the disbelief in Ponsonby's eyes.

'It may take time,' she continued, 'but he will. On the other hand if the relationship between them was just carnal attraction, I'm afraid he may well do something silly in the very near future.'

'I hadn't thought of that,' Ponsonby said.

'"Oh the toil we lost and the spoil we lost/and the excellent things we planned/belong to the woman who didn't know why/and did not understand."'

'Should I recognise that?' he asked.

'Kipling,' she said. 'Whether your boy in Moscow stays in place all depends on the girl.'

Outside Broadcasting House in Portland Place, Ponsonby pulled in to the kerb. He leaned across Dr Nathan to open the passenger door with his right hand, so that he was almost embracing her, his face only inches from hers.

She shivered as he picked the photograph off her lap with his other hand. There was a wolfish intensity in the grey eyes boring into hers. She thought for a moment that he was going to kiss her and knew that she would not resist.

Ponsonby was wondering what kind of body was

concealed inside the man's waistcoat and shirt she was wearing. He pushed the passenger door wide open and sat back. 'You've been a great help,' he said with a smile.

'Women!' Ivanov ejaculated at the next meeting in the office on Kuznetsky Most. 'I've had three wives and two long-term mistresses, plus all the bits of pussy I run around with now. And I'll tell you one thing, Feldink: if I'd ever found one like Rada, I'd have settled down to a pair of warm slippers by the fireside long ago. Frankly I can't see what made a girl like that fall for you, but she's a jewel.'

'With a gigantic flaw.'

Ivanov gestured exasperatedly. 'For perfection, wait till you get to heaven. Listen, your wife had a complicated childhood: her mother drinks at Olympic standard and has lived with more men than I can count – on a steady downward slide ever since Arkady Sergeyevich kicked her out. She dragged the kid through some pretty bad scenes before sending her back to live with her dad. With an upbringing like she had, a girl with her kind of looks was bound to get into trouble sometime. Better sooner than later. That way, she's got it out of her system.'

'What's to stop her going back to all that mess of drugs and prostitution?' Tom asked.

'You.' Ivanov shook him by the shoulders. 'Rada grew up a lot during her year in Irkutsk, but the biggest change in her life was when you came into it. That's why Arkady Sergeyevich thinks you're the best thing since zip flies were invented. As a favour for my old pal, I had Rada watched quite a bit when she first came back to Moscow – and I can tell you, the only men she was ever alone with were you and her father. Did you ever have the slightest reason to suspect she's two-timing you?'

'No,' Tom admitted.

'To live in this country,' Ivanov advised, 'you have to think and feel like a Russian. If the present moment is good, we enjoy it without worrying about the past or the future. So forget what Rada did before you knew her. Live with the woman she is now. One way and another, you've got it made, Feldink.'

.8.

The mystique of mushrooms in Russia is akin to the reverence accorded to wine by the French. Instead of *appellations*, Muscovites compare species and argue over the right moment to pick them and how they should be cooked. Instead of vintages they remember years when this or that variety was particularly delicious.

In every group of mycophiles opinions are divided as to which species should be eaten raw on the spot, and which must be cooked. Some say it is sacrilege to fry certain rare green mushrooms which must be boiled in salt and pepper, laced with garlic and onions. Others hold that the only fungi worth picking are small red ones which are chopped up into tiny slivers, fried in butter until they have shrunk to almost nothing and nibbled with draughts of vodka throughout the dark months to stave off winter ills.

To find a particular mushroom in optimum condition Muscovites will travel a long way. On mild wet autumn weekends there is an exodus from the capital when what looks like half the population heads by bicycle, motorbike, car and train into the country in search of edible fungi.

Some head for pine forests to look for delicate white mushrooms with umbrella tops which only grow there; others swear that the tastiest of the edible fungi are the red ones covered in fever spots which are only to be found in birch woods; others again spend the whole day seeking a few handfuls of the ones known as 'little foxes' or the sticky, dark-tipped fungi called 'butter-covered' or the apyata mushroom which grows on shrubs, not in the ground. But these preferences are the differences of schisms whose essential doctrine is the same great truth.

Foreigners who live there attribute the Russian obsession with foraging for mushrooms to the famines which have ravaged Russia and the neighbouring countries repeatedly throughout recorded history, but it can be traced back much earlier than that: to the scavenging of the nomadic tribes who roamed steppe and tundra in prehistoric times, from whom the Slav races are largely descended.

Tom awoke one autumnal Sunday morning when it was still dark outside. Rada was already awake and dressed, which in itself was unusual. She found it hard to get up in the morning. Twice that week he had left for the university with her still dozing in bed.

'Come on,' she said, handing him a mug of coffee. It was Maxwell House, a present brought back by her father from a conference in Los Angeles the previous week.

'Come on where?'

Excitedly she announced that her father had telephoned to say that he and Ivanov were going on a mushroom hunt and had invited Tom and Rada to go with them. Tom's first reaction was incredulity that such a townie as Professor Sibirsky should want to scramble through the rain-sodden forest with a penknife in one hand and in the other a *lukóshko* – the little cylindrical wicker-work basket invented to keep the most delicate mushroom in perfect culinary condition until the hunter gets home.

'It's raining,' he said, after one look out of the window. 'They'll get soaked.'

'Who cares? Warm, wet weather makes the best mushrooms.'

Somehow she persuaded him to get dressed. Because he had no driving licence, she drove the red Lada. After they had picked up Arkady Sergeyevich from the Pyatnitskaya Ulitsa, Tom had to sit in the rear seat so that Rada's father could stretch his legs in the front.

In the centre of town the streets were deserted, but by the time they reached the outer suburbs traffic was building up until it seemed that every ancient Zhiguli, Polish Fiat or East German Trabant had been pressed into service in the hunt for mushrooms.

On the highway leading south and west towards Minsk, even the normally intrusive GAI traffic police in their concrete and glass observation towers seemed in festive mood, watching through binoculars as the stream of mushroom hunters flowed away from the capital, with none of the officious checking and rechecking of papers that frequently interrupted journeys into and out of Moscow.

Tom took little part in the conversation. At work, he and Rada existed in an undeclared truce. At home, they had hardly spoken during the fortnight since the wedding. He did not notice where they were heading as Rada left the highway and turned south-east. For several kilometres they skirted the edge of what had been a private estate before the Revolution, bordered with a high stone wall topped with three strands of barbed wire. At a checkpoint manned by bored KGB troops, Ivanov was waiting for them. In his car was a vivacious, dark-haired and dark-eyed girl of less than half his age who was chatting with the guards through the open window. Tom recognised her as one of Rada's friends who had been at the wedding feast.

Rada followed the other car through the checkpoint. After a kilometre on the cobbled road, they turned off and bumped along unpaved tracks to park eventually in a clearing where everyone got out to don galoshes or rubber boots and old anoraks. Even the two girls were dressed in their oldest clothes. There was an excited party mood, from which Tom felt excluded, watching the others get ready.

He accepted a slug of Ivanov's vodka, which burned in his empty stomach.

'Have another,' said the major. 'It's good stuff. You won't buy that in any liquor store.'

In an atavistic ritual of the hunt they stood in the drizzle eating chunks of salami on rye bread, washed down with more vodka, and listening to Ivanov's boasts that this was the best place within a hundred miles of Moscow to find mushrooms because the public was not allowed into the estate. Under the Soviet system even mushroom hunting could become a privilege reserved for the élite.

As they headed into the woods, Ivanov spoke more quietly for Tom's ears alone. 'You recognise where we are?'

Receiving a shake of the head in reply he commented, 'You're no countryman, my friend.'

The party separated, with Sibirsky insisting that he would find a short-seasoned green-capped mushroom which might – just might – be out that day. Ivanov disagreed, saying that it was too early in the season for this particular species and that anyway he had looked for it on the estate in previous years with no luck.

Tom wandered away from both parties, still feeling low. He came to a fence on the other side of which were several substantial wooden dachas, each different in style from the others. They were unified only by the elaborate decorative fretwork around the windows. One of them especially attracted his eye because of the strange shingle-clad cupola on the roof. It was almost certainly the place where he had lived during the debriefing. There was no sign of life within.

He walked deeper into the woods and sat on a fallen trunk in the lee of a huge oak tree, where he was out of the rain.

There he dozed off to be awoken by Ivanov sitting down beside him. Between the trees, they could see Sibirsky and the two girls a hundred metres away, on their knees in the fallen leaves.

Tom took the proffered bottle and swallowed another slug of Ivanov's vodka.

'Still depressed?' commented the major.

Tom shrugged. A sudden blow from Ivanov's elbow sent him sprawling on the wet earth. Beside his face the spirit was running out of the bottle and soaking away into the ground. He twisted round to pick it up and found his hand crushed into the soft earth by Ivanov's foot.

'Sort your priorities out,' he said. 'Fuck the vodka, Feldink. We can buy more of it any time. What you can't buy more of, is life. That's glugging out of the bottle just as fast as the booze, take it from me.'

A strong hand pulled Tom to his feet and brushed him down.

'Get this,' Ivanov said. 'You're a damned lucky guy. If you hadn't had an idle, womanising boozer like me assigned to your case, you could still be sitting in that fucking dacha over there, waiting for one of my more conscientious colleagues to sign your release papers.'

Tom nodded.

'Instead, you've got a good job, a nice place to live and a beautiful woman who loves you, so pull yourself together and enjoy the present. It doesn't matter what happened in the past, right?'

Ivanov picked up the bottle, swallowed what remained of the vodka and tossed it into some bushes before walking off to join the others.

Tom watched him go.

Although the physical affair with Rada had been mind-blowing, the only reason he had gone along with her father's plan for the wedding was because of Ponsonby's advice to get hitched. So what did that make him? Hardly an innocent betrayed. He had used Rada and her father, exposed them to possible sentences of fifteen or twenty years in a labour camp. It was about time he gave something in return, instead of sulking like some immature kid over what Rada had or hadn't done before she knew him.

As though sensing his thoughts, Rada stood up and looked in Tom's direction. She took a couple of paces towards him before stopping in her tracks, wary of making any advances. For the first time Tom wondered what he was subconsciously trying to do, by punishing her. If he continued, it was quite conceivable that he would drive her back into the comforting embrace of heroin.

She turned away to kneel down beside her father who was holding up something – presumably a mushroom – for Ivanov to see.

'Vanya, come over here!' the major's new girlfriend called out excitedly. 'We've found hundreds of them.'

Sibirsky put an arm around Rada's shoulder and hugged her. 'Come see what we've found,' he called to Tom.

In a moment of revelatory clarity Tom realised that he felt a lot more for these Russians on their knees in the leaves, enjoying the spontaneous pleasure of a mushroom hunt on a wet Sunday morning, than he had ever felt for his family spending Sundays so righteously on their knees in church.

'Fuck Ponsonby!' he said to the trees.

Rain dripped from the branches, dislodging leaves heavy with moisture, which fluttered down to the ground. All distant sounds were damped by the wetness. Even the four people on their knees were silent now, engrossed in the search. There was just a swishing of dead leaves and the crack of an occasional twig as Tom walked between the silver trunks of the birches, heading towards them.

Rada looked up as he stood over her. The usually immaculate hairdo was tangled and wet; her carefully manicured hands were grubby and there were smears of mud on her cheek. In the lap of her skirt lay a dozen or more of the green mushrooms her father had been eulogising earlier. She lifted one of them for Tom to sniff. It had a delicate perfume that teased his memory, made harder to identify by the salty smells of autumn all around, with the powerful odours of rotten wood and wet leaf-mould predominating.

'*Drózhzhi*,' she told him. 'It smells of yeast.'

Tom pulled her to her feet, ignoring Sibirsky's yell of protest as the precious green fungi were spilled on the ground.

'*Tebyá lyublyú*,' he said: I love you. He did not know or care whether it would be the next day, the next week or in ten years' time. The present moment was all that mattered.

Arkady Sergeyevich gave a strangled cry: 'You're trampling on my mushrooms!'

'Fuck the mushrooms,' Tom retorted. 'That's better than trampling on someone's emotions.'

He buried his face in Rada's hair, bejewelled by droplets of rain. Wishing that they were alone, he inhaled the smell of her shampoo and felt her body trembling against his, her hands clawing at his back to hold him tight against her.

From a thousand miles away, they heard the voice of Ivanov's new girlfriend: '*Smotrí, Vanya. Oní obá plakáyut!*' Look, they're both crying.

'*Eto tólko dozhd*,' Tom said: it's just the rain.

He held Rada close and lifted his face to the sky which was broken up by a thousand interlaced branches beneath the grey overcast. Then he closed his eyes, the better to feel the raindrops on the lids and the rivulets of rain trickling down his cheeks. The moisture on his lips tasted salty, but he repeated, 'It's just the rain.'

PART VI

.1.

Apart from the copies he came across in university libraries and a few on the shelves of Dom Knigi, Tom never discovered what became of the massive print run of *Clarifying Confusion*.

The longer he lived in Russia, the less he asked questions like why? or how? In any case, Rada had a simple explanation: to have printed fewer than 100,000 copies of such a work would have been a political insult both to the subject and to her father, a respected academic and Party member, who had written the foreword.

Another lesson Tom learned was how wealth built up for members of the Soviet élite. A year after publication of the book, they had still spent less than half of the royalty cheque, despite Rada's extravagances, which included a trip to Paris with her father. From this she returned with twenty kilos of excess baggage – all clothing she had bought there.

A two-week holiday for Rada and himself on the Black Sea coast near Yalta – only a pebble's throw from the former Tsarist summer palace of Livadia – had cost virtually nothing because they stayed in a luxury villa belonging to the Writers' Union. Air travel by Aeroflot, then the monopoly carrier in the Soviet Union, was spartan but so cheap that peasants could travel 2,000 kilometres to sell a suitcase of oranges and end up with a profit.

Given the shortages of everything from foodstuffs to clothes, it would have been hard to spend much more than their two modest salaries if Rada had not enjoyed access in her father's name to the *beriózhka* hard-currency shops where she bought Western goods. When Tom walked out of these emporia for the privileged beside her with arms full of their purchases, he learned not to see the long, hopeless lines of less fortunate citizens in the street queueing for such basics as razor blades, soap or toothpaste. The only item in limitless supply in every food shop was *mintai* – a kind of canned fish which tasted so bad that it was rumoured to have been refused even by starving cats.

Despite occasional moments of familial intimacy, like the boat trip on the Moskva River, Professor Sibirsky remained a man of mystery to Tom. After his frequent unexplained absences, catalogues of icon auctions at Sotheby's and Christie's would appear in the apartment on Pyatnitskaya Ulitsa, with prices noted in the margins in Sibirsky's careful hand. Western newspapers and magazines – including publications that were forbidden in the USSR – were left casually lying around in the apartment too. Tom deduced that, like many Russians who travelled abroad, Sibirsky was doing work for the KGB on the side, which afforded him privileges denied to most.

At the Department of Soviet History, Sibirsky's deputy Makarova grabbed the reins of power more and more firmly. Luckily for Tom, she appeared to have decided that his star was in the ascendant if not yet quite as red as the ones crowning the Kremlin walls. He grew used to the grovelling obsequiousness with which she asked him to autograph copies of his book for her friends, almost curtseying with gratitude as she gushed, '*Pozdravláyu vas, továrisch proféssor. Eta sámaya vázhnaya kníga.*' I congratulate you, comrade professor. It's a most important book . . .

The regular meetings with Ivanov were now reduced to one a month. The twenty-minute chats over glasses of scalding black tea in the office on Kuznetsky Most were increasingly taken up with Ivanov's objections to Mikhail Gorbachev's reforms. Like many of his countrymen, he saw the liberalisation measures hailed in the West as a social breakthrough in terms of dangerous meddling with the status quo.

As ethnic conflicts flared between Azeris and Armenians in Nagorny Karabakh and the whole massive structure of the Soviet Union began to crack apart, Ivanov knew whom to blame: 'Gorbachev and that smart wife of his may be clever, but possession of an American Express gold card is not the secret that will hold together an empire of 150 million Russians and 150 million aliens – Balts, Asiatics, Ukrainians, Muslims, all of whom hate our guts.'

He was fidgety that day, and kept getting up to walk round the office – a condition which Tom had come to associate with a new woman in his case officer's life. Ivanov placed a finger across his lips, tiptoed to the door and threw it open. He looked out into the corridor, then closed the door carefully before taking from his wallet a photograph of a woman who looked to be in her fifties. Elegant and haughty, with sculpted features and hair pulled severely back into a bun, she held herself like a model on the catwalk.

'My latest girlfriend,' the major confided. 'She's a former dancer at the Bolshoi who is the wife of a Politburo member.'

'Very nice.' Tom handed back the picture, wondering what had happened to the major's previous nymphet.

Ivanov licked his lips as he put the photograph away. 'She fucks like a rattlesnake. Her training as a dancer has given her muscles where I've never found them before in a woman. When her husband's out of town . . .'

'Should you be telling me all this in here?' Tom wondered. He pointed at the walls.

'Broken,' grinned Ivanov. 'Nothing works any more, haven't you noticed?'

It seemed the right moment for Tom to ask a favour. 'In that case, perhaps you can help me. I'm working on another book with Rada and Arkady Sergeyevich. Tentatively entitled *The Railway War*, it's an account of the strategic uses of the Trans-Sib during the Civil War. The problem is that we can't get hold of any accurate maps. As you know, even the street plans of Moscow are useless.'

'The discrepancies are for reasons of national security.' Shutters came down over Ivanov's eyes and the avuncular *roué* turned back into a uniformed *aparátchik*.

'That's rubbish,' Tom pointed out. 'With satellite photography, American intelligence must have accurate maps of all the major towns from Leningrad to Vladivostok. So what's the point in continuing to print inaccurate ones for your own citizens?'

'We lost thirty million dead in the Great Patriotic War.' To Ivanov it sounded like an explanation. 'The fact that every map the *Wehrmacht* got hold of was misleading, maybe saved ten million other lives.'

'But Hitler didn't have satellite photography.'

'You won't change our maps,' said Ivanov obstinately. 'Any more than you'll get us to print real telephone directories.'

'Exactly!' said Tom triumphantly. 'We, the public, can't have telephone directories but you and your colleagues do. So you must also have accurate military maps without the deliberate mistakes.'

'It's possible.'

'I want you to do me a favour, Ivan Petrovich.' Tom took from his briefcase several maps of different sections on the Trans-Siberian railway, on each of which he had marked with red ink a number of inaccuracies. In some cases entire towns of fifty thousand inhabitants and more were missing and the railway was shown up to a hundred miles away from its correct position.

'If I promise not to tell the *Hauptkommandantur der Wehrmacht*, will you get a pal inside the organisation to go over these sheets and correct them for me in the interest of historical research?'

'Railways are strategic objects,' Ivanov grumbled. 'The request is not as simple as you think.'

'Don't be ridiculous!' Tom raised his voice despite their relationship. 'The Pentagon has better maps than these. So who are you fooling?'

'Forget it.'

Tom shrugged. Both Sibirsky and Rada had told him that the request was pointless. He was putting the maps away in his briefcase when Ivanov saw the camera inside.

'You still carry that thing around?' he asked. 'It'll get you into trouble one day. Get rid of it, Tom.'

'Don't give me advice, Ivan Petrovich,' Tom retorted. 'Or I might point out that fucking the wife of a Politburo member when he's out of town could be a lot more dangerous to your health than smoking sixty a day.'

Ivanov stubbed out his tenth *papirós* since the beginning of the interview. 'Some pleasures,' he grinned, 'are worth the risk.'

Back at the small office on the Lenin Hills which he shared with Rada, Tom found her crouched over a series of maps, red pen in hand. The longer they worked together, the better they functioned as a team. He was constantly surprised how content she was to do all the hack work and to keep Makarova off his back. And sometimes, he had to admit, the best ideas were hers.

'How did you get on?' she asked absently, her attention concentrated on the map.

'Ivan Petrovich wouldn't play ball.'

'You should have left it to me.'

'And how would you have handled it?'

Rada felt smug. 'To get anything from a macho stud like Uncle Vanya, you have to flatter him, imply no one else could do it, tell him how clever he is.'

'You're probably right,' Tom agreed. He leaned over her desk and recognised the map on which she was working as a different edition of one of those he had shown to Ivanov. On at least half a dozen points, he could see that it was more accurate than the version Makarova had obtained for him from the university library. Being completely bilingual by now, it did not strike him immediately that the place names on this one were all in their English versions.

Rada swivelled her chair and parted her legs to pull Tom close. Burying her face in his clothes to inhale the smell of him, she sighed, 'It's been a long day for those of us at the sharp cutting edge of the grindstone.'

Tom pulled her head up so that he could see the smirk on her face.

'Stop teasing,' he said. 'Where did you get this map?'

She changed to English in case anyone was listening through the open door: 'From my father.'

'And where did he get it?'

'You remember Levitskaya, the girl who used to give him singing lessons? She's married to another refusenik, a captain in the Israeli army. He wanted to do a favour in return for the way my father helped her get out of Russia. Somehow he got hold of several CIA maps like this one.'

It was, thought Tom, a typically Russian solution to a Russian problem.

He pulled Rada to her feet and kissed her. 'What will I do without you?' he said.

She hugged him with her eyes closed. 'It's only for a few months,' she said. 'And anyway, after the birth, I can work with you at home just as well as I do here.'

*

When I learned she was pregnant, I had argued that it was

too early in our relationship to encumber ourselves with a child. The real reason I wanted her to have an abortion had more to do with the nightmares I was having.

There were weeks – sometimes months – when I didn't think once about Ponsonby and the mission. Then, for no particular reason that I could identify, I'd awake sweating in the night after a vivid dream in which I was taken by surprise, surrounded by men in dark suits, who twisted my arms behind my back, handcuffed me and threw me into the back of a black Volga. Being dragged along the echoing basement corridors of the Lubyanka, I saw Rada and her father in different cells. 'How could you do this to us?' they cried.

Lately the dream had another participant: in the cell Rada was screaming as a pair of faceless women warders tore a child from her arms and took it away to some State institution where neither of us would ever see it again.

Because of the difficulty in obtaining reliable contraceptives in the USSR, abortion was available free and on demand. But when I urged Rada again to have the pregnancy terminated, she refused even to think about it. 'I want my father to see a grandchild,' she repeated obstinately. 'It might give him a reason to stay alive.'

A massive heart attack the previous month had left Sibirsky short of breath after the slightest effort. Instead of walking upright he shuffled along with hunched shoulders. His complexion was grey, he had lost weight and had no appetite.

On our first visit to him in hospital, Rada had voiced her anguish to me: 'I could understand it if this had happened to Uncle Vanya. He's overweight, smokes and drinks too much and fucks everything that walks past in a skirt, but why to my father? He's slim, doesn't smoke, neither eats nor drinks to excess, so why?'

There was no answer.

.2.

The only light in the room was the funereal greyness fil-
tering in through the windows and the faint glow of the
tiny candles burning in front of the icons in the hallway.
Outside, there was hardly a soul visible on the empty sweep
of Pyatnitskaya Ulitsa. Beyond it, on the flat expanse of the
frozen Moskva River where the snow-covered ice was grey
from the fallout of a whole winter's airborne pollution, a
few dark figures sat huddled where they had sawn holes for
fishing.

At four o'clock in the afternoon it was dusk already. To
protect themselves from the cutting wind, some of the ice-
anglers had fashioned tents of plastic sheeting. They sat
inside them with oil lamps making the plastic glow from
within like great golden lanterns set out at intervals on the ice
for a mysterious winter festival.

Ivanov had been invited to the meal but not shown up. He
was often late on Sundays and usually arrived with a tired

but smug expression on his face that indicated a new conquest. Like a perverse solar cell picking up energy from the cold and dark instead of light and warmth, he seemed recharged by the winter weather.

For Sunday lunch the old Tartar housekeeper had prepared *manty*, large Siberian dumplings stuffed with meat and herbs, which had been one of her employer's favourite dishes. Sibirsky was supposed to follow a special diet which did not include greasy dumplings, but in any event his palate was not tempted. He had picked distractedly at the food on his plate while leafing through the first draft of *The Railway War*. In the momentary elation that came from finishing their long research project late the previous night, Tom and Rada had brought it with them for his comments before sending it to Gosizdat.

Rada was not feeling hungry and had eaten little. Increasingly worried about her father's health, she had taken to leaving the university early most afternoons and sat with him in the apartment on Pyatnitskaya Ulitsa until Tom came to take her home. If he asked what they had talked about, she replied, 'Sometimes he doesn't say anything for an hour or more. He just sits and stares at his icons. There's something on his mind, but he won't talk about it.'

Tom watched now as Sibirsky left the table and walked slowly from end to end of the wall covered in icons, examining the many faces of the Mother of God. In front of some, small candles had been lit in little red glass holders. By the flickering light, the stylised faces came alive and took on individual personalities. Some returned his gaze boldly while others coyly hid their eyes from him. He was aware that either Tom or Rada had said something to him but since the heart attack there had been a roaring in his ears which stopped him hearing properly what people said. The doctors had been unable to explain or cure the phenomenon; it was the Mother of God who had whispered to him that he was hearing the sands of time running out of the broken hourglass of his life.

Hers was the only voice Sibirsky heard clearly now. 'Tell them soon,' she had warned him more than once. 'Or else it may be too late.'

A week later, Sibirsky had some colour in his cheeks. There was an air of conspiracy between him and Ivanov, who was already there when Tom and Rada arrived. The meal had been set in the kitchen. Ivanov always insisted that it was the only place where Russians could talk. He refused ever to eat in Sibirsky's well-appointed dining room, disparaging as bourgeois irrelevancies his friend's elegant silver and china, the expensive Finnish furniture and the Western hi-fi.

The housekeeper had been given the day off to visit her married daughter in Kazan so Ivanov had brought food from some favourite *gastronom* and laid it out as a cold buffet. When Tom and Rada arrived he was poring avidly over the manuscript of *The Railway War*.

'What do you think about it?' Tom asked.

'Brilliant,' Sibirsky replied.

'It must be, if a philistine like Ivan Petrovich is bothering to read it.'

The joke fell flat. Tom sat down to eat and found that he was the only one at table. Rada was not hungry, Ivanov was immersed in the manuscript and Sibirsky was putting one of his favourite CDs – a Vladimir Ashkenazy recording of Rachmaninoff's C Minor piano concerto – into the hi-fi.

During the Civil War, the Trans-Siberian railway had been an elongated battlefield which extended over six thousand kilometres east-west. The only way for Whites and Reds alike to transport men and matériel across these vast distances to each confrontation was aboard *bronepoyézdy* – the heavily armoured trains that thundered night and day along the tracks. Leapfrogging tactics were developed by both sides: first the Whites would outflank the Reds on the line and get behind them to cut off their supplies. Then the Reds would execute the same trick, which made the respective troop movements difficult to unravel: on a particular date the Red forces might be where one would expect to find the Whites and vice versa.

It had taken months of hard work for Rada and Tom to piece together a comprehensive and coherent picture of all the rapid advances over hundreds of kilometres followed by equally rapid reverses, with death the price for every failure.

Ivanov finished reading the manuscript and put it down, impressed. Sibirsky picked it up and weighed it in his hand. 'This is the choreography of a dance of death. It's a significant piece of scholarship, in my opinion.'

'So you'll talk to Gosizdat for us about publication?' Rada asked eagerly.

Her father shook his head. 'I already did. They said that the subject had already been adequately covered in *Clarifying Confusion*. I'm sorry.'

Tom looked at the sheaf of paper that represented so much work; it suddenly seemed very slim. 'Are you telling me that we've spent all these months working on a fool's errand?'

A look of conspiracy passed between Ivanov and Sibirsky.

'Not at all,' Rada's father said. 'I'm just telling you that there never was a commission for a book. The idea of one was just a plausible cover for your research as far as people at the university were concerned.'

'Why?' Rada asked.

'Because the real reason had to be kept secret.'

'From them?'

'And from Tom.'

'So what's changed?'

'This.' Sibirsky placed his hand on Rada's swollen belly. 'It makes him one of the family, doesn't it?'

'Did you never wonder why I made everything so easy for you?' Ivanov asked.

I reminded him that he had once said something about me being lucky to be allocated to a lazy womanising bastard.

He grinned. 'No Russian would ever believe what a major in the KGB told him.'

'Which just proves I'm not Russian,' I retorted. 'Now what's all the mystery?'

'I'll tell you,' Sibirsky said. 'For years I have been patiently trying to fill in all the blanks about what actually happened on a particular stretch of the Trans-Siberian at the end of the Civil War. Vanya was the only person to know the real reason for my researches. When you walked in, he realised immediately that you must have had access to sources we could never tap and might be able to fill in our blanks.'

'It was a Friday afternoon,' said Ivanov. 'All the other guys wanted to get home, so nobody argued when I said I'd handle you.'

'The following day he sent me the copy of Clarifying Confusion which you had brought with you,' Sibirsky continued. 'Within a couple of pages, I realised that you had brilliantly exploited all our research and cross-referenced interviews with a couple of hundred émigré White officers and civilians – all of which gave you a comprehensive oversight which I could never have achieved. I told Vanya that you were exactly the person we had been seeking.'

'For what?' I asked.

'How would you like to be very rich?' Ivanov grinned at me.

'I've never thought about it,' I said truthfully.

'I have,' he laughed outright. 'Lots of times. And, with a little help from you, Feldink, all four of us will end up millionaires.'

'All five?' Rada queried.

'We're talking of a lot more than $5 million,' said Sibirsky.

.3.

'You always told me that you had never known your parents,' Rada commented. 'You said they both died in the Ukrainian famine when you were two years old.'

'It's a lie,' Sibirsky confessed. 'My father was a Tsarist naval officer who went over to the Reds in 1917, and served in Dzerzhinsky's embryo *Chrezvecháinaya Komíssia* – the original Cheka, which became OGPU, then NKVD and now the KGB. He was arrested and shot during the great purge of 1937.'

'And your mother?' Tom asked.

'She died the same year – and for the same reason – in a camp on Solevetsky Island, north of the Arctic Circle.'

'Then why the orphan story?' Tom wondered.

'Until Khrushchev rehabilitated the victims of Stalin's purges at the Twentieth Party Conference,' Ivanov explained, 'telling the truth would certainly have damaged Arkady Sergeyevich's career.'

'And afterwards?' Tom asked. 'He's had plenty of time since.'

Sibírsky spread his hands apologetically. 'There wasn't much to tell. My parents amounted to no more than a few blurred memories – until I summoned up the courage a few years ago to ask Vanya to unearth their files as a favour to me. It was during the time Rada was in Irkutsk. The future looked so bleak that it seemed important to make sense of the past.'

Rada gave her father a hug. 'And when you came back to Moscow,' he said, 'there were happier things to talk about than the death of an unknown grandfather for the crime of being a radish.'

The term was used to denote a turncoat who behaved outwardly as a Red but remained a White inside – in his political convictions.

'In the case of my father, the accusation was unjust. He devoted the greater part of his adult life to the Revolution. He was a selfless servant of the Party. However, during his examination in the Lubyanka, it was discovered that he had been a junior lieutenant in the Tsarist Navy and not a lowly petty officer, as he had claimed on joining the Cheka. At the time, a detail like that earned the death penalty.'

'Did they need a reason?' asked Rada rhetorically. 'Seven million souls vanished into the Gulag during the great purge for no reason at all.'

Ivanov disagreed: 'In each case, guilt was established according to the canons of the law which then applied. Nobody was executed before the relevant paperwork had been completed. And afterwards the files were meticulously preserved. They still exist.'

He remembered his own sense of awe on seeing the sub-terranean archives at the headquarters of the *Glávnoye Upravlénie Lágerei* near Magadan on the frozen Sea of Okhotsk. Seemingly endless kilometres of shelves were crammed with dusty but well-indexed files, each of which was the sole memorial to a human life. Who could say how many millions had been sacrificed to the original ideal of an earthly paradise and how many other millions were the victims of Stalin's paranoia? All were equally dead.

'It was thanks to Vanya,' Sibirsky said, 'that I learned most of what I know about my father.'

'You say you did this research when Rada was in Irkutsk,' Tom interrupted. 'That was 1981. The Twentieth Party Conference was in 1956. Why wait so long?'

'When the thaw began after the death of Stalin, it was gradual, not overnight. And, like most Russians, I found it hard to believe I had the right to ask questions after so many years of keeping silent.'

'Twenty-five years is a slow thaw.'

Sibirsky held up a hand for patience. 'Let me tell this my way. I was born in '31, so I was only six years old when my father was arrested. Picture me as a small boy, living with my grandmother and mother in the claustrophobic boredom of a one-roomed apartment with shared kitchen and communal toilet somewhere in the yellow brick wilderness of what are now Moscow's inner suburbs.'

'If your father worked for the Cheka – which was the OGPU by then – surely the family was entitled to better accommodation than that?' Rada ventured.

'Probably,' Sibirsky agreed. 'But my father was too busy hunting down the enemies of the Revolution to claim privileges for his wife and child. He spent months at a time away from us, travelling the length and breadth of the Soviet Union on official business. His infrequent visits home never lasted for more than a night or two. I remember them because of the bedtime stories. He used to take me on his knee and tell me of the places where he had been and the things he had seen: Tamurlaine's tomb in Samarkand, mummified Scythian warriors in full armour dug out of the permafrost in Siberia, a perfectly preserved mammoth revealed by a melting glacier in Kamchatka.

'On his last visit he must have known that his days were numbered, for the stories were different and each one was told for a reason. I learned that millions were starving to death in the famine areas of the Ukraine even as we talked . . . and how, on the Trans-Sib during the Civil War, he had seen whole lineside villages wiped out – right down to the last scrawny chicken – purely for target practice as an armoured train steamed past, neither side knowing whom they were killing or being killed by. He had seen naked corpses of men, women and childen who had been sprayed with water in the middle of a Siberian winter by that madman Grigori Semyonov – deliberately turning them into human icicles so that he and his men could knock off projecting body parts to keep as grisly souvenirs.'

In the gloom, Tom winced. 'Great bedtime stories for a boy of six, Arkady Sergeyevich. Their nightmare coefficient must have been way above that of giants and witches. How did you sleep after your dad's fairy tales?'

Unable ever to sit still for long, Ivanov was in the hallway, straightening some icons that were slightly crooked on the wall. Sibirsky delayed his reply for a moment, listening to Ashkenazy play the opening of the third movement.

'It was,' he said, 'my adolescent curiosity about those last stories – which spanned the period from the Revolution to my father's death twenty years later – that led to my specialisation in Soviet History. But for that obsession, I should have become a historian of religious art, which would have been a more fulfilling path, although certainly less well rewarded materially in our society as it then was.'

'And did all those bedtime stories ring true, once you were in a position to check them out?' Rada asked.

'They were all true,' Sibirsky nodded soberly. 'My father had invented nothing.'

'What's this got to do with *The Railway War*?' Tom asked.

'Tell them about the night your father was arrested,' Ivanov prompted.

Sibirsky took a deep breath. 'I was still awake when they

came for him at three a.m. He was dozing in a chair, fully dressed with me on his lap. When he heard the knock, he got up and put on his coat and his uniform cap with the red star over the peak. He did not say a thing to the men who had come to take him away or to us, but just walked out of the door.'

'He didn't kiss you goodbye?' Rada asked. 'Or your mother?'

'No.'

'Then perhaps he didn't realise that he was under arrest?'

'Oh, he knew.' Sibirsky was quite definite; he could see the scene as clearly as when it was happening in front of him, half a century before. 'When they insisted on taking my mother away with them too, I heard him shouting up the stairwell, "But she doesn't know a thing about it, I tell you!" Oh yes, he knew.

'That's why he had kept the final story until the very last moment. It ended only half an hour or so before the knock on the door. He had woken me up especially to hear what he had to say after he was certain my mother and grandmother were asleep.'

Over Rada's protests, Ivanov poured a generous measure of Courvoisier cognac into a balloon glass and handed it to Sibirsky who took a sip and continued, 'My father was talking about the final days of Admiral Kolchak, the commander of the White forces in the east.'

'. . . in 1920,' Tom filled in for Ivanov's benefit. 'On the Trans-Sib, somewhere near Irkutsk.'

The dimly lit kitchen took on the ambiance of a tutorial as Sibirsky's faint voice resumed the situation: 'On the Whites' side, General Dennikin had pushed the Reds back to within one hundred and sixty kilometres of Moscow. If he could have taken the capital at that moment, total victory would have been his, the infant Soviet Union would have been strangled at birth – and the history of the twentieth century would have been very different.

'In my opinion – but I've always kept it to myself because it goes against the myth of the predestined invincibility of the Red Army – it was ironically Dennikin's initial success that gave victory to the Reds. Instead of being dispersed and with their lines of communication overstretched like the Whites', the Red forces, pushed back by reverses on all fronts, were briefly concentrated in a relatively small area. Thus Trotsky was able to regroup and strike in any direction he chose.

'When he saw that he had committed a gross strategic error, Dennikin resigned and handed over command of the White forces in the west to Baron Wrangel. At the time, Kolchak's White army was 3,000 kilometres away in Central Asia and had no hope of linking up with Wrangel's forces. The two White armies were pushed farther and farther apart until Wrangel was trapped in the Crimea and forced to evacuate what remained of his army by sea to Turkey.'

'. . . where they starved,' Rada interjected, 'except for the thousands of men who volunteered to enlist in the French Foreign Legion.'

Sibirsky nodded. 'In the east, the White forces were harried mercilessly by Budenny's Cossack cavalry, the so-called worker Cossacks. According to my father – and your research bears this out, Tom – Kolchak retreated in good order along the Trans-Sib, carrying the White treasury aboard his armoured train. When he was eventually cut off to the east of Irkutsk, he hid the only valuable thing that was left, in order to deny it to the Reds. It's never been found.'

'What was it?' Tom asked.

'An icon,' said Ivanov. 'The most valuable icon in Russia.'

'My father interrogated Kolchak after he had been captured by the Red forces,' Sibirsky continued. 'He learned from him that the Whites' treasury of gold and silver coinage had been exhausted. All that was left was a handful of the Romanov family jewels and this one icon: the Virgin of Kazan.'

'And did your father find out where it was hidden?' Rada asked.

Sibirsky shook his head. 'Kolchak died before he could be made to divulge its whereabouts.'

'Kolchak died . . .?' she repeated slowly. 'Is that a euphemism for saying that my grandfather tortured the man to death?'

Sibirsky was staring through the gloom at the faintly lit faces of the Mother of God, the fount of all forgiveness. In one of his midnight conversations, he had pleaded for his father's soul in the Biblical formula: 'He knew not what he did.'

'It was routine,' he said now to Rada. 'In civil wars especially, both sides use torture to get information. You know that.'

He walked into the hall and took one of the larger icons off the wall. It measured about 50 centimetres high by 40 wide.

'The Virgin of Kazan,' he said. 'This is a very good nineteenth-century copy.'

He handed it to Tom who held it up to the light coming in from the street. On the painted wooden panel the Mother of Christ was coyly holding her head on one side with a Mona Lisa-like smile while the child nestled blond curls against her face. The haloes, painted in gold leaf, gleamed in the dim grey light from outside.

'Until the state became officially atheistic after the October Revolution,' Sibirsky continued, 'the Virgin of Kazan was carried through the streets of St Petersburg every year on her feast day, the eighth of July, from the Nevsky *lavra* to the Kazan cathedral where she stayed for the next twelve months. As the faithful prostrated themselves in front of the procession of acolytes, monks and priests, nobody apart from a few scholars knew that the precious icon was a fake.'

'So where was the original all this time?' Tom asked.

'No one knows for sure,' said Sibirsky. 'It disappeared in the wake of the revolution in 1905. There was colossal social upheaval, as you know. I have a private theory that it travelled east in the personal baggage of a nobleman who was exiled for his part in the uprising. Many of them settled with their families and servants in considerable luxury around Irkutsk. If I'm right, that's how it came to be in Kolchak's hoard of loot.'

'And it's never been seen again?' Tom queried.

'After the Great Patriotic War the icon was thought to have been rediscovered in western Europe among other art treasures looted on Goering's personal orders. It was eventually purchased by the Russian Orthodox Church in the USA. I've seen their icon and I'm not convinced. I think they bought a very good fake.'

Sibirsky kissed the icon before hanging it back on its hook and switching on all the room lights in the apartment, which changed the mood entirely.

'So,' said Tom. 'You set up the idea of the fake book in order to give us a cover for tracking down the real Virgin of Kazan?'

Sibirsky nodded. 'My father asked me to recover it when I was a grown man, to restore it to its rightful place in the Kazan cathedral – and to say a prayer for his soul before it. I think he hoped that I might atone for his sins in that way. "I have worshipped false gods," were his words on that last night, "and caused much suffering to my fellow men in the name of an impossible dream."'

'Exactly how much is the genuine icon worth?' Tom asked.

Sibirsky waved a hand at the row of London and New York auction catalogues on one of the bookshelves. 'My informed guess is that it would fetch at least $25 million in today's market. It could be worth double that, but not less.'

'Oh my God!' exclaimed Rada.

'I'll never understand you people,' said Tom slowly. 'I

thought you wanted to restore the icon to the Kazan cathedral, to atone for your father's sins? Now you're talking about selling it to the highest bidder. How's that going to redeem his immortal soul?'

Sibirsky grimaced. 'All in all, I don't owe my father much. I think that, if we have a duty in this life, it's to the future generations, not those who came before.'

He stood behind Rada and put a hand on each of her shoulders. 'The point of studying history – or so it seems to me, Tom – is that by looking intelligently at the past we may come to see the future more clearly. Patterns repeat. Men don't change, nor do nations. I think my country is in for another period of turmoil very soon. When that happens, I'd like to know that my daughter and her child are safely out of it, living in the West with you and enjoying the kind of security that a lot of money can buy in your society. With all the research you've done, one thing is certain: nobody has ever been in a better position to find it – and probably no one ever will be again.'

Tom laughed. The idea of finding a treasure that had been lost for seven decades was a lot more exciting than having another book disappear without trace into Gosizdat's maw.

'There's one thing I don't understand,' Rada said. 'How can we smuggle such a valuable icon out of Russia?'

'Show them,' Sibirsky said.

Ivanov removed the copy Virgin of Kazan from the wall and turned it round. Taped to the back were two official-looking pieces of paper. Tom deciphered the signatures: Pavlova from the Hermitage Museum and Vasilyev from the Tretyakov Gallery, the two greatest authorities on iconography in the whole world.

'After my heart attack,' Sibirsky explained, 'I asked these two old friends to look at my copy of the Virgin of Kazan, pretending that I thought it was the original. With great regret they told me what I already knew. They obviously thought I had gone gaga.'

'I'm not with you,' Tom confessed.

Sibirsky finished his brandy, enjoying the suspense. 'Their signed attributions state unequivocally that it is just a late nineteenth-century copy. When you find the original; just stick those pieces of paper on the back and hey presto! You can walk out through the customs with it under your arm.'

'So all you have to do,' finished Ivanov, 'is find the bloody thing!'

. 4 .

My first sight of Lake Baikal was spellbinding. Like
everything else in Siberia, it was vast. The far shore was
hidden by the curvature of the earth. The peaks of a range
of high, snow-capped mountains floated on the horizon,
showing where it was. All around me was the noise and
activity of a seaport; it was hard to grasp that I was looking
not at an ocean, but at the largest freshwater lake in Asia,
which contains one-twentieth of the drinking water on the
planet's surface.

The rich lake, as 'bai-kul' translates from the local
Buryat tongue, is 640 kilometres long, 1.5 kilometres deep
and up to 80 kilometres wide. It lay right across the path
of the Trans-Sib and the difficult terrain on its shores
presented some of the worst engineering problems in the
entire journey from Moscow to Vladivostok. Although the
rest of the line was completed before the First World War,
rolling stock and passengers had to cross the lake on
ferries for several years until the Circumbaikal link was
constructed after the Revolution.

Looking at the vast expanse of water, I realised that either Sibirsky's memory was defective or his father had been lying when he said Kolchak had been cut off by the Reds 'to the east of Irkutsk'. It would have been necessary for the retreating White forces to cross Lake Baikal by ship in order to reach the continuation of the railway on the other side. And if the remnants of the White army had made it as far as the eastern shore, they could have effected a fighting withdrawal across the nearby Chinese border – in which case some of them would have escaped to tell the tale. Since not a soul had apparently survived the final stand, my instinct was that Kolchak's armoured train must have been trapped on the wrong side of the natural barrier, so that his forces were wiped out to the last man to the west of Irkutsk.

I wondered whether the wily Commissar Sibirsky had deliberately reversed the compass direction when telling his son about Kolchak's last stand, in case pressure was put on the boy to tell what he knew. Had he hoped that, when adult, Arkady Sergeyevich would detect so gross an error? There was no way of knowing.

It had taken three months to organise my trip, ostensibly to deliver a lecture at Irkutsk University. Belying its reputation as a land of snow and storm, Central Siberia in July was in the throes of its short summer. Clad just in a tee-shirt and shorts, I was sweating from the sultry heat.

To prolong the relief from the slight breeze which was blowing off the lake, I walked along a rickety wooden landing stage which projected 50 metres or so into the water. I suppose it reminded me of the boardwalk on Toronto Island, and that's what triggered the thoughts of Karen. Dimly in the water I saw a faint image of her face, hidden behind dark glasses, and heard her say again, 'Goodbye, Tom.'

I shivered. I was looking down at what seemed to be a white human body, trapped between the pilings of the jetty.

It was hard to see properly because of iridescent patches of oil floating on the water. Then a head broke surface. It was like that of a hairless dog with huge brown eyes. Rings spread out across the glassy surface as the nerpa, or freshwater Arctic seal, dived again, frightened by the shriek of a factory whistle.

Nearby a huge and monstrously ugly paper mill was spewing sulphurous yellow water from its waste pipes directly into the lake, its chimneys belching smoke and steam through defective or non-existent filters. In the shunting yard that adjoined the mill, railway workers were assembling a long train of goods wagons, each loaded with two massive rolls of paper. There was not a trace of grass to be seen anywhere; the ground seemed to be one vast cindered car park, littered with industrial refuse and rusting machinery.

I folded up my maps and stuffed them back into my briefcase before making myself comfortable behind the wheel of the Lada 4WD which I had hired at the airport. I wished that Rada had come with me, but she had insisted on staying in Moscow in case the birth was early.

After an hour's driving the twentieth century in the form of Irkutsk's steel mills and the lakeside paper mill was left well behind. Tom was driving through a landscape that had not changed in the last hundred years. The metalled road had ended just outside the sprawl of suburban cottages and he found himself following a dirt road that wound through thinning forest with small villages at irregular intervals. The small wooden houses on either side of the road, each set in its plot surrounded by a rickety fence, had not changed inside or out since the Revolution. Any one of them could have served as Grandpa's cabin in a stage set for *Peter and the Wolf*.

When even the dirt road dwindled to a rutted cart track that wound between isolated clumps of trees and finally petered out altogether, Tom used basic Russian and sign language to ask the way from two Buryat horsemen in pointed felt hats, seated on sturdy, short-legged ponies.

Their directions left him bumping across the trackless steppe country in second and third gear, trailing a cloud of fine dust in the air behind the Lada. A rock concealed in a clump of grass tore the silencer loose, allowing an unmuffled roar to escape from the labouring engine. Stopping to see what he could do about the noise, Tom found that the exhaust pipe was the wrong model and had been cobbled together with pieces of flattened tin can, and secured with wire and binder twine in a typically botched repair job. Once it was cool enough to handle, he wrenched the remainder of the silencer from its makeshift mounting and threw it into the back of the vehicle, discovering only then that there was no spare tyre.

It would have been prudent to turn back and find one before venturing further across the featureless rolling grassland but an unaccountable excitement made him drive on, keeping to a compass bearing which he hoped would lead to the first of ten locations marked on the map in Rada's neat hand. Each was the site of a documented massacre during the Civil War. Any one could be the place where Kolchak had been tortured to death by Sibirsky's father.

Tom drew a blank at the first four. It was mid-afternoon when he neared the fifth site, intending to head back to Irkutsk for the night after checking it out and there to pick up a spare tyre before heading further into the wilds next day.

When it appeared through the heat haze, the *byvshi dom* – or 'former house' as it was described on the map – was such an unlikely sight that at first he took it for just another mirage suspended in mid-air above the featureless plain which seemed to stretch northwards to the Arctic Circle.

The facade of an Italian Renaissance palazzo floated

above what seemed like shimmering water. In front of it, faint images of gondolas drifted past on the fantasy of a Venetian canal. The boats turned into a grazing herd of half-wild ponies as he drove nearer but the prospect of the house itself became even more improbable. Anchored firmly to the shallow soil of Central Asia was a carbon copy of some Italian nobleman's family home, built here at the whim of a rich fur merchant in the 1890s. This, thought Tom, must surely be the most incongruous bastard to be spawned by Peter the Great's love affair with Italian architecture.

With brakes squealing from all the dust trapped inside, he pulled to a halt in front of the elegant double flight of stone steps which curved up to the front door. The ponies had galloped away in alarm as the noise of the Lada drew near. When Tom switched off the engine, their hoofbeats were already fading into the distance. Gradually Tom became aware of the low susurration of a million insects in and above the dry grass.

The facade of the palazzo was crowned by a line of vivid green Italian tiles which perched on the eaves overhang. Bleached by the pollution-free air, the wind and the sun, the white plasterwork looked newly painted, except where several lines of pockmarks marched across the whole facade. Around the gaping holes where the doors and windows had been, the imported white Carrara marble facings had been badly shattered by sustained heavy machine-gun fire. One side or the other had fortified the place and fought hard, thought Tom – presumably for their lives.

He took shots from different angles, using a Pentax with zoom lens that Sibirsky had brought back as a present after a trip to Hong Kong. From the front, the house looked almost habitable, as though at any moment a servant would come out of the open front door and down the steps to enquire the intruder's business.

From the side, the house revealed itself as more of a film

set than an illusion. Behind the facade, hardly anything remained standing. Sparse steppe grass grew on uneven mounds of rubble, formed when the house had been burned to the ground. From the mounds charred timbers jutted out at all angles. A piece of wall with an elaborate plasterwork cornice still clinging to it hinted at the luxury that had been there. The brickwork of the main chimney stood in isolation three storeys high, with gaping holes showing where the marble fireplaces had been wrenched away from the masonry, all except for the topmost one, which must have been too difficult to remove. In the centre of what had been the entrance hall, a once-elegant balustrade in wrought iron-work, still gilded in places, rusted its way drunkenly heavenward with three steps clinging to it uselessly, halfway up.

Tom changed to an extra-wide lens and took several exposures, deliberately using the optical distortion to exaggerate the trompe l'oeil effect. He picked his way up the steps and through the front doorway, to stand on the threshold looking at the rolling grassland beyond. A cloud of large brown flies took off from a heap of horse dung, buzzing noisily.

In the hazy distance, a line of telegraph poles on the horizon showed where the longest railway line in the world ran east to Vladivostok on the Pacific coast and west to Moscow.

To the east of the house, trees had been planted at some time to make a park; now only a dwarf forest of amputated stumps remained. On the other side of the house, some rotten stakes showed where a paddock had been made, perhaps for the children's ponies. The outlines of a tennis court and what looked to have been a sunken water-garden with a dried-up fountain were just discernible.

Tom clambered across the ruins of the house to the dilapidated stable block. Time seemed to have done the most damage here; the buildings had not been torched when the main house was burned down, but there were gaping holes in the roof and broken windows banged in the small puffs of breeze, giving a general sense of desolation.

There were some chickens rooting around near the doorway of the coachhouse, watched by two black cats who were preening themselves in the sun. As Tom's eyes adjusted he saw, sitting in the shade of the wicket doorway, a small and ancient woman. The top half of her body was shrouded in several shawls despite the heat. From her shapeless and dirty skirt projected a pair of yellow plastic boots. Covering her head was the ubiquitous red-and-white *babushka* scarf that all the old women wore throughout the Soviet Union. This particular scarf framed a wrinkled, wind-tanned face that looked about a hundred and ten years old. A pair of rheumy blue eyes were watching the intruder.

Tom waved a greeting. '*Zdráftsvuyite!*'

'*Otkúda vy?*' she called back.

'*Iz Moskvy.*'

She nodded matter-of-factly, as though visitors from Moscow turned up every day in the middle of Asia.

'*Nu kto vy?*' she asked: who are you?

'*Anglískii istórik.*' Why not? Tom thought. In this surreal setting he could claim to be Margaret Thatcher or President Reagan and the old crone would not know any different.

'And what are you doing here, English historian?' she wanted to know.

Tom replied in English, 'Looking for a treasure, would you believe?'

He peered through the broken glass of the coachhouse. '*Byli aftomobíly,*' she called in a cracked voice. 'They took them all.'

'Who took the cars?'

'*Bolsheviki, konyéchno.*'

It was not unusual for the very elderly whom Tom had interviewed to talk of Bolsheviks, meaning the Communists. He took a few more photographs, including several of the old woman sitting in the sun with her cats and the chickens. He stood facing away and held the camera sideways, so as not to alarm her.

Then he pulled out his mini cassette recorder to dictate some brief notes about the Venetian palazzo-that-never-was for Rada to type up on his return. It did not take long. 'Another blank,' he ended in English. 'Who knows if Admiral Kolchak got within a hundred miles of this place?'

'Would you like a cup of tea?'

That most English of sentences stopped me in my tracks. I turned round. The only person in sight was the old crone.

'There's no one to hear,' she said, again in English.

Her wrinkled face showed a faint amusement at my surprise. 'No one for miles and miles.'

'Thank you,' I said. 'I'd like a cup of tea very much indeed . . . if it's not too much trouble.'

It took her an age to stand and shuffle, leaning on a stick, into what had been the tack room of the stable block. I followed her inside, restraining the questions raised by her knowledge of English. Her accent intrigued me; it was odd but not Russian.

Mouldy harness hung on pegs driven into the walls. The place was roughly fitted out with a bed, a sofa and an old iron stove. On a plank shelf by the sink was the remains of a meal. Pervading everything was a stink of cat urine and worse. Taking a breath was like inhaling the air in the feline house of a zoo.

'I have only Russian tea, I'm afraid,' the old woman apologised. The cats had followed her inside and were rubbing themselves around her gumbooted calves as she filled a grimy saucepan by working the lever of a cast-iron pump beside the hollowed-out stone sink.

There was a fire in the pot-bellied iron stove, with a small heap of wood beside it. I took the pan from her and put it on top of the single cooking plate. Moving slowly at the careful pace of the very elderly, the old woman was searching on the shelf for a tin of tea.

Most of the glass in the single window of the tack room had been broken and replaced with layers of brown paper. Once my eyes had adjusted to the gloom, I saw that the shelves above the sofa were stacked with books in English. They were all paperbacks, published in Leipzig around the turn of the century. I'd come across the Tauchnitz edition before, in second-hand shops in Moscow. Each book bore the legend: 'This Collection is published with copyright for Continental circulation, but all purchasers are earnestly requested not to introduce the volumes into England or into any British Colony.'

I took one down at random. It was an 1896 copy of a romance by Mrs Humphrey Ward. Among the other authors' names on the shelf were Thackeray and Swift but also popular Victorian and Edwardian writers like Dickens, Ouida, H.G. Wells and A.E.W. Mason.

'There was a time I could have quoted you whole chapters,' the old woman said. 'I was a great reader, but it's years since I've been able to see well enough. Still, I like to feel the books around me. They prompt memories that are almost as pleasurable as reading used to be.'

Experience told me not to rush her, but to let her ramble on in her own good time.

'They burned most of the books.' Her voice was clear and well-modulated but she chopped and changed from English to Russian and back so frequently that I had difficulty following her, to begin with.

'Savages always do that, you know,' she confided. 'It's because they're frightened of the power of the printed word. Such a pity! There was a wonderful library here in the old days.'

She turned her head in the direction of the main house, as though she could see it as it had been. 'We had books in German, French and Italian – as well as Russian, of course. The ones you're looking at are some of those I saved after *the fire. I read them all many times over the years in order . . .'*

She hesitated and turned her head towards me. 'Can one say, to keep up my English?'

I told her one could and sat down on the evil-smelling sofa, keeping very still and feeling like a hunter watching his prey emerge from cover. It couldn't be coincidence, finding her at a probable site of Kolchak's last stand. Had I cracked the problem with which Sibirsky had grappled unsuccessfully for decades?

'I had to hide the books for so many years,' she confided. 'Now, hardly anyone comes here, apart from the village women who bring me food each week and collect my pension for me. And they are so ignorant, I don't suppose they can even read Russian. But they have good souls, as we used to say.'

The rheumy eyes focused on mine, as though still undecided how much to tell me. 'And I suppose it's not a crime, to have foreign books now. Stalin is dead, you know.'

I took the tea from her trembling hand. The chipped willow-patterned gravy boat had fly specks on the lip of the china and numerous greasy brown tidemarks lower down. From the way the cats watched when I raised it to my mouth, I had the feeling that it was their dish. So I pretended to take a sip and asked her where she had learned to speak such good English.

'In Southend,' she said.

'And what were you doing there?'

'My mother kept a boarding house on the sea-front.'

She sat down painfully on the other end of the sofa. I could almost hear her bones creak.

'And how did you get from Southend all the way here?' I asked softly.

'Oh dear,' she sighed. 'It's such a long story, young man. Are you sure you want to hear it?'

'Very much.'

'Because you're a historian and I'm a living relic from the past?'

That's putting it mildly, I thought. And I didn't know the half of it, yet.

.5.

The old woman was silent for several minutes while Tom waited patiently for her to collect her thoughts.

'My father was killed at Second Ypres,' she began hesitantly. 'And when all that dreadful business was over . . .'

'The Great War, you mean?'

She nodded. '. . . my mother took me back to France with her after the Armistice.'

'Back to France?'

'I didn't tell you that she was French. An aunt had died and left her a small family pension in Nice. There we met the Antonovs – or at least Madame Antonova and the children who had been staying on the Riviera during the Revolution, to be safe. There was quite a colony of Russians there in those days. They built their own Orthodox cathedral, you know.'

'Forgive me interrupting . . .' Tom wanted to get every detail in the old woman's story straight. 'These people – the Antonovs – were staying in your mother's pension, right?'

'Oh no!' The old woman smiled at the thought. 'They were much too grand for that. Real swanks, mother called them. Madame Antonova had taken a suite at the Carlton in Cannes.'

'When was this?'

'Just before my seventeenth birthday. I was just two years younger than the century, so it would be in the summer of '19.'

'And how did you meet Madame Antonova and her children?'

'She had advertised in *Nice-Matin* for a governess who could – keep up, that's the word – keep up her children's French and English after they came home to Russia. Being bilingual and needing a job, I thought it would be an adventure. And Mother said it was a golden opportunity for me to see the world.'

Tom pressed the Record button on the cassette recorder and pointed it at the old woman. When she asked what it was and he explained by playing back her question, her only comment was, 'What's happened to people's memories?'

'Let me get this clear,' Tom said. 'Do I understand that you came here with this family – the Antonovs – in the middle of the Civil War?'

'We came by ship – the long way round via Vladivostok. At that time, it was thought that the Whites had won the war and that anyway Irkutsk – four thousand miles from Petrograd where the trouble had started – would be quite safe.'

'In 1919?' he queried. That did not tally.

She shook her head; in her memory dates were tangled like her knitting wool the day the kittens had been playing with it. Which kittens? Not the ones who were grown up now. Oh no, it was long before these scrawny farm cats who were bothering her for their supper. Two Siamese kittens in Southend, she remembered now. And the wool – the precious wool from an unpicked cardigan – had been ruined. It was for a scarf and socks to send to her father in the trenches for Christmas – the Christmas of 1915.

'When was this?' Tom repeated. 'When did you come? It couldn't have been in 1919 because of the fighting.'

It took her an effort to remember what he was talking about. 'Let me see. I had been the children's governess for a whole year before Madame Antonova decided it was safe to come home.'

'So it was in 1920, near the end of the Civil War?'

'Yes.'

Tom checked that the tape was running. The old woman was a modern historian's dream: a family governess transplanted from Edwardian England and stranded in the middle of Siberia for seventy years . . . What a source for any researcher to stumble upon!

Kolchak's death had taken place two years after the end of the Great War, at the time when every mine in Britain was closed by a strike caused by the coal owners' refusal to pay two shillings to a man, one shilling to a youth and ninepence to a boy under sixteen for a ten-hour day underground. Terence MacSwiney, Lord Mayor of Cork, had just died at the end of his hunger strike and the IRA was already killing British soldiers, especially the hated Black and Tans. In India, another hunger-striker by name of Mohandas Gandhi had persuaded the Congress Party to adopt his policy of non-violence as the only way of driving the British out of the sub-continent. In Syria, Britain had just betrayed and abandoned to his fate T.E. Lawrence's war-time friend and ally, Prince Feisal. In Germany, both economist John Maynard Keynes and the up-and-coming politician Adolf Hitler were denouncing the Versailles treaty for their different reasons. And in Irkutsk, closer to the Pacific port of Vladivostok than to Moscow, an eighteen-year-old English governess to the pampered children of a rich fur merchant was about to be swept into the maelstrom of civil war.

'May I ask your name?' Tom said for the record.

'Oh, how rude of me!' A frail hand patted his arm in apology. 'It's Addison. Marie Helen Addison. How strange to say that aloud after all these years.'

'You have another name?' Tom asked. There was no way a solitary Englishwoman could have survived the xenophobia and the purges of the Thirties, so somehow Marie Helen Addison must have become . . .

'Olga Timofeyevna Akhmanova,' she filled in the blank. 'Now they just call me *stárshaya sumashédshaya* – the old madwoman.'

Miss Addison was looking at Tom quizzically. 'You haven't introduced yourself, young man.'

'I'm sorry,' he apologised. 'My name's Tom Fielding.'

'Tom, short for Thomas?'

'It's short for Thomas Winston Churchill.'

'Are you a relative?'

'If you mean of Churchill, no. He was a hero of my father's. That's why I was named after him.'

'Oh dear,' she said. 'We pinned so much hope on Mr Winston's interventionist forces. It seemed they would turn the tide against the Reds, but it was not to be. How is the gentleman?'

'I'm afraid he's dead.'

'Everyone's dead,' she said. 'Everyone I ever knew.'

As the afternoon wore on, Miss Addison frequently backtracked and repeated things she had already told Tom. But there were also huge gaps in her narrative, which his prompting could not persuade her to fill in.

He was running out of cassettes and had only one spare battery left. Despite that, he reversed his original plan of returning to Irkutsk for the night and coming back next day because of the risk of the old woman changing her mind about talking to him, as happened sometimes with the very elderly.

For supper he ate a stale sandwich and some chocolate,

left over from the picnic lunch he had eaten in the Lada, and drank some mineral water rather than trust the brownish fluid that gushed from the pump. Miss Addison had spent an hour feeding her cats and was sitting on the sofa, waiting for him, when he braved the fetid air of the tack room again just after dusk. For lighting she had an ancient hurricane lamp that added paraffin fumes to the other smells. The wick was trimmed very low and gave only a feeble glow.

To save the battery, Tom did not switch the recorder on at first.

'Tell me what happened the day the fighting reached Irkutsk,' he suggested.

Miss Addison pulled the cats nearer to her for their warmth.

'Do you remember that day?' he asked, to jog her memory.

She had her eyes closed. 'I'll never forget it, Mr Fielding. I was just thinking . . .'

After a minute had elapsed, he prompted her, 'You were thinking.'

'I was wondering where to begin. Perhaps the previous day?' Her eyes opened and she sat up straighter with a briskness that put Tom in mind of her as the bright-eyed young governess she had once been, telling a bedtime story to the children in her care. 'Well, Mr Antonov was living in town, you know – at the other house. Because of the news that came from the west, along the telegraph line which ran beside the railway, he decided that it was too dangerous for the family to stay on at Borzhoi.'

'That was the name of this place?'

'Yes. He thought the estate too isolated, you see. So he sent his driver to bring us into town. We shut the house up and left in two motor cars with a great deal of baggage. The estate servants stayed behind of course. In Irkutsk we thought there would be safety in numbers. I say we. Well, nobody consulted me, a mere girl of eighteen. I was called

Mademoiselle, never by my proper name. Like the other servants, I did what I was told. It was Madame Antonova and her husband who made the decisions.'

'What were conditions like in Irkutsk under siege?'

'For a few days, it seemed that once again the fighting would recede. Every hour there was a new rumour: the Reds were coming, or else the Whites had beaten them at a great victory in some place no one had heard of. Madame ordered me to keep the children to their lessons, in order to distract them, but the two boys were impossible for me to discipline: Mikhail was twelve and as imperious as his father. His ambition was to become a cadet in the Preobrazhensky Guards and personally hunt down the Reds who had murdered the royal family. His brother . . . Now, his name I don't remember. Isn't that strange? He was a nice boy but, being two years younger, he hero-worshipped Mikhail and copied everything his brother did, so he gave me a lot of trouble too. The boys were tall for their ages, with blond hair. Their younger sisters were blonde too. I'm glad to say that the girls were very polite and obedient with me, most of the time.'

Miss Addison stayed silent for several minutes, gazing into the past.

'And what was life like in Irkutsk when you got there?' Tom repeated.

'There was a shortage of food because of hoarding.' Her thin hands caressed the cats now purring on her lap. 'It was said that the poorer people were eating dogs and even cats and rats. Of course we had plenty to eat.'

'And what happened when the fighting reached the town?'

Miss Addison looked puzzled. 'There was no fighting in Irkutsk.'

That was not quite true, as Tom knew. But then individual witnesses' recollections – even of a mundane traffic accident – varied widely according to where they had been at a given moment.

'What happened, Mr Fielding, was that one of the gardeners at Borzhoi was despatched by the estate steward on horseback to give us the news that Admiral Kolchak's armoured train had broken down near the house. This meant that the White troops could not arrive in force in Irkutsk until the following day at the earliest, which was alarming news for us, as you can imagine.'

Tom nodded sympathetically.

'Oh!' she said. 'That poor gardener . . . His name was Timofei. I can see him still. He arrived in a state of considerable agitation, having been mistaken for a Red spy by a patrol of Kolchak's Cossacks. They had fired on him and given chase but luckily he had been able to elude them, thanks to knowing the countryside better than they. Poor Timofei!'

'So you were at the town house,' Tom nudged her back on track. 'You got the news that Kolchak's *bronepóyezd* was broken down here. Then what?'

'Mr Antonov was at the warehouse down by the steamer terminal, where he was trying to despatch across the lake as many bales of fur as possible before the town was cut off,' Miss Addison continued. 'So Madame Antonova told the second chauffeur to get her car ready and drive her to the warehouse in order to give her husband the news. Shortly after she had left, we heard cheering and a few shots. Thinking that Kolchak's train had arrived after all, Mikhail insisted on going down to the station to see what was happening, although his mother had forbidden any of the children to go out. His younger brother went too. I followed them, begging the boys to come back. People were on every street corner, talking excitedly in little groups, all heading for the main street, where the noise was coming from.'

The purring of the cats and the soft popping of the wick in the lamp were soporific. Tom pressed the Record button and sat back with half-closed eyes, letting the old woman's voice bring her memories to life for him too.

PART VII
Summer 1920

.1.

The firing was coming not from the station, which lay in the southern outskirts of the town, but from the north. Out of nowhere a column of Reds had appeared, having outflanked Kolchak's men by forced marches over hundreds of kilometres of forest and swamp. There was no organised resistance in the town; the sporadic shooting which had excited Mikhail Antonov was from a succession of military non-events. A volley announced the summary execution of a White deserter stupid enough still to be in uniform. A single shot rang out as a looter murdered a householder trying to protect his property. Another sounded as a soldier took pity on a lamed horse and put it out of its misery.

Marie watched the men's faces as the head of the column shambled past her vantage point outside the town's only department store. It was the first time she had seen soldiers at war. There was no parade-ground smartness here, nor even a pretence of marching in step. Their legs were muddy up to the thighs, their hands filthy and their faces hollow with fatigue. Only the weapons had travelled first class.

Had her father and his comrades looked like this when they came out of the trenches? she wondered.

The officers – or commissars, as they were called in the Red forces – were on horseback or in motor cars. Their men seemed disciplined enough, Marie decided – just hungry and very tired. From some of the humbler houses, women and children ran out with food and drink for the soldiers. The first improvised red flags appeared, hung out of upstairs windows or draped across the recently installed public utility cables that looped from pole to pole along the street.

The crowd on the wooden sidewalks grew more and more numerous. Marie was attempting to persuade the two boys to return home but they defied her, sitting on top of a circular advertising kiosk where they had climbed to shout abuse at the Reds. A policeman in civilian clothes hauled them down and ordered them home to prevent an incident.

'We don't have to obey you,' said Mikhail rudely. 'Our father is Councillor Antonov.'

'I know who your father is,' was the man's reply. 'That's why I'm doing you a favour, young sir. Now get on home before they arrest you or something worse happens.'

A muffled thudding of unshod hooves on the dirt road surface and a jingling of harness followed Marie as she hurried after the boys, hampered by her heavy ankle-length skirt; in Irkutsk, decently dressed women still wore fashions that Queen Victoria would have thought proper.

As the horsemen drew level, Marie caught up with the two Antonov boys, standing on tiptoe in an effort to see over the heads of the crowd.

'The Cossacks are here,' Mikhail shouted to her.

'Will they rescue us from the Reds?' asked his brother.

'These are the traitors,' Mikhail sneered. 'The ones they call worker Cossacks. They fight for the Reds.'

To Marie's eyes, the heads of the horsemen appeared to float jerkily along above the heads of the crowd. To show that they were not regular troops, each Cossack took pride in dressing differently from his fellows. While the riders did not look as fatigued as the men on foot, their shaggy, short-legged mounts were poor-looking beasts, compared with the plump, well-groomed ponies that Marie was used to riding on the Antonov estate at Borzhoi.

She shivered as her eyes met those of one of the riders, a short, angry-looking man with a clean-shaven chin below a black moustache. A large astrakhan hat perched on his head and he had two rifles slung across his shoulders, with bandoliers strung criss-cross over his red shirt. In his right hand was curled the Cossacks' favourite close-quarters weapon – the *knout* – a particularly vicious kind of whip, as feared by their victims as the sabre they all carried slung from their belts on the left side.

At a road junction, for no reason that Marie could see, the man in the red shirt lashed out with his *knout* at a bystander. The lead weights sewn into the tip of the lash left the target moaning on the ground with one eye torn out of its socket and his cheek cut to the bone after just one slash. Marie dragged the boys away from the spectacle, aware of the horseman with the red shirt staring hungrily after her as he stood in the stirrups, re-coiling his *knout* for another blow.

Her relief on reaching the Antonov home and seeing that both cars had returned was short-lived. Inside the house was bedlam. The under-cook was weeping and screaming in the kitchen where the second chauffeur, to whom the hysterical girl was engaged, was yelling at her to shut up. There was a smell of wood smoke from the back garden and she could hear the sound of axes and the whinnying of horses and the jingling of bridles coming from the same direction, interspersed with shouting and drunken laughter.

'Where have you been, Mademoiselle?' Madame Antonova shouted as soon as Marie and the boys entered.

Her normally immaculate coiffure awry, she gripped the governess's shoulders and shook her savagely. In a more than usually confused jumble of languages, she screamed, 'You are very wicked girl! I am beside myself with worry. *Je te défends* to let the boys go out *i chto slucháyetsa?* As soon as my back is turned . . .'

She released Marie and turned to her sons. 'Mischa, you and your brother must stay upstairs and keep away from the windows.'

'Lock the doors, Mademoiselle,' called Mr Antonov, running down the stairs with his wife's jewellery case in his hand.

'Leave them open,' his wife contradicted. '*Les Casaques sont des fauves* – wild beasts they are. They will smash the doors down if we close them. Listen to *le bruit qu'ils font dans le jardin!*'

Mr Antonov was mopping nervous sweat from his forehead and panting, his eyes wide with fear. 'Whatever they want, give them,' he shouted at no one in particular. 'By tomorrow they'll be gone, God willing. They'll run when Kolchak's men get here. Nothing matters but to stay alive until tomorrow.'

He hurried into his study where the wall-safe stood open. Before he could lock the jewellery case inside, they heard several shots in the garden and the noise of breaking glass upstairs.

Madame Antonova screamed, 'My boys!'

Lifting her skirts, she ran upstairs and was halfway to the first floor when her elder son reeled into sight on the landing. There was blood pouring down his face from a scalp wound and his left hand was clamped round his right arm as he tried to staunch the bright red blood pulsing from the torn arteries in his chest and arm.

He fell at the top of the stairs, his father's heavy silver-plated Colt .45 revolver falling from his hand and clattering down the steps, all the way to the bottom. As his mother bent over the lifeless body, she saw the form of her younger son lying in a crumpled heap by the shattered window of his bedroom.

'Mama! Mama!' her two daughters were screaming downstairs, despite Marie's efforts to calm them.

The back door burst open. With a stream of abuse two Cossacks entered. The first had a half-empty bottle of brandy in his hand. He fired a revolver several times at the crystal chandelier in the hallway, covering the floor with shards of glass which crunched beneath his booted feet.

The other was shouting, 'Tsarist pigs! Who shot at us? Hand him over immediately.'

He stooped and picked up the Colt, pointing it at the nearest person, which happened to be Marie. She was kneeling down with her arms around the two screaming girls, trying to comfort them.

'You,' he said. 'Outside.'

She stayed where she was.

Deliberately, he cocked the hammer with his thumb.

'You cowards,' she said, looking up at him. 'You shot two children – boys of ten and twelve. You should be ashamed.'

He looked from her to the body on the stairs and the sobbing woman beside it, then ran up to the first floor, kicking Madame Antonova out of the way. In the bedroom, he shot the moaning boy on the floor twice in the head and shouted something out of the shattered window to his fellows in the garden below.

The second Cossack was in the study using his *knout* reversed to belabour Mr Antonov, knocking him to the floor in front of the still open safe. The handle of the whip, studded with brass nails, was raising huge welts on the backs of his victim's hands which were clasped over his head. Tiring of the game, the Cossack coiled the whip and stuck it in his belt. He took a swig of brandy and used his revolver to shoot at Mr Antonov who was crawling out of the room on all fours. The first shot missed and took a splinter out of the door jamb. The second bullet shattered the crawling man's right femur. He screamed in agony that was abruptly terminated as a third bullet caught him in the base of the spine, shattering three vertebrae and severing the spinal column, paralysing both legs before tearing its way through his large intestine and finally lodging itself in his right lung. His hands scrabbling futilely at the carpet, Mr Antonov lay in the doorway, moaning softly, with blood trickling from his open mouth. With his booted foot another Cossack kicked him over onto his back, then stooped to tear the rings from the dying man's fingers.

The house seemed full of armed men now, rampaging from room to room, smashing furniture and pictures in their hunt for alcohol. One man swallowed the entire contents of a cut-glass decanter of whisky from the sideboard in the dining room, then hurled it into the fireplace where it smashed to pieces, while another upended above his head a bottle of 1907 vintage Médoc, spilling most of it over his face and tunic. More bottles were being brought up from the cellar. In the kitchen, the two cooks were being forced at gunpoint to prepare a meal for the horsemen encamped in the garden. Upstairs there was a scream from one of the maids and the sound of a door splintering, then laughter and more shots.

Marie grasped the two girls firmly by their wrists. They had stopped crying and were silent although shaking visibly, their faces white with terror. She pulled them with her and pushed a way through the throng of sweating, stinking, shouting men. Halfway up the stairs Madame Antonova sat rocking the dead body of her elder son, her face and hands red with his blood.

'Mischa!' she kept wailing. 'Mischa, my son!'

'Forget your sons!' Marie let go of the girls' hands for a moment in order to shake her employer. 'You can do nothing for them, Madame, but your daughters need you.'

Her employer could not hear. She was staring around in shock at the wrecking of her home. Two paces away, a pair of Cossacks naked to the waist were fighting over a mauve satin blouse from Paris which both wanted to wear. The fabric tore and one man reeled backwards, smashing the balustrade and falling backwards onto the press of men below who were using sabres to hack curtains from their rails in order to use the material as cloaks. In the bathroom, a Cossack was on his knees, quenching his thirst with handfuls of water scooped from the patented flushing toilet and laughing with pleasure each time it refilled. Others were coming out of the bedrooms with arms full of clothes and bedding.

A face that Madame Antonova knew was shouting at her to forget her dead sons. Another pushed the first face out of the way and screamed at her: 'Pig!'

The senior chauffeur had taken off his livery jacket and boots. Barefoot and with his shirt open to the waist, hoping to pass for a Red sympathiser, he tore the body from her arms and hurled it down the stairs.

'Kill them all,' he was shouting. 'The Tsarist pigs have weapons hidden behind a false wall in the cellar. I'll show you where.'

Hands grabbed the woman at whom he was screaming, as well as Marie and the girls, pulling at them, tearing their clothes, hitting them. The victims stumbled through the gauntlet of blows downstairs and outside into the garden, which was unrecognisable. The once neatly trimmed lawn with its white-painted wrought-iron furniture and carefully tended flower beds had been transformed into a Cossack encampment, with men lounging on velours-covered armchairs and horses grazing on the flowers and shrubs. A pile of hay had been looted from somewhere and dumped in the clematis-covered belvedere, transforming it into a stable. There was a hoarse cheer from a dozen throats and a crash as a double bed was heaved over the first-floor balcony to land on a rose bed beneath.

'Kill the Tsarist pigs!' a few men were chanting, led by the chauffeur. Others, only a few yards away, carried on sleeping or unsaddling their horses or eating – taking no notice of the small group intent on bloodshed who roughly thrust their four victims against the sun-warmed wall of the house.

A thin man with a scarred face stepped forward from the impromptu execution squad and said something official-sounding about crimes against the people for which the penalty was death. The only one of the four victims who could hear him was Marie. Madame Antonova was in a trance, unable to see or hear even her own daughters clinging to her skirts, screaming and weeping with terror.

Marie pulled the two girls to her. She knelt down to place her face on a level with theirs, putting her arms around them. 'We must say our prayers,' she said.

'*Odná minútka!*' The scar-faced man stepped back grudgingly. 'One minute is all I give you.'

Marie pulled the girls closer, forcing them to turn and face her so that they did not see the men threatening them and the weapons pointed at them.

'Now close your eyes, girls,' she said. 'Put your hands together like we always do and say after me, Our Father, which art in Heaven . . .'

First one and then the other uncertain voice joined in. Dear God, Marie prayed privately, please make the sight of two little girls saying their prayers touch these savage men's hearts.

She kept the words going when the children's voices faltered – but slowly, literally praying for time in the hope of divine intervention. Above the blonde curls so close to her face she could see an argument developing between the man with the scar and a newcomer, another Cossack. He had his back to her but seemed to have authority of some kind.

'. . . for ever and ever, amen,' they finished more or less together.

Did you hear us, God? Marie wondered.

'Shoot the others,' the newcomer was saying. 'But I want the younger woman for questioning.'

When he turned round, Marie saw that her saviour was the man in the red shirt who had been staring at her in the parade. He stretched out the *knout* in his right hand, looped the bloodstained thong around her neck and pulled her aside as a ragged volley crashed out and the three bodies in their white summer dresses fell together in a heap on the ground at Marie's feet.

Two of the bodies lay still but the younger girl, who was only five years old, opened her eyes and lifted one hand as though to ward off a blow. Momentarily deafened and unable from shock to move hand or foot, Marie watched the muzzle of a rifle part the blonde curls. Then another shot blew away the side of the child's head, lifting her small body and throwing it across her mother's legs.

Stunned, Marie stared at the bright red splotches on the clean white linen of the three matching summer dresses. It looked to her tear-blurred vision as though God had thrown a bouquet of scarlet roses from on high to say He was sorry.

.2.

The man in the red shirt led her like a dog on a lead through the carousing mob in the garden. More worried about the red stain on her skirt than what was going to happen next, Marie stumbled after him, nearly falling with each savage jerk on the *knout* as he dragged her via a gap smashed in the fencing into the next garden, which belonged to the house of the Japanese consul. The Antonov children had always been curious about the people who lived there. The consul, Mr Yasumoto, had worn Western dress, always removed his top hat and bowed politely when meeting his neighbours in the street. His wife had rarely appeared in public but been seen from time to time by the children, when they peered out of upstairs windows and caught sight of her dressed in brilliantly coloured kimonos, flitting through the garden like a gorgeous butterfly.

Several of the men now drinking the consul's looted *sake* in the garden were wearing those kimonos, roughly cut down to serve as shirts belted at the waist and hanging down outside the trousers. Of the Yasumoto family there was no sign.

The house was in less of a mess than the Antonov home because Marie's captor, whom the others addressed as *hetman* – the traditional title of the leader of a Cossack horde – had chosen it as his quarters.

He led her into the kitchen where the Yasumotos' terrified cook was trying to prepare a meal for a group of Cossacks despite continual molestation. With a string of oaths the *hetman* chased the other men out of the kitchen and ordered Marie to help her with the preparation of his meal.

'I'm a governess, not a cook,' she said, her heart beating fast and her palms clammy with fear.

He seemed amused at her defiance. 'If I say cook, you cook.'

'I don't know how.'

His dark eyes bored into hers. 'What kind of woman does not know how to cook?' he sneered. 'Are you an aristocrat?'

'No,' she said. 'I'm a British citizen.'

Marie had read many cheap romances in which fearless English heroines faced down their native captors in far-flung outposts of the Empire.

'If you will kindly take me under your protection to the house next door,' she said in a trembling voice, 'I shall show you my British passport, sir. And when all this unpleasant business is over, you will be rewarded by the proper authorities for rendering me assistance.'

The *hetman* started to laugh and continued until he was bent over out of breath and holding onto the door jamb for support.

'You don't realise, *anglichánka moyá*,' he said, straightening up at last. 'We are changing the world. There are no more proper authorities and this business, as you call it, will never be over.'

He waved the coiled *knout* in a circular motion above his head to indicate all the killing and looting going on around them. 'This is the future. There are no more proper authorities.'

'Not in Russia, perhaps,' Marie agreed, feeling weak with

fear. By standing very straight, her eyes were level with his. 'But the British Empire spans the globe. The new government in Moscow would be wise not to antagonise it by maltreating its citizens.'

Abruptly he tired of playing with her and yawned, showing a mouthful of yellow teeth. 'You cook,' he ordered. 'Or this will be your lover.' He patted the *knout* tucked into his belt. 'After ten of its caresses on your tender skin, you will be out of your mind with pain. Which is it to be?'

Remembering the man in town whose face had been laid open to the bone with one lash, Marie said, 'I'll cook.'

She turned away from him, and felt the handle of the *knout* poking her chignon, flicking away the two tortoise-shell combs so that her hair fell loose down her shoulders, nearly to her waist.

'And when I have eaten,' the *hetman* said, 'you will have the honour of serving the Revolution in my bed.'

With a savage prod of the *knout* handle he spun Marie round. His left hand ripped open the front of her blouse, feeling her bodice and the skin above it as though she were some beast in a market that he was thinking of buying. Aware of the cook watching, Marie felt the crimson flush of embarrassment spread from her face down her neck to her bosom. She clenched her hands by her sides, wanting to run away or hit the *hetman* but knowing that either course would be fatal.

'You're as beautiful as you are frisky,' he said, coming closer. 'Are you a virgin?'

Her silence was the answer. 'Well, enjoy your last day,' he grinned.

Marie found her tongue at last. 'If you're going to kill me anyway, why should I bother to cook your meal?'

'My mare was like you when I first caught her,' he said. 'Full of spirit until I broke her to my will. Don't worry, *anglichánka moyá*. I meant only that today is your last day as an unbroken virgin.'

*

The two maids were from peasant families. They had grown used to serving food to drunken men in their own homes before they had gone into service, so they accepted as normal the slaps and groping and the lewd jokes that grew more pointed as the evening wore on.

Marie stayed close to the *hetman*, standing behind his chair most of the time, reaching the food at which he pointed and pouring wine into the crystal goblet from which he was drinking. It was the best way to ensure that none of the other Cossacks dared touch her. She filled and refilled the goblet, hoping to get him as drunk as the others, but the *hetman* insisted on watering his wine so it had little effect on him, so far as she could see.

As his companions got steadily more drunk, he watched with an expression of contempt when they fell from their chairs to the floor, paralytic with alcohol, or stumbled in pursuit of the girls, now topless and half drunk themselves from the liquor with which they had been plied.

Marie would have liked to believe that the scene in which she was taking part was a bad dream of some kind. Less than twelve hours before, her greatest worry had been not to get on the wrong side of the volatile Madame Antonova; now the entire Antonov family lay dead and unburied in and outside the house next door.

When he had eaten enough, the *hetman* stood up and growled, '*Sledí za mnói.*'

Accustomed to obedience from women and horses, he left the dining room without turning round to make sure Marie was following. From spending years of his life in the saddle, his legs were bowed; his gait was more of a controlled lurch from side to side than a normal walk. The stairs were lit by gas brackets, as was the consul's bedroom. In it the simple Japanese furniture had been left in place. A *futon* occupied the centre of the room. The *hetman* unbuckled his belt and dropped it with his *knout* and sabre on a priceless black lacquered chest.

'Close the door,' he ordered. 'I don't want those drunken fools bursting in here while I'm taking my pleasure.'

Marie complied and stood aside as he heaved a Western-style chest of drawers against the door to block it closed. There was a key in the lock but either he did not understand its purpose or mistrusted its strength.

'Now,' he said, throwing himself on the *futon*. 'Come here.'

She took a deep breath and unpinned the torn front of her blouse. The whole plan she had worked out while supervising the preparation of the meal depended on undressing herself without his interference.

'No,' she said. 'You've done enough damage to my clothing. I'll undress myself.'

She had often lain awake at night imagining how it would be, the first time a man touched her to the sound of violins and poetry. She had envisaged the act of giving her virginity as some wondrous gift to a gentle lover with soft brown eyes and softer lips who would transport her with promises of undying devotion and hold her tenderly through the night.

The reality was this, she thought: a hard-eyed middle-aged killer to whom she was a female beast to be subjugated, used as he wished and then maybe slaughtered for sport. Well, so be it. If that was the way it had to be, then she would couple with him – but like a tigress. Let him beware of her claws, for he had set the rules . . .

She laid her blouse within reach of the *futon*.

'*Bystro*,' he grunted, fondling his crotch: get a move on!

She unfastened the waistband of her skirt and let it fall on top of her blouse. The *hetman* had never seen a woman wearing underwear. Fascinated, he watched Marie's petti-coats drop to the floor and then her drawers, only losing patience when she stood naked before him except for her lightly boned cotton bodice.

Trying to imagine how a whore might keep a man at

arm's length in such a situation, she pulled the swell of her breasts upwards so that the nipples showed above the top of the bodice. She saw the *hetman* lick his lips, fastening his eyes on the twin rosebuds he intended to pluck that night. In deliberate striptease she took off first one stocking and then the other, dropping them on the pile of clothing while his eyes devoured her.

She stood just out of his reach, clad only in her bodice. Her hands were trembling and kept fumbling the hooks and eyes down her back. At last she took off the bodice, turning to keep her body between it and him. Carefully, she rolled it up around the whalebones and placed it on the top of the pile of clothes.

She closed her eyes before kneeling down on the *futon* but she could not close her nostrils, which were filled with the stink of him: a compound of horses and urine and stale sweat. She felt his bridle-hardened hands on her soft breasts and told herself that Mr Antonov was right: nothing really mattered except staying alive until the morrow.

The *hetman* tore his way into her with a laugh at the single cry of pain she could not repress. With hands clenched and teeth biting her lower lip until it bled, Marie lay beneath him. He took her a second time within minutes and then rolled off her to lie on his back, snoring.

Through the uncurtained window she could see the low clouds reflecting the light of a house burning not far away. Drunken laughter competed with the noise of timbers exploding with the heat and masonry falling. The noise outside grew less as the house burned itself out and men collapsed in drunken sleep where they fell. Horses whinnied in the gardens and occasionally there was the sound of blows or a woman's cry of pain.

When she judged that most of the Cossacks were sleeping, Marie stretched out her right hand towards the pile of clothes on the floor. Inch by inch her hand crept closer to it until her fingertips found the rolled-up bodice which she began slowly to unfold, terrified of making a noise at the last moment and waking the man she had to kill.

Once the slim-handled fish-gutting knife was in her hand, she sat up cautiously, jerked the blanket off the *hetman* and raised the knife high. She aimed for where she thought his heart must be and brought the knife down with all her strength. The tip skated off a rib bone and lost momentum, penetrating the skin for no more than an inch.

With a raucous intake of breath, he opened his eyes wide, his strong hands reaching for her. For a moment that went on and on, Marie thought the blade was too wide to pass between his ribs. Her eyes locked with his as the *hetman*'s hands clamped on her forearms like steel bands. In desperation she raised herself up, putting all her weight on the knife handle, pushing down and twisting it until it slid into his chest up to the hilt.

Then his grip relaxed and his mouth opened wide to ask the last question of his life. '*Pochemú?*' he gasped.

'*Potomú-chto ya dévushka a ne lóschad,*' she replied: because I'm a girl, not a horse.

.3.

The dead man's head was arched back with the mouth open in the hideous rictus of death, his yellowed teeth gleaming in the gaslight. Marie shuddered and pulled the blanket over the body beside her in order to hide the sight. She wanted to be sick but repressed the violent gagging for fear of making any unnecessary noise, listening to the sounds of the house for several minutes before deciding that none of the men in the other rooms had heard anything amiss. Only then did she open the French windows and step out onto the balcony.

The burning house must have been one of the many in Irkutsk constructed almost entirely of wood; it was now just a huge pile of embers glowing at the end of the road. By the light of the quarter moon between the intermittent clouds, the dim outlines of men sleeping in the garden, wrapped in cloaks or blankets, could just be made out. The pony which the *hetman* had personally fed and watered was tethered to the fence halfway down the garden. So far as Marie had been able to tell by dint of repeated glances through the kitchen window that afternoon, it was the best-looking beast of the lot.

But where was its saddle? Marie was no Cossack, able to ride bareback if need be. She sighed with relief on seeing it thrown athwart the fence only a few feet away from the animal and wondered how long it would take her to saddle and bridle the pony.

She went back into the bedroom and felt revulsion creep all over her skin as she pulled on the dead man's baggy Cossack trousers, stiff with dried sweat in the seat and insides of the thighs. Next came the red shirt which the *hetman* had been wearing. It stank of him, but that was to the good. The more she looked like him, the less attention she would attract from anyone who happened to be awake; the more she smelled like him, the likelier it was that his pony would let an unknown hand bridle and saddle it.

The *hetman* had not been much taller than Marie but he had been far sturdier than the slim girl who now wore his clothes. In order to keep up the heavy trousers, she cinched the belt in tightly, way before the first hole, and pulled the bottom of the shirt down outside the trousers. Instead of buttons the shirt had ties of cloth to keep it closed. Her fingers kept fumbling them in her haste.

She caught sight of her hair in a wall mirror. Where were her combs and pins? Still lying scattered on the kitchen floor, probably. But the long blonde hair, of which she was so proud, was a giveaway. There was only one thing to do: cut it off.

She tried pulling the knife from the dead man's chest, but it would not come free. So she took his sabre from the scabbard, found the blade razor-sharp, and watched her image in the mirror as handful after handful of hair was pulled across the blade and fell to the floor. Staring back at her from the glass was a wide-eyed boy in baggy trousers and red shirt. The astrakhan hat, greasy with sweat, was too large for her head. The dead man's boots were also useless, so she put on her own lace-up black ankle boots and was ready to leave.

She tossed the hat down to the ground and grasped the trellis up which a wisteria climbed to the roof of the house. There was only one way to find out whether the wooden slats were strong enough to bear her weight. From habit, she bent to pull up her skirt in order to throw a leg over the balcony railing, before realising that wearing trousers gave her an agility she had never known before. A minute later she stood in the shadow beneath the balcony while the garden was bathed in moonlight. The ponies were all looking in her direction. She hoped no one was awake to wonder what they were staring at – and that the animals would not neigh or disturb the men sleeping among them.

Then the moon disappeared behind a cloud and she slipped across the garden and took the bridle off the fence. By tossing its head, the pony threw it off twice. She was standing between it and the fence, for concealment. Repeatedly it crushed her against the palings so that she had to push it away with one hand at the same time as trying to put the bridle on with the other. By the third attempt, she was drenched in sweat; it seemed impossible that she had not woken any of the men sleeping in the garden.

At last the bit was in the animal's mouth and the buckle fastened. There was a chinking of metal as the pony chewed to get the bit comfortable, making a noise that sounded like an alarm bell to Marie's ears. Still none of the sleeping figures moved, so she slipped the halter free and reached for the saddle, dropping it gently onto the animal's back before reaching beneath its belly for the girth strap.

Suddenly drenched in light as the moon came out from behind a cloud, she froze, willing the pony not to move and reveal her crouched against the fence. It turned its head and nuzzled her face wetly while she whispered, 'Good horse. Good horse, don't move. Oh, please don't move.'

Then the moon disappeared and she buckled the girth

beneath the pony's belly with a prayer that the *hetman* had broken it of the vice of puffing itself out when being saddled. If not, the girth would be loose and the saddle would slip at any pace faster than a walk, throwing her to the ground.

She led the pony through a gap where the fence palings had been torn out for firewood. In the street there were forage waggons parked at all angles, but no sentries posted so far as she could see. Reasoning that the most alert guards would be on the southern side of town – from where Kolchak's attack was expected in the morning – Marie headed northwards, in the direction from which the Reds had come.

As soon as she thought it safe she mounted the pony. Having only ridden side-saddle before, it felt strange to be astride her mount, which pricked up its ears and moved into a trot as her heels tapped its flanks. She held the Cossack hat on the back of her head with one hand, hoping that in the poor light she looked like a man. Although the danger was not yet past, she began to breathe more easily, now that so much of her plan had worked.

She left the town behind unchallenged, avoiding any main road and threading a roundabout route through the network of dirt tracks which peasants used to bring their produce into Irkutsk on market days. With one eye on the pole star and Orion for bearings, she headed first west and then south, keeping the lights of the town across the fields on her left side.

When she came to the railway tracks gleaming in the moonlight they seemed like a sign from heaven, showing her the way to go as clearly as the pillar of smoke and the column of fire had guided Moses across the desert. Yet she stilled the prayer that rose to her lips; God had not listened to her impassioned plea for two innocent children, so she would not speak to Him now.

As the lights and noises of the town faded behind her, all Marie had to fear – or so she told herself – was the comparatively slight chance of running into a skirmish party or a scout. Failing that, the next human face she saw should be a friendly one.

'Halt! Who goes there?' The age-old challenge stopped the tired pony in its tracks.

Exhausted by her experiences and lulled by the motion of her mount, Marie had dozed off after dawn, awoken and dozed off again a dozen times. She opened her eyes to see a mounted man levelling his rifle at her fifty paces away. From his dress, she could see that he was a Cossack. In momentary anguish she wondered whether the pony had turned round while she was asleep and headed back to Irkutsk. The day was grey and overcast, so she had lost all sense of direction.

Then she saw, behind the sentry, the immobile black metallic bulk of Admiral Kolchak's armoured train, sitting uselessly astride the line. Further away and to the south, lay the Antonov country house at Borzhoi.

Relieved that the man pointing a gun at her must be a White Cossack, she called back, '*Ya drug.* I'm a friend.'

She let the bridle drop onto the pony's neck and kicked it to a walk, riding forward with both hands in the air. Halfway to the sentry, there was a pounding of hooves on turf as five other Cossacks rode out of a nearby clump of trees and surrounded her. Marie's relief turned to alarm. They knocked her roughly to the ground and rode round in a tight circle, leaning low from the saddle to shout at her and threatening her with drawn sabres and their *knouts*. Her hat had fallen to the ground. She shouted back at them that she was a friend but they were making too much noise to hear her.

'Who are you?' they yelled. 'You are not one of us, so you must be a Red.'

Winded by the fall, Marie crouched on the ground with hunched shoulders, trying to get back her breath. She staggered to her feet, only to have a pony's haunch barge her sideways off-balance and knock her down again. This time she stayed down. Through the wall of horses' legs she saw another rider dismounting. He had polished boots and a tunic jacket over riding breeches. On his epaulette was the insignia of a Tsarist captain. His face was clean-shaven, apart from a small neatly trimmed moustache. On his head he wore a peaked uniform cap instead of a Cossack's astrakhan hat.

'Bring the fellow to me!' he ordered.

One of the Cossacks in the circle bent from his saddle, and grabbed the collar of Marie's shirt, intending to haul her to her feet. The badly fastened belt gave way and fell to the grass, leaving him waving a red shirt in the air while a half-naked girl stared up at him, one arm across her breasts and the other holding up her trousers, which were in danger of falling down. The mounted men roared with laughter, jeering at her embarrassment.

The captain strode between them, snatched the shirt away and handed it back to Marie. 'Where have you come from?' he asked sternly as she struggled to cover herself.

All the ties had been torn off the shirt. She held it closed with one hand and refastened the belt round her waist, then tried to smooth her badly cropped hair which stuck out at all angles.

'From Irkutsk,' she stammered.

'Impossible,' he snapped. 'We've had scouts out since yesterday morning. They reported that all routes into the town were heavily defended.'

'Not on the north side,' she said. 'I escaped that way and then headed west and south to pick up the line of the railway.'

He swore in exasperation; twelve hours earlier, that information might have made all the difference. 'What's your name?' he asked curtly.

For no reason except total exhaustion, she answered in

English: 'Marie Helen Addison. I'm a British subject, employed as governess by Councillor Antonov, whose house you can see over there on the estate of Borzhoi.'

The change in the man facing her was total. He clicked his polished heels and bowed. 'Captain Yussupov, Dimitri Andreyevich. Thirteenth Imperial Cossack Cavalry. At your service.' His English was faultless.

'I have cousins who live outside Cheltenham,' he smiled. 'The Sinclair-Smythes. Perhaps you know them?'

Marie shook her head numbly.

'Or perhaps we have met?' Captain Yussupov suggested. 'I was in England for most of the racing season of '13. Were you at Ascot? Or perhaps it was at Epsom for the Derby when that unfortunate suffragette woman fell beneath the King's horse?'

'No.'

'Really not? My cousins told me that everyone who was anyone went to Ascot.'

Marie's head started spinning. 'Forgive me,' she said. 'I'm not feeling very well.'

The captain snapped his fingers and the dismounted Cossack who had been holding his horse's bridle walked it up to them. He vaulted into the saddle and stretched down a hand to lift the exhausted girl effortlessly up in front of him. Marie's own pony was standing by the tracks with its head down, too tired even to graze.

Closer to, the *bronepóyezd*, with the two huge locomotives at its head standing silent and steamless, revealed itself as virtually a town on wheels. It was a mobile garrison capable of accommodating two and a half thousand men with all their weapons, supplies and horses. Until the fatal breakdown it had both housed them and transported them across Central Asia at speeds of up to 100mph.

The trucks in which the Cossacks travelled with their mounts had sides which could be let down to serve as ramps, permitting two hundred armed horsemen to be disgorged at the gallop within seconds of the train coming to a halt.

The roof of each carriage sported two sandbagged heavy machine-gun emplacements and the sides of the compartments were armoured from top to bottom with thick steel shutters from the firing slits of which more weapons poked. Outside the train, men strolled about in the grey morning, cleaning weapons, feeding horses and preparing their own food. A party of dispirited Red prisoners under armed guard were digging a deep ditch, uncertain whether it was to be a latrine or their own grave. At the rear of the train a small handful of women in nurses' uniforms were tending the wounded on stretchers.

As they trotted across the parkland towards the house, Marie started to weep. From his cuff Captain Yussupov took a clean white linen handkerchief that smelled of eau de cologne.

'I can't help it,' she apologised to him, dabbing at her tears. 'It's just the relief at being safe.'

'If that's the trouble,' he said quietly, 'your tears are somewhat premature, Miss Addison. I fear we'll all be dead, come this time tomorrow.'

.4.

The ground floor of the house was busy with all the comings and goings of a military headquarters: clerks sat at
desks writing on pieces of paper which messengers took
away. Then other messengers arrived with new pieces of
paper. Outside, sentries presented arms as officers passed;
orders were given and acknowledged with crisp salutes.

After being given a drink and some biscuits to eat, Marie
was kept waiting under guard for an hour without being
allowed to go and change her clothes. At last she was shown
into the library where Admiral Kolchak, in a high-collared
dark blue uniform, was sitting in Mr Antonov's buttoned
leather armchair by the fireplace. As he rose to greet her,
Marie saw a stoutly built bald-headed man of forty-five who
looked fifteen years older.

'*Pozdravláyu vas*,' he rumbled, holding out a hand to
shake hers. 'I congratulate you, Miss Addison. From what
Captain Yussupov tells me, I understand that you are a
remarkably brave and resourceful young woman.'

'It wasn't courage,' said Marie, 'but desperation which drove me to do what I did.'

The admiral motioned her to a chair, which Captain Yussupov held as she sat down. Marie had never been invited to take a seat in the library before.

'Dimitri Andreyevich has told me your story,' said Kolchak, seating himself opposite her. 'But I want you to tell it to me again, describing in detail everything you saw and heard on the way here.'

Unable to decide what was important and what not, Marie told them everything. Neither the admiral nor his elegant aide seemed to find her appearance strange or the situation odd. When she briefly recounted her rape by the *hetman* and how she had killed him, they nodded. Such tales were commonplace to them after three years of civil war. From time to time the admiral glanced at a map on the circular drinks table beside his chair, across which Yussupov's finger was tracing the stages of Marie's nocturnal journey.

'It doesn't amount to much, I'm afraid,' she finished. 'I was too tired to take notice of anything, once I had left the town behind me. Have I been any help at all?'

The admiral sighed. 'From your description of the Reds' forces, their numbers are far too great for us to attack with any chance of success, now that the train is out of action.' With the nearest workshop facilities in Irkutsk in Red hands, there was no hope of his engineers making even temporary repairs before the Bolsheviks attacked next morning.

'Then what will you do?'

'Sell ourselves as dearly as possible,' smiled the admiral. 'What else is there to do?'

'You could surrender,' Marie said.

'Some will,' he agreed. 'But there are many like Yussupov and myself who would be better off dead than captured.'

'Then,' said Marie, 'there was no point in my escaping from Irkutsk. I might as well have stayed there, to suffer whatever fate had in store for me.'

'On the contrary, Miss Addison,' said Kolchak. 'I view your arrival here as an act of God, for you are the one person under my command at this moment who can carry out a mission of the utmost importance.'

Another aide had entered and was whispering in the admiral's ear something about skirmishers and contact.

'I'll brief you later.' Kolchak stood to indicate that the interview was over. 'Meanwhile Captain Yussupov will find you a room where you can wash and change your clothes. Then you must eat and get some rest, Miss Addison. What I am going to ask of you will demand all your considerable reserves of courage and resourcefulness.'

Upstairs, the first room into which Yussupov conducted Marie was Mr Antonov's bedroom. There was an Imperial Russian Navy admiral's dress uniform laid out on the bed, with a servant polishing a gilt-hilted ceremonial sword in the adjoining dressing room.

'It's quite all right,' said Marie. 'I know my way around the house far better than you, captain. I'll use my own room.'

At the foot of the stairs leading to the second floor, Yussupov stopped. 'But these are the servants' quarters,' he said.

'I was the governess.'

He looked embarrassed. 'Forgive me. I had forgotten.'

She was halfway up to the next floor when he said, 'Miss Addison, would you do me the great honour of dining with me tonight?'

Marie turned. She could feel herself blushing. 'I'm not sure that would be proper,' she said hesitantly. 'After all, given our respective positions, Captain Yussupov . . .'

He came up the stairs towards her. 'These are exceptional circumstances, Miss Addison. And if you'll forgive me being far less than gallant, may I say that it would give me much greater pleasure to eat my last meal with a very attractive live governess than with all the dead princesses in Russia.'

He stood for a moment, two steps below her, and Marie

saw that he was younger than she had at first thought – only a year or two older than herself, at most. His face had been prematurely aged by the strain and hardship of the long fighting retreat. Looking up at her, he had the air of a school-boy asking a favour.

'In the exceptional circumstances,' she said gravely, 'I shall be pleased to accept your invitation, Captain Yussupov. But surely you will be too busy to sit down to a proper meal, with all the preparations for the battle tomorrow?'

Conscious of their proximity, Yussupov moved a couple of steps lower. 'Downstairs you see the appearance of a func-tioning military headquarters,' he explained. 'Everyone is going through the motions of preparing for battle because that's what soldiers are trained for – and because it's easier than simply sitting here and waiting for the Reds to wipe us out. In fact nobody is really doing anything useful at all.'

Marie awoke at dusk after sleeping for nine hours solid. In the familiar surroundings of her own room, she listened to the unaccustomed noises coming through the attic window. There were no children's voices; instead the sound of horses and men on the move and shouted orders drifted up to her.

Memory seeped back, filling her mind with images that made her sit up and cry, 'No!'

There was a jug of water by the large china bowl on her washstand. She used all of it and another jugful from one of the maids' rooms to get herself clean. If the family had run-ning water and a flushing toilet on the floor below, in the attic bedrooms where the servants slept such convenience would have been considered a waste of money.

Marie's own clothes were all in Irkutsk. In any case, she had no dress suitable to wear to dinner with Captain Yussupov, so she put on a clean cotton shift from one of the maids' rooms and went cautiously downstairs to the first floor in search of some appropriate clothing. In Madame Antonova's room a man in the uniform of an Imperial colonel was asleep on the bed, fully dressed and with only the collar of his tunic undone. Marie crept past him and into the dressing room. Having worn cast-off items of her employer's clothing – whose value had been deducted from her small salary – she knew that they both took the same size in dresses, gloves and shoes.

In Hollywood, stars like Mary Pickford were experimenting with the first bras and showing their knees in public; in London, fashionable socialites were wearing Liberty bodices which gave them the freedom to dance the newly discovered tango. Madame Antonova's wardrobe was of an earlier era; most of the dresses would be impossible to put on without the aid of a maid. Marie also had to discard the corsets, which would require a second pair of hands to lace them, in favour of a simple bodice. From the rail where the dresses hung, each in its linen mothproof bag, she chose a plain cream-coloured silk ball-gown with matching gloves and slippers before remembering an organdie and taffeta extravaganza that Madame Antonova had had made just before they left France and never worn. It was far from the latest fashion, being modelled on the dress worn by the girl in the picture *A Dance in Town* by the painter Auguste Renoir, who had just died in Nice.

Marie took it out of its bag and held it in front of her, to see the effect in the full-length gilt-framed mirror. The evening light made the pale lilac tint of the material, ruched and gathered from the waistline right down to the floor, glow with a luminosity of its own. Looking at herself from different angles, Marie imagined – as in the painting – a man's arm around her waist . . . Captain Yussupov's arm.

For several minutes she hesitated at the impudence of wearing such luxury. Then she thought, why not? In such exceptional circumstances, to use the captain's words, why not?

Without a maid to help, getting into the dress and fastening its myriad tiny hooks and eyes all up the back nearly defeated her. It was a relief to concentrate on the feminine details of her appearance. The effect of the dress was marred by her badly cut short hair, so she set to with a comb and a pair of scissors to tidy it as best she could.

The colonel was still asleep when she walked through the bedroom and down the stairs. At the bottom, Captain Yussupov was chatting with an officer in major's uniform, whom he presented to her as Prince Alexei Romanov, his cousin.

'*Mes hommages, Mademoiselle Addison*,' the prince said, kissing the back of Marie's gloved hand.

She felt quite dreamlike, drifting in the rustling taffeta ball-gown into the candlelit drawing room, with her hand on Yussupov's arm. The table had been set for two, with the best crystal, porcelain and silver.

Kolchak and his staff officers were eating in the dining room next door. Through the connecting doors, Marie could hear the sustained buzz of quiet conversation and the occasional burst of laughter as someone used humour to keep despondency at bay. She and Yussupov were waited on by his personal servant. The food he brought from the kitchens was looted from the Antonovs' pantry, but badly cooked. The wine was a vintage French champagne.

'No point in leaving the bubbly for the Reds to guzzle,' said Yussupov.

When the first bottle was empty, he opened another. At some point in the conversation – Marie could not remember when or how – he had asked her to call him Dimitri and equally solemnly requested permission to call her Marie.

'But if your cousin's a prince,' she said, 'then you're a prince too, surely?'

'Princes,' he laughed, 'are ten a penny in Russia, you must know that.'

He put one of the new-fashioned flat gramophone records on the turntable of the large wind-up Victrola. As the needle came down on the black surface and the Destiny Waltz began, he held a hand out in invitation to Marie.

She glided around the room in his arms. Catching sight of herself in a gilt wall-mirror, she thought, I *am* the girl in the painting.

When the music ended, they wandered out into the garden. Few men were sleeping that night. There were lights away to the north where the *bronepóyezd* sat useless on the tracks, and lanterns in the park to the east of the house where men were chopping down trees to make barricades and digging trenches. In the deserted moonlit water garden, Marie sat on the stone ledge that ran around the basin of the fountain while Yussupov recited poems in Russian by Lermontov and Turgenev, followed by some verses by Lamartine and Wordsworth in French and English.

'Poetry and violins,' Marie said softly. 'And a prince with brown eyes.'

Perhaps it was the effect of the poetry, but Yussupov's professional detachment seemed to have deserted him. He looked wistfully at Marie, as though realising the awful truth that it is always too early for a young man to die.

It was she who led him back through the moonlit garden to the house for one last waltz. At the end of the music, Yussupov left the needle scratching in the empty scrolling round the centre of the record. Looking into Marie's eyes, his lips only inches away from hers, he said, 'I'm so glad that we met in these exceptional circumstances.'

He stepped back, bowed and raised her hand to his lips. Marie pulled the hand away and slid off the lilac coloured silk glove, in order to feel the kiss on her skin.

When he straightened up and met her eyes again, the young captain looked more boyish than ever. 'This is a terrible thing to ask,' he stammered. 'I am emboldened to do so only in the knowledge that dusk will almost certainly see both of us dead.'

Marie waited for him to finish.

'I've never kissed a woman, apart from my mother and sisters. And I don't want to die, not knowing.'

It seemed to her at that moment such a small thing for a man to ask, just before going out to his death. Millions of the men slaughtered in the First World War and the civil war that followed had been virgins, but that was no reason for this one to die *not knowing*.

Marie made no resistance as he gathered her inexpertly in his embrace and lifted her face for his kisses. She felt his desire growing. Instead of pulling away, she moved closer, moulding her body to him and opening her mouth to his tongue. It did not matter to her whether his desire was for her or whether any pretty young woman would have satisfied his need. But since he could not say the words, it was she who whispered, 'Make love to me.'

There was a party of officers playing bezique in one bedroom. In another a major with bandaged head sat alone, writing a long letter that would never reach its addressee. In a third, a machine-gun team was setting up a Maxim gun at the window.

Marie led Captain Yussupov up to the second floor and into her bedroom. Their roles were now completely reversed: he seemed almost frightened at what was happening, while she felt calm and fully in control. She kissed him on the lips and put his hands on her breast and around her waist, then unbuckled his belt and unbuttoned the flap of his breeches until his flesh was in her hand.

And when he came, hot semen burning its way out of him and into her palm, Marie kissed the look of anguish from Yussupov's face. She felt a thousand years older than him: as old as the ocean receiving a river's tribute. How stupid, she thought, that people make such agony of this good comfort.

To stop him saying anything, she closed his mouth with her lips again and pulled him down onto the bed, until she was on her back with him lying over her, urgently pulling up her gown, feeling his unaccustomed way through the layers of feminine underwear and then parting her legs to thrust himself deeper and deeper into her.

She was glad that he was bigger than the *hetman*, glad that he could hurt her, make her cry out and efface for a minute the memory of the previous night. When he had finished and lay trembling on top of her, she soothed him with words a mother might use to her child.

At the first bugle call for the dawn stand-to, Yussupov struggled into his uniform. He hesitated for a second in the doorway, looking back at Marie still lying on the bed in the now crumpled lilac dress.

'You don't have to say anything,' she said.

. 5 .

The first sounds of combat came from the direction of the armoured train. This was only a diversionary feint. As Admiral Kolchak had explained in his briefing of Marie, the Reds' main thrust would be made through the parkland towards the softer target presented by the house.

Listening to the battle develop, Marie crouched on the primitive wooden bed in the coachman's room above the stables. Her face and hands were filthy with dung and soil. So was the rest of her body; after taking off the organdie and taffeta ball-gown she had tanned her skin and dyed her hair with some walnut furniture stain found in the scullery and then rolled naked in the midden before putting on a coarse and soiled shapeless woollen dress which had belonged to the coachman's daughter. Its owner, a retarded girl of eighteen, now lay beside her father in a roughly dug grave behind the stable block. On the disturbed earth lay the two men from Kolchak's bodyguard who had dug it, each with a bullet from the admiral's pistol in the nape of his neck.

Marie tried not to think about them; there was so much

horror that they were simply a part of it. As the firing grew more intense, the coughing of light and heavy machine guns contrasting with the cracking of individual rifle shots, she wondered where Captain Yussupov was and whether she would receive some spiritual message at the moment he died as lovers were supposed to do.

Resistance to the east ceased before midday. Marie heard the thudding of unshod hooves growing nearer. Some of the White defenders had hidden in the stables from which futile refuge they were hunted into the open by dismounted Reds. Oaths mingled with screams and horses' neighing as men's arms were hacked off by the Cossacks' sabres and heads were severed from bodies. Sporadic shooting continued while the survivors were being finished off, then the sounds of battle moved away in the direction of the house where the last stand was being made. Away to the north, where the armoured train was still holding out, a heliograph flashed pointless messages which no one read.

Marie whimpered and cowered away when the first Cossacks came into the room where she lay. Act for your life, the admiral had told her. She recognised the cruel faces of two of the Cossacks who had been with the *hetman* at the Japanese consul's house, but they took no notice of her. Emboldened, she ventured outside after the fighting in the stable yard ended. Men stared, but once they smelled her and heard her talking nonsense and laughing to herself like a crazed child, they crossed themselves, backed away and left her alone.

The main house was burning now. Figures could be seen inside, silhouetted against the flames as men stood up to make better targets of themselves in the hope that the Reds would take pot shots at them. The besiegers held their fire, preferring to watch their enemies burn alive or jump out of the windows as human torches to roll screaming on the ground, begging to be finished off with a *coup de grâce* that never came.

It was evening when Kolchak was brought under guard by an OGPU detachment to the stable block where Marie was huddled in a corner of the yard, muttering to herself. The political troops were cleaner than the others, having travelled to the battle in motor transport. In charge of them was a tall, blue-eyed young man whom the others addressed as 'továrisch komissár'.

He stood over the stretcher on which Kolchak lay. The admiral's face and one arm were badly burned. White bone was showing through the charred flesh where his right wrist had been, the hand having been hacked off by a sabre before he could shoot himself in the head to avoid being taken alive. The stump had been roughly cauterised by fire to stop the White commander bleeding to death.

Although obviously in agony, he was refusing to answer questions. Marie watched in horror as the commissar pistol-whipped the burned face of the man on the stretcher. At last Kolchak spoke, taunting his captors with details of the icon which they would never find.

'And why?' he yelled to the night sky. 'Because I should forfeit my soul, were I to disclose to the godless where the Virgin of Kazan is hidden.'

Deliberately the commissar placed his revolver against the elbow of the injured arm and fired a bullet into it. Kolchak's whole body spasmed, rolling off the stretcher into the dung-heap where he lay face down, twitching involuntarily until lifted and placed back on the stretcher, to be held there by four men.

'Gdyé ikóna?' Where, where, where is the icon? The same question was repeated again and again by the tall commissar, until Marie wanted to scream the answer and see the man on the stretcher put out of his misery.

Another bullet shattered Kolchak's other elbow. At last he screamed – a long, inhuman noise like the bellowing of a bull being tormented by the picadors in the ring.

'Chort vozmí!' he yelled at the man tormenting him: may the devil take you!

Agonising minutes later, the next bullet shattered the admiral's right knee-joint. A fourth blew away his left knee-cap but still the man on the stretcher defied his captors.

By now Marie was numb. She had seen and experienced so much horror during the last three days that her senses were at last suspended. She watched the continued torture without conscious emotion. When Kolchak finally died, still cursing his tormentor, just before midnight, she felt no admiration for his courage, only relief.

She heard the tall man with the red star on his cap say, 'Someone has to know where it is.'

Each time his men finished questioning a prisoner in the stable yard, another shot announced that they had drawn a blank.

The danger of which Kolchak had not warned Marie was starvation. Before decamping, the Reds had foraged for men and horses so thoroughly that there was virtually nothing edible for miles around.

She found Yussupov's body under a pile of corpses both Red and White, near the *bronepóyezd* where the fighting had been fiercest. It took all her strength to drag it free from the other bodies and heave it onto a wheelbarrow from the stable yard, on which she wheeled it back to the water garden for burial beside the fountain which now no longer ran.

There was no point in prayers; instead, she spoke a few lines from Lamartine's poem *Le Lac*, which he had recited for her in the same place, so few hours before. The words tell of a bereaved lover's thoughts as he returns alone to a lake whose beauty he once shared with his beloved, but they meant nothing to Marie. She buried the body and recited the poem because they were things that might one day have a purpose, if feeling ever returned to her life.

In the same dreamlike condition she saved the volumes in English from the piles of books that had been used by Kolchak's men instead of sandbags to build a couple of futile machine-gun nests in front of the house. Other bodies lay in small clusters, as far as the eye could see. From miles around, black crows arrived to caw and fight and peck out the dead men's eyes and tear away the soft flesh of their faces, but there was nothing that Marie could do to stop the grisly scavenging.

Early on the second day after the battle she heard hoof-beats. A squadron of Cossacks rode up to the house through the ruins of the park where all the trees had been felled. At their head, she recognised the tall man with the star on his cap. Following them the long way round came two motor lorries, bringing prisoners taken in Irkutsk whom the commissar set to work. Some dug graves and buried the bodies; others were put to digging through the ruins of the house, which were still smouldering in places where the rubble was deepest. They had with them some metal rods with which the commissar tapped the exposed flooring, listening for the echoes of a cellar that never came, for the house had been built on solid earth. Next he turned his attention to the stable block with the same result.

When they paused for their midday meal, some of the Cossacks threw scraps from their own meagre rations for the mad girl, as they called Marie. To encourage them to throw some more, she amused them by grovelling in the midden after their crusts and ate a few, thrusting the others into the pocket of her dirty skirt for later.

Becoming aware of the tall young commissar's eyes on her, she retreated into a corner of one of the loose-boxes and crouched there with her pathetically small hoard of scraps. She heard boots on the cobbles outside and did not look up when his shadow fell across the floor.

'And who might you be?' he asked.

She giggled and flinched away as the commissar walked closer and squatted beside her. He took one of her hands in his and examined it. The skin was stained and filthy, the nails were broken and there was a festering blister in the palm of her right hand where the spade had rubbed the flesh raw while she was digging Yussupov's grave.

The commissar shouted questions at her, grew angry at her silence and hit her with the back of his hand before dragging her outside. Men gathered round to see the sport.

'What do we know about this creature?' he asked them.

One of the prisoners who was a local man volunteered that he had heard of an idiot girl who had been the daughter of the coachman on the Antonov estate.

'Are you the idiot girl?' the commissar asked, thrusting his face close to Marie's.

She whimpered as his hands grasped her arms painfully hard and spat into his face when he would not let go. He released her with an oath and wiped the spittle off his face. Slowly and deliberately he drew the revolver that he had used on Admiral Kolchak and put it to her head. Marie waited for the shot. Because her feelings were frozen, locked away deep within, she experienced no fear. And when she spat, this time into his eye, it was not conscious bravado but simply the senseless act of an idiot.

His backhand swing knocked her to the ground. Dazed, Marie saw two of her teeth lying on the filthy cobbles of the stable yard, knocked out of her mouth by the pistol barrel as the blow connected. Blood dripped from her badly cut lip.

'Use her,' she heard the commissar order the watching men. 'If she knows anything, that'll make her talk.'

They objected, saying that she was an animal, not a woman – and too filthy to rape.

'Then throw her in the fountain,' he shouted at them. 'Drown the bitch if you want, but make her talk – if she can.'

Hands dragged Marie to the water garden, where they pulled off her filthy dress and threw her naked into the basin. Two men jumped in after her and held her head under water until she was nearly unconscious. Each time she surfaced, vomiting water from her lungs and stomach, she saw the pale blue eyes of the commissar watching her closely.

In the end he grew bored, mounted his horse and rode off. Most of the Cossacks followed, leaving behind only a dozen of the worst – those who were excited at the prospect of gang-raping a mad girl. Two of them held her down over the edge of the basin while the others took turns to use her now clean body for their brief pleasure. Staring down at the reflection of her own suffering face in the water, Marie submitted. It was that or have them force her face beneath the water's surface again and this time drown her for good.

Some took her one way and some the other. By the end they did not even have to hold her down. When the last man had used her, he mounted his pony and delivered a lash across Marie's buttocks with his *knout* as a farewell. The cut flesh twitched and a moan escaped Marie's bleeding lips but she did not get up.

For a long time after the Cossacks had ridden off, she lay across the stone ledge where they had left her, staring into the water. There was no more suffering on the face that stared back at her; it was as empty of emotion as that of an angel. Only the chill of evening roused her enough to turn around and sit up. The suspension of feeling now included most of her own body. There was no hunger, no cold, no soreness, no pain. She was just a mind floating in space tenuously connected with the suffering flesh by the fountain.

PART VIII
Summer 1986

.1.

Miss Addison seemed not to hear Tom's voice. Her lips were clamped tightly shut and her eyes darted left and right as though she were seeing the events of which she had been talking more clearly than the present. He wondered whether he had pushed her too far into the trauma of the past. Receiving no reply to his questions whether she was all right, he turned out the oil lamp and left her alone with the cats and her memories.

Outside, the clean night air – only a few degrees above zero – was like a cold shower after the fetid stench of the tack room. Sitting in the Lada, Tom watched the dawn come up. A dozen or so mares with their foals were grazing not far off, with rabbits hopping between them and stopping every so often to sit bolt upright as though listening to the dawn chorus of birdsong coming from an isolated clump of trees. It seemed impossible that such an idyllic scene had been the setting for the violence and bloodshed of Kolchak's last stand. Then a long goods train of a hundred wagons or more trundled across the horizon on the very rails where the admiral's *bronepóyezd* had broken down. Birdsong was replaced by the distant snarling, squealing and clattering of the train's old-fashioned linkages as it rolled on its slow way eastwards to Irkutsk. Disturbed, the rabbits went to ground and the ponies galloped away, with the foals racing after the mares in their effort to keep up.

Until the last battery ran out, Tom listened and re-listened to the tape of Miss Addison's account, cross-checking all the details he could with his and Rada's research on the fighting around Irkutsk. Searching through the rubbish at the bottom of his briefcase, he found some stale biscuits which tasted musty but they were all he had, so he ate them and drank the last of the mineral water before going back to the stable block.

Passing by the dried-up fountain, he walked over the grave without noticing it; the mound had long since sunk level with the surrounding earth. Only a rough wooden Orthodox cross told him that a body lay beneath his feet. He picked up the broken-off lower cross member and traced with a fingertip the indentations where someone had burned a name into the wood with a red-hot poker; the combined effects of time and weather made it impossible to decipher.

At some point during the night the cats had gone out to hunt, leaving Miss Addison alone in the tack room.

'Thank you for talking to me,' Tom said gently. 'Your eyewitness account has been extraordinarily helpful. I hope it was not too hurtful, reviving all those memories.'

Noticing that she was shivering, he pulled the shawls up over her shoulders and put a blanket over her knees, then filled the blackened kettle at the pump over the sink, only to find that the stove had gone out and there was no other way of heating water to make her a cup of tea.

'No,' she said, when he started to relight the fire with some kindling. It was the first word she had uttered for several hours. 'The stove's temperamental. Two of the village women will be here at noon, bringing my rations for the week. Better leave it for them to do.'

Tom sat down beside her. He was certain that the gist of her story was true, and equally certain that she had left many gaps in the narrative, either from a desire to conceal the truth or just the natural confusion of memory in the very elderly.

'Don't think me hostile,' he said, 'but my job as a historian is to get at the truth – and you haven't told me the whole truth yet, have you?'

'Haven't I?'

'For example, I find it a little hard to believe that you could act the part of a mad girl so convincingly.'

'I didn't have to act all the time,' she said simply. 'I think I was genuinely mad for quite a long while after the Reds left. I'd seen children whom I knew shot in front of my eyes, their blood spilling on my clothes. I'd killed a man with my own hands and watched another being tortured to death. And all that other business . . .'

She shook her head. 'For several months I *was* Olga Timofeyevna Akhmanova. But for the memory of those hours with Captain Yussupov, I think I should have drowned in a sea of misery.'

Tom was about to call her bluff. The cheap romance she had spun him about her night of love was transparently fictional. And yet, it had kept her sane – or helped her regain her sanity. So did it matter whether it were true or not?

'Akhmanov!' he exclaimed. 'That's the name on the cross. And yet you say that the body you buried was that of Captain Yussupov.'

'I could hardly put the name of a Tsarist officer on the cross. And I needed . . . not an alibi but a reason for staying here. They took me away, you know. Three times I was locked up in a mental hospital but each time I escaped and walked back to Borzhoi, pretending that the grave was my father's . . .'

'The coachman's?'

'. . . and that I was obsessed with tending it. In the end they left me alone here.'

'And what was the real reason you kept coming back here?'

'Where could I go?' she asked rhetorically. 'Even after the Civil War had ended, where could I seek refuge, Mr Fielding? Do you think I was in any condition to walk two thousand miles across the mountains and the Gobi Desert to the nearest British officials in Peking?'

In London, Tom had interviewed many White Russian émigrés introduced to him by Brodsky. Men, women and children had walked as far as 2,000 miles from Russian garrison towns on the Amur River to safety in Shanghai after the Revolution. Some had been robbed of all their possessions by bandits; others had been fed by penniless peasants and nursed back to health by them when they fell ill on the journey. But none had travelled alone. A single girl of nineteen trying to cross the Gobi would either have died of thirst and hunger on the way or been enslaved by a tribe of nomads.

'Was that the real reason?' Tom asked.

When she stayed silent, he tried another angle: 'The commissar. I need to know more about him. You described him as being young, tall and thin, with blue eyes. Did you hear anyone use his name?'

She shuddered. 'They called him *továrisch komissár*, you know. The Reds didn't use personal names very much.'

'But did anyone call him by name? Please try and remember.'

Miss Addison turned her face away.

'Please,' said Tom, misinterpreting the gesture. 'This is important.'

'Kolchak knew him,' she said at last. 'At the time I wondered how a Tsarist admiral and a Bolshevik commissar could know each other. Yet there was a horrible intimacy between them and Kolchak knew the man's name some-how.'

'Perhaps the commissar had been in the navy before the Revolution?' Tom suggested.

Miss Addison was not listening to him. She still had her head turned away, as though to catch the echoes of the dying man's agony. 'It was the last thing the poor admiral said when they were torturing him on that stretcher out there. He screamed, "In the name of the Virgin of Kazan I pray God to curse you, Sergei Nikolaievich Sibirsky – you and your children and your children's children – for what you have done this day!" And then he died.'

There was now only one piece missing from the puzzle. 'If it's any comfort to you,' Tom said, 'I happen to know that Commissar Sibirsky was arrested and executed in Stalin's great purge of 1937, so I suppose you could say that the curse worked in his case.'

'Now that was a terrible man, Mr Fielding.'

'Stalin?'

'Sibirsky.'

Tom stood up and stretched his cramped limbs. 'There's one other thing I'd like to clear up, Miss Addison.'

'I'm tired.'

'Just one thing,' Tom promised. 'Then I'll leave you alone. When you arrived at Borzhoi after your ride through the night, Kolchak told you, quote I view your arrival here as an act of God, for you are the one person under my command at this moment who can carry out a mission of the utmost importance, unquote. That was a strange thing for a military commander to say to a young girl just before making his last stand against overwhelming odds. What was the mission he entrusted to you?'

Miss Addison started whimpering, her mouth twitching, and covered the movements of her lips with one bony hand while the other tried to hide her eyes from him. For a second Tom saw Olga Timofeyevna Akhmanova in the flesh; Marie

Helen Addison was an actress trapped in the part she had played to perfection for the last seventy years.

Very gently he pulled the gnarled old hands away from her face and held them until she was calm.

'It's all right,' he repeated. 'We'll do this another way. I'll tell you what I think happened and all you have to do, is nod your head if I'm correct. Have you got that?'

'Yes,' she whispered.

'When you arrived here that morning, Kolchak knew that there was no escape for him or his men. There was however one important duty he still had to perform. All over Russia, millions of icons were being destroyed on Lenin's orders. In Kolchak's care was perhaps the most valuable of all. To save it from the iconoclasts, he could have simply buried it and killed off the witnesses. But if he hoped that one day the Whites would be back and Russia once again a Christian state, he'd want to make sure the icon could be recovered by posterity – a course of action which necessitated trusting one person with the secret of its hiding place. Am I getting warm?'

Miss Addison gave no reaction, so Tom continued. 'When you came along, Kolchak realised that a young woman as brave and resourceful as you had proved yourself to be, would have a better chance of escaping interrogation under torture than any man in his retinue. So he either showed or told you where the Virgin of Kazan was hidden and then rehearsed you how to act the part of the coachman's daughter.'

Miss Addison turned her head away again.

'Where did Kolchak hide the icon?' Tom asked. 'Not in the open, for there were too many pairs of watching eyes. Not in the main house, for that was thoroughly searched afterwards – the rubble was sifted shovelful by shovelful, I think you said. And yet it must be hidden somewhere on this estate. Why otherwise would the coachman and his idiot daughter have been killed to give you an identity that would enable you to stay here?'

Tom followed Miss Addison's eye line. One of the cats had just jumped onto the old cast-iron stove, which was cold now. The base of the stove, he saw, was raised slightly off the floor on a thick flagstone which stood proud of the others.

.2.

I felt like shouting, 'Eureka!' but I didn't want to alarm
Miss Addison so I kept my voice quiet.

'Is that why you allowed the fire to go out?' I asked.
'Because you couldn't tell me any other way after all these
years of silence?'

She did not reply, nor take any notice when I walked to
the stove, wrapped my arms around it and heaved it slowly
sideways. If it was hard to shift for one man on his own,
the stone on which it stood must have taken all the strength
of Kolchak's two bodyguards to move with lifting tackle,
seventy years before. In the interim, it seemed to have
become of a piece with the flags beneath. I sweated and
grunted with exertion but could not lift it or slide it in any
direction, no matter how hard I tried.

In the back of the Lada I found a torch, two tyre levers
and a jack. The flag yielded to the tyre levers sufficiently
for me to wedge a log underneath, which in turn made it
possible to slide the jack into position and raise the heavy
slab a few inches. Then I could see the problem. Beneath

the flagstone yawned a circular well shaft; several rusted metal pegs had been cemented into the underside of the stone to key it in position, so that the only plane in which it could be moved was vertical.

With the jack at the limit of its extension, I wedged more logs in place, to bear the weight in case it should slip, then inched my head and shoulders towards the hole. The batteries in the torch were nearly flat but in its faint beam I could see the rungs of a rusty iron ladder descending the brick-lined shaft on one side, while on the other a narrow lead pipe ran up to the pump in the sink. If Commissar Sibirsky had not been a town-dweller, he might have wondered where the water in the sink came from.

With the torch gripped in my mouth to leave both hands free, I wriggled into the narrow gap beneath the flagstone until I got stuck and could move neither forward nor back. I panicked with the realisation that any further movement might dislodge the logs and allow the flagstone to fall and crush me. Miss Addison had gone outside to sit in the sun with her cats; in any case there was nothing a frail old woman could have done to help.

From my climbing days I remembered an old cavers' trick and concentrated on relaxing my tense chest muscles and breathing out as far as I could to reduce the thickness of the ribcage. At last I slipped through the narrow gap, only to find myself with another problem. I was hanging on to the ladder with both hands, head down at the top of the shaft while the weight of my legs twisted them through 180 degrees! My feet scrabbled for purchase and found the rungs of the ladder. Chest heaving from the exertion, I nearly dropped the torch and caught it just in time with one hand while the other clung to a rung for support.

When my breathing was more or less back to normal, I shone the torch downwards and saw below only the black surface of the water. Had I guessed wrong, after all?

The rungs of the ladder were cold and scaly with rust,

*but it felt solid enough. I started to climb down and
continued until – maybe ten metres below the floor of the
tack room – I found myself looking into a small, brick-lined
gallery that led off the main shaft of the well. I knew what
it was: an ice well – a pre-electricity cold store where large
blocks of ice cut in winter would last throughout much of
the long, hot Siberian summer.*

*For Kolchak it had made the ideal place to hide the
treasure.*

*At that second I wasn't certain what I was looking at,
of course. A part of my mind was wondering how much
oxygen there was down there – and how long the batteries
would hold out. Then I realised that the large, dusty box in
front of me was a brassbound military chest of drawers
that split into two halves for easier carrying. On the inlaid
brass nameplate was inscribed in Cyrillic script: A.V.
Kolchak. I had found the admiral's travelling chest!*

*I could see in the dim light of the torch that my hands
were trembling as I pulled open the top drawer. It was full
of maps covered in arrows with dates and notes in red ink –
presumably written by Kolchak's own hand. The second
drawer contained clothing. In the third was a loaded,
grease-packed Colt .45 revolver, Kolchak's signed Last Will
And Testament and a large leather pouch containing
jewellery – which I supposed to be the final remnants of the
Whites' treasury. The other drawers were stuffed with
documents. There were movement orders, copies of
despatches in code and en clair – and more maps marked in
the same faded red ink, plus Kolchak's own private diary.*

*The chest was a historian's dream, a time capsule that
could open up the entire eastern front of the Civil War
for modern study. I wasn't sure whether my difficulty
in breathing was from the poor air or the almost
overwhelming excitement at what I had found.*

*I had forgotten all about the icon until I knocked it over
by accident. It had been leaning against the back of the*

chest, wrapped with military neatness in layers of oilskin.
When I undid the string and peeled back the oilskin I saw
the face of the Virgin of Kazan, with the same scaled-down
man-child leering on her lap as in the copy that hung on the
wall of Arkady Sergeyevich's apartment in far-off Moscow.

The light went out. I shook the torch but it made no
difference, so I wrapped the icon up again by touch, shut
all the drawers and climbed back up the ladder in total
darkness. I squeezed through the gap below the flagstone
and stood in the old tack room, taking deep breaths and
feeling not so much high as stunned by the importance of
my find. I had come looking for an icon and found the
Holy Grail.

Recalling Miss Addison's warning that someone was due to
bring her week's rations at midday, Tom lowered the flagstone and heaved the stove back into its usual place, refitting
the old iron stove-pipe and rubbing grime into the scratch
marks made when sliding the stove across the floor.

The noise of metal scraping on stone woke Miss Addison
from her doze in the sun. She hobbled back into the tack
room and asked Tom when he was going to come back for
the icon. He told her that he had not decided.

'There's a pistol down there, Mr Fielding,' she said. 'It
belonged to the admiral, you know. He said it might be more
use to me than ever it would be to him, but he was wrong.
The poor man could have shot himself, if he had kept it. Do
you suppose it still works?'

Tom knew nothing about firearms, and told her so, wondering what was on her mind.

'My cats,' she said. 'I don't think I shall live through
another winter. So if I'm not here when you come back for
the icon, will you put them down for me? I wouldn't want
them to suffer after I'm gone.'

It seemed easier to say yes than to find an excuse.

Miss Addison looked up into Tom's face. 'D'you know,

Mr Fielding, I feel most wonderfully relieved. The burden is yours now. Thank you so much for coming.'

From 'Would you like a cup of tea?' to 'Thank you for coming,' Miss Addison had spanned the gamut of polite Edwardian English conversation.

On the return journey to Irkutsk, Tom diverted north and south, deliberately adding kilometres to make it harder for anyone to work out the radius of his trip. After hitting the metalled road, he detached the leads from two of the spark plugs and limped back to the airport on two cylinders, returning the Lada with complaints about the condition of the roads, the maintenance of the vehicle and Irkutsk in general. Accustomed to dissatisfied clients, the beautiful Kirghiz girl behind the counter waited for this tirade to end before asking calmly, 'Apart from all that, did you have a good trip, comrade?'

Soviet long-distance lines were always busy, occupied with priority calls on Party and KGB business. Informed by the local operator that his booked call to Rada would come through in two days, Tom changed the number and gave that of Ivanov's office. In less than an hour he was put through. The tinny quality of the line made the voice at the other end sound as though Ivanov was sitting inside a dustbin.

Tom asked him to do a favour and call Rada to tell her that he was catching the evening flight back to Moscow and would see her at their apartment in the morning.

'She won't be there,' was the reply.

'What's wrong?'

'Nothing's wrong. She's in hospital. You're a father, Feldink. Congratulations!'

'Are you disappointed it's not a boy?' Rada asked. She looked tired but blissful.

I shook my head. 'How could I be disappointed?'

'A Russian husband would be.'

'I've told you before, I'm not Russian.'

'Do you think she looks like me?'

Frankly, the infant swaddled in Rada's arms looked to me like all the other babies in the ward. 'Just like you,' I said.

'I want to call her Svetlana. Svetlana Tomasovna, is that all right? Or do you want to give her a Western name?'

'Svetlana is beautiful,' I said. 'She's a Russian girl. She should have a Russian name.'

'I'm so tired,' Rada said. 'It went on a long time.'

I squeezed her hand and promised to come back and see her the next day, then slumped on a bench in the corridor outside the ward. The twelve-hour flight from Irkutsk had included three hungry and thirsty hours on the ground at Novosibirsk while parts were unbolted from another aircraft and used as spares to get the Moscow flight airborne again. For the last three-hour leg of the trip I had sat in the gangway after giving up my seat to a pregnant peasant woman, travelling to Moscow for hospital treatment.

Throughout the flight I had been slowly coming to a decision which the sight of my daughter in Rada's arms confirmed. Like Kolchak and Miss Addison before me, I was now the guardian of the icon. To recover it after all the years it had been hidden and then simply sell it to the highest bidder would make a mockery of all the suffering that had kept the Virgin of Kazan safe for so long.

How had Kolchak's curse been worded? '. . . on you and your children and your children's children.'

Although I wasn't superstitious, it seemed that selling the icon would be tempting fate to betray me – and Rada and the child.

The decision meant that I should also have to leave all the admiral's papers at the bottom of the well. For a historian that was a hard pill to swallow, but it was the price that had to be paid.

It would mean confessing failure to Rada, but she was unlikely to grill me in her condition. As to Sibirsky, he had spent so many years himself looking for the icon that he could hardly complain at my failure. And Ivanov? Well, it rather suited me that he should think me incompetent.

Once my mind was made up, I felt very peaceful and fell asleep on the bench in the hospital corridor, despite all the comings and goings. I woke to find Ivan Petrovich shaking me. He had a large bouquet of flowers and beside him stood Arkady Sergeyevich. For a moment I could not understand what they were doing there. In the dream, the mother of my newborn child had been Karen. It was a long while since I had been able to recall her face but as I woke up it was so clear and so real in my mind's eye that I could not place either Ivanov or Sibirsky for a moment.

Dear Fran,

You're right, Etna is all I dreamed it would be! And you're right also that I was leaving something out of my recent letters. It's a guy, of course . . .

I don't know what you'd make of Luigi. I've known him since my first trip to Sicily, but only as the handsome, rather aloof but always charming, head of the Italian side of the team. A typical Mediterranean boss, I thought, flirting with the girls, collecting all the kudos for the work we do, always dressed like a movie star, driving expensive cars and arriving with politicians or press people in tow.

And now he tells me that he was shy of me! He wanted to get to know me before but couldn't find an opportunity until I was (for one night) the senior person on the British side. He invited me to dinner at the villa where he stays on the coast outside Taormina. It's owned by some rich relative of his, I can't untangle Italian families – a cousin of an aunt by marriage, something like that. The rest of us have rooms in local hotels, but Luigi has to do it in style.

He'd said something about discussing the method of classifying gas samples, so I arrived at the villa by taxi staggering under the weight of two seasons' crop of computer print-out. Luigi looked quite baffled, poor man.

He had omitted to mention that there would be about twenty other people there, plus a small orchestra playing in the garden and servants carrying trays of drinks. The guests were all in evening dress, the women covered in jewellery. And there's me wearing beach sandals and a cotton sundress – it's pretty hot here even at night right now. I felt like the girl in the bra commercial who forgets to put her dress on, i.e. ever so slightly under-dressed.

So what did Luigi do? Disappeared for a moment and came back in a shirt and shorts. He abandoned the party and drove me to a restaurant in his red Alfa. (He has another, white one on the mainland.) We ate by candlelight at a beach restaurant with guys dressed as fishermen singing at the tables and playing mandolins. I was still trying to talk about sample sites and spectrum analysis over the *antipasti*. He didn't say much, just looked and looked. By the start of the main course even I realised he wasn't interested in talking shop.

'Tomorrow,' he said, putting his hand on mine. 'Tomorrow we shall discuss all that. Tonight we shall talk about you.'

I didn't eat much and we drank a couple of bottles of local white wine with the meal. The moonlight, the music . . . well, you can guess the rest. We ended up back at the villa. The party was still going on but we crept into his wing of the house like two kids at summer camp – giggling, on tiptoe and holding our shoes in our hands!

In the morning we seemed to have the whole villa to ourselves. God knows where everyone else was. The place was like a film set: white pillars, bougainvillea everywhere, the pool sparkling above the blue of the sea.

Luigi made some excuse about having to fly back to Bologna that morning and I thought, oh well. Imagine my surprise, as we used to say, when I got a call in my hotel room that evening: when could we meet again?

Maybe you'll disapprove, because he's married of course. I always said I'd never fool around with a married man, but here I am, spending two nights a week with a lover almost old enough to be my father. Luigi has two teenage kids and a wife he'll never leave. Your sister's a scarlet woman, Fran. You see why I didn't write earlier? Put down in black and white, the tale diminishes in the telling.

Am I in love with him? I really don't know, but I feel very good. And what does he feel about me? Almost every day when he's not here, he calls. But does he and do I? Somehow we never get around to the sort of conversation where you have to tell lies – which suits me fine. Do you understand?

Write me soon.

Love, K

.3.

Ivanov was a Muscovite to the core, as uneasy away from the capital as a Madison Avenue man in Minnesota or a Cockney in Cornwall. 'You must be crazy,' was his reaction.

'I've always wanted to do this,' Tom argued. 'Don't forget I've spent years researching events which took place on the complex of lines that make up the Trans-Siberian railway, without ever taking the train myself. It's about time I knew what it was like.'

'You should stay here. Rada may be trying to reach you.'

'That's the point,' Tom argued. 'With her and Svetlana in Washington for the next fortnight, maybe longer, now's the best time for me to make the trip. You don't think Rada will mind missing this little adventure, do you?'

Ivanov chuckled at the idea of a girl dressed as smartly as Rada wanting to sit on a dirty old train with Tom for a whole week when she could fly to Vladivostok in eight hours long-haul and have only a crease in her skirt to show for it.

Tom picked up the stamped and signed *própusk* from the

KGB office in Kuznetsky Most later that day. The travel permit authorised Comrade Feldink, Tomas Mikhailovich to leave his place of work for the purpose of travelling to Vladivostok via rail.

There were two hours before the train was due to depart. Back at the apartment he dressed for the journey in a cheap anorak and a pair of Polish fake-Levi jeans. For once he checked his appearance in a mirror and wondered whether, by some osmosis, he could at last be mistaken for a Russian.

'I think you could,' he murmured to the man in the glass, who agreed.

The postcard from Leningrad sitting in the mail-box when he had got back from taking Rada and Svetlana to the airport with Arkady Sergeyevich had read simply, 'Thanks for everything. Having a great time. Mischa.'

In the steam-room at the baths, an almost unrecognisable Brodsky had been waiting. Sporting a neat goatee beard and moustache, he looked as though he had shed several pounds during the hours he had been there. He slipped into Tom's hand a small piece of paper, but was so nervous that he fumbled and dropped the towel held modestly round his waist. Blushing pink with embarrassment all over his hairless chest, he snatched the towel up off the wet floor, before vanishing into the steam without a word, to leave Tom looking at the where and when of the long-awaited meeting with Ponsonby.

With a temporary moustache and short-back-and-sides haircut making him look unwittingly more than ever like his predecessor, Captain Trevor Barton, Ponsonby had been suffused with the excitement of what he called *the Big One*. He had welcomed Tom to the safe apartment with a rugby hug and nearly kissed him: 'This is it, dear boy. We have the Go.'

They drank a bottle of Johnny Walker Black Label between them during the all-night briefing which included a short lesson in how to use a Minox 8mm camera, small enough to be concealed in the palm of Tom's hand.

'The forwarding arrangement is for film,' Ponsonby had

stressed. 'So, if Viktor tries to give you any original documents, copy them on the spot or as soon as you can afterwards – then get rid of them. Understood?'

The only other equipment was a battered old fibre suitcase of a type that could be bought in any second-hand market in Russia. Lifting it, Tom was surprised by the weight, most of which was due to the alterations to the case that Ponsonby demonstrated with schoolboy glee. They included a false top and bottom for the money, and an incendiary device which would destroy both the suitcase and its contents if anyone else attempted to open the inner compartment.

The Trans-Siberian was the longest journey in the world without customs or security checks. 'So why all the James Bond gadgetry?' Tom asked.

'Because the auditors insist, dear boy.'

'The auditors?' It didn't seem real.

Ponsonby patted the case. 'There's $500,000 in there. Over the years we've had a few instances of cash grabbed on the way to rendezvous by muggers. Now the internal auditors insist on every courier taking reasonable precautions.'

In the crowded Metro, Tom could not resist repeatedly leaning down to touch the handle of the suitcase and make sure it was still on the floor beside his feet. The old adrenaline-trip was as strong as on that first time in GUM: his brain raced as though someone were feeding him pure oxygen through an invisible tube. He scanned the faces of the other passengers, to see whether any were familiar; the surveillance had dwindled to a few days each month and usually Tom could pick out his followers, if he bothered to look for them. Most of the people in the carriage were pale-skinned Muscovites, silently avoiding each other's eyes, apparently glued to their copies of *Pravda* and *Izvestia*, but when Tom came up out of the Metro at the Yaroslavl station – the western terminus from which the Trans-Siberian trains start on their 10,000-kilometre journey to the Pacific Ocean – it seemed that every one of the national groups which made up the USSR had sent some representatives to the chaotic assembly which filled the main concourse.

Brown, white and yellow skins jostled each other; European clothing rubbed against Asiatic robes and quilted *bushláty* from Siberia; voices clamoured in a hundred different languages, most of them totally incomprehensible to a Russian; children, wide-eyed with excitement at being in the capital, sat side by side with grandparents tired out by days of travelling. Whole families perched or lay on their piles of baggage so that the overall effect was like some enormous ongoing refugee camp. High above the throng of travellers, huge smoke-grimed glass chandeliers dangled from the vault but did little to light the enormous space.

'*Vnimánie!* Look where you're going!' The shout came from a family of three generations of Crimean Tartars who were making their own way home from Uzbekistan after half a century of exile: Stalin's revenge for the way some of their people had welcomed the *Wehrmacht* as liberators from Moscow's yoke in 1942. Caught between ill-matched train connections, or maybe just too exhausted to continue the week-long journey in 'hard' class without sleeping for a few hours lying down, they had staked a claim to an area of floor space by arranging their entire worldly belongings into a rough stockade within which they sat, sawing slices off oily salamis and carving chunks from enormous loaves of black bread as if they were eating the evening meal in the kitchen at home. An old man lay snoring in one corner; in another twin babies suckled at their mother's breasts.

'*Izvenítye.*' Tom side-stepped past the impromptu barricade and made his way through the throng to the platform where the train known as *Rossiya No. 1* was waiting to depart. *Rossiya No. 2* did the journey in reverse direction, east to west. Since the entire trip took seven days, there were at any one time a total of fourteen *Rossiya* trains on the line. Most, like this one, were composed of twenty green carriages, each embellished with a plaque bearing a golden hammer and sickle on a yellow globe. It stretched away along the platform to where a brutish VL80 (Vladimir Lenin class) electric locomotive was being coupled on at the front. In each carriage were coal-fired samovars that would provide tea throughout the journey. The primitive refreshment arrangements made the train seem almost alive as it shuddered from the coupling, belching smoke and farting steam into the fuggy atmosphere of the station.

At the door of his carriage, Tom was stopped by a pair of officious women in Air Force blue uniforms. The two unsmiling *provódniki* could have auditioned for the parts of the ugly sisters without make-up. The stout middle-aged one had a mass of peroxide blonde hair which had an odd greenish tint to it. The younger one – who looked little older than a schoolgirl – had a bad case of facial acne. The older one took Tom's ticket and held it suspiciously with fingers whose nails were covered in several layers of chipped bright red varnish.

'Where is the rest of your group?' she demanded sternly.

'I'm travelling alone,' Tom replied.

'Alone?' She eyed him up and down like a detective about to arrest a child molester, then jerked her head in permission to climb aboard. The empty two-berth compartment that had been reserved for him smelled of unwashed feet and garlic from the previous occupants. As the train swayed its way out of the station and across the points, heading for Kazan and all the immensities of Russia and Siberia beyond, drizzle slashed lines of water down the dirty window. On the other side of the glass, the cloned apartment blocks and factories looked bleaker and more depressing than usual.

To allow some less tainted air into the compartment, Tom jammed the door open with his foot until told to shut it by the senior *provódnik*.

'Why?' he asked.

'Regulations,' she glared, daring him to contradict her.

'Then please open the window.' It was locked; he could see the key dangling on her belt.

'*Nyet*,' she said.

'Regulations?' he guessed.

'*Da.*'

She was the epitome of the petty bureaucrat who made everyday life in Russia into an obstacle race. If he defied her, he risked getting nothing to drink for the entire journey and probably no blankets either – for the *provódniki* controlled all refreshment and bedding.

Tom gave way gracefully. '*Izvenítye*,' he said solemnly. 'Forgive me, I didn't know. This is my first time on the Trans-Sib, comrade.'

'Well, you know now,' she smirked.

How much to give in Russia, was something Tom had never worked out. Usually he let Rada take care of bribes; like most Russians, she seemed to know within a kopeck the right amount in roubles or dollars to slip to anyone from whom she wanted a service.

Tom held out a $5 bill.

'What's this for?' the *provódnik* asked suspiciously. It was illegal for Soviet citizens to possess foreign notes or coins, which did not stop dollars circulating clandestinely as a parallel currency.

He gestured to the empty bunk. 'I'd like to be alone.'

'Why?' The one-word question contained all the Russians' suspicion of anyone who desired privacy – there was not even an adequate translation for the word in their language.

Tom patted the bulging briefcase. 'I have a lot of work to do.'

She crumpled the note and sniffed it. Some people thought that forged dollars smelled fresher. As it vanished into her pocket, she muttered, 'I'll see what I can do, comrade.'

An hour after leaving the greyness of Moscow, the train rumbled into the outskirts of a small town in bright sunshine and Tom found himself looking out onto a forest of blue and gilded spires and domes. Sparkling in the sunlight, they were crowned with golden crosses and studded with glittering stars. This was Zagorsk, the religious capital of Russia and headquarters of the Orthodox Church. Tom wondered what the iconoclast Commissar Sibirsky had thought of the sight when he saw the glittering domes and crosses each time he travelled on the Trans-Sib, which was the only fast way of getting to Irkutsk in those days.

There was a knock at the door. Tom opened it to find the peroxide *provódnik*, holding a blanket. Instead of the frown she had been wearing when he climbed aboard, she gave him a startling smile which transformed her hard face into that of a jolly games mistress, strict but essentially good-humoured. The smile revealed several black metal crowns among her teeth, which rather spoiled the effect.

'Anything else you want,' she said in a friendly voice. 'Just let me know.'

After she had gone, Tom made up the lower bunk and lay down, suddenly assailed by doubts. There were all the small operational worries about recognition, checking whether the man he was to meet might be under surveillance and so on – but they were dwarfed by the Big One, to use Ponsonby's own phrase. If the material involved this time was worth half a million dollars, the penalty for being caught with it would be equally big-time.

The timing of the mission could not have been more inconvenient. Sibirsky's main day-to-day problem had been diagnosed as arrhythmia. Since in the USSR only members of the Politburo qualified for pacemakers, Rada had taken him to the US to have one implanted. They had taken Svetlana, now two years old, with them for the trip.

What kind of father am I? Tom asked himself. A labour camp would unquestionably be the death of Sibirsky, for no camp doctor would bother about replacing batteries in the pacemaker of a condemned *zak*. Just as surely, even a few years in a camp would destroy Rada's youthful beauty for ever. And what about Svetlana? What kind of life would a two-year-old child have in the Gulag?

And then the moment of sanity was lost as he heard a knock on the door of his compartment and another dose of adrenaline surged through his brain, blocking all reason.

In the corridor stood the *provódnik* with a glass of scalding black tea in her hand. Tom thanked her, closed the door and sipped the tea, watching the flat landscape flash past: vast, unhedged collective fields, clumps of woodland, small villages unchanged since before the Revolution. As Lenin had said in a rare moment of humanity, it was the most boring landscape in the world.

The choice, Tom knew, was his. There was nothing to stop him getting off at the next stop, taking the train back to Moscow and dumping Ponsonby's suitcase – money and all – in the Moskva River. Or he could walk into Ivanov's office and earn Brownie points by offering to betray the man called Viktor, to whom he owed no loyalty.

But he knew he would do none of those things. The fact was that he felt more alive since reading the brief alert message on the postcard from Leningrad than he had since he first came to Russia. The core of him wanted not out, but in – all the way, cost what it may.

Like a gambler or addict, Tom apologised mentally to Rada and his daughter: *This time, I swear, will be the last.*

His eyes kept straying back to the underside of the bunk above his head, where the suitcase lay. At the briefing, he had allowed Ponsonby to convince him the auto-destruction device was a good idea. Now he was not so certain. In the event that some officious functionary insisted on opening the case, it would be easier to try and talk his way out of having half a million dollars illicitly in his possession than to face the responsibility for having burned, maimed or possibly blinded a servant of the state. Apart from any other consideration, the penalty for that was death.

'Fuck the auditors!' Tom said in English. 'At least I can make one sane decision.'

I stood up and disarmed the incendiary mechanism.

At the briefing which Ponsonby had delivered so concisely and smoothly in the safe apartment, everything had sounded straightforward and organised, but the truth was that for the joe at the sharp end even the most routine run could lead to disaster. It was all very well for Ponsonby, who risked nothing, to make promises like, 'After this, we'll get you out, Tom. Home for Christmas, as the man said.'

Had that been a Freudian slip? I wondered. In the safe apartment, the reference had escaped me; there were too many other things to absorb. Now I recalled the phrase as being Field Marshal Sir John French's promise at the start of the 1914–18 War. Most of the poor fools who had believed the field marshal were dead before Christmas and the unwounded survivors did not come home for four interminably long years.

There had been no time during the briefing to ask exactly what arrangements had been made for my return home. Was 'home' the sinecure in some provincial English university I had been promised that night on the downs in Bristol, or was it life with Rada and Svetlana in Moscow? Thinking in those terms, I knew that I could not leave them behind. Perhaps Ponsonby could arrange for them to come too?

And what about myself? Was I certain that I wanted to go back to Britain? Despite the inefficiency, the frustrations and limitations on personal freedom that Russians took for granted, I had become used to living in Moscow. Even the occasional clumsy surveillance no longer bothered me; it seemed to confirm that I was a part of things.

Ivanov used to joke half-apologetically: 'We have to train the new boys somehow.'

In an indefinable way I now felt more at home in Russia than I could ever remember feeling in Britain. It was something to do with the fact that, having ensconced myself in Soviet society – and not in some insulated enclave for foreigners – every day's living was an achievement. Each meal, each item of clothing purchased, even a book had value because it cost effort.

Just after Rada and I moved into our apartment, the concierge said to me, 'Comrade Feldink, I've heard that, in the West, one can buy anything in the shops. Is that true?'

'If you have the money,' I replied.

'How boring,' she said. 'Never any surprises.'

I knew what she meant. The truth was that, for someone as privileged as I was by virtue of being Sibirsky's son-in-law, life in Russia was different from living in the West but not worse. So where did I belong? It was a question I had not addressed for a long time.

To oblige me the provódnik locked the compartment with her key at dinner-time so that I did not have to worry about my luggage. From a corner seat in the restaurant car, I could see the door while I ate my plateful of a mess called 'bifsteks' – slices of anonymous meat with mashed potatoes and a tasteless gravy.

Afterwards, I walked along the corridor – never too far away from my compartment – in order to stretch my legs. I wondered, not for the first time, at the passivity of the Soviet masses. It was as though the swirling throng of heterogeneous people who had pushed and shoved their way aboard with all their belongings at the Yaroslavl station had been tranquillised by some potent bromide in the tea that came out of the samovars on Rossiya No. 1. The 'hard' class passengers sat staring blankly out of the windows; in the 'soft' class compartments the more privileged travellers sprawled, fast asleep on seats and bunks. Only a few children playing in the corridors seemed not to be drugged.

I returned to my compartment to find the door unlocked. Startled, I yanked it open to see that the peroxide provódnik was in the act of remaking the bed. After getting rid of her, I wondered whether her attentions were going to cause complications later on.

.4.

Of all the many alternative routeings between Moscow and Vladivostok, the longest was the one on Tom's ticket. Adding more than 1,000 kilometres to the journey, it diverged from the direct route near the city of Kuibyshev and ran south-east under the name Trans-Turan as far as Tashkent. Clattering over the catch-points as they came into the outskirts of the Uzbek capital, Tom tried to listen to the commentary on the train's PA system.

'Population over two million . . . industries include manufacture of mining machinery, textiles, leather goods . . .'

The noise of the points ensured that few passengers could hear the complete commentary. While the train skirted what had been the shores of the Sea of Aral – now reduced by ill-advised irrigation schemes to two shrinking, polluted lakes – Tom had chatted in the restaurant car to a German railway buff. According to him, the noise problem was due to outdated couplings between the carriages: Russian railway design was fifty years or more behind Western technology in this area. Monitoring his own shifting allegiances, Tom had been aware of a temptation to retort that Russian rockets were a great improvement on the original German models.

Looking out of the window on the remote chance of seeing Tamurlaine's tomb, he thought how proud Commissar Sibirsky would have been of the Party-line commentary. Arkady Sergeyevich's father must have travelled on the same tracks if he had been able to describe to his son first-hand the great tourist attraction of the city.

There was no mention on the PA of the brilliant crippled Mongol leader who defeated the Golden Horde and sacked Delhi, or that the city had only been Russian since 1865. Nor was there any whisper of the earthquake that devastated the region as recently as 1966.

At Tashkent the line changed name again and became the Turk-Sib – a title reflecting the Turkic peoples through whose lands it ran, heading east and then north to join the Trans-Sib proper east of Novosibirsk. After four days on trains, Tom was affected by the numbness that overcame all Soviet long-distance travellers in the end. Each meal seemed to be the last one miraculously reconstituted, with the only difference that, in place of the perennial *bifsteks* on the Trans-Sib, passengers on the Turk-Sib were served equally tasteless stringy boiled chicken at every sitting.

Tom dozed and ate and stared out of the window, wondering how the drivers kept alert, day after day. The snow-capped Kirghiz Khrebet mountains came into sight to the south, providing novelty for an hour or two until they too became a part of the brain-numbing monotony. Browsing through an old copy of *Fodor's Guide* which he had brought along as reading matter, Tom agreed with the comment that trains were not to be recommended for travel in Central Asia.

Alma Ata, the capital of Kazakhstan, merited an entry in the *Guinness Book of Records* for the capital city with the most bizarre name. It meant 'father of apples'. Woken by the noise of the train clattering over the points outside the main station, Tom lay half-asleep, trying to recall why the place was so called. There was a knock on the door. He opened it in vest and shorts, expecting to see the *provódnik*, and found himself instead eyeball to eyeball with a shortish, overweight man in nondescript clothes and a leather cap who said, 'Keep me in sight.'

He slipped into Tom's hand a twin of Ponsonby's post-card from Leningrad before vanishing along the corridor, elbowing his way through the tightly packed throng of passengers noisily assembling their baggage and jostling their way off the train.

Tom dressed in a hurry and grabbed both his cases. Clambering down stiff-legged to the platform, he craned his neck without success for a sight of the man with black hair in the crush of bleary-eyed travellers bunched up at the narrow exit, where two militiamen were watching but not stopping people or asking for papers. Acutely aware of the suitcase in his right hand, he walked out of the station and stood, straining his eyes to see anything in the darkness outside the small pool of light cast by a few streetlamps. A cloud was passing in front of the full moon. In the darkness a brief flash of headlights drew Tom's eye to a black Moskvich saloon parked in the gloom across the road.

Ponsonby had been vague about the actual handover, saying only, 'Viktor has carte blanche to do things his way. That's been agreed.' However, Tom had assumed that the contact would be effected on the train. He had calculated that the time necessary to check the contents of the suitcase and complete the handover should be less than a minute. No pro would seek to prolong the vulnerable moment when they were both together by a second more than necessary, so what was Viktor playing at?

'*Bystro!*' he hissed as Tom walked up to the car: quickly.

Tom got in. Expecting to be asked to hand over the suitcase, he was startled to hear the motor being started.

Viktor crashed the gears twice, putting the Moskvich into reverse. '*Yob tvóyu mat!*' he swore. 'This is my wife's fucking car.'

'Where the hell are we going?' Tom asked.

'You'll see. Did you bring the camera?'

'Yes.'

They turned north, away from the lights of the downtown tower-blocks, and passed the airport. Beyond it loomed the snow-capped peaks of the Mountains of Heaven, looking deceptively near in the moonlight.

'The train stops at Alma Ata for two hours, in order to change engines and clean the carriages,' Viktor announced. 'We've plenty of time.'

'This is insane,' Tom remonstrated. 'I'm not going to spend two hours with you. Two minutes should have been more than enough.' He lifted the suitcase off his knee. 'Stop the car. Check the money now and give me whatever it is you've got for me.'

'It's not here,' Viktor replied. Naked fear of his house being searched made him prefer having the documents themselves in his possession for a night, rather than own a camera, which might be regarded as incriminating – but he was not going to tell Tom that.

'My camera's broken,' he lied. 'You've plenty of time to photograph everything at my home.'

They shot across an intersection against a red light.

Had Ponsonby guessed this might happen? Tom wondered. Was that why he had been so vague about the reason for the Minox?

'Slow down,' he said urgently, 'unless you want to get picked up by a GAI patrol car.'

As Viktor's driving grew more erratic, the old familiar nightmare took shape. On Tom's knee was a suitcase containing $500,000. Beside him was exactly the kind of traitor for which three-quarters of a million KGB informers were constantly on the lookout – a man who was taking a Western agent to his house where Top Secret documents were waiting to be photographed.

Tom checked the rear-view mirror for lights behind. There were none. He told himself that, if it was a KGB set-up, Viktor would have brought the documents or a film to the station. In a scene from a hundred Cold War movies he had seen on Russian television, the arrest would have taken place as soon as he got into the car. A squeal of brakes from several black Volgas pulling up, a dozen men leaping out of them, grabbing the suspect with unnecessary force and twisting his arms behind him, the snap of the handcuffs, the mouth forced open to see what might be hidden there, a couple of photographers shooting the evidence of arrest: the money and the documents. No, what was happening might be bizarre and unprofessional, but it wasn't a set-up.

Even so, when they slowed on the approach to a red light and a streetlamp showed Viktor's face beaded with sweat, Tom was tempted to get out of the Moskvich and walk back to the station. By heading for the lights of the city and with a bit of luck hitching a lift, he might still catch the train. It would serve Ponsonby right if he dumped the money and ran, but unfortunately all Tom's clothes and papers were in the case, so it would mean leaving them behind too.

And then the moment of opportunity was gone. Viktor jumped the light and accelerated across the junction in front of a huge articulated truck with Bulgarian number plates which missed the Moskvich by inches and screeched to a halt, air horns blaring a protest.

Shortly afterwards Viktor turned off the highway and was driving along a traffic-free residential road between modest individual houses set in wooded hilly country. There were lights at some of the windows, revealing normal family scenes inside: a group seated at table, a couple watching television, a small child no older than Svetlana being put to bed . . .

The Moskvich bumped off the metalled road and along a rutted track, narrowly avoiding a fallen tree trunk.

'Put the headlights on,' Tom shouted. 'You'll smash an axle, at this rate.'

'I know my way,' Viktor snapped. The tension was bringing on the old tightness in his chest; he wished he had brought his inhaler with him.

He drove up the side track that led to his one-storey brick-built dacha, turned off the sidelights and got out. 'Quickly,' he hissed. 'Follow me.'

Clutching the case, Tom hurried after him through the neglected moonlit garden and into the kitchen, where Viktor pulled blinds down at all the windows before switching on the lights. On the draining board were the unwashed dishes and pans from supper. On the large table that took up the centre of the room were two desk lamps and a briefcase.

'I've got everything ready,' Viktor said, sliding a sheaf of papers from the briefcase. 'Just don't make any noise.'

'You mean there's someone else in the house?'

Viktor tried to smile reassuringly. 'My wife's asleep, but don't worry – she's drunk. She won't hear a thing.'

Tom took a slug from an opened bottle of vodka on the draining board. According to the light meter, the lamps were more than adequate for the 400 ASA film that Ponsonby had supplied. He started photographing the pages of figures and diagrams while Viktor opened the suitcase and began counting the money.

Tom had used the first two rolls of film and was loading the third when he heard a toilet flush. In leaping up to turn off the lights, Viktor knocked over one of the desk lamps. They stood in the darkness, listening to the sound of dragging footsteps coming nearer. The door opened and a large female figure stood in the light from the hallway, wearing a cotton nightdress and swaying unsteadily.

'*Chto éto takóye?*' Viktor's wife asked: what's going on?

'It's all right, Marina,' he said. 'Go back to sleep. A friend just dropped by for a drink.'

If he had given any other reason for Tom's presence, she

might have returned to bed and remembered nothing in the morning.

Instead, she mumbled, 'I'll join you,' and switched on the room light.

Like many long-term heavy drinkers, she functioned quite well even with a lot of alcohol inside her. 'That's no friend,' she said. 'I've never seen him before. And what's this?'

She waved an arm to encompass Tom, standing wide-eyed by the table with camera in hand, the briefcase, the lamps, the documents and the caseful of money. They were the props from the dénouement of the many Soviet spy films which she too had watched on television.

'*Ty spión!*' she said to her husband: you're a spy!

In the films, the traitor admitted his guilt and was led away by the heroic KGB men while the patriotic wife watched, weeping with shame and being comforted by her neighbours.

Real life was different.

Viktor panicked, grabbed a wooden rolling-pin from among the dirty dishes on the draining board and brought it down on the back of Marina's head. Sheer inertia kept her on her feet for a moment. Before Tom could stop him, Viktor hit her again, harder. And again.

Horrified, Tom watched the woman fall to the floor and lie still with a trickle of blood coming out of her ear.

.5.

Tom knelt down to feel the woman's flabby chest. The layers of subcutaneous fat made it impossible to know if there was a heartbeat. He tried the wrist and found no pulse.

'You've killed her,' he said.

'What could I do?' Nosarenko gasped. 'She would have informed on me – on us. And then what?'

He felt no remorse, only fear for himself as he groped his way down the corridor to use the inhaler in the bathroom and splash cold water on his face, trying to think coherently.

'We have to get rid of her,' he called to Tom. 'You must help me.'

By the time he came back into the kitchen, Tom had shovelled the remaining documents into the briefcase and thrust his clothes and papers into the suitcase, emptied of the stack of notes which stood on the table. The camera and films were in his pockets.

'I've got to get back to the train,' he said. 'You can pretend that she slipped and fell against the corner of a cupboard. Say the floor was wet. It happens all the time.'

Viktor was staring at the body on the floor, amazed that a few blows on the head could remove from his life the woman to whom he had been tied for so many years.

Tom shook him. There was still an hour before the departure time of the train, but he wanted to get away – to be anywhere else but in that kitchen with a very nervous traitor and a dead woman. 'Let's go,' he said.

Viktor's panic was over. He was pleased with the idea that had come to mind. 'I don't want detectives roaming all over the house,' he said. 'They might find something. We have to get her out of here and make it look as though it happened somewhere else. Help me carry her.'

'Where to?'

'To the house next door. They keep animals in a sort of zoo. She liked them. I'll say she was drunk, went to feed them and had an accident. Come on, you take the head.'

He switched out the lights and took hold of Marina's feet. Reluctantly Tom put down the suitcase and got his hands beneath her shoulders. They lurched down the steps to the garden with their burden: 105 kilos of flabby flesh and bone.

Nervous of being overlooked, Tom asked, 'Won't the neighbours see us? It's only ten o'clock.'

'They're away for the weekend,' Viktor panted. Even after using the inhaler he was having trouble breathing but his brain was clear. 'And the next house after theirs is five hundred metres away, round a bend, so we're quite safe.'

They staggered through the moonlit garden, tripping on roots and stones. Viktor kicked open a wicket gate that led into the next garden and they lurched between a pair of heavy wooden gateposts and into a wired enclosure, where he gasped, 'We can put her down now.'

Tom straightened up to see that they were in a tunnel made of heavy-gauge steel mesh that looked like a reinforcement trellis for concrete. Nearby were other enclosures and cages. A rank smell of carnivores and decaying meat hung in the cold air.

When a floodlight came on, activated by a proximity switch, he thought for a moment that they had been discovered. Viktor pushed Tom ahead of him through the gate which slammed behind them, locking itself automatically. He hurried to the shed at the end of the cage and hauled on a chain which lifted a sliding door. Tom saw first one dog and then a second emerge, blinking at the light. They were emaciated animals, who glared at him with baleful yellow eyes.

Not dogs, he realised, but Siberian grey wolves, as big as Alsatians but leaner and meaner. There were four of them in the enclosure now: four pairs of unblinking yellow eyes checking out the two men on the other side of the wire as they slunk up to the body lying on the ground, confused by its familiar odour.

Tom turned away. Even if Viktor's wife were dead, he did not want to watch. As the first wolf sank its teeth into the woman's breast, the sudden violent pain brought her back to consciousness. She opened her eyes and saw the wolves standing round her, then screamed, uncertain whether she was having a nightmare. Another wolf sank its teeth into her ample buttocks. She lashed out and caught it on the nose. Unused to living prey, it backed off momentarily. Clutching her bleeding breast, Marina Nosarenko rolled and scrambled to her feet, sheer desperation propelling her past the startled wolves.

The first scream made me turn round. I could not see the woman, only the wolves snapping and snarling at each other over her body. Then I saw her lurch to her feet, clutching herself. The wolves must have been as surprised as I was because they drew back, allowing her to stagger to the fence. She grabbed the uprights of the gate, by which I was standing, and screamed at me, fingers scrabbling to undo the catches. 'Rádi Bóga! For the love of God, help me!'

Instinctively I tried to open the catches so that she could get out of the enclosure, only to find Viktor pulling me away.

'Leave her! Leave her!' he was shouting.

I gave him a huge shove which sent him reeling but it was too late. The moment of opportunity was past. By the time I had my hand on the lock, the wolves had renewed their attack, teeth slashing in fury as they tore at her face, arms and legs. I managed to get a hold on one of her hands, as though to pull her bodily through the mesh to safety, but the combined weight of the wolves and their victim was too much. I lost my grip and had a split-second image of her face with wide-open mouth as she fell to the ground in a welter of grey fur and teeth, screaming in wordless agony until a pair of powerful jaws closed on her throat and tore out the vocal cords.

'I could have saved her,' I shouted at Viktor.

He did not reply but walked round to the other side of the enclosure, where the wolves had dragged their prey.

There was no question of helping the woman by now, but I could not stand there as he was, just watching. I slipped the loaded Minox out of my pocket and removed the close-up lens with hands that were shaking and slippery with perspiration. The click each time I wound on the film was lost beneath the growling, the scuffling of paws in the dirt and the panting of the feeding wolves.

An awful bubbling groan escaped the lacerated trachea as the woman's one undamaged eye recognised Viktor, standing in the light. Still she moved, one arm flailing helplessly in the air, her body held completely clear of the ground by the wolves tearing at her flesh while he stared at the scene in gruesome fascination.

He dropped me back at the station with two minutes to spare. Numb with horror, I don't think I said a word on the way. Once aboard the train, I spent the first hour of the journey to Novosibirsk on my knees in the toilet, vomiting in delayed nervous reaction to the horror I had witnessed.

*Then I stripped out of the suitcase what remained of the
incendiary device and false lining, throwing the pieces
through the small ventilation window at five-minute
intervals, until I was satisfied that the case had nothing to
distinguish it from a hundred thousand others.*

*Returning to the compartment, I found that the train
was now so full that, despite the bribe to the provódnik, the
second bunk was occupied by a middle-aged insomniac
Polish geologist, travelling to Irkutsk.*

*She was one of those people who had an explanation for
everything. 'It's the meat they serve on the train,' she said
when I walked in, smelling of vomit – and looking pretty
shaken up. 'It takes a lot of passengers that way, especially
Westerners. If you work in Central Asia for long, your guts
get used to it. Me, I could lick the floor in a Uzbek shit-
house and never get ill.'*

*Happy to talk all night, she insisted on regaling me with
her theory that the cooks on the Turk-Sib sold any good
meat on the black market and served up inferior or even
condemned meat which they had bought at lineside
markets for a fraction of the price. Then she started plying
me with personal questions: why had I taken the train
instead of a plane, why was I living in Russia, and so on. I
pleaded renewed stomach pains and returned to the
stinking toilet, to be alone with my thoughts.*

Captain Mustafin wrinkled his nose. He had seen some
repulsive sights during his years of service in Alma Ata CID,
but nothing to equal this. The remains of Marina Nosarenko
reminded him more of the leftovers from a barbecue than the
body of what had been a walking, talking, feeling, living
person just a few hours before.

The wolves had been shot by a police marksman who had
taken no chances and used a Kalashnikov 74 on short burst
at close range. The bodies lay in a heap of bloody pelts, piled
up at one end of the enclosure. Several carloads of police in

and out of uniform were standing about, smoking and staring at the scene. Most of them were not even on duty. The
official photographer had finished his work but a couple of
officers were taking snapshots for their personal albums.

Mustafin walked the fifty paces to Viktor's dacha. In his
hand was a photograph of Marina on the beach at Yalta. It
had been taken three years before, and showed her bulging
unprepossessingly out of her swimsuit. She stood several
inches taller than the short, dark-haired man beside her and
must have weighed as much as a well-muscled six-foot male.
Mustafin decided there was no way that her husband could
have carried his wife from the dacha to the cage, or even
dragged her that far. If the body had been dragged, it would
have left a deep track gouged in the soft leaf-mould underfoot. Mustafin had looked for that when he first arrived, but
by then some of his sensation-seeking colleagues had already
trampled all over everything.

In the kitchen, Viktor was sitting by the telephone on
which he had called the local KGB sector office, shortly after
dawn, asking them to contact the police. Playing the
bereaved husband, he was wheezing badly and kept mopping sweat from his forehead.

'How could your wife have got into the enclosure?'
Mustafin asked.

'It shouldn't have been possible.' Viktor clutched the captain's sleeve. 'When Comrade Minsky started to keep the
larger animals – the wolves, the tiger, the bison and the
deer – he paid the city zoo manager for advice. One of his
contractors built the cages and the runs, moonlighting for
cash. The safety devices had to be imported from the West.
They cost him a fortune.'

Mustafin's bland brown eyes travelled across Viktor's
face; there were no scratches. He looked at the neatly
trimmed nails of the fingers drumming on the kitchen table;
there was no hint of flesh trapped there. He had spoken by
telephone to the nearest neighbours and to the owner of the

wolves. All had agreed that Marina was a drunkard, perfectly capable of getting herself killed in this way. There was, in short, no reason for suspicion except his own instinct and the odd fact that the bottle from which she had last been drinking had been wiped clean of all fingerprints, including hers.

Viktor's shoulders slumped. 'She'd had too much to drink,' he told Mustafin, lowering his eyes as though ashamed of the admission. He knew that the neighbours would corroborate Marina's drinking habits. She had sometimes disturbed them in the middle of the night by knocking on their doors, pleading for alcohol.

'How drunk was she?' Mustafin asked.

Viktor did not appear to have heard. 'She insisted on driving us out here last night. I was scared she would crash the car. She cut red lights and nearly hit several vehicles. When we got here, for God knows what reason she wanted to feed the animals, there and then. I said it was too late, they could wait till morning, but she used to get fixations about trivial things – it was a part of her condition, I suppose.'

Mustafin nodded.

'I was having a bad attack of asthma,' Viktor wheezed. 'So I went to bed about midnight and left Marina drinking in the kitchen.'

He pointed to the nearly empty bottle of vodka. 'She must have gone out there, drunk as a Cossack and . . .' He gestured helplessly.

Mustafin was a Kazakh. One of only seven million whose country was as large as the whole of Europe, he belonged to a racial minority in his own land. As much as to any talent for detective work, he owed his successful career to a philosophy of never making trouble for an ethnic Russian if he could avoid it. He had no intention of locking horns with a full colonel in the élite KGB Rocket Forces.

'I suppose so,' he agreed. 'But there'll have to be an autopsy, colonel.'

'D'you need me there?'

By the time the wolves had been driven away from the carcase and shot, all that was left of Marina was the empty ribcage, cracked skull, the pelvis and some leg bones. With no organs to work on, the forensic examination would be a pure formality.

Mustafin shook his head. 'Just so long as I can reach you, if need be.'

Viktor wrote down a telephone number beginning with the prefix of the KGB Semipalatinsk switchboard. 'This will get you through to my office at the *Vostok 4* test range. The number is not to be divulged to anyone. After your investigation is complete, you will destroy this piece of paper and forget the number. Understood?'

'Absolutely, colonel.'

.6.

Changing trains at Novosibirsk, I said goodbye to the garrulous Polish woman and paid another bribe to obtain an empty two-berth compartment where I could be alone to ride the thousand-odd kilometres to Khabarovsk and Irkutsk.

I had no idea of the exact significance of the sheets of figures and technical drawings I had photographed in Viktor's kitchen, nor what was the norm for payment, but the amount was worryingly high. If the documents Viktor was selling to London were really worth $500,000, they might be the key to unlock the current stand-off in the arms race. Was that what Ponsonby had meant by calling the mission 'the Big One' in his moment of unguarded euphoria? As far as I and the rest of the human race was concerned, nuclear stalemate was far healthier than a situation where either side had the kind of advantage that made a pre-emptive strike an attractive proposition. The pawns in the game of realpolitik being played by Ponsonby

*and Viktor were millions of innocent people . . . like Rada
and Svetlana.*

*So what am I doing? I asked myself. Do I owe a loyalty
to Britain because I was born there? Shouldn't my allegiance
rather be to my wife and child?*

*It seemed very shallow to have played the game of
espionage for kicks without thinking of the possible
consequences. The longer I thought about it, the more
attractive became the idea of destroying the films.*

*I remembered the night in Leningrad when Karen had
told me I was a fool to have got myself mixed up in
Ponsonby's game. If I had destroyed those films then, none
of this would have happened . . .*

*All the Rossiya trains ran on Moscow time. After the
midday meal was served at 4 p.m. local time, I borrowed a
book of matches from the provódnik. When I flushed the
toilet and saw the charred remains of the two films
disappearing onto the track below the train, I knew that it
was the best decision I had made in my life.*

*I intended destroying likewise the film inside the Minox,
wanting to rid myself of everything to do with that ghastly
scene, yet some instinct warned me not to. Instead I decided
to hide it in the safest place I knew.*

*At Irkutsk, a taxi took me from the railway station to
the airport where the same sloe-eyed Kirghiz girl hired me
the same Lada 4WD. This time I checked that there was a
spare tyre and tool kit, before driving off. It was mid-
morning when I left the outskirts of the town behind me
and mid-afternoon when I arrived at the byvshi dom. The
magic of my first visit was missing. The two-dimensional
facade that had looked like a Venetian palazzo was now
just a ruined wall, no different from the remains of a
million other 'former houses' in the immensity of war-torn
Siberia.*

*Outside the stable block I called Miss Addison's name
but there was no reply. In the tack room, the scrawny cats*

*came to rub themselves around my legs, miaowing for
food. They followed me outside to where I guessed she
would be. There was a second grave by the fountain, at the
head of which someone had stuck in the disturbed earth a
simple Orthodox cross bearing the legend Akhmanova,
Olga T. – and the date: 4th June 1986. She had died the day
after my first visit.*

*An hour later, the Minox camera was at the bottom of
the well and the film lay sealed in a plastic document
folder, tucked inside the oilcloth that had protected the
Virgin of Kazan for seven decades. Recalling my promise to
shoot the old woman's cats, I unwrapped Kolchak's
revolver, wondering whether it still worked. Two of the
cats were peering curiously over the lip of the well when I
looked up but I could not have brought myself to shoot
them, even if I had been competent with firearms. So I
wrapped the revolver up again and left it where it was.*

*It was dusk when I threw the tools into the back of the
Lada and shooed the cats out of the vehicle. About to drive
off, I noticed an animal watching from the edge of a clump
of trees half a mile away. It could have been a large fox or a
dog. I wondered how long it would be before I could close
my eyes at night without seeing the yellow eyes of the
wolves and hearing the screams of the woman they had
torn to pieces alive in front of me.*

The empty apartment seemed very large without Rada.

On the phone from Washington, she sounded excited
and happy: 'The operation was a success, Tom. It's incredible: a tiny little machine no bigger than a torch battery
implanted in my father's chest muscles and already he's a
different man. He's up and walking. He even climbed a
flight of stairs today without getting out of breath. Isn't it
wonderful?'

'And how are you?' Tom asked. 'I need you. Come back
soon.'

'Don't worry. We're having fun. Svetlana wants to talk to you.'

After listening to his two-year-old daughter's simple chatter, Tom hung up more convinced than ever that he had done the right thing.

He was woken three times that night by the telephone ringing. Each time a man's voice asked to speak to Mischa from Leningrad and Tom said in Russian, 'Go away and leave me alone.'

In the end, he left the phone off the hook but sleep would not come. The one thing he had not worked out during his long train ride was how to get Ponsonby off his back.

The violence of the approach took him by surprise. He was waiting on the crowded platform of the University Metro station that evening on his way home when two young men in leather jackets pinioned him between them and hustled him into the tiny office of the platform attendant. It was done so professionally that few people noticed – and those who did looked the other way, thinking that Tom's assailants were KGB men.

For a moment Tom thought so too. Then he saw Ponsonby, similarly dressed to the two younger men. By the look of him, he had not slept since the briefing meeting. He was defying orders by being there in person and had an even shorter fuse than usual. Red-eyed and tense, he snapped, 'What the fuck are you up to, Tom? Where the hell is it?'

'*It* doesn't exist,' said Tom. 'There never were any secret documents. Your pal Viktor conned you.'

The two leather jackets were blocking the open doorway with their wide backs, so that no one could see in.

'You gave him the money?' Ponsonby asked.

Tom laughed. 'Too right, I did.'

With a jab of his powerful forearm Ponsonby thrust Tom back against the wall. 'Don't fuck with me! What happened?'

Tom told a simplified version of the meeting in Alma Ata: 'And when I got into the car, he pointed some kind of

automatic pistol at me and said, "Hand over the money!"
What the hell could I do?'

'Jesus Christ!' Ponsonby was furious.

His face only inches from Tom's, he hissed, 'Are you
trying to make me believe that Viktor set up the whole long-
running scenario as a way of bilking British Intelligence out
of half a million dollars?'

'That's what it looks like, Clive.'

Ponsonby's right fist slammed into the door, narrowly
missing Tom's head and leaving a streak of blood on the
woodwork. Alarmed by the noise, one of the watchers turned
round, only to recoil at the fury on Ponsonby's face.

'I'll be in touch,' he snapped at Tom. 'Shit! Shit! Shit! Shit!
Shit!'

After they had gone, Tom walked back onto the platform.
Not a single person looked at him; nobody wanted to know.
He took the train to Arbatskaya and headed for the baths, to
spend the night there, drinking *samohón* moonshine and
eating raw onions with a lonely ex-miner from the Donbas
whose emaciated pale white body was half-covered in blue
scars where coal dust had got into cuts received underground, so that it looked as though a mad tattooist had
experimented on him with marbling techniques from head to
foot. Every sentence was punctuated by a cough as he told
Tom how he had been pensioned off at the age of forty-eight
to die from dust in the lungs.

Just before leaving, Ponsonby had muttered the promise,
'We'll be in touch about getting you home, Tom. Just stay
cool.'

And Tom had said, 'Don't bother, Clive. Home is where
the heart is. Deal me out. I'm staying here.'

With those words he had crossed the Rubicon.

*

'You'll have to lure your boy back,' said Madeleine
Wharton. She cursed her predecessor, who had retired with a
knighthood after bequeathing her this and other time-bombs

at a no-papers briefing exactly an hour before he left Century House for the last time.

Ponsonby stood in front of her desk. With his moustache shaved off but hair still *en brosse*, he looked, she thought, exactly what he was: an overgrown football hooligan. There were too many officers like him in the Firm, but somehow she had to live with them even though their thinking was rooted in the past.

'There's no way you'll get at the truth any other way,' she decided.

Ponsonby had only met the new director-general a few times and found it hard to come to terms with her as his boss. A tall, thin woman who could have been elegant if she had paid more attention to clothes, her gaunt frame showed little femininity. But she was a woman; and in Ponsonby's book, women made good analysts but not executives. His own plan of action had been to kidnap Tom, take him to a safe house and sweat the truth out of him. Madeleine had coldly pointed out that Tom was a Soviet citizen and the risk was unacceptable.

She got up from behind her desk and toyed with the six red roses arranged in a crystal vase on her windowsill. 'Do you suppose that it's Fielding who's taken you for a ride, Clive?'

'It's possible,' he grunted.

'If so, he'll presumably surface sooner or later, living on the fat of the land in some Western country with which we have no extradition agreement – and we'll have to ask him some polite questions for the record, if he'll agree to talk to us.'

'Tom is fundamentally straight,' Ponsonby argued. 'I tell you, if he had been intending to screw us, I'd have known. There has to be another explanation.'

'Was there anything odd about his behaviour at the briefing in the safe house?' she asked. 'Had he been drinking, for example?'

'He was as sober as a judge.'

'Is it possible he's been turned and is working for the other side?'

'Why would they invent such a crazy story?' Ponsonby asked. 'The comrades create the best tailor-made legends in the business. This one's so threadbare you can see through it.'

'Could he have simply gone native, with his wife and child? It's happened before.'

Ponsonby had to defend Tom in order to protect himself. 'That's every sleeper's problem to some extent. Even Lonsdale was genuinely sorry that he could never return to Britain. And Rudolf Able missed hamburgers and baseball after he was swapped for Francis Gary Powers. So if – I say, if – Tom's loyalties are a bit mixed up, it's only to the same extent as a foreign correspondent on extended mission.'

'They move foreign correspondents every two or three years for exactly that reason,' Madeleine pointed out acidly.

Toying with her single piece of jewellery – a Victorian floral cluster brooch – she moved to the window, to put more distance between them.

It was time for the Firm to move out of this sordid building. Century House had been designed for a simpler age. With all the additional layers of glass for security and bombproof netting on the ten lower floors, it was increasingly difficult for anyone to see out, never mind in. We're like goldfish, she thought, going round and round in a bowl, seeing the world through glass ever more darkly.

'I never liked Operation Viktor from the start.' Her voice was, if anything, quieter than that of the old man. Ponsonby could hardly hear the words, 'It smelled.'

'You sanctioned it,' he snapped, not prepared for his boss to walk away and leave him alone, facing an Internal Enquiry.

'My predecessor did.' She spun round and glared at him. 'I simply inherited it with several hundred other ongoing projects, some good, some bad. Whatever the explanation, $500,000 is a lot of money we're missing. There'll have to be an IE, Clive. In your own interests, I think you should prepare a very full report. And be sure to let me see the draft before anyone else reads it.'

.7.

The messages from Mischa grew less and less frequent until by mid-winter of 1988 Tom assumed that he had been written off on whatever balance sheet was drawn up annually by Ponsonby's auditors.

His old dream of being picked up by the KGB now alternated with the new nightmare of watching a living woman being torn to pieces by a pack of wolves. Most nights he awoke sweating, her screams in his ears, and with his heart beating as though he had been in a race. The only way to keep the dreams at bay was to start drinking earlier and earlier in the evening and fall into bed drunk.

Misunderstanding the reason for Tom's depression, Rada persuaded her father to use *blat* on his behalf at the university. Tom was promoted to senior lecturer in the department of twentieth-century history at Mosuniv on Sibirsky's retirement. To his surprise, Rada decided to resign on the same day, arguing that Tom's new salary was enough for both of them.

'I only ever pretended to be an academic for my father's sake,' she said.

'As long as you're happy,' Tom said uncertainly. He was trying to cut down on the booze, but every time he did the death of Viktor's wife replayed in the midnight cinema of his mind.

Aware that he and Rada were drifting apart, he mumbled, 'I thought modern women wanted children and a career.'

'Why do I have to conform to other people's stereotypes?'

'You'll get bored, alone with Svetlana all day.'

'I have no work ethic, you'll see.' Rada quoted the old Soviet joke: '"We pretend to work and they pretend to pay us." I've stopped pretending, that's all.'

*

On 9 November 1989 at midnight the Berlin Wall was breached in the first blow of a bloodless revolution that changed overnight and for ever the political geography of Europe. The social and economic unrest predicted by Sibirsky spread like a cancer through the greatest empire of the twentieth century; within a few months the USSR had disintegrated. The chaos was epitomised on 7 February 1990 when the Communist Party of the Soviet Union voted itself out of the monopoly of power on which it had insisted for seventy-two years at the cost of tens of millions of lives.

In the cutbacks at Mosuniv that spring, Tom – being one of the last appointments – was one of the first to be told he was no longer required. Like most redundancies, it was shattering. Since all the universities in what had been the Soviet Union were in the same financial straits, there was no chance of finding another job. One of Tom's friends, made redundant at the same time, took a job driving a taxi for a living; another became a cook in a cooperative restaurant.

The drinking that had made most evenings a blur now began earlier and earlier in the afternoons. Tom realised just how far it was possible to drift away from the person one lived with when Rada stunned him one afternoon with the announcement that she had solved their financial problems by taking a job working for an American fast-food company which was opening new outlets in Moscow and several other cities. Converted at the black market rate, her initial salary in dollars was more than ten times what Tom had been earning as a professor.

'I didn't even know you were looking for a job,' he protested.

'We've talked about it,' she said shortly. 'At least, I've tried discussing it with you but you never listen.'

'And what'll we do with Svetlana?' he asked.

'There are more good day nurseries in Moscow than New York. I read that in a magazine somewhere.'

'I don't want my child to be brought up by strangers.'

'Then why don't you look after her?' Rada suggested. 'You're at home all day, doing nothing.'

When he asked what her work would involve, she looked vague. 'I'm a sort of bilingual secretary to the big boss.'

'A Yank?'

'And how! Vito thinks the solution to every delay is to pay people more and they'll work harder. He doesn't understand that Russians work less, the more you pay them. He needs me as an interface between American methods and the Russian workforce.'

'Vito?' Tom queried. 'What kind of name is that?'

'His parents were Italian.'

'I'd like to meet the guy.'

'It wouldn't be a good idea,' Rada decided after one look at her husband. Unshaven, with no shirt or socks on and a glass in his hand at four o'clock in the afternoon, he was not someone she wanted to meet her new employer.

'Why not?'

She turned away from him. 'I've told Vito that I'm divorced. He's a workaholic. He wouldn't have hired a woman with domestic obligations.'

At Sibirsky's suggestion, Tom began work on another book: an hour-by-hour documentation of the collapse of the Communist dream. Even so, the days were long. Rada started work early and rarely returned before late evening, six days a week. The best moments in Tom's day were with Svetlana.

He found himself arguing more and more with Rada. Sometimes he sounded, even to his own ears, like a house-bound housewife: 'Svetlana never sees you. It's not fair on the kid.'

'Face facts.' Rada looked tired. She sat on the bed with hardly enough energy to undo her new lace-up boots. 'Since I was promoted, I earn double my starting wage, paid in dollars. We're better off than most people in Russia, Tom. You know I have to go along with the hours Vito wants me at my desk – or lose the job. He could easily replace me.'

'There's something else,' said Tom. 'I only ever see you on Sundays. The rest of the week, you come back at ten o'clock or midnight and fall asleep before I can even say, "*Dóbry vécher*." Whatever happened to our sex life?'

'I'm tired, Tom.' Rada hung her dress on a hanger and went into the bathroom to finish undressing. 'You work a fourteen-hour day and you'd be tired too,' she called through the closed door.

Inevitably the suspicion built up, eating away at Tom each time Rada phoned to tell him not to wait up for her. It culminated when she announced that she was working out of town and would be away for several nights running. That evening he paid a neighbour to baby-sit and waited in the street outside her office in the Arbat. At any hour, the pedestrian precinct was busy: gypsies playing folk music, caricaturists making lightning sketches of passers-by, hawkers selling gimcrack souvenirs, currency changers hustling tourists. It was easy to lose himself in the queue winding away from the plate-glass shopfront, above which glared the neon logo of the fast-food company.

Rada came out earlier than he had expected. Feeling cheap, he watched as a secretary ran out after her with some query which Rada answered briskly, looking at her watch. In a white long-sleeved silk blouse, red midi-length skirt and black patent boots, she stood out among the drably dressed crowd like a lighthouse on a dark night.

Halfway along the Arbat, she took a call on her mobile phone. Catching a glimpse of her face in a shop window, Tom thought, that's the way she used to smile at me.

At the end of the pedestrian precinct, Rada got into the red Lada and swerved out into the commuter traffic in her usual style, leaving Tom to follow in an unlicensed cab that was cruising by. Ten minutes later he was paying off the driver opposite the entrance to an underground car park beneath a new block of expensive apartments into which Rada had driven. Two hours passed before she left the building arm in arm with her boss, a fashionably dressed, fast-talking Italian-American from Detroit who used his hands to make points the whole time.

Tom wanted to believe that they had been working upstairs, but something about Rada's face as she acknowledged the salute of the smartly uniformed doorman, told him otherwise. He slunk back into a doorway as her boss held the door for her to get into a new BMW, parked in front of the building. After they had gone, Tom bought a bottle of vodka and sneaked into the garage, where he spent the night in the Lada. He was still there next morning when Rada, wearing an angora sweater and a different skirt from the previous day, opened the door and started with surprise.

'How much does Vito pay to fuck you?' he shouted at her. 'Do you get overtime for night-duty?'

She stared at him in amazement. 'Tom? What are you doing here?'

'You're my wife!' he shouted.

Smelling the drink on his breath, Rada said coldly, 'At

last you look and stink like a hundred per cent proof Russian husband.'

'And you,' Tom said unsteadily, 'look like a high-priced whore.'

'I'm surviving the best way I can,' Rada snapped. 'Now go home and I'll talk to you this evening.'

'Oh, don't let me interrupt your sex-life,' he snarled. 'If Vito needs your services, that's fine by me. Perhaps you've forgotten that you used to have a daughter as well as a husband?'

They were both outside the car now. Tom grabbed Rada's arm.

'Let me go,' she said as remotely as if a stranger had touched her up in the Metro.

'Who is this guy?' A security guard had come up behind them and pinioned Tom's arms behind him.

'It's okay,' said Rada. 'I know him.'

Tom hacked the man's shins with his heel and pulled free. The guard swore and came at him, mouthing threats, until Rada pushed between them and thrust a five-dollar bill into his hand. 'Please,' she said. 'I can handle this.'

He backed away with a promise: 'If I see you in here again, shit-face . . .'

'I need to talk,' said Tom, when they were alone.

'What about?'

'Us?'

'Us?' Rada's voice rose in indignation.

She pulled a make-up mirror out of her bag and held it in front of his face. His hair needed a cut, he had not shaved for a couple of days and his face was haggard with red-rimmed eyes.

'That's you,' Rada said. She took the mirror away. 'Now look at me, Tom. Go on, look!'

I looked at her as though she were a stranger – and saw a stunningly beautiful young woman with an expensive coiffure, immaculate make-up and clothes that would cost a fortune in the West, never mind in Moscow.

I shut my eyes to blot out the truth but it was as though the lids were a camera shutter; the image was already imprinted on my memory and would not go away.

'How can there be any us?' I heard Rada say. Her voice wasn't quite so harsh now. 'Go back to the West, Tom. It's where you belong. Life is easier there. You may look like a Russian – and even smell like one right now – but inside you're just not tough enough to be one.'

I knew she was right.

.8.

Two days later, Tom came back from shopping to find the baby-sitter in the hallway, looking worried. Behind her was a stack of his belongings, dumped on the floor.

'Your wife was here,' the woman said. 'She's taken the child and left this.'

She handed him a letter on official headed notepaper, written in legalese. It informed Feldink, Tomas M. (1) that Mikhailova, Rada A. had applied for a divorce from him; (2) that custody of the child of the marriage would be granted to the said Mikhailova, Rada A. because she was able to provide for the child, whereas Feldink, Tomas M. was without work or lodging; and (3) that any further attempt on his part to molest Mikhailova, Rada A. or to get in touch with the child would be referred to the militia and render him liable to arrest and automatic exile from Moscow.

When Tom tried to let himself into the apartment to use a telephone and call the number on the letterhead, he found that the locks had been changed. He threw his useless keys on the floor in impotent rage and kicked the pile of clothes, books and CDs down the stairs. From a coin box in the street he called Sibirsky's number.

'No, I don't know where they are,' said his father-in-law.

Tom was sure he could hear Svetlana crying faintly in the background.

'I'm coming round,' he said.

'Don't do it,' counselled Arkady Sergeyevich. 'I don't know what happened between you two, but Rada is furious. She isn't kidding about the militia, Tom. Her boss has them in his pocket. Cause any trouble and you'll just get yourself arrested and exiled to Minsk or Yaroslavl where you can't do a thing. Take my advice, calm down and leave her alone for a while.'

'But she's got Svetlana!'

'The kid's safe, I promise you.' Safer than with a drunken father, he seemed to imply.

Tom spent that night in the baths where the Donbas miner shared a bottle of vodka with him. He shrugged when he heard Tom's tale of woe and echoed Sibirsky's warning: since losing his job, Tom had no residence entitlement in Moscow and could be deported immediately if he got on the wrong side of the law.

It seemed that Ivanov was the only person who could help, but unbeknown to Tom, he had problems of his own. The last two monthly meetings had been informal. Ivan Petrovich, looking suddenly older and with no girlfriend in tow, had come for Sunday lunch at the Pyatnitskaya Ulitsa and assured Tom that there was no need for him to go to the office on Kuznetsky Most. That morning, Tom found out why. In Yeltsin's massive cutbacks, 75 per cent of the KGB's counter-espionage personnel had been sacked; only the First Directorate with its international responsibilities had been kept more or less intact. Ivanov was one of the victims.

Tom swallowed his pride and walked the four miles back to the apartment where those of his belongings that had not been looted by the neighbours were in the dustbins at the rear of the block. In an old address book, he found Ivanov's private telephone number and rang it.

'I can't help you,' said Ivan Petrovich. 'I know where Rada and the kid are, but if I tell you where, I'll be helping you to stick your head in a noose. And don't try hanging around Rada's office or her boss's place. He's hired bodyguards to keep you away.'

'How do you know all this?'

'I'm one of them.'

'Oh Jesus!' Tom exclaimed.

'That's the way it is. The whole of our society is in turmoil. Everyone's on the make. Without a lot of money, there's nothing you can do, Tom. Take it from me. D'you think I like watching the back of a smooch like Vito Danello?'

After a pause, Ivanov offered, 'I could have a word with some old pals, if you like. I'm pretty sure that no one gives a fast fuck if you should want to fly out on the next plane to London. Rada's right. In the circumstances, that would be the best thing to do.'

'My home's here where my kid is,' said Tom obstinately. 'Anyway, I don't belong anywhere else. The problem is that I've got no money. If I get picked up on the street, I'm done.'

'You want a handout?'

'I want a job.'

'What kind of job?'

'Anything.'

'Maybe I can fix something.' Ivan Petrovich did not sound too hopeful. 'Call me back in half an hour.'

Ivanov was driving a late-model Mercedes saloon when he picked Tom up.

'Nice car you've got, Ivan Petrovich,' Tom said. 'Bodyguards must get paid well.'

'There's no point in being one of the hounds when you can be the leader of the pack,' Ivanov grunted.

'That's what you are?'

'I look after security for Vito Danello's fast-food chain.'

'What's this job you've found for me?'

'You'll see.'

Housing Estate 17 was fifteen miles from the centre of the city but might as well have been on the other side of the moon, which it closely resembled in sheer bleak misery. Piles of damaged materials and broken machinery littered the dirty snow between the unfinished blocks. Ivanov handed over some money to a woman overseer who signed Tom on as night-watchman.

The job – as Ivanov had pointed out during the drive – was at the bottom of the social ladder but would at least entitle Tom to stay legally in Moscow. It also provided him with an unofficial roof over his head: it was possible to sleep during the day in one of the poorly designed prefabricated apartments that were being erected to house the city's over-spill. There was no electricity and no running water yet installed in Area 11 of Housing Estate 17, but it was better than sleeping rough.

'If I think of anything else useful, I'll be in touch,' Ivanov promised. He had driven a hundred metres down the unmade road when another thought struck him and he reversed the Mercedes, bumping over the re-frozen slush to where Tom was standing.

'If you move from here,' he said, 'let me know. That way, if there is any news about Svetlana, I can always find you.'

The bulk of the labour force on the site was made up of women and girls from the country, taking on work that no Muscovite wanted because a job was the only way for them to qualify for a Moscow residence permit. Some of the younger girls were living illicitly in the unfinished buildings. At night they sat around a blazing brazier, muffled in anoraks, and swapped hard-luck stories. Their lives were rich only in rejection and loss. Sometimes one of the girls would play the balalaika or a guitar. The sad and wistful songs they sang were not modern, but the folk music of Russia. The simple harmonies which they managed by instinct expressed something of their yearning for a better life – or at least a simpler one when a boy and a girl could wander through the birch forests hand in hand and kiss in the moonlight, believing in happy-ever-afters.

The hopelessness of his life mirrored in theirs dragged Tom down and down. In return for shutting his eyes to a little pilfering at night, he was fed once a day on the same simple peasant food that the women prepared for themselves. Most evenings, whatever the weather, he walked two miles in order to reach the nearest beer hall. It was a sordid unheated urinal of a place where, for 40 kopecks, drunks and down-and-outs bought half-litres of watered-down *pivo* from a dispenser in dirty reused cardboard cups.

It was hard to sleep during the day because of the noise of drills and cranes and concrete mixers. When he could get hold of it, Tom used vodka to knock himself unconscious. It was the only way of switching off the new nightmare, in which Rada and her lover were driving off in the gleaming new BMW with Svetlana leaning out of the rear door, waving goodbye for ever to Tom. He kept shouting after the car that the door was not properly locked, but no one heard. Then the door swung open and the child fell out onto the roadway just as the pursuing wolves drew level. Vandals had stolen the BMW's rear-view mirrors, so that neither Rada nor the man at the wheel could see the pack closing in on the defenceless toddler. As they drove away, laughing together, Tom knew that only he could save the child. 'Daddy!' she cried as he ran and ran towards her without ever getting any nearer, although his lungs were bursting with the effort. There was no chance of reaching her before the wolves did.

The dream was always silent, apart from that one word: 'Daddy!'

*

'Get in,' Ivanov said, as he pulled up alongside in an even newer model, just after Tom had come out of the boozer.

'I have to make a phone call,' Tom mumbled. Each night at 7.30 he called the number that was written in felt pen on the tiled walls of the beer hall. The telephone of trust, as it was called, functioned similarly to the Samaritans in Britain. Each night a middle-aged woman asked what sort of day Tom had had and listened as he rambled on for a few minutes before hanging up and going back to the wasteland of Area 11 of Housing Estate 17, there to punch the time clock in the watchman's hut.

'Not tonight, you don't. You're coming with me.' Ivanov pulled Tom inside the car and accelerated away from the kerb.

'My birthday?' Tom queried, looking at the 200-gram bottle of vodka that was shoved into his hand.

'If it was,' Ivanov growled, 'by the look of you there'd be a hundred candles on the cake.'

Tom upended the bottle and sat back in the seat with eyes shut, feeling the alcohol hit in his brain. It was the best drink he could remember. The bottle was empty long before the car pulled up thirty minutes later outside a private hospital on the garden ring road, mainly used by foreigners. Ivanov and the doorman had to half-carry Tom inside.

'Where are we going?' he kept asking as they walked him into lifts and along corridors.

Each time the reply was, 'You'll see.'

He sobered up a little in the dentist's chair when the nurse was tying a plastic bib under his chin. 'What am I doing here, Ivan Petrovich?'

He watched without interest as the dentist tied a rubber tube around his left arm. He had such a hard job to get the vein to stand out for the injection that Tom apologised. A nurse in a white uniform handed him some tablets and a cup of water, which he swallowed docilely. The drill whirred, probes clattered onto the porcelain dishes, the suction glugged and wheezed. Tom gazed at the light above his head and tried to think what he was doing there.

'You can get up now,' the dentist said.

Tom stood up obediently – and just as obediently lay down on a gurney. 'What was all that about?' he asked as two men wheeled him along a corridor.

Ivanov's face appeared to be floating upside down. 'We had to take out all your fillings, in case they had given you a suicide capsule.'

Ivanov's lips were moving but the voice in Tom's ears was Donald Duck's and the words did not make any sense.

'Who would do that?' he asked. 'The women on the site? Do they hate me that much?'

Somebody was laughing; he thought it must be himself.

'You're going home,' Ivanov said when the gurney had stopped moving. 'Sleep well.'

'*Spi mladénetz, moi prekrásny . . . báyushki-bayú . . .*' Tom started singing the lullaby but could not recall the words.

'Tomorrow you'll be back in the land of your fathers.' Ivanov tapped him on the shoulder. 'I'll see you in the morning.'

'I need a drink,' Tom called. But Ivanov did not seem to be there so he tried to get off the gurney, only to find that his head, arms and legs were strapped down tightly.

'Let me get up!' he shouted. 'I need to take a slash urgently.'

'Do it where you are,' a strange man's voice replied. 'It's a rubber mattress. Be my guest, like all the others.'

For a while Tom resisted the urge. Finally he let go and felt the warm wetness creep between his thighs to form a pool beneath his buttocks. By the time the pool of urine started to cool, he was already crying at the degradation of it all.

Next morning, a male nurse shaved Tom and made him take

a shower before getting dressed in clean clothes. He recognised the garments as his own, but all of them were several sizes too large. He had lost count of the injections he had been given; even the unfilled cavities in his teeth caused no pain. He was aware of what was going on around him and could talk normally but seemed to have no will of his own.

After yet another injection he was aware of being in Ivanov's Mercedes – on the rear seat, his hands cuffed together. In front, Ivanov was arguing about money with a man who spoke fluent Russian with an English accent. Beside the Mercedes was a BMW. It looked to Tom like the one that belonged to Rada's boss but he could see nothing inside through the tinted windows.

The Englishman sitting in the front seat talking with Ivanov had the hopeless face of a sad spaniel and something of the same beaten look as Brodsky. The argument ended and Ivanov re-counted the money while the Englishman opened the door and motioned Tom out. 'Come on, old chum,' he said. 'They want to get this thing airborne.'

Tom looked up at the fuselage of a British Airways Boeing 737. The air was full of kerosene fumes and noise. The other passengers had already boarded via the telescopic walkway but there was a mobile service stairway against the open rear doorway, up which the sad-faced Englishman nudged Tom, step by step. At the top, Ivanov unlocked the handcuffs.

'Enjoy your thirty pieces of silver,' Tom said.

'Get a move on,' called Ponsonby's man. He was standing inside the aircraft, beside a stewardess who was waiting to close the door.

Ivanov glanced down at the BMW, in which there was still no sign of life. Looking embarrassed, he took a small plastic bag of soil from his pocket and thrust it into Tom's hand.

'Remember the day we went picking mushrooms?' he mumbled. 'This came from there. It was Rada's idea.'

Against the noise of aircraft engines, it was hard to catch

what he was saying. As though in slow motion, Tom saw the door of the BMW open and Rada step out. She stood, looking up at him for a long moment before raising her hand in a hesitant wave. Then she got back into the car which drove off immediately.

'Hang on to the good memories,' said Ivanov. 'You'll need them.'

He embraced Tom briefly, kissing him on both cheeks Russian-style, before running down the steps which were immediately pulled away by a tractor.

In a curtained-off compartment at the rear of the aircraft there was a row of reserved seats. Tom took a last breath of Russian air and sat down as the door was locked shut by the flight attendant. She bent over Tom to make sure that his seat belt was fastened and the man with the spaniel's face gently removed the plastic bag from Tom's hand.

'Soil?' he queried.

In the old days before the railways, the *zaks* who had been sentenced to Siberia had to walk there. They used to kneel down when they arrived at the frontier in the Urals and scoop up the last handful of Russian soil they would ever touch, so it could be placed in their coffins when they died.

'Just soil,' said Tom.

'I expect they'll let you have it back, when it's been analysed.'

Once they were airborne, Ponsonby's man called the stewardess and ordered four double whiskies, placing three on Tom's drinks tray and keeping one for himself.

'Enjoy every drop,' he advised. 'It's going to be a long, dry summer where you're going, chum.'

PART IX

.1.

The red brick Georgian country house where Tom was confined was set well back from the road and surrounded by a neglected garden. High hedges and thick shrubberies effectively insulated both the house and its occupants from prying eyes behind an impenetrable screen of green leaves.

Tom had the feeling of being cut off from the world. The sense of isolation was enhanced by the total ban on his reading a newspaper, hearing a radio or seeing television. Having arrived at night in a blur of alcohol and drugs, he had no idea whether the house was north, south, east or west of London, nor how far he had been driven from the airport to get there.

Occasionally, depending on the direction of the wind, he heard distant traffic noises and the sound of tractors nearer at hand. He measured the passing of the weeks each time he heard the tolling of a single bell in a village church not far away. It reminded him of being dressed up in school uniform on Sunday mornings, talking politely with the parishioners before and after the service and trying not to yawn openly during his father's long sermons. Afterwards came the ritual family lunch, his father carving some large bird or a joint of mutton at the table, punctuating the conversation with accusations: 'I couldn't hear your voice in the psalm, Margaret,' or 'You didn't join in the Lord's Prayer, Tom. I want to know why.' The sparse praise was almost always reserved for Tom's elder brother: 'You read the lesson well, Adrian.'

The sleepless nights of alcohol withdrawal were long, especially when a new scenario tormented Tom's imagination. In it a small girl was ill and alone in a Moscow hospital, crying for her father. Her age was indeterminate and Tom could never see her face but the setting was so realistic that he could smell the disinfectant in her room and hear the echoing footfalls of the nurses and orderlies in the corridor outside. He flew into Sheremetyevo, knowing that she had not long to live. Ivanov was at the immigration desk, waving Tom's cancelled Russian passport and refusing him permission to enter the country. On the return flight, Ponsonby tore up Tom's British passport so that he had no right to enter Britain either.

It was a relief when morning brought another session with his confessors. With no logic that Tom could discern, most of the debriefing was carried out by Brodsky, sometimes backed up by the man with the sad-spaniel face, whom Tom christened Mr Noyes – because all he ever said at the sessions was 'No' and 'Yes'. Sometimes Ponsonby turned up. When he was alone and the weather permitted, he would conduct his sessions outside the house, presumably to avoid microphones.

'I know you're lying,' he told Tom again and again. 'Why don't you make it easy on yourself? I don't give a fuck about the mission now. That's all ancient history. But I want to know what you did with my half million dollars.'

Instinct prompted Tom to confine himself to an expanded version of the story he had given Ponsonby in the Metro station. Thus it was always the same account: 'He pulled a gun. I handed it over. He told me to get out of the car and drove off. That's the last I saw of your bloody agent or the money.'

And so the weeks passed. The guards were a team of fit young clones in tracksuits and trainer shoes who managed to look both bored and alert at the same time. Each day, two of them accompanied Tom for an hour's exercise in the gardens. Cars came and went on most days but the only people Tom was ever allowed to see were his interrogators, the security men and the middle-aged couple who did odd jobs around the house and cooked endless curries, which was all the minders ever seemed to eat.

Tom's repeated requests to see a lawyer were met with a bland assurance that, so far, there were no charges against him. He was, it seemed, simply helping with enquiries.

'Helping whom, Mr Brodsky?' he asked again and again.

'The government, of course.'

'But what department or ministry do you represent?'

'I'm not allowed to say.'

When Tom mentioned the Habeas Corpus Act of 1679, Brodsky shrugged. 'You're a Russian citizen. I'm not sure the law applies to you. In any case, it would be necessary for a judge to issue the writ – and no judge knows you are here.'

Twice Tom attempted to walk out of the grounds. He had no real expectation of escape but hoped by causing an incident to force a decision out of someone.

The first time was in broad daylight after an argument with Brodsky. Before reaching the gate, he was politely but firmly led back to the house by two of the clones. On the second occasion he waited until after being locked into his room at night and then climbed out of the window and shinned down a drainpipe. He had almost reached the boundary wall when two clones materialised in front of him, alerted by one of the infrared alarms which he had unwittingly set off. To make the point that Tom had annoyed them, they beat him up quietly and systematically on the spot, taking care that each blow landed where bruises would not show. Winded and retching, he was dragged upstairs and locked in a smaller bedroom at the top of the house which had bars on the windows.

Dr Nathan's first visit came on the sixth Sunday of Tom's debriefing. The distant bell for morning service had just stopped ringing. At that moment of the week, with nothing to read and no other entertainment, even Brodsky's questions would have been a welcome relief for Tom.

One of the guards unlocked his bedroom door and said, 'On your feet. You've got a visitor.'

In the sun-filled drawing room, Dr Tessa Nathan sat wreathed in cigarette smoke, back-lit against a window. For a moment, Tom failed to recognise her. She was wearing a flower-patterned summer dress and criss-cross sandals with one-inch heels. A dab of lipstick, some eye shadow and a discreet use of mascara made her look startlingly feminine, in contrast with the unisex person he remembered.

'Why don't we take a stroll in the garden?' she suggested. 'You must be fed up with being grilled in stuffy rooms and it's such a beautiful day.'

Once outside, she headed for the maze because: 'It symbolises the twists and turns of life, I always think. Mind if I call you Tom?'

The weather was warm and showery. One of the guards was following them, a discreet twenty paces behind. Tom wondered whether some sophisticated listening device was picking up the crunch of their feet on the gravel path and relaying it to Ponsonby, crouched like a spider where all the electronic strands converged. Had the cries – his own cries – that woke him from disturbed slumber that morning been recorded, listened to and discussed by strangers already? Was that why Dr Nathan had come? Or was she there to find a way round his defences that had escaped the masculine brains pitted against him? After all the weeks of being probed and watched, Tom had the feeling of being a living, breathing public building, into which anyone could come and poke around at will.

As they entered the maze, Dr Nathan remarked, 'At least they've dried you out here, Tom. Or will you go back on the booze when you get the chance?'

'Probably,' he said. The only game he could play was to say the opposite of the truth whenever plausible.

Clouds were building up for the next shower. He took off his sweater and used it to wipe dry a slatted wooden seat so that they could sit down. Surrounded by green privet hedges in all directions, they seemed alone even though the minder was doubtless somewhere within earshot. Tom noticed that Dr Nathan seemed impatient, lighting each cigarette before she had finished the previous one and looking at her watch surreptitiously.

The conversation was rambling and imprecise: an exploration of sorts. When it touched on guilt, he said, 'I don't have any. I'm the one who's been screwed, but no one seems bothered by that.'

'I gather there's some money gone missing.'

He laughed. 'Do I look like a man with a half million dollars in the bank?'

'Loyalty,' she said later, 'is a very primitive emotion, Tom. It's what binds together the family in the cave and makes possible the hunting band and the war party. We talk of symbols – queen and country – but really it's family or tribe we betray.'

'I don't have either.'

'I thought they lived in the Lake District?'

'I wrote to my parents,' he said.

She probably knew anyway, so he told her: 'I was allowed to send one letter, using an accommodation address for any reply. My letter came back, with the envelope marked "Return to Sender".'

'Perhaps they've moved to a new address?'

'I recognised my mother's handwriting.'

'That must have hurt.'

'Pain,' said Tom, 'is all a question of thresholds. Put a bullet through someone's kneecap and he'll forget about his toothache.'

After the nth glance at her watch, Dr Nathan stubbed out her final cigarette on the leg of the bench and stood up. 'I must be going. Is there anything you'd like me to bring you, the next time I come?'

As all prisoners in solitary confinement know, there are moments – in the early hours, after a few days of being left alone or during the infinitely long weekends – when they come close to talking because morale plummets from sheer loneliness. The art of successful interrogation lies in exploiting these moments of weakness and arriving with a small present like a cigarette or a drink – or even just a friendly word. Well-timed human warmth can be more effective at unlocking secrets than thumbscrews or the rack.

Dr Nathan's job was to assess Tom's weaknesses, but that day she had something more compelling on her mind. When she left he was escorted upstairs and locked in his room. He heard the noise of a car travelling fast up the gravel drive to the house and craned his head between the bars on the window. The driver braked hard and skidded to a halt in a shower of gravel with half the car showing round the corner of the house. Tom could see the top of a low-slung red sports car and part of the bonnet.

A man's shirtsleeved arm emerged from the open driver's window and a finger beckoned. Dr Tessa Nathan MD ran across the gravel with the step of a young girl. Her face was flushed and she looked fifteen years younger as she opened the passenger door to slip inside the car with a flash of stockinged legs. Listening to the roar of the Morgan's exhaust growing fainter, Tom had no doubt in his mind that the arm and the beckoning finger belonged to Clive Ponsonby.

*

HM Prison Wandsworth was a black hole defying time and geographical co-ordinates where normal values were turned upside down. Some of the warders were vicious sociopaths, some of the criminals decent men whose lives were simply out of control. The majority were social inadequates, exploited by the prison aristocracy of hard men who handed out beatings for offences that even a capricious medieval monarch might have pardoned.

The real victims of the system were the screws. Tom's cell-mate in the remand wing was a professional burglar in his mid-thirties with a wife and two young children. As he said, 'We get out when we've done our time, mate. Those poor bastards have to stay inside for life. No wonder they're sour.'

Advised by his legal aid solicitor that the best tactic when faced with a prosecution under Section 2 of the Official Secrets Act was to plead guilty in the expectation of a sentence of two years on each charge, to run concurrently with remission for good behaviour, Tom agreed. He learned – also from his cell-mate, who was more helpful than either of the lawyers had been – that although Parliament had abolished capital punishment for murder, it remained on the statute books for one offence only. The single crime for which a man could legally be executed in Britain was treason. And the place where the sentence would be carried out was Wandsworth, where the condemned cell and execution chamber were kept in working order with regular maintenance and tests. It was all part of the pressure Ponsonby was applying.

Prisoner-on-remand Fielding W.T.C. was charged with fraudulent conversion of government funds, visiting a prohibited foreign country without permission, disclosing classified information to a possible enemy and retaining classified documents without permission. Only afterwards did he learn – from another prisoner, likewise a victim of the Act – that the judge had been chosen for his record of favouring the security services, that the jury had been picked from a list vetted by MI5 and that the defence counsel had been drawn from a panel of barristers with security clearance and a record of never biting the hand that fed them. The entire trial lasted less than four hours, and was held almost entirely in camera at the request of the prosecution: '. . . for reasons that touch upon the Defence of the Realm, my lord.'

The hearing was a verbal game played between the bewigged barristers and the judge, a grey, shrivelled man peering over half-moon glasses like a short-sighted mole, whose pursed lips expressed a dislike of the accused from the first moment. No one had explained the arcane rules of the game to Tom. He listened to the elaborate mock fencing of the two barristers with a growing sense of alienation. It was hard to stay aware that the ball they were kicking around the court was himself.

At the end of the trial, Ponsonby appeared, sitting at the back of the court to hear the judge deliver a sermon on treachery before taking apparently personal pleasure in handing out the maximum sentence on each count, to be served not concurrently, but consecutively. Stunned at the prospect of eight years in prison, Tom stumbled twice as he was led down the stairs to the cells beneath the court. His barrister was nowhere to be seen. The solicitor appeared and said one word: 'Sorry.'

In the interview room at Wormwood Scrubs next day, Ponsonby, wearing a smart three-piece blue suit and regimental tie, looked amused to see Tom in ill-fitting prison uniform. He threw a copy of the *Daily Telegraph* onto the bare metal table in front of Tom and murmured, 'Enjoy your brief moment of fame, dear boy.'

The paper was folded to a two-paragraph report on an inside page to the effect that T.W.C. Fielding, a former employee of the MOD, had been found guilty of offences under the Official Secrets Act and sentenced to eight years' imprisonment. Under the British censorship system of

D-Notices, no British newspaper printed any further information about the case, nor ever would.

Anger erupted. Tom threw the newspaper back at Ponsonby. 'If you call me *dear boy* one more time, I'll smash your teeth in,' he snarled. 'You fucked me and it was rape. I don't have to pretend I enjoyed it like poor Tessa Nathan.'

Ponsonby's eyes gave nothing away. 'Go on,' he dared. 'If it'll make you feel better, take a swipe at me.'

'One day I will,' Tom promised. 'But not while you have all the advantages.'

Ponsonby nodded curtly at the warder standing by the door. When the man had left the room, he said, 'Forget the trial, Tom. It was only to make you see reason. I know you're lying about the meeting with Viktor. Tell me what actually happened and I'll do a deal.'

He snapped his fingers. 'I can get your sentence reduced on appeal to two years suspended, just like that.'

'Is the law so pliable, Clive?'

Ponsonby's smile displayed his perfect teeth. 'To hell with the law. The judiciary is an organ of the state.'

Tom stood up and knocked on the door, asking to be taken back to his cell.

'Who was that Savile Row shit that was baiting you?' the warder asked on the way back to Tom's cell. He was one of the older prison officers, nearing retirement, with the face of a man who had seen and heard a million variations of man's inhumanity to man.

'He's just a figment of a bad dream,' said Tom.

'Well, don't let the effing figment get to you,' was the screw's advice. 'It'll cost you six months' remission if you hit the bastard.'

'It would almost be worth it.'

'Nothing's worth it, believe me. Do your time, get out and don't come back.'

.2.

'I wanted to visit you earlier,' said Tom's sister, 'but they always refused my request.'

'Not *they*,' said Tom. 'It was me. I refused to let you come.'

'Father was right, then. He said that you must hate us all very much.'

'He was wrong, Megs. I don't hate you.'

'Then why wouldn't you see me?'

'Closed prisons are not places for a nicely brought-up girl to visit,' Tom explained gently. 'I didn't want you to see your own brother behind bars, wearing prison uniform.'

They were walking in the grounds of Longfield open prison, to which Tom had been transferred after serving his second year at Winson Green Prison in Birmingham. Like the other prisoners at Longfield, he was wearing his own clothes, so that outwardly there was nothing to distinguish them from the visitors that Saturday afternoon. A game of cricket was being played on the sports pitch between the

home team and a local eleven, small family groups were pic-
nicking on the lawn and couples were strolling in and out of
the gate.

Tom had taken his sister on a tour of his room, the cafe-
teria, the library, the workshops and the classroom where he
was teaching an 'A' level course on the origins of the Second
World War.

'This place is like school,' she said brightly.

'Apart from the blue and white *HM Prisons* sign by the
gate,' he agreed, 'and the fact that exeats are few and far
between.'

'Mummy will be so pleased that you're teaching again.'

'It staves off the boredom for an hour or so.'

They walked among the rose beds that were the governor's pride. Megs examined the blooms closely and bent to
read the name plaques planted beneath each bush as though
that was what she had come for.

'Did you tell anyone you were coming to see me?' Tom
asked, meaning the family.

'I talked it over with Mummy, of course.'

'And?'

'She said it was a matter for my conscience, whether I visited you or not.'

Tom watched a visiting batsman score a boundary. 'How
is your conscience, Megs? Troubled at going against your
father's wishes, even at your age?'

Tom's sister took a handkerchief from her handbag and
started twisting it between her hands. It was a habit he
remembered.

'It's hard for him,' she said. 'You know how patriotic
Father is, how ashamed he must be to have a traitor in the
family.'

'He sees everything in black and white,' Tom snapped.
'It's time he grew up.'

'He suffered for his country,' she said defensively. 'It's
not easy for him to accept that you went to Russia and gave

them classified information. He said, "If Tom's actions were due to a sincere belief in a different political system – albeit an atheistic one – I could try to understand. But to steal government funds . . .'"

'And how does he know that I'm guilty as charged?' Tom interrupted.

'Because you had a fair trial.'

Having mixed so long with convicted men, Tom had forgotten that people like his parents believed in the infallibility of British justice. 'And do you think I'm guilty, Megs?'

The handkerchief was now a tormented rag. 'I don't know what to think. But even if you are, you're my brother.'

'Oh, God!' he burst out. 'You're all so bloody innocent. Do you still go to church every Sunday?'

'Of course.'

He rounded on her. 'Because you want to? Or because Our Father will be angry if you don't go?'

'You're being unfair, Tom. Unfair to me and him.'

'I probably am,' he admitted, calming down. 'So, tell me about yourself. How's work?'

Her grimace made him want to hug her. It reminded him of the timid schoolgirl whom he had walked home from school each afternoon throughout one whole winter because she was frightened to cross a council estate on her own and brave the torrent of obscenities that the local children reserved for a vicar's daughter.

'The job's boring,' she admitted, 'but it's very safe and the pension's good.'

The moment of warmth was gone. 'You're thirty years old – and already you're worried about a pension?'

'I can't say a thing right, can I?'

'I'm sorry,' Tom apologised, aware that he was venting a backlog of frustration and anger on someone who did not deserve it. 'What about your private life, Megs? Have you got a boyfriend?'

She shook her head. 'No one special at the moment.'

'No one you could take home and expect to pass Father's scrutiny?'

'It's not like that.'

'I think it is.' Tom could feel the anger building and tried to hold it back, aware of the courage it had taken for her to defy her parents by coming to see him.

'You've gone back to live at home?'

She nodded. 'I think Mummy's less lonely with me to chat to. Anyway, I never liked living on my own.'

Taking in the flat shoes, the unfashionably long skirt, the drab colours she chose to wear and the unbecoming hairstyle, Tom saw that already his sister had a spinster's walk. She *looked* like a vicar's unmarried daughter who had espoused a safe job in local government and would one day probably abandon it in order to stay at home and look after her ageing parents.

'It's time you cut loose,' he said. 'Start living your own life, Megs. Otherwise you'll end up like Mother, neutered and sterile, wondering where her life went.'

She looked at Tom as though he had hit her. Again the image was of the frightened girl in school uniform. He put his hand on her arm to say he was sorry but she turned away from him with a muttered, 'I shouldn't have come. You're not the brother I knew. God bless you, Tom.'

*

'You're getting very bitter,' said Tessa Nathan.

She sat in the library at Longfield lighting a cigarette beneath the No Smoking sign.

Tom opened a window to let the smoke out. 'I was screwed,' he said over his shoulder. 'Why shouldn't I be bitter about it?'

'Because that way, Clive wins twice over,' she said quietly.

'How do you make that out, Dr Nathan?'

'Once by keeping you in here for however long it is. And again because he'll have diminished the quality of your life for ever, if you let the bitterness work on you like this.'

'What do you care? Isn't Ponsonby paying for your trip up here today?'

'I'm a doctor, Tom,' she said. 'Not the best kind maybe – but still a doctor with a duty to patients.'

'And I am a patient, Tessa?'

'You will be – not mine perhaps but someone else's – the way you're going.'

'Being treated for what illness?'

'A condition loosely termed *terminal bitterness*.'

'Then what do you suggest?' He leaned on his knuckles and glared at her across the plain deal table. 'Going to church every Sunday? I've done that, when I was a kid. It didn't work.'

'You could try writing everything down,' she said.

'So that's the idea? I write it down. Someone photocopies it when I'm doing my daily workout . . . and Ponsonby gets the story that way.'

She ignored the sarcasm. 'Use a computer. Put a password on the file and nobody can access it except for you. Can you use a word processor?'

'I use the one in the library to prepare my lecture notes, but I don't know any tricks like passwords.'

She laughed. 'You couldn't be in a better place to ask for help. How many of your fellow-inmates are here for computer fraud? A dozen or more, I should think.'

The tension went out of Tom. He never forgot why Tessa Nathan was paid to come and talk with him, but even so the conversations with her always made him feel good. After each visit he felt as though a breath of sanity had blown away some of the residue of anger that was building up inside him.

'I'd need to buy my own PC,' he said. 'And you know what the pay is like here.'

'I've got an old Apple Mac. You can have it, if you want.'

'Why are you doing this for me, Tessa?'

'You shouldn't be here,' she said. 'I don't know all the

details but Ponsonby screwed you, one way or another. Don't quote me, but I'm sure of that.'

'So your offer is an anti-Ponsonby gesture?'

'There's a bit of guilt in it too,' she admitted. 'It's partly my fault you got mixed up in whatever you are mixed up in. Oh, let's just say it's more of a gesture of solidarity between victims of the same oppressor.'

'I wondered,' said Tom. 'All those flowery dresses . . .'

'Laura Ashley did rather well out of me for a few months,' she sighed. 'And all that waiting for the telephone to ring . . .'

'So what's your personal therapy?' Tom asked. 'Or is that an improper question to ask one's favourite shrink?'

It was the first time he had heard her laugh outright. 'Helping a fellow-victim, perhaps. So do you want it, or not? The Apple Mac, I mean.'

'I'll give it a try.'

'Okay.' She emptied the travelling ashtray into a plastic bag. 'I thought you'd say yes. I've got it outside in the car. If I may give you a word of advice, Tom – start at the very beginning and don't hurry.'

'Time,' he said, 'I've got plenty of.'

'And stop making sarcastic remarks like that.'

'Is that an order?'

'It's a condition.' She placed her hand on his. 'I give you the computer and in return you promise to mount your own personal anti-bitterness campaign. Do we have a deal?'

Tom thought about it. 'Seems like heads I win and tails I win.'

'Be a winner,' she said cheerfully. 'Let's show the bastard he doesn't always come out on top, eh?'

They walked together to the car park. 'I'm not sure this is going to work,' Tom said, hefting the Apple Mac off the rear seat of her Volkswagen Scirocco.

'Nonsense.' Tessa lit another cigarette. 'You've written two books. Just write everything down. Treat it like a first-person novel. That way you can explore your own motives and feelings without having to guess at other people's. It could be really therapeutic.'

'I misjudged you.'

She looked up at him holding the computer and wondered whether she had left it too late.

'The vital thing,' she said, 'is not to misjudge yourself.'

Tom sat for a long time looking at the blank page on the screen. Start at the beginning, Tessa had said. But where was the beginning?

He got up and paced his room. It had to be neat and tidy for the daily inspection, so he had become used to keeping it that way, day and night, in order to save work. Accidentally kicking the bedside rug crooked, he bent down from habit to straighten it immediately. Someone was playing house music a few doors away down the corridor and the television was on in the next room. He had taught himself to ignore other men's noise during the years in prison and told himself to concentrate.

What about the first meeting with Ponsonby at the Institute? No, beginning there would leave out a large part of the relationship with Karen. If the whole point of the exercise was to come to terms with the person he had been and accept responsibility for his decisions and actions, then Karen must be part of the beginning.

The memories began to sift themselves. The music had finished and the television been turned off when he sat down and started to write:

I walked out of the bookshop at the top of Park Street. It was the first really hot day in June 1982. The newspaper headlines prophesied the imminent end of the Falklands War. I'd been trying to pin Ashmole down about the renewal of my contract and was hoping to catch him on the way to lunch at his club near College Green.

At the bottom of the hill, I stubbed my toe and looked

up to see the Fat Boy sitting on one of the benches with this girl talking to him. It wasn't exactly love at first sight. She was skinny, looked like she'd just been jogging and was wearing a pair of ghastly spectacles that I later persuaded her to get rid of.

Ashmole, as usual, got my name wrong . . .

.3.

'Je-sus, you must be bored out of your mind in this place!'

Karen's frank reaction to a tour of Longfield's facilities made Tom laugh, defusing the tension and uncertainty that spoils so many prison visits. Her attitude was the reverse of the way his sister had tried to look on the bright side of things.

'I can do everything I want,' he said, 'except walk out of the gate and not come back.'

'How much longer have you got to do?'

'With remission,' he said, 'I could be out on probation in twenty-six months, two weeks and three days.'

She whistled. 'I'd go crazy if it was me.'

'Here it's not so bad, but in the Scrubs, banged-up for fourteen hours at a stretch, I thought I'd go nuts,' he admitted. 'Slopping out in a stinking queue of men in the early morning, counting the days one-two-three and knowing that I might still be in that same cell when I'd got past 2,000 . . .'

'So when exactly do you get out?'

'It depends,' said Tom.

'On what?'

'In theory, on the parole board. In fact, on that bastard Ponsonby.'

'Who's he?'

'He's the cat to whom I play mouse.'

'That guy! I'd forgotten the name. Well, he really screwed you. You must be very bitter.'

'I'm working on it.'

On the sports pitch the football match was nearly over, with the referee lecturing one of the home team about unnecessary violence. One of the linesmen, seeing Tom strolling past, jeered at him for letting the team down but Karen called back, 'Blame me, guys. It's my fault.'

The chorus of whistles, interspersed with a few obscene remarks, shocked her into awareness that beneath the superficial normality of the scene were dark depths of sexual frustration and physical violence. There were no iron bars, but these men were caged all the same.

She had hesitated for a whole week after getting Tom's letter, addressed to her care of Toronto University. It was the first news she had had of him in years. The image of him locked away from society for so long shocked her into writing a reply the same day. His second letter made her realise that he had changed a lot. On her side, curiosity mingled with compassion as the correspondence grew.

She watched him now watching the players on the field for the few remaining minutes of the game, and liked what the years had done to his face. With the stodgy food and little exercise, Tom had put on weight in the Scrubs and Winson Green. After losing it, lines had remained on his forehead and around his eyes, which erased for ever the expression of dilettante arrogance that had annoyed people when he was younger. His hairline had also receded and nature had given him a few silver highlights in his hair.

Overall, Karen thought the effect was a considerable improvement.

Half-watching the players on the field, Tom was thinking how the years had done Karen a few favours too. Her features had broadened and softened; she wore her hair longer and in a more feminine style. And the body that had been slim as a boy's now had curves in all the right places.

As the teams ran off the pitch after the final whistle, he said, 'I didn't ask how your husband is.'

Karen blinked at the word *husband*. 'If you mean Larry, we got divorced after three months. Now he has the wife he deserves and two pretty little daughters.'

'It didn't work out?'

'I cried every night on my honeymoon,' she said flatly. 'That's not an auspicious beginning to any marriage.'

'You cried because of me?'

'Was it hell because of you!' She glared at Tom. 'I cried for Larry. It was such a rotten thing to do to a nice guy.'

'I seem to have a genius for complicating my own and other people's lives . . .'

Karen was not going to contradict him. It was an extension of his thought when she prompted, 'Tell me about the girl in Russia.'

'How did you know there was one?'

'There had to be a girl.' She was watching his face closely. 'I don't believe you defected. More likely you fell in love with a Russian girl and decided to stay there. So what was she like?'

'Beautiful. We had a kid – a little girl called Svetlana. She's just had her seventh birthday.'

Catching the fleeting expression of pain on his face before he turned away, Karen wanted to reach out and touch him, but the memory of the whistles and jeers held her back. She contented herself with asking, 'Do you hear from them?'

Tom shook his head. 'I sent a birthday card but I don't

know whether they'll let her see it – or even what my name would mean to her if they did.'

'Who's they?'

'Her mother lives with one of the new fat cats over there: an American hamburger king. I suppose Svetlana's been brought up to think of him as her father.'

'When did you two split up?' Karen asked softly. 'Was that why you chose to come back to England?'

'I didn't choose to come back. I was sold.' For a moment the bitterness rose like bile, until Tom repressed it. 'I don't want to talk about that.'

'Is that a way of saying, it's none of my business?'

'I didn't mean that at all,' he protested. 'If I could talk to anyone, it would be you.'

They were alone on the deserted pitch. He grabbed Karen by both arms and pulled her towards him, wanting to be close to another body for a moment of shared warmth, but she misunderstood and slipped away, keeping her distance.

'Don't get me wrong,' she said with a half-laugh. 'My boyfriend is Sicilian and very jealous.'

Tom made a gesture of apology. 'I just felt good seeing you again, that's all.'

'Me too.' Karen was inspecting the running track and thinking how much fitter Tom looked than when she had known him before.

'You used to be a flabby scholar,' she remarked. 'Now you're in better shape than I am.'

'Every morning I do an hour's workout in the gym. Every afternoon, rain or shine, I run for an hour.'

'Good for you,' she said over her shoulder, walking ahead. 'That way, the bastards are not calling all the shots.'

'You used to run, I remember.'

'Now I run to fat,' she grinned, turning unselfconsciously to pat her hips.

The changed hairstyle and the discreet use of make-up made her hard for Tom to be close to after the years of abstinence. Even in jeans and an unzipped anorak Karen was turning him on. He could not take his eyes off her breasts, which were larger than he remembered; her figure was altogether more curvaceous.

Catching the hungry stare, she pulled her anorak closed and made a joke: 'It's all that pasta I eat when I'm working on Mount Etna.'

Tom thought that asking about her boyfriend might be a way of deflecting his lust before it spoiled the fragile contact between them. He learned that Professore Luigi Della Porta was a seasonal lover, for when she was working in Sicily on Mount Etna.

'The rest of the time he lives with his wife and kids in Bologna and I teach geology at the U of T.' Karen shrugged. 'Two vulcanologists make for a fiery relationship, so it could never be permanent.'

It was starting to drizzle. On the lawn in front of the governor's rose garden, visitors were starting to pack up picnics and say their goodbyes.

'I was reading in *National Geographic* magazine about the volcanoes on the Kamchatka peninsula,' Tom said casually.

'I saw the article. Good pictures.'

'There are some pretty important volcanoes over there: Tolbachik, Klyuchevskaya . . . Had you ever thought of taking a look at them?'

'Trouble is, the Russians make too many bureaucratic problems.'

'Not now,' he disagreed. 'Wave a fistful of dollars and your opposite numbers in Petropavlovsk will welcome you to Kamchatka with open arms.'

'What makes you think I have a fistful of dollars? Vulcanology is a poor science – except in the immediate aftermath of an eruption that has claimed a lot of lives.'

'Think about it,' he said. 'I know your Russian's wobbly but I'll lay a hundred to one that it's better than most of your colleagues could manage.'

'Wouldn't I have trouble, being from an émigré family?'

'Ever heard of xenophobia? Russians prefer dealing with other Russians, no matter what they may have done in the past. You know, if you move now you could be the first Western vulcanologist to publish a paper on Siberian volcanoes.'

Tom saw immediately that he had touched a chord.

'You could have something there,' Karen said thoughtfully. 'I've been getting the message that my obsession with Etna is boring my colleagues and that I ought to publish something more original if I want to get the chair that's been promised me when my boss retires in three years' time.'

'If I can help set things up in Siberia . . .' Tom threw the offer away. ' . . . just let me know. I've got a second-hand computer which I'm using to put together a course of lectures on the collapse of the Soviet Empire. That still leaves me with plenty of spare time. With the fax module, I could handle your correspondence from here. I'd need the governor's permission but I'm sure he'd give it, in the interests of international co-operation between scientists, etcetera, etcetera. I'd be more than happy to help out with translations, advise you how to fill in forms, how much to offer people, and so on.'

'You'd be willing to do all that?' Karen sounded wary.

Understanding the reason, Tom said, 'Put yourself in my place. By giving me some real work to do, you'll be doing me a favour.'

She was thinking that Tom's idea was pivotal. If it failed, she had lost nothing. If it came off, she would be able to publish something really original. It would also give her an excuse to keep in touch with him on a regular basis without any emotional implications.

'I'll come over and have another chat when I've had time to think it over,' she said. 'If that's okay with you.'

'Any time.' Tom grinned. 'You know where to find me.'

He had forgotten how fast she could move. The kiss on his lips was delivered and over before he could return it.

'You're such a fool,' she said. 'Why'd you do it?'

'I didn't.'

'I mean, why'd you get mixed up with all this? D'you want to tell me about it?'

'One day,' he promised.

He walked Karen to the visitors' car park and watched her drive away in a hire car. A bell was ringing for the evening meal but he felt too zipped-up to eat. He changed into his running strip and did ten circuits of the cinder track without even feeling the rain on his face and body. Even after he had showered and changed, the elation did not lessen.

Like many men locked away from society for a long period, especially those who consider themselves innocent, he had become obsessed that the world owed him retribution for the prime years of his life which had been spent in prison. It seemed in retrospect unbelievably naïve to have kissed goodbye to a fortune by leaving the icon at the bottom of the well. He had found it; therefore it belonged to him. What did he owe to Rada and the others? What had they done for him, except betray him, sell him back to Britain and place him at Ponsonby's mercy? What did he owe anyone?

But how to reclaim what was his by right? To get into Russia, all he needed was a stolen but genuine passport in another name – which would be easy, for a man with the connections Tom had made in prison. The problems came later. With the collapse of the USSR many things might have altered in Eastern Europe but the traditional xenophobia of the Slav mind would be unchanged. Passport controls, visa requirements and all the endless snooping and checking up on foreigners had not been introduced by Communism but been just as rife under the tsars.

The best idea he had thought up so far for getting the icon safely out of the country was to help set Karen up as a foreign scientist who routinely came and went to some remote part of Siberia. Using her as cover, he planned to sneak himself onto her team for one visit, take an internal flight to Irkutsk, recover the icon and smuggle it out, concealed among the team's scientific equipment.

After which – or so the fantasy went – he would be rich for the rest of his life.

Riding a mental high that would not go away, Tom lay awake that night until dawn, wondering whether Karen would take the bait.

'I'm sorry,' Ponsonby said. 'But we had to open it. The letter got held up for a couple of days in my In tray, so I thought it no more than decent to drive down here and let you have it without more delay.'

He had timed his arrival to catch Tom when the staff and prisoners were all at lunch, so that they were alone in the library at Longfield. Dressed as smartly as usual, he sat rock still, watching Tom read and re-read the letter through eyes that refused to focus on the paper in his hand.

Anticipating interception, Rada had written in English, using silver ink on mauve paper:

Dear Tom,

You can know Svetlana is well when you see this photograph of her. I hope you like it.

In your letter you talk about after you come out of prison. You must know that is all over. I have my life and you have yours. Svetlana is part of me, not you. If you want to visit her here some days, that is okay but no more than that. You know, you have only yourself to blame for what happened between us, Tom. When I am finding out how you are using me, my love is finished. But I don't write apologies.

I hope you are healthy now and not drink so much, which would be good for you, I think. Anyway, my father sends his greetings and also Ivan Petrovich. And Svetlana, she says prayer for you each night.

The photograph was signed *To Daddy with Love*. Tom thrust it into his shirt pocket and tore the single sheet of mauve paper into smaller and smaller shreds. He scooped the pile of paper off the plain deal table and tipped it carefully into the waste-bin beneath.

He kept his voice level. 'Lately, I've worked some things out, Clive. The state I was in, those last few months in Russia, I couldn't think straight. But just recently I've been putting a lot of energy into working out what happened and who's to blame. I wondered even at the time what that business with the dentist was all about. It had to mean that Ivanov knew I had been working for you all along, because no innocent immigrant gets to have a suicide pill implanted in a tooth filling. And the money I saw Ivan Petrovich counting at the handover was not the price of shipping back an ordinary citizen. You paid way over the odds for me, so he obviously knew the true nature of the goods being sold. The question is, who told what to whom and when?'

'Delusions of grandeur, dear boy. We bought back a lot of defectors after the Wall fell down. Not just you.'

Tom ignored the interruption. He scooped the pieces of mauve paper out of the bin and watched them fall through his fingers like petals from a flower that had been beautiful and was now dead. Then he stood up with his back to Ponsonby, looking out of the window at the neat gardens and the governor's house beyond.

For a long time I had suspected that Ponsonby had started flushing me out of cover very soon after the meeting on the Metro station when I declared my intention of not returning to Britain. That phrase of Rada's about me using her had to mean that one of Ponsonby's running dogs had found a way of telling her that I was a spy who had married

*her just to provide myself with cover. It was nicely
calculated, I granted him that. He must have gambled that
Rada was an essentially decent person who would not shop
me to the KGB. But no wonder she had thought I didn't
love her and gone looking for someone who did. With a
marriage breaking up and nothing to live for in Russia,
most foreigners would have run for home. It might even
have worked with me, if I hadn't had Svetlana.*

*When I challenged Ponsonby with what I had worked
out, he chuckled, 'Get a grip on yourself, Tom.'*

*It was an odd quirk of his that he never actually told me
a lie. When he didn't want to divulge something, he
avoided the question.*

*I said something like, 'Don't worry. I'm really in
control.'*

*Then I turned, pulled him to his feet and in one fluid
motion smashed my left fist into the bridge of his nose. It
was a moment to remember: four years of frustration and
impotence went into that blow. He subsided onto the chair
with a gasp of pain, both hands clutching his broken nose
and with blood pouring over his clean shirt and immaculate
suit.*

'You've just lost six months' remission,' he groaned.

'Twelve,' I suggested. 'Make it twelve, Clive.'

*As his hands came away from his face in surprise, I hit
him again in the same place, making him yelp in agony.*

*I felt almost peaceful, seeing the bastard bleeding and in
pain, and handed him my handkerchief to mop up the
mess. I wanted him to understand the reason why I had hit
him, so I said without raising my voice, 'That's for calling
me "dear boy". I warned you what I would do.'*

*'You're fucking crazy!' he snarled, head back and trying
to staunch the flow with my handkerchief.*

*I grabbed a handful of his hair and pulled his head down
so that he could see me, and said in the same calm tones,
'As for the damage you did to my life – and to Rada's and*

Svetlana's – I can't think of an adequate way of repaying that. But if I ever do, Clive – believe me, I'll come looking for you.'

Until that moment I had not been 100 per cent sure. The brief look of fear in his eyes told me I had been right, so I took my hands off him before I did any more harm and walked out of the library, back to my room.

.4.

'I don't like what I remember of them,' Karen said on one of her subsequent visits, 'but shouldn't you try to heal the rift with your family – both for their sake and yours?'

'You sound like my favourite shrink,' said Tom. 'She's been trying to get me to write to them – oh, in a very subtle way – for months.'

'Then why don't you?'

'Because I know them.'

'That sounds bitter.'

'You're right,' said Tom after a moment. 'I should make an attempt at contacting them – if only for Megs' sake. I feel badly about her. She came to see me when I was very mixed up. The poor girl couldn't handle it.'

A little later, Tessa Nathan pointed out that Tom had not used a single sleeping-out permit. 'I recommend you should, Tom. You have to face the fact that, after nearly four years inside, you've become institutionalised. The weekend pass system is designed to smooth the transition back to normal life which otherwise, believe me, can be shattering.'

The reply from Tom's sister said simply:

Father had a small stroke last month and has finally agreed with the Bishop that it is time to retire and let the new vicar take over 100 per cent. Apparently Father could pass away at any time. Mother thinks that it would be a pity if he dies without giving you his blessing.

Because of various commitments the first time we can all be together is on Whit Sunday. Please arrive at 1.15. We shall lunch at 1.45 precisely. You know how Father hates unpunctuality.

The call from Karen reached Tom at lunch-time on the Friday.

'You're where?' he asked. He was standing in an acoustic booth outside the canteen. It was hard to hear what she was saying against the background noise.

'I'm at London airport, on my way to Sicily,' she repeated. 'Siberia's taking up so much of my time now that I'm saying goodbye to Etna. If there's any chance of seeing you, I'll stop over in England for the weekend.'

The first visit to Kamchatka had gone well, she said. Tom wanted to know what formalities the geological team from Toronto had been subjected to on flying from Anchorage to Petropavlovsk. There were a thousand questions he wanted to ask, but casually in a conversation, not over the telephone or by fax. So he offered to cancel the trip to the north, but Karen persuaded him to let the arrangement stand and suggested that she could accompany him.

'I've never seen the English Lake District, Tom. Who better to show it to me than you? I can pick up a rental car at the airport, collect you and we'll drive up there together.'

'It sounds like a dream,' he said.

'I could even come and meet your family, if you want.

Perhaps that would make it easier for everyone. Sometimes an outsider . . .'

'No thanks,' Tom cut her off. 'My father would probably anathematise you as the topless whore who held my hand when I took my first steps on the slippery road to sin.'

'Have it your way,' Karen laughed. 'While you eat Sunday lunch at the manse or whatever you call it, I'll amuse myself, doing the tourist sights in the nearest town. How's that?'

Whit Sunday was a cool, blustery May day. Tourists and weekend trippers strolled through the streets of Keswick, buying postcards and ice creams. Hardy hill walkers were bundled up in thick anoraks, wearing backpacks as they clumped around the town in boots and hairy wool socks into which thick trousers were tucked.

Tom and Karen braved the rain showers to walk up Skiddaw's bleak flanks after breakfast. Afterwards they drove down to the lakeside where a few rowing boats bobbed peacefully at their moorings. Beneath the catkin-burdened willows, they drank the two cans of Labatt's Ice Beer which Karen had brought from Toronto as a present. Watching the seagulls wheeling over Derwentwater and swooping down to catch in mid-air the pieces of bread that picnickers were throwing for them, Tom grilled her gently about the trip to Siberia, forgetting about the time until Karen pointed out that he was going to be late. He wondered aloud whether people in normal families specified an exact time of arrival for a visit to aged parents which entailed a long journey.

'Relax,' Karen squeezed his hand. 'Give those guys a break. Remember the parable of the prodigal son? This being the sabbath, it could be you're in for a tearful reconciliation. So let's go!'

She dropped Tom at the gates of the Old Rectory at exactly 1.10 p.m. and drove off, heading south to visit the disused graphite mines at Seathwaite while he was with his family.

Tom walked past the new vicarage, a modern house built at the bottom of the drive. There was the sound of children's voices coming through an open window. On the washing carousel children's clothes were hung out to dry although it was Sunday. The small, fenced-off garden was an untidy jungle of uncut grass, toys, bicycles and gardening tools. At the top of the drive all was order and quiet, the gravel weedless, the lawn neatly trimmed. Poking out of the garage doorway was the freshly waxed bonnet of his father's vintage racing green Bristol. There was a gleaming new black 800 series Rover saloon parked by the front door and, beside it, a rusting and dented blue Ford Escort that, Tom guessed, must belong to his sister.

He opened the front door to hear a murmur of voices in the sitting room. From the rear of the house, the two grizzled Labradors came running, too old now to jump up at him and stand on hind legs, licking his face, but still excited by his remembered smell. Calming them, Tom saw that everything in the hall was exactly as it had been; nothing in this house ever changed substantially. Even the sight of a new towel on the heated rail in the bathroom, he recalled, had once precipitated an outburst from his father.

Hearing the door and the dogs, Tom's mother came out of the sitting room, smiling. 'It's lovely to see you,' she said a little hesitantly. 'Come on in.'

Kissing her cheek, Tom saw Megs watching him through the open doorway of the sitting room. Behind her stood his brother Adrian and sister-in-law, Kim. They could have been actors chosen by an agency to play the parts of a back-bench Conservative MP and his wife. Twinset, pearls and the perennial lacquered Maggie Thatcher hairstyle for her; navy blue three-piece pinstriped suit for him, even on a Sunday.

The new Rover outside must be theirs, Tom realised; the cars were made in Adrian's constituency. They had all been to church for the eleven o'clock service – that was why he had been told not to arrive earlier. From the way everyone was standing, he had the impression that his father had been in the room and had just left by the other door which led to his study. There was an awkward lack of spontaneity when his mother excused herself to finish preparing lunch.

'I'll give you a hand, Mummy,' said Megs brightly.

'No, you stay and talk, dear. I can manage.' Tom's mother disappeared back into her realm, the kitchen.

Megs took Tom's hand and squeezed it. 'I'm so glad you came,' she said. 'How many years is it since we were all together for Sunday lunch?'

He grinned at her gaffe. 'Trust you to say the wrong thing, sis.'

She blushed and looked so awkward that he gave her a hug before crossing the room to kiss his sister-in-law's cheek. Her frigid embrace – hands on his arms – was actually a way of keeping him at a distance.

'Tom,' she said, pasting on a thin smile. 'How are you?'

'Very well,' he said. 'An open prison's as good as a health farm, if you put your mind to it.'

'Oh, cut that out,' said Adrian.

'Why?' asked Tom. 'Prison's where I've been for the past four years. Not that I expected you two to come and see me.'

'Please!' Megs' voice was full of reproach. 'You know they would have come, if only Daddy hadn't been so upset by my visit.'

'You're thirty-five years old,' Tom snapped. 'And Adrian's forty-five. Does it really still matter what Our Father does or doesn't want you to do?'

'Have a sherry,' said his brother heavily. 'And let's try not to raise our voices, shall we? As you know, Father's not well. I think we owe him a pleasant Sunday lunch, eh?'

Tom accepted the glass of Sainsbury's cream sherry. There was never anything else alcoholic in the house, he recalled, except for a bottle of port at Christmas. For the first time in a long while, he yearned for a glassful of hard liquor in his hand.

What am I doing here? he wondered, listening to his sister-in-law's anodyne comments about items in the Sunday papers while his brother discussed point-to-points with Megs. From the dining room came the clatter of dishes and from the study, silence.

Tom laid a silent bet with himself that the meal would consist of overdone roast beef with Bisto gravy, roast potatoes and parsnips, followed by trifle. His father would carve the joint at the head of the table and say, 'A good piece of beef this week, Mother.' And she would glow briefly at this small praise. Then Kim would ask how the gravy had been made and affect interest in the reply. Megs would sit beside her father and pass him the cruet and the gravy boat a millisecond before he asked for them. And at the bottom of the table the vicar's wife would be looking anxious, uncertain whether she had yet learned to cook a Sunday lunch to her husband's satisfaction.

And so it was.

.5.

Karen drove on auto-pilot, thinking more about Tom than the scenery. Halfway along Derwentwater she stopped the car by the lake, took a sheet of paper from her briefcase and started a letter.

Dear Fran,

I've just spent twenty-four hours with Tom. Tomorrow morning I say *au revoir* to him and head for Sicily and Luigi – to say *addio* to both man and mountain. Professionally, it's time I said goodbye to Etna. Emotionally, it's time to move on from Luigi. The relationship has been going nowhere for years, but then in all honesty it always was. We were colleagues first and foremost and lovers only for convenience.

So why am I breaking up with him now? Is it because of Tom coming back into my life? You warned me about having anything to do with him for a second time, but if you could meet him you'd see how much he has changed from the person who tricked me in Leningrad. He's a very different guy now. I think suffering has made him a better person. On each visit here we come a little closer to each other. And in addition I have him to thank for setting up the relationship with the Siberians. Not only was it his idea, but I'd never have gotten to first base without him smoothing out all the problems.

She stopped writing. I'm pleading for him, she thought. Why? Whatever happens between Tom and me is no one else's business; we have to work it out for ourselves . . .

It would have been so easy and so natural to have let him slip into her room as they exchanged a goodnight kiss the previous night on the landing of the little country pub in Borrowdale where they were staying, but she did not want their coming together – if they came together again – to be a casual slaking of lust or even the mutual comforting of two friends who had known each other a long while. She wanted it to be slow and thought out and for some very good reason that could make it work this time. The very first step, she had decided, was that Tom had to tell her the truth – all of the truth about everything. On one thing she had made up her mind: that she would never let him lie to her again.

She crumpled up the sheet of paper and stuffed it into the ashtray. 'No use, Fran,' she said aloud. 'I have to do this on my own.'

During his long silences on the mountain that morning when they were alone with the rocks and the wind and the sky, she had wondered what Tom was thinking about. He had been trying to put into words for her his plan to recover the Virgin of Kazan but whichever way he rehearsed the beginning of his story, it sounded like an apology for tricking her once again. Unlike Moses, he had come down from the mountain with no message for Karen or anyone else.

Kim and Adrian had spent most of the meal telling the old

man about their daughter's new pony, the rosettes she had won at gymkhanas and their son's prowess on the sports field at a minor public school. Tom spoke only to Megs and his mother, except for one exchange with Kim. Throughout the meal, the Rev. Michael Fielding did not give away by word or the slightest gesture that he was aware of his younger son's presence.

It was quite a masterly performance. Tom wished he could have made a videotape to show to Tessa Nathan. The title would have been something like *Dysfunctional Family's Joyless Meal*. With a commentary by Woody Allen, it could have been played as comedy.

Having finished the second helping of dessert, his father folded his starched linen napkin, rolled it up and slipped it into its ring with precise gestures, as though performing a ritual at the altar. 'For these and all Thy other gifts, we thank Thee, O Lord,' he intoned before standing up and reaching for his walking stick.

'Thank you, Mother,' he said. 'Excellent trifle.'

'Isn't this all rather childish?' Tom spoke before his father could leave the room. 'I mean, playing ostriches at your age, Father!'

The Rev. Fielding turned to look directly at him for the first time. 'As far as I am concerned,' he said coldly, 'I have one son and one daughter.'

There was silence after the study door closed behind him.

'Oh, why did you do that?' asked Tom's mother. 'We had such a nice family meal.'

'Did we hell!' exploded Tom. 'We're not a family. We're a collection of humanoid puppets manipulated by a nasty old man.' He was aware that he was one of them, behaving in a way he would not have chosen to.

'That's unfair, Tom,' said Megs. 'Mother tried very hard to make a special occasion.'

'It's my fault for coming,' said Tom. 'I should have known what it would be like.'

'Father's only got a few months to live.' Adrian stood up and made sure that the communicating door was closed. 'He doesn't know about it, but in the check-up after his stroke they found an inoperable cancer of the prostate.'

'Well, I'm sorry about that,' said Tom. 'But if I don't exist, there's not much I can do to help him.'

'The point is that there will be a little bit of money coming to us,' said Kim brightly. 'And we all thought . . .'

'Coming to you,' Tom corrected her. 'Father's hardly likely to leave anything to a son who doesn't exist.'

'You've had a tough time,' she said, watching him with her head tilted to one side.

Her voice took on a little-girl quality and rose several tones in pitch. 'So Adrian thought he could have a chat with the bank manager and raise a spot of cash – you know, in anticipation of the legacy.'

From the way the others at the table were watching him, Tom knew that everything had been rehearsed.

'If I put it to him, he'll be stroppy,' Adrian would have said. 'You tell him, darling.'

And Megs – poor crushed Megs, still trying to please everyone, just like her mother – would have nodded and gushed something like, 'You're so good at this sort of thing, Kim.'

'. . . and you could emigrate to Australia, Tom,' the offer ended. 'Had you thought of that? With a lump sum to give you a new start in life.'

'Or the west coast of Canada,' Adrian suggested. 'There, anyone with $60,000 or more to invest is welcome, Tom. And that's where the action is these days – round the Pacific rim.'

'Take it from Adrian.' Kim nodded. 'He knows.'

'Follow the Chinese, Tom,' said Adrian pompously. 'They're getting out of HK before Beijing takes over. They know where the big money is to be made. Follow them and you can't go wrong.'

'What do you think of this offer?' Tom asked his mother.

She smiled nervously. 'Well, it's very generous of Adrian and Kim.'

'No, it's not.' Tom put her straight. 'They're both shitting their pants in case somehow I hit the headlines one day, despite the way my trial was hushed up. That might compromise my dear brother's chances of political advancement. Of course, he could have come to see me in prison at any time during the last four years and offered a suitable bribe, but word of his visit might have reached the Press because both cons and warders are terrible gossips. He could have invited me to his home this weekend to meet my nephew and niece, except he's probably told them I'm dead – just another skeleton in the family cupboard, like sad-gay Uncle Tim who hanged himself out there in the garage and was never mentioned again. So poor bloody Megs was the Judas-goat, leading me into this trap with her talk of Father blessing me on his deathbed. I should have known.'

'Tom,' his mother remonstrated, 'you've learned some very coarse language in prison.'

'That's not all I've learned inside, Mother. But who planned this farce?'

He looked around the table, his eyes settling on his sister-in-law. 'Most likely it was Adrian's brain, sitting there next to him, who came up with the idea of a fake family Sunday lunch. I was right, wasn't I, Kim? You thought I'd be so grateful at being allowed back into the fold for a few brief hours that I'd be unable to resist your grimy little subterfuge. Well, you failed to allow for Our Father's principles. I don't like the man or what he stands for but at least he has integrity.'

'Have you quite finished insulting us all?' Adrian asked calmly.

'I'm sorry, Mother,' Tom said.

She was staring at the tablecloth in front of her. He could not work out what she was thinking.

'I told Adrian you'd see through it all,' she said at last. 'He was always trying to trick you when you were boys, but it never worked.' She got up to start clearing away the dishes.

Tom was halfway down the drive when he heard Megs calling, 'I'll give you a lift into town.'

By the sound of it, she was having trouble starting her car, so he walked back to the house.

'Blasted thing,' she said. 'It floods. Something wrong with the carb. It'll be all right in a minute.'

'Sorry, sis,' Tom said, patting her arm. 'I know you meant well.'

'Now you think I was in league with them.' She looked about to burst into tears. 'It wasn't like that at all, Tom. I really thought Adrian and Kim wanted to help.'

'Talk of the devil,' he said.

His sister-in-law was coming out of the front door, holding her cardigan together with one hand, against the cool breeze. Still wearing the same plastic smile, but using her normal voice, she said, 'Thanks for the compliment, Tom dear. But before you storm off down the motorway, shouldn't you at least know how much of the ready you're turning down?'

'Because every man has his price?'

'Every man I've met.' Kim shivered and pulled the cardigan tighter. 'It's not a lot but we can probably raise 50K. No strings. Think about it.'

Tom watched her walk back into the house. 'She and Adrian,' he said, 'are a perfectly matched couple: a triumph of computerised mating.'

'They never seem to quarrel,' Megs murmured.

Tom looked down at her. 'What about you?' he asked. 'I never had time to find out how your life is.'

'Oh, the job . . .'

'Not the bloody job,' he shouted. 'You! You're a pretty woman.'

Watching her blush, he asked, 'Still no regular boyfriend?'

'All the best men are married.'

He grabbed her arm through the open car window. 'I wasn't talking about marriage. Haven't you ever heard of fun, sis? You've spent the whole of your adult life looking for a man who'd be acceptable to your father. The guy doesn't exist. The next time a bloke wants to get his hand up your knickers, forget that miserable old bastard who's dying in there, jump into bed and have some fun before it's too late.'

This time her face went white – with anger or horror, he could not tell.

'I've never been spoken to like that before,' she stammered.

'That's why I said it.' Tom refused to relinquish his grip on her arm. 'I love you, Megs. Seeing you living in this house of the walking dead hurts me like hell. Renounce your vows of chastity and misery. Jump over the wall and come back to the world, please.'

There were tears in her eyes now. 'I think you'd better leave,' she whispered.

He turned for one last look at the house. There was the pale blur of a face behind the net curtains at the study window, where the Rev. Michael Fielding was watching, unable to say even 'Hallo' to a son he had not seen for nine whole years. In the kitchen, Tom's mother was bent over the sink, washing the dishes without delay because her husband liked what he called 'a tidy house at all times'. In the open front doorway, Kim and Adrian were standing side by side, his arm around her waist, both their faces expressionless. And Megs, the one he cared most about, was hunched over the steering wheel of her malfunctioning car, hiding her face from him and silently destroying yet another handkerchief.

'How did it go?' Karen asked.

She was standing in a shaft of sunlight that was pouring

through a break in the clouds. Tom noticed that she had been back to the pub and changed from her walking clothes into a matching Paisley pattern shirtwaister blouse and long flowing woollen skirt, with knee-length boots.

The skirt was blowing in the breeze, as was her hair, tinted red by the sunlight. At that moment Karen looked to his eyes more beautiful than any model in the pages of a fashion magazine. He walked up to her, full of an impulse to take her in his arms, shut his eyes and hold her tight against him – but stopped a few paces away, held back by the invisible barrier she had placed between them the previous night.

'Was it as bad as you feared?' she asked.

He broke the eye contact, walked past her without replying and stood at the water's edge.

'All happy families resemble each other,' he said. 'Each unhappy family is unhappy in its own way.'

Recognising the quotation, Karen murmured, 'Anna Karenina.'

'Yes.' Tom was watching the pool of light. It travelled across the lake like a searchlight beam, illuminating couples in rowing boats one after another. Karen's footsteps sounded on the pebbles behind him and he felt her fingers intertwine with his.

'You tried,' she said softly. 'That's what matters.'

'I might as well not have bothered,' he said bitterly.

'That's not true. For the first time in years you made a gesture to someone that showed you cared about them. If your family rebuffed you, that's their loss but it doesn't diminish your gesture. Tell me how it was.'

'How were the graphite mines, interesting?'

'I didn't get that far,' she said. 'Too many things on my mind, so I stopped and looked at the scenery instead.'

Tom did not speak for several minutes, by which time the cold wind was making Karen regret not putting on her anorak. She was about to let go of his hand, to fetch it from the car, when Tom began recounting every sad minute of his visit home without looking at her once.

She was freezing long before the end but she stayed still, listening. He's talking to me, she thought. He's really talking. One day he'll tell me everything else.

.6.

In a closed prison it was possible to ignore the fact that other men had visitors; on Sundays at Longfield girlfriends and families were there for all to see. It was the children who disturbed Tom – especially girls of about Svetlana's age. To avoid seeing them, he spent most sabbaths closeted with the Apple Mac – pounding the keyboard on what Tessa Nathan now referred to as *The Virtual Novel* – and leaving his room only for a punishing morning workout in the gym and an afternoon session on the running track that lasted for two whole hours.

That Sunday his routine had been interrupted, the usual morning schedule put aside in favour of a priority fax-chat with Karen. Just arrived on Kamchatka, she had had a host of small problems that needed Tom's intervention. By lunchtime GMT they were resolved and the final message read:

Thanks for everything, genius! What would I do without you? Volkov, the pilot you fixed for us, is some

character. He flew most of our supplies to Mount
Tolbachik this afternoon. And, guess what! He
deliberately diverted over the crater and says there's a
minor eruption taking place, so we're in luck!

Love, K

It was through a curtain of sweat dripping from his eyebrows
that Tom saw a familiar figure waiting at the finish line as he
came to the end of his tenth lap round the track. On the last
couple of circuits he had been dimly aware of a splash of red
in the visitors' car park where the Morgan was parked, but
was too concentrated on his stride and breathing to make the
connection.

Ponsonby was dressed for an English country house weekend: polished brown brogues, cavalry twill trousers, Harris
tweed jacket with leather patches at the wrist and elbow and
a matching tweed cap. Beneath the cap, the sharkish features
gave nothing away. Aware from Karen's comments how
much his own appearance had changed in the thirteen years
since they had first known each other, Tom was glad that he
had managed to put one dent in Ponsonby's otherwise
immaculate bodywork: his nose was bent to one side where
the cartilage had set crooked.

'Perhaps you've already seen the Sunday papers?' he asked
as Tom came to a halt, chest heaving.

'No.' Tom turned his back to pull on his tracksuit.

'If you had,' said Ponsonby evenly, 'you'd have seen a
familiar face. Have a shower and get changed, but quickly.
I'll wait for you over there by the cricket pavilion.'

Tom spun round. 'I don't have to take orders from you!'
He wondered whether Ponsonby's habit of looking above
the head of the person to whom he was talking was just
another mannerism or whether it was the result of a lifetime
of manipulating people which made it impossible to meet
someone's eyes.

Ponsonby's gaze drifted down to settle on Tom's face.

'Then regard my suggestion as a prelude to an offer you won't want to refuse.'

It was starting to drizzle as Tom jogged away to the showers. Visitors were running for cover. Ponsonby looked at them disdainfully as he walked slowly across to the shelter of the pavilion. Beneath its eaves he took his gold hunter watch from the pocket of his canary yellow waistcoat and consulted it, working out distances and times. Replacing the watch, he patted the bulge of documents in his breast pocket and waited, hands clasped behind his back, rocking gently on his heels.

Tom returned wearing jeans, a sweatshirt and a light anorak over the top. He pushed the hood back and willed Ponsonby to look him in the eye again. 'What brings you slumming to Longfield, Clive?'

'Read this.'

Tom took the neatly folded news section of a Sunday paper. Since childhood, he had read newspapers from back to front. It was a quirk that had intrigued Tessa Nathan while she was exploring every theory from early weaning to bed-wetting and masturbation-guilt in her efforts to explain what she had in those days insisted on calling 'your decision to betray your country'. As far as Tom was concerned, it was the natural way for a left-hander to read a newspaper.

He scanned the sports page first and found nothing, then glanced at the weather report, which suggested that the sky should be sunny and cloudless, with an air temperature of 32 degrees Centigrade. The truth on that August afternoon was the first rain in six weeks and a temperature 15 degrees lower.

He browsed through the columns of progressively harder news, working towards the front page. Even in a half-screen reproduction of an agency mug-shot at the top of page three, there was no mistaking the dark button eyes and the thick shock of dark hair that erupted from just above the eyebrows and continued all the way back to the collar of the open-necked shirt. He was looking at the face he had last seen outside the station in Alma Ata.

The shock was so great that he had to read the beginning of the article twice before its meaning sank in. The man who had watched his own wife being torn to pieces by wolves was now President of the fledgling Ukrainian Republic, having taken advantage of a political crisis to ride a voteslide in the previous week's elections that made him overnight the most powerful politician of his country.

President Viktor Nosarenko's first act on taking office was an official visit to Washington, where he was asking the World Bank, the White House and anyone else who would listen, for several billion dollars in aid to redevelop his country's neglected agricultural and industrial infrastructure. As the writer pointed out, Ukraine had been the granary of Eastern Europe until the Soviet collectivisation programme in the Thirties turned the country into a wasteland within a single decade of centralised misgovernment that culminated in a famine which killed millions. Sixty years afterwards, less than a quarter of the once-fertile wheatland was back in production. Simply to feed itself, Nosarenko's country urgently needed the help of foreign agronomists, biologists, chemists – and a lot of investment in fertilisers, modern machinery and methods.

Despite soaring inflation Ukraine was not exactly asking for help on bended knees. At least 1,800 intercontinental ballistic missiles, implanted in bombproof silos, had been left behind by the retreating Russian forces on the break-up of the Soviet Union.

International inspection teams had logged the numbers and whereabouts of the missiles. American welders had flown across the world to cut them in half and Russian technologists been driven in by the busload to deactivate the warheads, but the fact remained that the nuclear armoury made a formidable bargaining counter for a Ukrainian President haggling with a White House whose incumbent was already worried about the leakage of radioactive material from the ex-Soviet Union.

'And this.' Ponsonby took back the newspaper and handed Tom a glossy weekly news magazine, folded to a page where the same face gazed unsmilingly at the reader.

The article beneath it reported a rumour that Nosarenko's blitzkrieg electoral campaign had been financed by selling to the Serbians a substantial quantity of Red Army artillery and tanks, which they had used to crush the Bosnian Moslems in the latest round of ethnic cleansing that scarred the former Yugoslavia.

Tom looked up. Ponsonby was standing in the drizzle with his back turned. The rain-bedewed tweed cap turned slowly round. If there was a message in the steely grey eyes beneath the curved dark eyebrows, it was hard to read. He took the magazine from Tom's hand and dropped it with the newspaper into a waste-bin on the pavilion wall.

'Why did you come?' Tom asked.

'You must realise, old boy,' Ponsonby drawled, 'that it's time to stop playing games with me. You have to face the fact that there are some very dirty players after that ball you're holding. Kick it into touch while there's still time – unless you're really tired of living.'

Tom refused to be fazed. 'I asked why you came.'

'On his way to Washington, Viktor made an unofficial stopover in London. He's suddenly a very important man and the PM couldn't wait to shake his hand behind a triple security screen on the hard-standing at Brize Norton. So when Viktor asked the man from Number Ten to arrange a chat with my revered D-G, the answer was, "Yes, sir. No, sir. Three bags full, Mr President."

'The D-G caught the next Concorde to Washington. There, Viktor said that he had stood by his side of the bargain when he offered to spy for Britain. He said that you had never handed over the cash we owed him for the material he supplied and that he wanted it now. The D-G kept her cool.

She said we had another version of events: that Viktor held you up at gunpoint and took the money without ever handing over the material we were paying him for.'

'And which story do you believe, Clive?'

'Viktor confirmed exactly what I had held all along to be true, but let's not argue about that again. The reason why I'm here now is that our Ukrainian friend agreed to let bygones be bygones providing . . .'

'. . . that your people tell him where to find me.'

'You got it in one,' Ponsonby nodded. 'On her return from Washington and after consulting the PM on Friday evening, the D-G ordered me to pass details of your present whereabouts to Viktor Nosarenko's private telephone number in Kiev without delay.'

'Which you did?'

Ponsonby smiled thinly. 'Luckily the British weekend supervened. Since even Burgess and MacLean owed their getaway to their watchers working a five-day week, I saw no reason to break such important precedent. The President will receive my message via our man in the embassy in Kiev first thing tomorrow morning.'

Ponsonby grinned, showing his teeth. 'How does that feel? If I were in . . .'

'But why you, Clive?' Tom goaded him. It was vital to know who stood where on this chess board. 'Indeed, why did anyone from London come to warn me? If you really thought I'd screwed you, why not stand back and let Viktor come and get me?'

The casual drawl was dropped as Ponsonby's face contorted with anger he could no longer suppress. He grabbed both sides of the collar of Tom's anorak cross-handed, and pulled his arms apart savagely, putting pressure on the carotid arteries and cutting off the oxygen supply to Tom's brain.

'Do you know what I went through professionally, because of the way you fucked up, Tom?' he hissed. 'Jesus, I recruited you and I was your control, so when you ran off the fucking tracks it was my fault all the way, with no one else to share the blame. Viktor was my star agent-in-place. Thanks to your balls-up, he never sent us another single item. You rubbished my career, Tom Fielding. In one month's time I'm due for early retirement on reduced pension. Put out to grass at the ripe old age of forty-nine! I think I deserve better than that.'

Tom broke Ponsonby's grip and stood, face pale beneath his tan, trying to get his breath back. 'Then why did you come?' he repeated hoarsely.

Ponsonby stepped back to put a decent interval between them. The English gentleman mask slipped back into place and the grey eyes focused somewhere over Tom's head as though watching the beaters work a grouse moor in the rain.

'Isn't it obvious? Even the Queen would split her skirt, bending down to pick up half a million dollars.'

Tom knew now where the conversation was leading. 'So what's the deal you're offering me, Clive?'

'You've got a choice. You can sit here until Viktor's debt collectors arrive and end up with a 9mm bullet in the back of your head. Or you can give the money to me and in return I'll give you this.'

He took from his inside breast pocket a brown envelope and slid out a British passport in the name of Colin Pearson, which he held in front of Tom. As he flicked through the pages, Tom saw a fresh Russian visa stamp. The face in the photograph was his own.

Ponsonby tapped the envelope in his pocket. 'I've got the lot: birth certificate, driving licence – a whole new identity, Tom. Give me the money and it's yours. This way, I'll be rich and you can look forward to dying of old age in a rest home.'

'What happened to the real Mr Pearson?'

'He was a pharmaceuticals rep who died in a crash on the M1 last year. I've kept his National Insurance paid up to date. He has two endorsements for speeding but otherwise he led a blameless life.'

Tom was not listening. If Viktor's people caught up with him, he was a dead man. His only chance of staying alive was to recover the film of the murder, make copies and publish them. And his only hope of doing that in time was to dupe Ponsonby into helping him recover both film and icon in the belief that he was going to end up with $500,000 in his pocket.

If they walked out of the gate that minute, Tom knew that he would not be missed until the roll call at 10 p.m., which gave them six hours' head start. There was nothing in his room he wanted to take with him. Even the computer discs on which he had stored a lecture course on the break-up of the Soviet Union were worthless now. If he got the icon and the film back to the West ahead of Viktor's hit team, he would be too rich to need them; if he didn't, he would be too dead to deliver another lecture.

'Let me get this straight,' he said. 'You're offering to break me out of Longfield and to come with me all the way?'

'Believe me,' said Ponsonby, 'I'm going to stay very close to you every inch of the way until we reach the spot marked with a cross on the old pirate's map. You get the passport and the rest of the bumph when I have the money in my hands – not before.'

'After which moment, you'll be the only person in the world who knows my new identity, of course.'

'Remember that,' Ponsonby grinned. 'Just in case you were thinking of double-crossing me.'

'And how do we travel, Clive?'

'At the Channel ports there are normally no Immigration controls now. The girl who issues your ticket may glance at your passport, but she won't be looking for Colin Pearson. If we move fast, we'll be at a French airport before Viktor's collection team starts heading this way.'

Tom shivered. 'The problem is, Clive, you're the last man in the world I'd choose to trust. I wrote to the bank where you pretended to be paying money into my account.

They replied that they had never had an account in my name.'

'Perhaps you got the number wrong.'

'I'm a historian. I don't get dates or numbers wrong.'

'It was there.' Ponsonby did not even blink. 'The Firm clawed it back when you went native. Damage limitation: there was no point paying you for a job you hadn't done. I wasn't consulted.'

'Either way, it doesn't build confidence.'

'You have no choice.' Ponsonby bared his teeth in a sharkish grin of satisfaction. 'If I were you, I'd be out of here like hot shit off a shovel. So make up your mind.'

'You're right,' said Tom. 'I have no choice.'

.7.

To silence Ponsonby's objections, Tom persuaded him that taking the quicker route to eastern Siberia via Moscow ran the risk of some sharp-eyed immigration officer at Sheremetyevo or Domodedovo airport recognising either or both of them. The real reason why he insisted on flying Paris-Chicago-Anchorage in order to catch the Aeroflot flight from Anchorage to Magadan and Petropavlovsk Kamchatskiy, was because of Karen.

If Nosarenko – who had the entire resources of the former Ukrainian KGB organisation on which to call – somehow connected her with T.W.C. Fielding, her name would be on the hit list. Stranded on a remote Siberian volcano with just a handful of scientists, she would be an easy target. So getting her to a place of safety was the first priority.

Once on Kamchatka, Tom planned to devote twenty-four hours to finding her on Mount Tolbachik and putting her on the first flight to North America, where she would be out of the line of fire. Only then could he concentrate on getting his hands on the icon and the film. Exactly how he would achieve that, he had no idea.

During the three long legs of the trip, he took advantage of the courtesy eye pads and earplugs to insulate himself from Ponsonby and everyone else. Even so, sleep was out of reach. After five years of living at the mind-numbing pace of prison life, it seemed impossible to do everything that had to be done before time ran out and Viktor's hit-team caught up with him.

Magadan airport was a seething mass of women. The new breed of post-Soviet traders were back from their weekly *kupil-prodal* run to Anchorage. Stout, hard-faced and loud-voiced, with uniform frizzed-out blonde hairdos, they haggled and bribed their way through Customs, struggling under the weight of oversize garbage bags and heavy suit-cases stuffed with underwear, summer dresses and food purchased in Alaska for resale to shops, friends and neigh-bours on the parallel market – this despite the fact that food prices in Alaska were the highest in the USA. To minimise the import taxes they had to pay, many of the women were wearing several layers of underwear and, as a result, were perspiring profusely in the airless Customs hall.

The smells of sweat, cheap eau de Cologne and garlic brought back memories. The noise and jostling which most foreigners disliked were oddly reassuring to Tom, as were the haggling and more or less open bribery going on all around. Exile and imprisonment had made him a stranger in his own land, which had changed much during the decade he had been away from it, but here, surrounded by aggressive on-the-make Russian-speakers, anything seemed possible. He breathed deeply, inhaling all the essence of corruption bodily and fiscal, and felt that he had come home.

Ponsonby noticed the change in his behaviour without understanding it. The man who had been content to let him book tickets and argue his way onto overbooked flights in Europe and the USA now took command. Tom shouldered his way through the crowd at the Aeroflot transit desk, waving a handful of dollars and grabbing the first tickets issued.

Flying into Petropavlovsk at midday, the ancient Ilyushin, crowded with tired but triumphant blonde women in nearly every seat – plus a few sitting in the aisle – bumped its way through an inversion layer of dirty hot air which hung over the town like a threat, the output of a dozen high filterless chimneys of chemical and industrial plants near the docks. Below the aircraft vast piles of timber stretched seemingly for miles, awaiting shipment before the ice closed in that autumn. Ships were being repaired and built in the yards, fenced around by outcrops of dark volcanic rock that vanished into the sea like giants' stepping stones leading nowhere. A black-painted nuclear-powered hunter-killer submarine was slinking out of harbour with half a dozen matelots on deck, enjoying a last cigarette in the lee of the sail.

Inland lay a range of vividly green hills, above which a bank of clouds stretched away to the northern horizon, broken only by the peaks of two volcanoes that loomed over the town. In the clear blue sky a thin plume of smoke rose vertically from the crater of one while Koryakskaya, its twin, lay sulkily dormant like a huge delinquent child promising never to be naughty again.

The quarter million inhabitants of the town – the largest on Kamchatka – lived in Soviet-era apartment blocks. From Tom's vantage point as the Ilyushin made its final approach they appeared to be dotted higgledy-piggledy between the sea and the hills, subject to no discernible zoning nor even linked by roadways in some cases. Karen had mentioned that they were spread out in this apparently random fashion to spread the risk when the next earth tremor shook this part of the Pacific ring of fire. Some of the many fault lines could even be seen from the air.

The grey buildings were soulless, ugly, cheap and as grim

as the winter that would swoop in from the Bering Sea in a month or six weeks' time at the most. And the town was looking at its best that day: in the brief but intense Siberian summer, every tree and bush spurred itself to complete the annual cycle of flowering, fertilisation and fruiting within a few weeks. During that brief span a thousand different species of flowering weeds – some growing as much as eight centimetres in twenty-four hours – did their best to hide soot-stained masonry and crushed cinder roadways. The lush new foliage of trees and bushes hid some smaller buildings completely.

On the drive into town from the airport the taxi passed a whales' graveyard where thousands of huge skeletons lay bleaching along the bleak shoreline. Seals gambolled in the wake of a rusty coaster. On a rock offshore, a solitary bull walrus driven away from some herd roared away his frustration, huge ivory tusks glinting in the low-angle sun.

From the peak of Nikolskoye Hill, Tom could see the miles of shipyards and docks that lined Avacha Bay, one of the world's great natural harbours and the real reason for Petropavlovsk's existence. At one quay cranes were hoisting from the belly of a huge factory ship, more rust than paint, hundreds of tons of king crabs caught on the fertile banks of the Sea of Okhotsk and already cooked and canned on board by the crew of 500 who were trudging wearily ashore after weeks at sea without a breath of fresh air or sight of the sky. A glistening white cruise ship was inching its way to the next berth, furling its electronically operated sails. The decks were lined with Japanese tourists gazing down at a fleet of coaches waiting to take them on a tour of the town. Flat-decked ferries to and from the Komandor Islands chugged across the black waters of the harbour, their sirens hooting mournfully in counterpoint to the sound of riveting and hammering from the shipyards.

'Miserable bloody dump,' was Ponsonby's verdict as they drove downtown.

The air temperature was barely 15 degrees Centigrade and there was a fresh breeze blowing off the sea, but the natives seemed determined to wear their summer clothes for the few weeks when this was possible. In light dresses and open-necked shirts they strolled along the streets carrying shopping bags, for the most part empty. So far, everything had been more or less as Tom remembered life in the USSR, except that more than a quarter of the faces around him were Asiatic – native Itelmen, Koryak, Even and Chukchi, with a sprinkling of Koreans and Chinese. His first real culture shock came on passing the gleaming Western-style Holkam supermarket – a joint Swiss-Dutch-Russian venture whose customers' new Mercedes and Volvos jammed the parking lot outside. Here the women who were studying the enticing window-displays through Ray-Ban sunglasses wore Western make-up and smart clothes while the men with them sported suits which had been tailored in Paris and London.

Thanks to the research he had done in Longfield while setting up Karen's visits, Tom knew his way around town. He directed the taxi to the Hotel Alyaska where he had booked the Canadian survey team for the first night of their current trip. It was a new building, staffed by Russians but managed by Poles, whose entrance lobby was crowded with attractive women aged from sixteen to fifty. They stood or sat quietly alone or in small groups, waiting to catch the eye of foreign hotel guests. A few of them were professionals; some were part-timers who went home to husbands and children each day; most were unmarried women and girls hoping for a reward more durable than a few dollar bills. Desperate to sell their one asset in the most lucrative market, they were prepared to become totally compliant wives for Western or Japanese businessmen in return for a new nationality and a permanent escape from the problems of keeping their heads above water in the social turmoil of the new Russia. One way or another, Tom thought, the women of the country were certainly not wasting any time in exploiting their release from the seventy-year tyranny of grim old men in the Kremlin who had kept them firmly in the back seat of a society whose constitution had been based since 1917 on sexual equality.

After checking in, Ponsonby changed money with a tout outside the hotel so that Tom could make some local calls from a phone booth in the lobby. Keeping one eye on him, Ponsonby prowled around, nostrils flaring as he sniffed the sex in the air like a shark in a swimming pool scenting blood. Wherever he looked, women's eyes met his gaze, some demurely lowered, some boldly challenging, but all sending the same message of availability. He felt like a sultan in his harem.

'Buy me a drink,' ordered Tom when he came out of the booth.

Ponsonby complained about the prices in the bar: $5 for a glass of canned Budweiser, paid in hard currency.

'Worth every penny,' Tom decided, swallowing his in two gulps.

He led Ponsonby away from the bar, where a statuesque blonde perched on one of the tall stools had aroused his interest. She bulged out of an absurdly tight and brief silver lamé dress. Her matching slingback sandals with four-inch heels looked more like weapons than footwear. As she talked, her breasts bounced quiveringly on a narrow shelf of wired undercups. She was more like a life-size sex toy than a real woman.

'I have a confession to make,' Tom said. 'I brought you here under false pretences, because I was telling the truth all along.'

Ponsonby tore his eyes away from the blonde's cleavage. 'What the hell does that mean, Tom?'

'Whatever Viktor Nosarenko told your boss, the truth is that I did hand the money over to him. There is no $500,000 stashed away, here or anywhere else.'

Ponsonby's eyes were pure ice. 'Nosarenko's a busy man.

Why is he so eager to track down a bit-player like you? You must have something he wants.'

Tom recounted everything that had happened in Alma Ata and at Borzhoi, wondering what was going on behind the busy eyes that roamed the women at the bar while Ponsonby took it all on board.

'Jesus H. Christ,' he said at the end. 'You are in really deep shit, dear boy. And if you think I'm going to help you recover a piece of film which shows the President of Ukraine as a raving lunatic who fed his wife to a pack of wolves, you're out of your tiny mind!'

'I need some mean bastard like you to watch my back, Clive. I'll make it worth your while. The icon's worth maybe $25 million. I'll give you half a million out of the proceeds of sale.'

'You're kidding,' was the response. 'Since Nosarenko doesn't know about the film, when the ex-KGB heavies with Ukrainian accents arrive, they won't be looking to deal. They'll just rub you out, together with anyone else you might have talked to. Being mistaken for a confidant of yours is going to be marginally more dangerous than climbing a lightning conductor in a thunderstorm.'

'I'll double your share in the icon.'

'The point of having a million bucks,' said Ponsonby grimly, 'is being around to spend it. Now, if you were able to pay me up-front, I might be interested.'

He walked across to the porter's desk where his case was still lying on the floor, picked it up, put it down again and came back to Tom.

'How long will it take us to collect the icon and the film and get the hell out of here?' he asked.

'There's a catch,' Tom said. 'You'll have to hang around here for a day while I get Karen safely out of the country.'

It was the first time he had heard Ponsonby really laugh. 'A catch? I knew everything was too good to be true.'

The ice came back into his eyes. 'Let me tell you

something, Tom – as a pro in this game. The only thing that matters right now is getting that damned film processed and syndicated to the world's press agencies. Once that's been done you can play Sir Galahad for the rest of your life. So if I were you . . .'

'You're not,' Tom cut in. 'It's my fault Karen's here, so I've got to get her out first, in case Viktor's people somehow tie her in with me. If you don't like it, you can stuff it up your arse and kiss goodbye to a million dollars.'

Ponsonby looked out of the picture window at the brooding mass of Koryakskaya. 'Where exactly is your Canadian girlfriend?'

'According to the helicopter pilot who's ferrying people and supplies to the survey team, she's on a site near the top of Mount Tolbachik.'

'And where's that?'

Tom pulled a map from his anorak pocket and pointed to the felt-pen circle he had drawn around the survey site. 'About two hours' flight north by helicopter.'

'Then let's go. It must be two hours to dusk. We should just make it to Tolbachik. Presumably the pilot can land back here at any time of night.'

'Trouble is, the weather.'

'It looks fine to me.'

'According to the met. people this is the only fog-free spot on the whole peninsula. North of here, Kamchatka is clamped down in fog that swept in earlier today from the Kuril trench. The pilot says we could take off but we'd have to return, so he recommends we get a night's sleep and hope the fog lifts at dawn.'

'Twenty-four hours.' Ponsonby made it sound like his decision. 'I'll give you twenty-four hours from now, Tom. After that, whether your girlfriend is safe or not, we redraw the rules.'

The bedside clock said 2 a.m. Tom switched on the light and

opened the bedroom door. In the corridor stood the night manager with two militiamen.

'Please come,' said the Pole in English. 'Your friend has had an accident.'

Ponsonby's bedroom looked as though a fault line had opened up beneath it. Bedding and furniture were strewn across the room. The body was lying naked across the bed, face down. A series of fresh and very deep red scratches across the back implied recent sex. There was no sign of his clothes or any other possessions. Even the toilet articles had gone from the bathroom.

'Is he dead?' Tom asked.

'Not yet,' one of the militiamen shrugged. 'It's an old trick – eye drops.'

Tom looked at the night manager for elaboration.

'Beta-blockers,' the Pole explained. 'One drop in your eye staves off glaucoma. A dozen drops in a glass of vodka are tasteless and a very effective knock-out potion. If she gave him two dozen, your friend won't wake up.'

Tom turned Ponsonby over and felt his wrist for a pulse. 'How long's he been like this?'

'I saw him in the bar with a tall blonde woman,' said the Pole. 'She's a known hustler. They left around one a.m.'

There was no pulse that Tom could detect. He shifted position and crunched glass underfoot. A tooth mug, with bright red lipstick on the rim, was lying on the floor in the middle of the room.

'Who gave the alarm?' he asked.

The Pole replaced the bedside telephone. 'Your friend somehow managed to get the phone off the hook.'

There was a flutter in the wrist. Tom leaned closer. A shallow exhalation brushed his ear. 'He's still breathing,' he said. 'Have you called a doctor?'

The Pole did not move. 'There's the question of who's going to pay.'

'Just get a fucking doctor,' shouted Tom.

'In the case of a foreigner, he'll want dollars before he even walks through the door.'

'No doctor . . .' The words slurred their way out of Ponsonby's mouth.

'An ambulance. Ring for an ambulance,' Tom begged. 'I'm taking this man to hospital.'

'And no . . . fucking . . . hospital.' The voice was a whisper but somewhere in the head lolling on the pillow, Ponsonby's brain was functioning despite the drugs in his system.

Tom lifted both eyelids, to find the eyeballs bouncing around in their sockets like unsynchronised balls in a pinmachine. With a groan, Ponsonby tried to stabilise his vision and focus on something but all he could see was a pattern of colours swirling around him. There was no sense of up or down. Voices came from some shapes which moved; others were silent and still, so he assumed they must be the furniture. Talking to the coloured shape leaning over him, he gasped, 'Make . . . me . . . sick.'

Tom rammed a finger down Ponsonby's throat and was rewarded with a thin trickle of mucus.

'Again,' came the feeble order.

This time an eruption of vomit spewed across the bed, the legs of Tom's pyjamas and the fitted carpet. The two militiamen were smoking by the door, looking bored by what was obviously a frequent occurrence.

'And again,' Ponsonby groaned.

When there was nothing left in his stomach he lay, chest heaving, staring up at the ceiling.

'What I usually recommend,' said the Pole, 'is getting a bottle of oxygen sent in and a saline drip.' He made it sound as though being slipped a possibly lethal drink was a normal hazard for Western businessmen staying in his hotel.

'No drip,' muttered Ponsonby. His voice was so quiet that only Tom could hear. 'No bastard's . . . going to stick . . . a needle in me.'

Tom used a towel to clean himself up.

The Pole waved the militiamen away. 'Your friend must be tough,' he said. 'Usually the victim doesn't wake up until the next day – if at all.'

'He's tough,' Tom agreed.

He looked around the room. He had in his pocket about seven dollars' worth of small change, left over from the telephone calls. His new passport and papers had been stolen, together with all Ponsonby's belongings. It was time to ask for help, but whom in the world could he trust?

.8.

'*Kto eto?*' Rada repeated. '*Kto govorít?*'

Tom tried to disguise his voice by deepening it and holding his hand half over the mouthpiece. 'I'd like to talk with Arkady Sergeyevich Sibirsky.'

'He's not in. Who's calling?'

'A friend who's trying to reach Ivan Petrovich Ivanov.'

There was a pause, then Rada said hesitantly, 'Tom?'

'Yes,' he admitted in his normal voice.

'Where are you calling from?'

'I'm at the Hotel Alyaska in Petropavlovsk Kamchatskiy.'

She sounded surprised. 'What are you doing in Siberia? I thought you were still . . .'

'Listen,' he interrupted. 'I didn't want to disturb you, but the number I have for Ivan Petrovich doesn't work and this was the only other one I could remember.'

'He's moved,' she said.

'I need to talk with him in a hurry. Can you give me the new number?'

'You can't reach him as easily as that. He's a very important man now.'

'So how do people reach him?'

'You call someone who calls someone else. Eventually Ivan Petrovich calls you back – if he wants to.'

'It sounds Byzantine.'

'That's the way our life is now, Tom. Give me your number and maybe in a day or two . . .'

'It's urgent. I can't wait that long.'

'Then you'd better tell me what it's about.'

The crowd of women clustered round the all-night drinkers at the bar gave Tom the idea of a code to use. 'I'm thinking of getting married again . . .'

Rada's voice rose in indignation. 'You rang to tell me that?'

'Please,' Tom begged. 'Stay with me. You know Arkady Sergeyevich's favourite virgin – the girl from Kazan? I've found one exactly like her, but the genuine article this time. I want to take her back to the West where she'll be worth her money in gold. And I need Ivan Petrovich's help to arrange the exit papers. D'you follow me?'

'I think so.' Rada was staring at the icon on the wall above the telephone. 'Are you telling me that you just found this girl?'

'I found her years ago,' Tom admitted. 'But it didn't work out between us that time. This time it will.'

The pips were going and he had no more coins in his pocket. It was infuriating to be talking about $25 million and not have a few pennies to prolong the call.

'I'll stay by the phone,' he shouted. 'Get back to me. Please, Rada. I need help fast.'

During the next fifteen minutes he stayed in the booth, hunched over the phone, with his free hand pressing the receiver rest down as he held an imaginary conversation with himself to keep other users at bay. On the first ring, he let it up and heard Ivanov's voice.

'You fucking foreigners are marrying all our best women,' growled the voice with the Moscow accent. There were traffic noises in the background. It sounded as though Ivanov were in a car with the windows open. 'Why pick one with problems? I can find you a thousand beautiful virgins: Kazaks, Tartars, Uzbeks, you name it.'

At first Tom thought that either he or Rada had not understood the message, until the jokey references to good lays and big boobs and tight little bums included the offer, 'Of course, if you're sure you've found the right one, Tom, I'll help you get this chick home. Give me a couple of days to make the necessary arrangements and I'll come in person to hold your hand and wave you off on your honeymoon.'

'There's a complication,' said Tom. 'I need help right now, Ivan Petrovich. A friend who came with me as best man has met with an accident.' Briefly he explained the details, ending, 'I don't know whether this is a coincidence or not.'

There was a pause while Ivanov clapped his hand over the telephone. Harmonics of other conversations, distorted electronically, drifted into Tom's ear. Then Ivanov was back on the line: 'Tell you what I'll do, Tom. I have some associates in Petropavlovsk. Within the next thirty minutes, they'll assume responsibility for your security. Tomorrow morning . . .' Remembering that Moscow was nine time zones to the west of where Tom was, he corrected himself. 'By mid-afternoon your time, I'll be with you.'

'How will I recognise your associates?'

Ivanov chuckled. 'They worked for the same company in the old times. You'll recognise them.'

'I'll make all this worth your while,' Tom promised.

'You can bet you will! I just talked with Arkady Sergeyevich. He says there's plenty for all of us, so I'm counting on getting my slice of the cake, and no mistake.'

Tom replaced the receiver. One of the women by the bar was looking expectantly at him. He pulled out his pockets to show they were empty and hurried back upstairs. The militiamen had been promised ten dollars apiece to guard the room until he got back. They were still arguing about payment when two hard-faced men in grey suits arrived.

'*My predstavíteli fírmy váshevo drúga*,' one of them announced: we are representatives of your friend's company. Standing well over six foot tall, he looked more like a wall on legs than a businessman. His companion was shorter but just as solid. They both had the emotionless faces, dead eyes and overbearing manner that came from years of pushing people around in the name of the KGB. The militiamen backed off as soon as they arrived.

'I owe these two gentlemen ten dollars apiece,' Tom explained. 'If you could pay them, they can go.'

He watched Big Wall peel two five-dollar bills off a roll from his hip pocket and murmured, 'I did say ten apiece.'

'I deducted my commission,' said Big Wall flatly.

The militiamen were already walking away along the corridor, disinclined to argue.

'*Yemú núzjno vrach*,' decided Short Wall after a cursory examination of the once again inert body on the bed: He needs a doctor.

The man in a white coat who arrived ten minutes later was very polite to the two men in grey suits. He gave Ponsonby an injection. Two hours later, the patient woke up to find himself propped up on clean pillows in a fresh bedroom and said, 'Christ, I could do with some breakfast!'

When the floor waiter brought a breakfast tray for four, Short Wall ordered the man to drink some of the coffee, sample the milk and eat one of the bread rolls before allowing him to leave.

Tom expressed the wish to go for a walk and get some fresh air.

Big Wall disagreed. '*Nyet*. You stay right here until our client arrives from Moscow.'

When Tom explained that he had a helicopter booked

and waiting to fly him urgently to Mount Tolbachik, he got the same answer: '*Nyet*.'

The dawn sky was clear and cloudless, perfect flying weather. Tom sat by the window, consumed with frustration as he watched the town come to life in the shadow of the twin volcanoes. He tried to tell himself that the delay did not matter in one sense, because Karen could come to no man-made harm on the top of a remote Siberian volcano.

Big Wall put the waiter through a similar routine with the lunch trolley at midday. It was 2 p.m. – nearly twelve hours after Tom's Mayday call – when the door opened and Ivanov walked into the room, accompanied by Big Wall's twin brother.

Ivan Petrovich had aged and was badly out of condition, with a paunch, bags under his eyes and skin that was short of ultra-violet and long on cigarettes and booze. Looking tired, he nodded coldly at Tom and threw at him a plastic shopping bag from the Holkam supermarket. 'My friends here traced the hooker who slipped your pal the drops.'

Inside the bag were both passports and all the personal papers, but no money. Even so, Tom was impressed. He listened to the rapid exchanges in *blátny yazyk* which zipped between Ivanov and the bodyguards; like yakuza or mafiosi, they had a language all their own. His clothes were expensive. On one wrist he wore a solid gold Patek Philippe watch set to Moscow time, and on the other a Corum Admiral's Cup watch showing the local time. His appearance was a measure of how he had prospered in the new Russia, from being a bodyguard himself to needing their services for his own protection.

With five men in the room, plus Ponsonby in the bed, there was hardly any room to stand, let alone talk. Ivanov led Tom outside. Two of the heavies followed, stationing themselves one at each end of the corridor, while the third stayed inside the room with Ponsonby.

'So you found the icon after all,' growled Ivanov. 'And now you want me to get it out for you.'

'Can you help me, Ivan Petrovich?'

'I can do anything for a price. Where is it?'

'That's my secret for the moment.'

'Let me put you straight,' said Ivanov. 'I checked up with some old pals in Moscow before catching the flight east. You're on the run, Feldink.' He pointed at the shopping bag. 'You're using false papers. You have no cash. Get real! You're in no position to bargain with anyone.'

He paused to let that sink in. 'I'll make you an offer for old times' sake. I'll give you $50,000 in cash the minute I have that icon in my hands, attested by Arkady Sergeyevich as the genuine article.'

'Sibirsky said the Virgin was worth $25 million.'

Ivanov lit a cigarette. 'Without my help it's worth fuck-all to a guy on the run who hasn't even got the money for a plane ticket. Okay, I'll be generous and say $100,000. If I were you, I'd take the offer and let me put you on the first available flight to South America.'

Tom heaved a sigh of relief; if Ivanov wanted to believe that he was in a hurry because he was on the run, that was fine by him; it saved explaining about Viktor. 'It's a deal,' he said. '$100,000 and you keep the icon.'

A couple tried to get out of the lift. Tom recognised one of the women from the bar, with a client. The heavy nearest the lift said, 'This floor is closed. Go away.'

Neither argued with him. The lift doors closed, taking them down to the ground again.

'Let's go,' said Ivanov.

Tom caught his sleeve. 'There's just one complication . . .'

When he had finished explaining about Karen, Ivanov's advice was the same as Ponsonby's: 'Forget her. Why waste time running after some chick at a time like this?'

.9.

Volkov, the helicopter pilot whom Tom had chartered to airlift Karen's team and their supplies from Petropavlovsk to Tolbachik, was a red-haired bear of a man in his early fifties. He was clad in an outsize Rentatent tartan shirt, oil-stained jeans and grubby trainers whose seams had split, allowing his bare toes to poke through. Three days' growth of gingery beard was itching his face, which he kept scratching. In contrast with the two walls who had driven Tom to the airport in the curtained rear compartment of a stretched black Mercedes, the pilot's face was open and friendly as he waved a come-aboard gesture to Tom through the stress-patterned Plexiglas of an ancient Mi-8 helicopter, whose dented fuselage was painted vivid Dayglo orange and blue.

Only after being told by Big Wall that Volkov was the best flier on Kamchatka, had Ivanov grudgingly conceded Tom what remained of the day to find Karen and put her on a plane to safety while he stayed behind to set up the logistics of the trip to Irkutsk.

'Don't do anything stupid,' were his last words to Tom. 'You're my investment now and I don't intend to lose you.'

Tom clambered over some crates of supplies for the survey team which were lashed down in the rear cabin and started buckling himself into a seat.

'There's a better view up-front,' Volkov shouted in between his pre-flight checks. 'Take the left-hand seat, but for God's sake, don't touch anything!'

Despite the huge body and shabby clothes, he was one of those pilots who made flying an art. His huge fingers flicked switches and nudged levers as lightly as butterflies kissing flowers. After exchanging a few casual words with the tower, he winked at Tom and said, '*Paidyómtye nu* – let's go!'

His trainer-shod feet danced on the pedals, his hands gripped and twisted the cyclic control stick between his legs and the collective by his side. The complex pattern of activity was so unlike driving a car or even a fixed-wing aircraft that his actions seemed to Tom unconnected with the helicopter's transit. Apparently by telepathy it lifted straight into a hover without any impression of movement, just the vibration of the engines and the noise reflected back from the ground skimming past beneath the Plexiglas panels that made up the nose of the craft. Lurching forward, it cleared the broken-down boundary fence by inches.

After an exchange of radioed insults with the pilot of an incoming Antonov jumbo freighter fifty metres overhead, the pilot handed Tom a headset and introduced himself, 'I'm Vladimir Vladimirovich Volkov from Vladivostok.'

Tom grunted, 'Feldink, Tomas Mikhailovich.'

'*Otkúda vy?* Where you from? Moscow? Leningrad? I can't place the accent.'

'England.'

'How come you speak Russian better'n I do?'

'It's a long story.'

Volkov's clear blue eyes, narrowed to slits by years of

gazing at blue sky and white snow, were summing Tom up. 'Been in one of these things before, Feldink?'

'No.'

Volkov patted the instrument panel affectionately. 'This beautiful beast is an Mi-8 – the all-purpose workhorse of the Red Army. Thirty years ago, when this one was built, the Mi-8 was the most heavily armed attack helicopter in the world, but now they're out of date as gunships. Like my old woman, they're too wide in the beam for modern tastes. They show up on an opponent's radar too easily – not like these sneaky little narrow-hipped tank busters, your McDonnell Douglas Apache and our Mi-28 and Ka-36 that pop up above the horizon, release a salvo of smart missiles and pop down again before anyone knows they're there. We learn by mistakes: Afghanistan taught us that wide-bodied craft like this were too vulnerable to the Stinger and Blowpipe missiles that your people and the CIA so kindly gave the mujaheddin. I lost a lot of friends to them.'

'You're talking way above my level,' said Tom.

'I am?' Volkov shot a quizzical glance at his passenger. 'That's funny, I had you figured for something to do with intelligence. If you're a civilian, all you need to know is that you're riding in a machine that's safer'n any Western helicopter. She's built by Russians. We can take punishment, so we build our machines the same way.'

Tom nodded. He was used to Russians boasting how their technology compared favourably with Western counterparts.

'You know, at one time,' continued Volkov, 'there were over 10,000 airworthy Mi-8s. That's more than even Bell Helicopter made of the famous UH-1 Huey, which tells you just how good she is.'

'You had this one a long time?' Tom asked. It was hard for him to say anything flattering about a craft with the paint worn off bodywork and controls. Some re-wiring had been done; cable joins were taped together and, instead of being passed through conduits, the wires were bunched and tied to anything handy with lengths of string. The seats were scuffed and foam poked out in places. Beside Tom's feet there were several rows of what looked like bullet holes in the body panels, with metal patches crudely riveted over them on the outside.

'Ten years I've had her,' Volkov answered. 'I bought her when she was pensioned off after service in Afghanistan. Like me, she's taken hits and has the scars to show.'

Tom noticed the burn scars on the back of both Volkov's hands and down one cheek. He wondered what 'taking hits' felt like, but remotely and with no idea that he would shortly find out.

'I'm told you fly search and rescue missions, land on glaciers and all that stuff,' he said. 'Does that mean you can put me down right at the camp on Mount Tolbachik?'

Volkov shook his head. 'There's a minor eruption going on at the moment, Feldink. What I'll do is, I'll drop you near the base camp. There's a helipad of sorts where I offload supplies. Then I'll go off to refuel at Atlasovo. It's a logging town about ten minutes' flying time to the north-east. I'll give you an hour to find your lady friend on the mountain – and then I'll have you both back in Petropavlovsk for dinner.'

There was something very reassuring about the genial giant with the gentle hands. Tom felt safe for the first time since leaving Dover. It was an illusion, he realised, but a pleasant one. He turned away to watch the scenery below. A landscape of unbroken bright green stretched as far as the horizon. Forests of spruce, larch, aspen and birch erased the memory of the ugliness of Petropavlovsk that only man could create. Gradually the trees thinned as the Mi-8 climbed higher and higher until there was nothing in sight but bare rock and volcanic ashfields, lava flows and columns of basalt. Kamchatka was a geologist's Disneyland.

Forty minutes into the flight, Volkov asked abruptly, 'You

been inside?' A grin disarmed the inquisitiveness of the question.

'What makes you ask?'

'Most people talk too much on their first trip – passengers, I mean. Guys who've been inside have learned to think with their mouths shut.'

Only another con would say that, thought Tom. 'Takes one to know one.'

'That's what they say.' Volkov's grin got broader. 'I did three years for killing a man in Afghanistan.'

Tom had grown used to cell-mates and men with whom he shared a table at meal-times talking about crimes they had committed. He showed what passed in prison for polite interest: 'You fragged him?'

A shake of the head as Volkov exchanged weather conditions with the pilot of a light aircraft passing them overhead, southbound from Atlasovo to Petropavlovsk.

'You shot him?'

'Didn't even waste a bullet.' Volkov jerked a thumb at the rear cabin. 'I pushed the fucker out the door. His name was Kotovich. A *stárshii serzhánt* armourer, he'd been selling SAMs to the mujaheddin. My best pal was shot down with one. If it had been a Stinger or a Blowpipe, I'd have said tough shit and got on with the job. But I couldn't buy that, so next day I said I was having trouble with one of the door guns, took Kotovich up for a ride – and splat!'

'And they gave you three years for that?'

Another shake of the head. Volkov seemed to be enjoying a private joke. 'I got three years for keeping my mouth shut, Feldink. If I'd admitted anything, I'd have got a bullet in the back of the head. It was my word against the co-pilot's. The bastard squealed on me. That's why I fly solo now.'

'I know how it feels,' said Tom.

'Chucking someone out at 200 metres?'

'No, keeping your mouth shut for several years, to stay out of worse trouble.'

'When d'you get out?'

Telling Volkov, it seemed almost funny. 'I walked out two days ago.'

'No kidding! You're on the run?'

'I suppose I am.'

Volkov whistled and punched Tom in the arm. 'I like you, Tomski.'

The playful blow nearly dislocated Tom's neck. 'It's mutual, Vlad,' he said, warming to the red-haired giant. 'Are all Siberian fliers as crazy as you?'

'Pretty much,' Volkov chuckled. 'My great-grandfather was a Cossack fur trader. Now, those guys were really tough. This was in the days of *yasak* – the tax the natives had to pay to Moscow in furs, 'cos they didn't have anything else of value. He married an American, so I'm one-eighth Yank.'

'You're kidding?'

'Nope. After Russia sold Alaska to the US in 1867, Moscow lost interest in Kamchatka, but a lot of American whalers lived here and some brought their wives. We even had a Yankee mayor of Petropavlovsk, name of Sandalin, sometime around 1880, I forget when exactly. I guess my great-grandfather stole some whaling captain's wife.'

'You know, Vlad, you're the chattiest Russian I've ever known.'

'Is that your way of telling me to shut the hell up?'

'No, it's true.'

'I'll tell you why, Tomski. Russians learned to keep their mouths shut under the Tsars and then Stalin and the purges and all that. Result: they don't open up easily. Now us over here, we carried on pretty much as we had been. After all, what could the fucking KGB do, send us to Siberia?' He chuckled richly at his punch-line: 'Fuckit, we were already there!'

They flew in silence for the next twenty minutes. Overflying the Valley of Geysers, halfway to Tolbachik, Volkov took his craft down to just above ground level, skimming through curtains of steam and dancing round jets of superheated mineral water a hundred feet high.

'Tourists.' He pointed to an identically painted Mi-8 on the ground. 'That's my son, the second-best flier in Kamchatka. The way I'm slowing up with booze and eating too much of my wife's cooking, he'll soon be better'n me. He just ferried in eighteen Japanese holidaymakers from that cruise ship anchored in Avacha Bay. They get out to take photographs and wallow in the radioactive mud baths over there.'

One huge hand pointed to a vast, bubbling mudfield. It was grey and blue and brown – every colour except green. A number of disembodied heads apparently floating in it followed the progress of the helicopter until it crossed a ridge and vanished from sight.

'And now you won't see any other evidence of the human race for a hundred and fifty klicks,' Volkov promised. 'You look tired. Go to sleep. I'll wake you when we're nearly there.'

'You were wrong, Vlad,' Tom said, ten minutes later.

To the east, flying parallel along the line of the coast itself, was a speck of black.

Volkov squinted at it for the second it took his practised eye to recognise the distant silhouette. 'M-24 Hip,' he said, 'from the airbase at Nizhny Kamchatsk. No external armament. Those bulges below the fuselage are long-range tanks, like ours.'

'A coastguard patrol?' Tom queried.

Volkov laughed. 'Our coastguards haven't any money for gas. They're grounded. That'll be some rich American hunter, looking for sport.'

'In a military helicopter?'

'If you've got dollars, Deutschmarks or yen, you can walk into just about any airbase of the ex-USSR and hire any plane they've got, fixed wing or helico. It's the only way for our pilots to get air-time. There's no money to pay for training flights otherwise, so if a rich foreigner looking for kicks wants to pay for the machine, the pilot and the fuel, they'll even let him drive a Mach 3 fighter.'

'How do you know that one's a hunter?'

'Because he's flying too slow for kicks. Might be tracking a sable. If he catches enough of them, he's paid for his holiday and his wife has a new fur coat into the bargain.'

'Is this the hunting season?'

'If you're rich enough.'

'You sound disapproving.'

'My old man first took me shooting when I was eight years old. In Afghanistan, I spent three years hunting men before they threw me in the stockade. Since I came back from the war I don't hunt any more. If a peasant lives by trapping and shooting, that's fine by me. This is a hard country. The animals kill each other for food and we kill them for the same reason. What I don't like are the *novyríchi*, Russian and foreign, who strafe moose herds and seal packs using chain guns and 30mm cannon in the nose of an attack helicopter, travelling at 300kph – just for the hell of it.'

Tom nodded.

'I didn't tell anyone else about this – not even my son.' Volkov shot a sideways glance at Tom, who was staring out of the windows. 'They called me out on a search and rescue mission last spring. A hunter from some South American country – Colombia, it was – had crashed on the pack ice. I found him.'

'Still alive?'

'The pilot was dead. The Colombian had survived two nights on the ice with both legs broken. I wasn't sure whether the floe he was on would take the weight of my machine – it was breaking up as it reached warmer water. So I set down like I was landing on eggs. I could see the cracks spreading through the ice as I reduced the lift slowly to zero. Looking back, it was a crazy chance to take.'

'Lucky for the hunter you came along.'

'Then I saw what had kept this sportsman from dying of cold for two days and two nights. It was the pelt of a female polar bear he had shot from the air. In the wreck was the pelt of her cub as well. I took the guy's rifle from him in case he loosed a pot shot at me as I took off, chucked it into the sea – and left him there to enjoy his trophies.'

'You sent someone else to get him?'

Volkov's silence was the answer.

. *10* .

A different silence pressed in from all sides almost tangibly after the Mi-8 had cleared the ridge and vanished from sight.

Volkov had flown off with a warning that the leaden sky meant an early dusk and bad weather on the way. 'Get your finger out, Tomski,' he had shouted as he left Tom standing beside the pile of supplies they had unloaded. 'I'll speed up the refuelling and be back as soon as I can. Make sure you're ready to pull out as soon as you hear me coming, otherwise we may have to sit out a snowstorm on the ground – and that could mean being immobilised on this godforsaken pile of rock for one, maybe two days.'

As Tom's hearing threshold dropped, he became aware of the noises of the mountain: boulders slithering down slopes themselves on the move, the creaking and groaning of the rocks, the hiss of gases escaping from cracks great and small. From somewhere high above, muted by folds in the ground, came the voice of the volcano – a rumble like a distant artillery barrage.

He started to walk up to the base camp just below the permanent snow line. It was a cluster of tents and plywood huts on a narrow ledge – one of the few flat places on the entire mountain, but with no place for the Mi-8 to set down, with its 70-foot diameter main rotor and overall length of almost 60 feet. Volkov had buzzed the camp after failing to raise anyone on the VHF radio. Curious faces had emerged from tents and huts and someone waved a recognition that transport was required.

Halfway to the camp Tom met a hard-top Lada 4WD bouncing down the rough track to pick him up. The Chinese Canadian girl at the wheel introduced herself as one of Karen's graduate students from Toronto. She recognised Tom's face from a photograph she had seen and asked, 'What are you doing here?'

'A good question,' said Tom. There was no reason for the team to be expecting him, so the alarm bells did not ring yet. 'How's Karen?'

'Oh, she's fine. But she got your message and left with the two guys you sent about half an hour ago.'

'What do you mean?' Tom grabbed the girl's wrist so hard that she braked the jeep to a halt with a cry of protest.

'I didn't send anyone,' he said. 'Where have they gone?'

She pointed down the track. 'They said your helicopter had made a bad landing at the logging camp in Atlasovo and that you were hurt. So she left in a hurry with them.'

'Did she leave any message?'

Something between fear and panic at Tom's intensity showed in the girl's eyes. 'I don't know. I was tagging a whole batch of gas samples for spectrometer analysis at the time. Maybe she talked to someone else.'

'Move over!' Tom ran round the Lada and got in behind the wheel, gunning the engine and skidding all four wheels in the refrozen slush until he got the feel of the transmission. At the camp he fired questions at everyone in turn.

'What did they look like?' Tom grabbed one of the

scientists who had been working with Karen when the two men arrived in an ancient ex-Army half-track.

The Russian had a Petersburg accent. 'Peasants,' he said. 'Loggers, maybe. I don't know. Could have been hunters – the locals all look the same to me.'

'Did they have Ukrainian accents?'

'They were both locals. I think the driver was a Koryak. The other man was a Siberian of some breed.'

'Were they armed?'

'Everyone's armed here, except us.'

'Where does the track lead to?' Tom asked.

'It forks about a kilometre after the helipad. Left takes you up to the crater. Right leads down to Atlasovo.'

Tom ran into Karen's tent, looking for any clue or message she might have left. There was nothing, so he grabbed her bag and stuffed her passport into it. There were no weapons to be had and no one could even find a pair of binoculars for him, so he thrust into the bag Karen's camera with a 400mm lens which she had been using to photograph the eruption from a safe distance.

Within minutes he was bumping down the track in pursuit. The estimate of distance turned out to be wrong by 100 per cent. Tom thought he had missed the fork and was about to turn back after two kilometres when he saw clearly in a patch of fresh snow the marks made by the half-track as it swung off the broad trail heading downhill and turned left towards the crater. He stopped and got out to steady the long lens of Karen's camera on the roof of the Lada. It was necessary to turn off the engine in order to kill the vibration so that he could focus the long lens. In the poor light he had problems seeing where the track went, as it snaked its way back and forth across the grey bulk of the mountain. After two minutes he was about to give up and drive on regardless when he saw a dot moving far above him. Through the lens he made out the long, low shape of a half-track in military camouflage climbing obliquely across a small snowfield. Once back on rock, it became invisible again.

Fighting his way up the badly graded track in first and second gear, using the four-wheel drive, Tom wondered how fast the vehicle in front could travel and how long it would take him to catch up, driving over such appalling terrain. He was tempted to head back to the camp and wait for Volkov's return. The helicopter would be able to overtake the half-track in minutes and Volkov would be a good man to have with him. But the weather was worsening; Volkov might be late – or even be grounded until morning. In either case Tom would have lost any chance of catching up, so going back was out of the question.

At a bend in the trail, he saw the half-track again, this time with his naked eye, much closer. That posed the question of what he could do when he caught up with two armed men, so he stopped the Lada and rummaged in the space behind the rear seat. There was a first-aid kit, survival blankets, sleeping bags, a Primus stove, water and food – but no weapon.

At this height, the clouds were threateningly near. Lightning generated by the ionised gases escaping from the main crater crackled between mountain and sky and the roar of continual explosions mingled with the thunder claps. One lightning strike was so near that Tom heard the moisture in the air boiling with a sound halfway between a sizzle and a whipcrack. Quickly he got back into the car; being virtually a Faraday cage, it was the safest place to be in a thunderstorm.

The half-track was out of sight again. He drove cautiously, aware that it might be very near, hidden by a bend or a dip in the track. Rounding a hillock of cinders, he found that it had stopped only a couple of hundred metres ahead, just before the track was intersected by a gully full of fast-flowing red-hot lava.

Luckily all the noises of the gale-force wind, the volcanic

explosions and the thunder had covered the sound of the Lada's engine, so he reversed out of sight and drove off the track, concealing the Lada behind a cinder outcrop. Grabbing the camera, he scrambled to the top and poked the long lens of the camera over. Zooming in and panning the camera, he could see all three faces clearly in the viewfinder. It looked as though the two men by the half-track were having an argument with Karen, threatening her with their firearms.

Tom swore. Without a weapon of any kind, he could do nothing against two armed men. He zoomed wide to check the overall scene and saw to his horror that the men were forcing Karen to walk up the track towards the gully. Refusing to turn her face away from them she was walking backwards, step by careful step.

After a particularly loud explosion in the crater, Tom saw both men duck a lava bomb which landed close to them. He whipped the camera back onto Karen just in time to see her take advantage of the distraction and make a run for it.

He stood up, no longer caring whether the two men saw him or not, and shouted, 'Here! Karen, over here!'

But she was running in the opposite direction – towards the gully glowing with molten lava. He saw her scramble up the side of the levee, stand on the top, arms flailing for balance – and then jump to what looked like certain death.

Sick at the thought that he had arrived too late to save her life, Tom lost his footing, slipped and fell to the ground, where he lay with head cradled in both hands, moaning, 'No, no, no, no, no!'

PART X

.1.

Karen shrank back into the ash and cinders on which she was lying. The Koryak, standing on the opposite bank of the gully, was so close that she could see the fire reflected in his eyes as he stared in her direction. He towered above her, lit against the dark sky by the hellish glare from below. With his jacket pulled up to shield the lower part of his face from the heat and those two eyes glaring at her, he looked more monster than man in that light. She told herself that he was blinded by the glare of the lava, but it seemed impossible for him not to see her. Like an animal fleeing the hunter, she wanted instinctively to scramble away from those two glaring eyes but forced herself to lie still. Keeping her fist withdrawn inside the khaki cloth of the anorak sleeve, she slowly inched an arm upwards to cover her face.

Her clothes were singeing now, filling her nostrils with a smell like burning hair. And still the man was looking in her direction, less than ten metres away. She held her breath until he turned aside to stare downstream at where her corpse would have been deep-frying in its own fat if terror had not given her leg muscles ten times their normal power and if the further bank had not started to roof over with a ledge of solidified rock that bore her weight for perhaps a second before breaking off and falling into the molten rock below. That brief respite had enabled her to regain balance just long enough to hurl herself forwards to safety and not fall backwards to her death.

The heat penetrating her jeans and burning the skin on the backs of her legs was excruciating. Fighting the pain, Karen dug her nails into her palms, holding her breath until the Koryak jumped back from the edge of the gully and disappeared from her sight.

From behind his mound of cinders, Tom watched him run back towards the half-track. Both men wanted to get away fast now that the job was done. They jumped into the vehicle and, remembering Karen's advice, began backing slowly and carefully down the track.

Karen had intended counting slowly to sixty before moving. At thirty she could stand the heat and the pain no longer and scrambled to her feet to beat at her smouldering clothes, knocking off the hot ash. She stood trembling, listening to the sounds of the mountain: the crackle and hiss of molten lava, the creaking of rock in motion and the thunder rolling from peak to peak. This close, the heat radiating from the rock of the levee was frightful. Shielding her face, she waited a minute longer, standing first on one foot and then the other, to cool the soles of her boots. Only then did she allow herself to scurry downhill and away from the place of horror, bent double to take advantage of the cover offered by the high banks of the gully until she could take the risk of standing upright.

According to her reckoning, the survey team's camp was no more than two kilometres distant, mainly downhill. She blanked out the immediate past by promising herself that, in an hour at most, she would be there – back in a sane world where men did not throw women into boiling lava, whatever else they did to them.

The driver of the half-track was having trouble handling reverse drive. By over-correcting, he slewed the tracks first one way and then the other. It seemed an age to Tom before the vehicle disappeared down the track and it was safe for him to run to the gully and scramble to the top of the levee.

Even with anorak zipped up and both arms held in front of his face, the heat was appalling. He shouted Karen's name at the top of his lungs but his voice was lost in the hiss and crackle of lava.

He backed away and leaped down the side of the levee. Numb with horror, he was halfway back to the Lada when he stopped in his tracks and tried to clarify what he had actually seen. A woman panicking and running to certain death? But Karen never panicked, so far as he knew. Even on that awful night in Leningrad station, she had not lost her nerve completely. And . . . she had spent her adult life working on volcanoes. Was it just remotely possible that she knew what she was doing?

He ran back to the levee. Again the terrible heat seared his skin until he brought both arms up in front of his face. It was hard to tell exactly where Karen had stood for that brief moment when he saw her silhouetted against the glow, arms flailing. In places it did seem possible for someone brave and desperate enough to jump across, so . . .

He squinted through the narrow slit between his arms. A hundred metres upstream, he could see the lateral vent from which the lava issued nearly at white heat. If he could some-how negotiate the Lada across the tortured surface of cinders and ash higher up the slope, was there time to make a search before darkness? How could he find his bearings on the other side with night coming on?

For the second time he climbed down from the levee. Before he had reached the Lada, visibility was down to less than ten metres and worsening as the blizzard got into its stride. The temperature was already well below freezing. In such weather conditions – even supposing that Karen had survived the jump – the odds were a million to one against finding her before she died of exposure. It was quite likely that he would himself succumb to darkness and cold. He might even drive through the solid crust and find himself in boiling lava. Tom hesitated before turning the key in the ignition. There was no doubt that the sensible course of action would be to drive down off the mountain while there was still some light and before the weather worsened.

After half an hour the blister on the back of Karen's right leg was as large as a hand and twice as thick. By a small mercy the hole burned in her jeans allowed the biting wind to chill her lower leg into numbness. It was almost completely dark now and she was still walking in an endless landscape of grey ash and pumice and whirling snowflakes, with no sign of the observatory.

On Mount St Helens, Etna or any of a dozen other volcanoes which she knew well, she could have found her way blindfold, but on Tolbachik she was a shocked and shivering stranger who had lost all sense of direction in the sunless gloom. The mountain covered more than a hundred square kilometres; even in fine weather and by daylight a person could wander on it for days and see no other living soul. Where had she gone wrong? The first deceptive downhill slope from the gully had led only to an unclimbable wall of old lava. Whichever way she turned led upwards, into the darkness and the thickening flurries of snow.

As the light finally went, Karen fell for the hundredth time, cutting her hands on some sharp cinders that poked through a thin layer of snow and tearing a hole in the right knee of her trousers. She could feel warm blood oozing from a deep gash below the kneecap. Winded, she stayed on the ground this time, looking numbly around at the featureless wasteland lit by a lightning flash. Her exhausted body wanted to crawl into the lee of a boulder and go to sleep, sheltered from the wind – even at the risk of never waking up again.

The thought of dying of hypothermia so near one of the hottest spots on the surface of the planet was almost laughable. Karen forced away the desire for rest and tried to stand up. An uncontrollable shivering started twitching her whole body spasmodically, preventing her from moving. How long, she wondered remotely, did it take a healthy adult female with a body weight of 145 pounds to die of exposure?

In between two shivering fits, she managed to press the light button on her wristwatch and saw with incredulity that less than an hour had passed since she had stepped out of the half-track. Until that moment she had been a respected member of the international scientific community who attended conferences and presented papers, an expert in her field who confidently expected to be offered a university chair in geology before her fortieth birthday. Now she was just a frightened animal drenched with perspiration, shivering with cold and shock.

Don't stop! Keep walking! She forced herself to stand and shuffle on, one outstretched foot feeling each pace in the darkness. The next time she pressed the light button, another thirty minutes had elapsed. The only choice was between this agonising, blind, tormented progress and sitting down to die.

What had interrupted her thoughts? she wondered.

It came again: a faint pulsing borne on the wind, hardly loud enough to hear. Only the rhythmic pattern of the sound distinguished it from the random noises of Nature. *Bip, bip, bip* she made out, coming from her right.

Karen turned her head in that direction. *Beep, beep, beep.* And again *bip, bip, bip*.

It was the only Morse code she knew: three longs and three shorts. She did not even know which was S and which was O, but the message somebody was sounding on a car horn was clear enough.

Her head moving from side to side like a radar scanner, she shuffled towards the faint sound. Sometimes the wind blew the distant hooting away and she had to wait in the darkness until it was audible again. Slowly it grew louder until she could see a glow which became a pair of headlights carving a beam through the flurries of snow.

Were they the lights of the half-track? She hesitated before walking out of the concealing darkness. Whoever was sounding the horn could be one of the men who had tried to kill her, waiting on the mountain to make sure she was dead. There was only one way of finding out. The alternative was to stay on Tolbachik and die of cold and exhaustion during the night.

She shuffled forward until she was standing in the beam of the headlights with her arms stretched out sideways. She tried to lift them above her head, but had not the energy to raise them that high.

'*Nye strelyáitye*,' she called. 'Don't shoot!'

The beeping stopped and the indistinct figure of a man walked into the light, seeming to move towards Karen in slow motion, tantalising her with his threatening male anonymity. The beam from the headlights projected his enlarged silhouette onto the mist and swirling snow-flakes, turning it into the figure of a great dark giant moving menacingly towards her.

Let me see your face, she wanted to scream. Then suddenly it didn't matter who he was. Her hands dropped to her sides. *Just let it all be over . . .*

She heard a voice call, 'Karen! Over here!'

The voice was familiar, but it belonged to someone she knew was on the other side of the world. I must be hallucinating, she thought, falling forward into the arms that were reaching out for her.

'It's okay, I've got you,' Tom said.

She felt like an old rag doll that had lost its stuffing; it was as though all the muscles of her body had gone on strike the moment she heard his reassuring voice. Her legs would not support her any longer. She clung to him, shivering and whimpering over and over again, 'Oh, Tom! Oh, Tom!'

.2.

Beneath her was the molten lava over which she swung on a thread of chance. The other side of the gully was impossibly far away; it seemed she would never reach it. Just as her feet touched the fragile crust and Karen tried to throw herself forward to safety, it crumbled beneath her weight. For a second that went on and on, she gazed down at her own certain death. From the moving, living, molten rock that roared like an animal insane with blood-lust, something evil was poking upward towards her. As it came clear of the glowing mass she recognised the twin barrels of the shotgun, pushing up towards her like a double steel phallus, to rape her with fire and lead. The rock was crumbling, crumbling, crumbling. She was falling . . .

Her eyes opened wide with panic to find Tom sitting beside her in the grey light of early dawn. She clutched his wrist, digging her nails in with a desperation that hurt him. The roaring became the noise of the gale outside their flimsy shelter.

'Two men tried to kill me, Tom.'

'I know.'

Karen shuddered at the memory. 'Why?' she asked. 'What had I ever done to deserve a death like that?'

Tom did not reply.

She sat up and looked around. They were in an emergency refuge she had had erected, in case any members of the survey team should be caught on the mountain in foul weather. It was no more than a plywood box: a two-metre cube heliported into position and lashed down with steel hawsers to resist the furious winds that lashed Mount Tolbachik, summer and winter.

Recognising her surroundings made it all the more difficult for Karen to reconcile Tom's presence. 'What are you doing here?' she asked. 'I thought you were in Britain.'

'I'll tell you in the morning.'

'Tell me now. How did you find me?'

'I trailed the half-track up the mountain. I saw the whole thing.'

'Why didn't you do anything to help?'

'Like what?' he grimaced. 'Those men were both armed. All I could do was watch through the telephoto lens of your camera. That's how I knew where to start looking for you, after they had gone.'

'Did I really jump across the molten lava in that gully?' It seemed incredible now, to have done what she had.

'You did.' Tom pulled the sleeping bags tight around her neck and willed her back to sleep.

There were a thousand things Karen wanted to ask him but her brain could not put the thoughts into words. It kept going back again and again to that moment when she was fighting for balance over a river of liquid death.

'Tom . . .' she began, but the questions drifted away. She felt so tired that a year of sleep would not suffice.

'Tom . . .'

'Later,' he said. 'Later.'

*

The gale had blown itself out in the night, winter held at bay for one more day by the rearguard of summer. The sun came up fast in a clear blue sky, climbing out of the low cloud that concealed the lower slopes of Mount Tolbachik and stretched as far as the Bering Sea, which showed as a pale metallic gleam on the eastern horizon.

Turning to the south-west, Tom saw more cloud. It seemed to go on for ever. Somewhere below it lay the logging camp of Atlasovo where he presumed that Volkov and his helicopter were still grounded.

To the north of the cabin, the volcano's peak rose as clear as a cardboard cut-out and as simple as a child's drawing: a triangle of grey rock and white ice with a stream of grey smoke coming out of the top. Beyond that the peaks of seven other volcanoes floated above the cloud, one belching smoke and another spilling red lava down its side from a lateral vent. Tom stopped what he was doing for a moment, and stood drinking in the breathtaking majesty and power of the view. The mountains of fire and ice adrift on a sea of cloud made him feel about the same size and importance as a speck of dust.

Awoken by the light pouring through the open door, Karen sat up and shielded her eyes to see Tom outside in the bright sunshine. He kneeled down in the snow, spreading out on the ground the orange aircraft recognition panel and the aluminised survival blankets from the Lada's emergency kit, weighting them down with large chunks of pumice to keep them from blowing away in the stiff breeze. Karen could hear the hissing of a Primus stove in the fireplace. A familiar smell teased her nostrils. Of all the things to wake up to, on the flank of an active volcano at the eastern tip of the Asian landmass, the least expected was the mouth-watering aroma of bacon frying. Saliva filled her mouth, reminding her that she had not eaten for twenty-four hours, during which time exhaustion and exposure had burned thousands of calories. Ravenous, she unzipped the sleeping bag and shrugged her way out of it.

The singe marks and tears all over her trouser legs made the unbelievable memories real. Her anorak was burnt right through in places. Her hands were filthy and cut by repeated falls. There was a huge flap of dead skin hanging on the back of her leg where the burn blister had broken.

She took the cup of cocoa from Tom and sipped the scalding fluid while he scraped slightly burnt tinned bacon, eggs and hash browns from the fold-up frying pan onto two plastic plates.

'I could eat them both,' she said.

'Go ahead. I'll cook some more for . . .'

He stopped in mid-sentence. The last sound he was expecting to hear before the cloud broke up was the insect drone of a distant helicopter, which proved that he still had a lot to learn about Vladimir Volkov. Mad Vlad, as fellow fliers called him, had taken a finely calculated risk, lifting off from the logging camp which was situated in a narrow, steep-sided valley, and climbing in tight spirals through swirling mist and cloud, knowing that death was lurking near in every direction.

Once above the cloud, his search was limited to those areas of Mount Tolbachik which lay above 2,500 metres. Everything below was shrouded in an impenetrable blanket of white, but that still left a lot of mountain to cover. He spotted Tom's recognition panels just before 7 a.m., radioed the news to the survey camp, invisible in the murk below, and swooped in to land neatly on the ledge of rock, blasting away the fresh loose snow and setting down exactly on the orange panel.

'What the hell is going on?' he shouted at Tom, standing with his arm shielding his face from the down-draught of the rotors. 'I radio the survey camp last night to make sure you're ready for me to pick you up before the wind gets too strong to risk a landing and they tell me you're lost up here in a blizzard. I call them up again this morning and they say you're still lost. Out on a mountain in weather like that, a townie like you could have died, you realise that?'

He caught sight of Karen standing in the doorway, shovelling food from the second plate into her mouth. 'So you found the yeti, Tom. Is that what you came for? I thought you had better taste.'

In her burned and torn clothes, with scabbed hands, filthy face and matted hair, Karen looked like some crazy who had been sleeping under bridges for years.

'We had problems,' Tom said. 'She . . . got lost and nearly fell into the crater.'

'Looks to me like she did fall in,' Volkov laughed. 'Either way, let's get her aboard and be airborne. I'm wasting gas.'

'I'm not going anywhere looking like this,' protested Karen. She pulled her bag out of the Lada and rummaged through it, looking for some clean clothes. 'The first thing I do is get changed out of what I'm wearing and have a wash.'

'We haven't got the time,' Tom answered, shouting to make himself heard above the noise of the engines and rotors.

'Two minutes,' she insisted, lugging the bag into the cabin. 'If you want to speed things up, heat me some more water in one of the empty cans.'

'What the hell is going on?' Volkov shouted.

'The lady wants to change her clothes.'

'Now I've heard it all. And what, pray, are you doing?'

'Heating some water for her to have a wash.'

'Well, pardon me.'

The rotors slowed to idle, the whine of the turbines dropped in pitch and then died away, lost in the immense silence. Volkov called, 'While you're at it, Tomski, call room service and get 'em to bring me a large regular coffee and two doughnuts.'

Twenty minutes later Karen was dressed in jeans, a sweater and a light anorak, with trainers on her sore and swollen feet. Her boots, burned and cut in a hundred places, had had to be thrown away, together with all the clothes she had been wearing. Tom had dressed the blister on her leg and swabbed her cut hands with disinfectant from the Lada's first-aid box, while Volkov took advantage of the delay to consume most of the ready-to-eat supplies in the Lada and tossed the rest on a you-never-know-when-you'll-need-it basis into an ancient plastic schoolbag he kept behind his seat.

Tom settled Karen in the rear cabin and threw in the half-empty holdall after her. She was trying to buckle herself into the seat when Volkov stuck his head through the narrow doorway in the bulkhead which separated the two cabins.

'Excuse my initial remarks,' he apologised. 'Tom didn't tell me you could speaka da Russki. You're looking a whole lot better now.'

There was something about Volkov that made it hard to take offence. Karen felt a different person after a wash in hot water and with some food in her stomach. She shook Volkov's outstretched hand and smiled, 'That's okay.'

Beneath the bluff exterior he was more sensitive than most people realised. His shrewd eyes took in the lines of stress on her face and put them down to the trauma of being lost on a mountain all night.

'Well, you can relax now,' he grinned. 'I'll have you back in civilisation in a couple of hours, ma'am. And, by the way, I radioed your team at the survey camp that you're safe and sound, so everyone can quit worrying.'

'Was that necessary?' Tom asked, shutting the cabin door.

'It's routine in search-and-rescue missions to stand every-one down when the missing person's been found.'

'Would anyone else have heard?'

'There are eyes and ears everywhere in these parts: Russian, Japanese, American.'

'I thought the Cold War was over?'

'The geography hasn't changed.' Volkov shrugged. 'The Yanks still keep two nuclear subs on station off Vladivostok, monitoring everything that leaves and enters harbour. I've seen their frigates top-heavy with radomes trolling up and down twenty-five miles offshore of Petropavlovsk. Every day American aircraft stuffed with COMINT gear fly along the Kamchatka peninsula, out of Adak and Shemya Islands in the Aleutians. Since I was using the international emergency frequency, the whole world could have been tuned in, for all I know.'

As the Mi-8 lifted off vertically in the cold dry air and spun round to head south with the sun pouring in the left-hand windows, Tom sat down beside Karen.

'Now,' she shouted at him, 'you can tell me what's going on.'

'Vlad will fly us to Petropavlovsk,' he shouted back. 'From there I'll take you to Magadan and put you on the first flight to North America.'

'I'm not a package, Tom,' she said. 'I'm a person. I said I wanted to know what's going on.'

He squeezed her hand. 'The less you know the better.'

Karen pulled free, undid her seat belt and turned to face him. 'Don't give me that chauvinist crap,' she shouted. 'Yesterday I damn near died! Out of the blue, you turn up. I'm not so stupid that I can't connect the two events, so before I go anywhere else I insist on knowing why those two men tried to kill me. I don't know who they were. I don't know why they did it. I know just one thing for certain, Tom Fielding: for the second time in my life you've dragged me into some scenario of life and death without my knowledge or consent. So start talking.'

Tom felt a tap on his shoulder and turned to see Volkov making signs that he should put on a headset. There was one lying on the seat opposite.

'What is it, Vlad?' he asked.

'We have company.' Volkov nodded to the north-east where a small black speck was growing larger, just above the horizon.

.3.

Tom changed seats with Karen and pressed his face against the scratched and discoloured Soviet version of Plexiglas. Through the window he could see nothing but blue sky and a few clouds, low down over the Bering Sea.

'What kind of company?' he asked.

'What does he want?' Karen shouted in his ear.

Tom shook his head. He was listening to Volkov's voice on the intercom: 'From the speed and the profile, I'd guess he's one of the Mi-28s from the field at Nizhny Kamchatsk – tank-busters with the NATO code-name Havoc. If so, he's a long way from home. Must have extra fuel tanks. He's just seen us and changed course, heading this way.'

'Another rich hunter?' Tom asked.

'Could be a tourist flying for kicks. We'll see.'

As Volkov brought the Mi-8 onto a new heading Tom caught a glimpse of the other craft in the sky behind them. Two minutes later, Volkov changed course again. The dot continued to grow bigger.

'What's going on?' Karen asked.

'There's another helicopter trailing us,' Tom told her.

Volkov keyed the radio, changing frequency several times as he asked the craft behind to identify itself. There was no reply on either civil or military frequencies. Could be the other pilot was just sloppy. Could be he was chatting with his co-pilot. Could be his radio was on the blink. Volkov ran through all the reasonable explanations. None of them accounted for the hairs standing up on the back of his neck.

He turned his head and caught Tom's anxious expression. 'Is there something you should tell me, Tomski? If so, let's have it.'

Widening the circle, Ponsonby had once called it. Tom took a deep breath. 'Karen didn't get lost on the mountain, Vlad. Two men took her for a ride. They wanted to throw her into some molten lava. It's only by a miracle that she escaped.'

Volkov gave a low whistle. 'Who did this?'

'I don't know.'

'But you're scared the guys in the Havoc may be friends of theirs?'

'*Mózhno*,' said Tom. 'It's possible. Do the extra fuel tanks mean the other helicopter is unarmed?'

'They'll have reduced armament,' was the reply. 'No smart missiles but probably six heat-seeking air-to-air rockets and a very efficient GSh 30mm cannon in the nose-pod.'

'How fast can we go?' Tom shouted.

'With this load, around 200kph, true airspeed.'

'And how fast can an Mi-28 fly?'

'Close to 300kph, but those extra tanks and the weight of the fuel will slow him down some. Even so, he could overhaul us without trying. And he's got the range to stay with us all the way to Petropavlovsk, if he wants to.'

Volkov changed course twice more before asking quietly, 'Are you guys belted in, back there? I think *nash drug* will be in missile range any minute now.'

Karen was having trouble with the unfamiliar seat belt

buckle. Tom gave her a hand and was reaching for his own seat belt when the Mi-8 flipped over onto its right side and dropped like a stone. The negative-G lifted him out of his seat and pinned him to the wall of the cabin. There was a loud *whoosh!* and an explosion nearby, which he felt like a kick on the other side of the thin metal panel. The helicopter levelled out and gravity forced an abrupt return to his seat, leaving him feeling as though he had been put through a tumble-drier.

'Y*ob tvoyú mat!*' Volkov swore. 'That motherfucker's really annoyed me now! I'll have to teach him a trick or two.'

'With what?' The only armament Tom had seen on board was a hunting rifle, clipped to the bulkhead behind the pilot's seat.

'We're going to play hide and seek,' Volkov announced. 'Hold tight!'

As far as Tom could see through the five windows that lined each side of the passenger cabin, there was nowhere to hide. The only breaks in the cloud layer below were where jagged peaks of bare rock and ice poked through. He recalled flying over the same murderous terrain on the trip north with Volkov boasting, 'I know this country like the back of my hand.' Please God it was true . . .

'Tighten your ring, Tomski!' Volkov yelled, as two more rockets left the stubby wing pods of the Havoc. Pushing the nose down, he dropped in a screaming powered dive straight into the cloud. Inside the Mi-8 everything went dark, with the exception of the glowing instruments on the flight deck.

Out of the window, as Tom's eyes adjusted, he saw a rock face streaking past, far too close for comfort. Beside him, Karen had her eyes closed and was gripping the arms of the seat so tightly that her knuckles were white. Her lips were moving in the Lord's Prayer.

'I didn't know you were religious,' Tom shouted in her ear. It was a stupid remark, but the first thing that came to mind.

'I'm not!' she screamed back, eyes still closed. 'But what the fuck else can I do?'

The pitch of the rotors changed as Volkov put the craft into a steep climb. The darkness changed to blindingly bright light as they broke through the cloud.

'*Gdyé sukinsyn tyepér?*' Ivanov shouted: where's the sonofabitch now? He was blinded by the light refracted by the web of stress lines in the Plexiglas; it was like staring into a searchlight.

'*Nalyévo!*' Tom shouted. On the left, clearly visible to him, the Havoc was five or more kilometres distant and heading away from them.

'Dive back into the cloud,' he urged. 'We may lose him altogether.'

It was a long time since Volkov had felt the anger that was building inside him now.

Combat spirit, his instructor pilot had called it when he was training at the huge helicopter base of Alexandria in Ukraine. He had enjoyed taunting candidate-pilot Volkov, calling him a slow-witted, good-natured Siberian peasant who would never be able to fly anything except geese and chickens . . . until the day Volkov, on his first solo flight, deliberately edged alongside him and overlapped rotors by half their length, with only two metres of vertical separation, keeping station relentlessly as the instructor tried to slide sideways and escape.

'How's that for combat spirit, motherfucker?' he had shouted over the radio.

It had been worth being grounded for eight weeks. If shoulder-fired SAMs in Afghanistan had not been downing pilots and machines at a pace never anticipated by the Soviet high command, he would not have been allowed to fly again.

Volkov turned in his seat and stuck his head through the narrow doorway, winking at Karen who looked terrified. Wanting to reassure her, he shouted for her benefit, 'Tom's pal from Moscow said I only get paid if I deliver you both back in one piece. I make a point of always getting paid, so I'm going to have to teach that bastard in the Mi-28 the final lesson in his flying career.'

'But we're unarmed,' she shouted back.

'So we let him see us.'

'And what will that achieve?'

'This time, he'll get closer,' Volkov predicted. He turned his attention back to the instruments and the few landmarks that projected above the cloud layer: jagged peaks of rock and ice, each of which resembled all the others to Tom's eyes. Twenty kilometres ahead lay the only real landmark – the smoking crater of another volcano, Kronotskaya. But the manoeuvre Volkov had in mind required accuracy in terms of centimetres, not kilometres. If he miscalculated, they would all be dead in a few minutes.

'Next time we pop out of the cloud . . .' He was thinking aloud. '. . . the other guy'll get closer still and I'll lead him into it. If I'm as good a pilot as I've been telling people all these years, we'll come back up into the sunshine and he won't.'

'What's he saying?' Karen asked, frustrated by her lack of a headset.

Tom grabbed a barf bag and thrust it into her hand. 'You'll need this. Volkov is going to try and persuade our pursuer to crash into a mountain.'

Karen's brain was spinning. She kept thinking about some gas samples she had been labelling the previous afternoon when she was interrupted by the arrival of the two men in the half-track. If someone else identified them incorrectly, it could spoil the whole season's research . . .

'He's fucking blind,' Volkov shouted over the intercom. He waggled the Mi-8 to catch the sun deliberately on the cabin windows and was rewarded when the vanishing dot turned and started getting bigger. Volkov held the Mi-8 on its previous bearing, allowing the Havoc to approach well within rocket range.

'Holy shit!' Even though he was expecting them, the sight of two more rockets burning their vapour trails across the empty sky between the Mi-28 and his own craft sent slivers of ice up and down his spine.

The Mi-8 lurched upward and then dropped like a stone as Volkov used a stall to get below the incoming missiles, hoping that the manoeuvre would look like a panic reaction to the other pilot, closing at a combined speed of over 500 kph.

Again the darkness and the belly-churning jerks and sudden drops, with the Mi-8 sometimes nearly vertical as Volkov twisted away from rock faces that loomed out of the cloud like the claws of giants trying to tear his machine out of the sky. There was a crash from beneath the cabin as the undercarriage hit solid rock. The Mi-8 lurched, shuddered and lost so much speed that Volkov had to take the risk of putting the nose down briefly, trading altitude for speed to avoid a real stall. Somehow he split his concentration between the lethal crags all around and the compass glowing in front of him to make sure they came out with the Havoc blind-siding them, behind the Mi-8 and in the sun.

'Keep a watch behind,' he ordered Tom. 'That's where he should be, thinking he's going to get us with that last rocket!'

Tom jammed his face against the window, squinting rear-ward. He was aware of Karen hunched over beside him, her face in the barf bag. Through the distorting curved Plexiglas the other craft was nearer than he had thought.

'*Yevó vízhu!*' he shouted: I see him!

'Where? Where?' Volkov shouted urgently.

The sun was burning holes in Tom's retinas. He forced himself to keep looking but saw only the blind spot.

Urgently he grabbed Karen's arm and shouted, 'Tell Volkov where he is! I can't see a thing.'

Motion sickness vanished in the urgency of the moment. She unbuckled herself and leaned across him. 'Behind us,' she shouted. 'Right behind us.'

'Level or high?'

'Above us.'

'Six o'clock high,' Tom shouted into the mic.

'Has he seen us?' Volkov asked calmly.

Tom thrust his headset at Karen. 'I'm blind. You talk him through.'

At that second the other craft altered course, going into a steep dive. '*Vot on pridyót!*' Karen shouted. 'Here he comes!'

'Steady,' said Volkov. 'I want to let him get real close this time. Tell me when he's a kilometre away.'

'How the hell do I know?' she screamed. 'He must be closer than that already!'

'Half a kilometre?'

'He's about there.' Karen was gripping the arms of the seat so tightly that it hurt and thrusting herself back into the seat as though it gave some protection. At the evil sight of the black camouflaged tank-buster heading straight for her, she wanted to curl into a ball and shrink back into her own womb to hide from this monster intent on killing her.

The cannon in the nose-pod rotated and elevated, seeming to aim right between her eyes. She could see a line of green tracers curving impossibly towards her. It was an optical delusion, due to both helicopters moving in three planes of space, but made the shells seem gifted with a living intelligence that enabled them to pursue the moving target of her vulnerable flesh. She winced as a series of thuds hit the fuse-lage and holes appeared in the cabin walls. A streak of white zipped from the Havoc towards the Mi-8, travelling even faster than the cannon shells. Before she could open her mouth to shout a new warning, Volkov threw his craft into a climbing turn and the rocket's warhead exploded behind and below them, lifting the helicopter bodily.

Dozens of small objects broke loose and flew through the air. A heavy tool box, released from its clips, hurtled across the rear cabin, smashing the door lock which was already damaged by the blast before disappearing into the white carpet below. The door slid back and jammed open. Karen was thrown to the floor. Grabbing desperately for anything to hold onto, she found herself sliding across the cargo space towards the open doorway, shouting for Tom to help her. First one leg and then the other was flailing in the void before she felt the neck of her anorak grabbed. Still half-blind, Tom was squinting sideways at her as he pulled her back into the cabin and onto the seat.

Throughout all this, Volkov was shouting, 'Where is he? For Chrissakes, someone tell me where the bastard is.'

Through the window Karen caught sight of the Havoc closing in again, two kilometres away to the right. Even in English, she was often confused between right and left. '*Naprávo!*' she screamed. 'Right, right, right.' *Please God, make it right . . .*

'Range?' Volkov sounded calm now. In a few seconds it would all be over, one way or the other.

'He's nearly on us!' Karen tried to sound equally calm, but it was impossible. 'This time he can't miss!'

'*Tsyp, tsyp, tsyp.*' Volkov imitated his old *babushka* calling the chickens to be fed on the farm where he had grown up – although the Havoc was now the hawk, closing in for the kill, and the slow-moving Mi-8 was the chicken.

'Come on, boy.' He willed the other pilot closer, alternately lifting the Mi-8 above the cloud tops and letting it side-slip into them as though having trouble with the controls.

Karen could see the head of the Havoc's pilot, his face dehumanised by the obscuring oxygen mask, helmet and wrap-around visor. Below him in the forward cockpit the weapons operator raised his right fist in an unconscious gesture of victory before pressing the firing button of the 30mm cannon in the nose. At that range, he could not miss.

Karen knew that if Volkov waited another millisecond, they would all die. 'Now, now, now!' she screamed into the mic. '*Davai! Davai!*'

The Mi-8 drifted sideways into the murk, jinked left and right, reappeared in the sunlight and plunged into darkness again with the Havoc on its tail. G-forces clamped Tom and Karen into their seats as Volkov stood the craft on its side and hauled it round vertical in a 180-degree turn for which it had never been designed and which nearly tore the Jesus nut right off. There was a whine of straining engines, alarm buzzers going and creaks of protest from the whole airframe, all of which was abruptly drowned by the more powerful twin turboshaft engines of the Havoc as it screamed past the open door, seemingly only inches away, at a collision speed well above 400kph. The combined length of the main rotors of both craft was 126 feet. Somehow they managed to pass each other with almost no vertical separation, heading in opposite directions between cliff faces only 200 feet apart.

The noise of straining engines and alarm buzzers was drowned by a huge explosion. The murk was lit by an unearthly orange light for a second and then went black. A blast wave kicked the Mi-8 sideways. Volkov, drenched in perspiration, was fighting the controls and laughing over the intercom, 'We did it! By God, we did it!'

Neither of his passengers could hear because they were both momentarily deaf. Tom was still unable to see straight ahead, but by looking sideways at her he could see that Karen's face was white with shock. He knew how she felt; there was a dark stain down his left trouser leg where he had wet himself from fear at some point, he could not recall when.

He took the headset back from her. He had to shout, even to hear himself. It seemed fatuous to thank a man who had saved his own life as well as theirs. 'How many times have you done that trick before, Vlad?'

The reply was scarcely audible: 'I've never done that before, Tomski. And never will again. D'you think I'm fuck-ing mad?'

.4.

Volkov nursed the Mi-8 the last few metres to land in front of the hangar proudly painted with the name *Volkov and Son* in Cyrillic and *Fuckoff's Flying Circus* in Roman letters. With a groan from the damaged suspension, the helicopter settled drunkenly on the ground, its rotors skimming lower and lower on the right as he reduced power and the weight came increasingly to bear on the bent strut where the wheel was missing. As 3,500 horsepower dwindled to silence and the rotors, unassisted by centrifugal force, bent lower and lower under their own weight, he watched anxiously until they came to a complete stop, clearing the ground by centimetres only.

Karen clambered through the open door and found herself looking at a semicircle of half a dozen solidly built men. Among them Tom noticed Big Wall; of Short Wall there was no sign. Two stretched Mercedes were parked beside Volkov's hangar, with some more men sitting inside.

Still feeling sick with shock, Karen grabbed Tom's arm. 'Who are these mafia types?' she asked in English.

Tom waved a greeting to Ivanov but received no reply. 'An old friend from Moscow,' he said. 'Plus some local associates.'

Volkov was on the ground, swearing at the twisted metal that had been the right undercarriage; it was easier than thinking what would have happened if the metal had not bent and torn – or if he had been a metre to the right or 50 centimetres lower.

'Where the fuck am I going to get a new wheel?' he shouted at Tom.

There was a hole between the synchronised elevator and the tail rotor drive-shaft, into which he shoved a fist. 'Two centimetres higher,' he grumbled to Tom, 'and we'd have lost the tail rotor.'

'Is that bad?'

Ignorance is bliss, thought Volkov. Without a tail rotor to balance out the torque from the main rotors, the Mi-8 would have spun its way down to the ground and screwed itself firmly and permanently in.

And again: '*Bózhe moi! Smotrí, Tomski.*' This time he was glaring at the jagged holes in three out of the five main rotor blades where the hollow aluminium spars had been torn open near the tips, revealing holes punched clear through the honeycomb filling. 'If I'd known about that, I'd never have had the guts to pull that last stunt. The stresses must have come near to tearing off the ends of the rotors and once that happened . . .'

There were more holes in the fuselage: all in a neat line that crossed the body of the Mi-8 miraculously avoiding any vital controls, the fuel tanks and the fuel lines.

Ivanov came forward. 'What the hell's happened to this flying heap of shit?'

'Somebody tried to blow us out of the sky,' Tom said.

'Get back on board,' Ivanov growled.

'What for?'

'Just do it.' He glared at Karen. 'And you.'

'I'm not getting back in one of those things again,' she said. 'Ever.'

'We're not going anywhere,' Tom told her. 'Ivan Petrovich just wants to talk in privacy.'

'That's my machine,' said Volkov. 'It may look like a heap of shit to you, fuck-face, but nobody gets in unless I invite them.'

'Then invite me,' suggested Ivanov.

Tom saw Volkov's fists clench and came between the two men. 'Please, Vlad,' he said. 'I owe you an explanation too – for what happened to your machine. Maybe this is the best place to talk.'

When the damaged door was as nearly shut as it would go, Ivanov unleashed his anger on Tom: 'I bankroll this operation of yours to recover an icon and give you permission to go and fetch this woman off some volcano. Next thing I hear, you're both lost in the wilderness all night. This morning, you're nearly blown out of the sky. So what gives?'

'Karen was hijacked by a couple of hoodlums who only missed killing her because she had the courage to jump over a stream of molten lava. Presumably the helicopter that jumped us this morning was sent by the same outfit. If she describes her assailants to your associates, perhaps we'll be able to trace them and know who we're up against.'

'Waste of time,' Ivanov muttered. 'There are more hit men in eastern Siberia than throughout the rest of the ex-USSR. After a hot job in Moscow or Petersburg, the killers head this way to cool off. The town of Cherski has become a resort for them, with a casino, whorehouses, specialised arms dealers and even firing ranges where they can keep their eye in whilst they're on holiday.'

He grabbed Tom by the shoulders and thrust him back against the bulkhead. 'What's more to the point is that whoever gave the order to rub out your girlfriend and shoot down Volkov's helicopter was not just some rival outfit going after the icon. So just what the hell is going on?'

'Calm down,' said Tom. 'First I want to know where Clive Ponsonby is.'

Shivering with cold in the small hours on Mount Tolbachik, he had worked out that the most likely person to have told Viktor's men where to find Karen was Ponsonby. How he had done it was another matter.

Ivanov released Tom. 'That's another thing – your pal's disappeared.'

'When I last saw him, he was in bed, under guard and had no clothes . . .'

'At some time in the night, he pretended to have a crisis. The minder I had left with him bent over the bed to see what was wrong and the next thing he knew, he woke up minus his handgun, plus a headache and two black eyes. Whilst he was unconscious, your friend' – Ivanov spat the words out – 'made a local phone call, after which two heavies with Ukrainian accents arrived at the Hotel Alyaska with some clothes and took him away with them – we don't know where.'

'Shit!' said Tom.

'I made some enquiries,' Ivanov continued. 'Your dark-haired friend had quite a busy time the previous night too. Before he picked up the blonde hustler who fed him the eye drops, he placed a call from a phone in the lobby to a number in Kiev. There was an exchange of recognition signals. Then a voice which we think belongs to the Ukrainian President came on the line.'

Ivanov threw at Tom a Sony mini-cassette dictating machine. He caught it in mid-air, pressed the play button and heard Ponsonby's distinctive drawling voice, saying in Russian: 'The price for divulging Fielding's present where-abouts is one million dollars up-front.'

Another voice replied, 'The price is not a problem, but I'm afraid we must collect the goods first.'

The quality of the recording was poor, but the second voice was the one which had said, that night in Alma Ata, 'It's all right, Marina. Just go back to sleep.'

Then there was silence on the tape. Tom switched off. 'What happened next?'

'The tape was reused.' Ivanov grimaced. 'Remember, this is Russia. Our national motto is: If we can fuck-up, we will. The one thing we know for sure is that Ponsonby left the hotel and returned two hours later, so presumably he continued the conversation with Kiev on a secure line in the meantime – as well as making arrangements for your girlfriend's cremation.'

He took the Sony back from Tom and slipped it into his pocket. 'Now get this very straight, Feldink. You invited me to come play in your paddling pool. I bring my bucket and spade and get in. Then what happens? I find we're not in a paddling pool – it's a life-raft in a shark-infested sea, and there's a hole in it! That may be the way you live, but it's not the way I want to die. So before we leave here you are going to tell me exactly what is going on.'

'And me,' said Karen.

'And me,' added Volkov. 'Some bastard has to pay for what was done to my lovely machine.'

Through the cabin windows Tom could see the local mafia thugs sitting on the bonnet of one of the Mercedes. With them on guard, the damaged helicopter was probably the most secure place to talk in the whole of Kamchatka.

He looked at the three people in the cabin for a long moment in silence.

Ivanov, with his KGB and mafia connections all over Russia, was one of the few people who could lay on the logistics required to outmanoeuvre Nosarenko. There was a conjunction of interests: he wanted the icon; Tom wanted the film that was with it.

Volkov – Tom was as certain of this as though he had known the man for a lifetime – was the best kind of friend to have on his side if anything went wrong.

But what about Karen? Did he have the right to drag her any further into this? The question was irrelevant:

Nosarenko had already designated her a target, even though she knew nothing about the murder. So there was no point in deluding himself that putting her on a plane to the USA would place her out of the line of fire. The safest place for her was in the eye of the shit-storm where at least she had Ivanov's mafia thugs to protect her.

And if Karen was in jeopardy, what about Rada in Moscow? He put that thought aside for the moment. First things first . . .

Tom sat down. 'Could your associates outside fetch us some lunch? This is going to take a long time.'

The remains of a *zakúzki* meal were spread out on the seats of the cabin, which smelled of beer, garlic sausage and pickled cucumbers. Volkov, certain that he could also smell jet fuel from some small leak, had forbidden smoking.

Without cigarettes, Ivanov was irritable. 'You haven't a chance of surviving this shit-storm,' he said. 'Nosarenko has intact the whole apparatus of what was the Ukrainian KGB – one hundred and fifty thousand full-time officers, plus his own Spetsnaz troops. Jesus, he even controls half the Black Sea Fleet. There's no hope of winning against odds like that. I'd be insane not to back out right now.'

'You can't,' Tom argued. 'Viktor is intent on silencing anyone who knows about the murder. He wanted Karen killed on the mere suspicion that I had talked to her. For better or worse, we're all in this thing together now. The only person who might get away with opting out is Vlad.'

'You're kidding!' Volkov sounded indignant. 'I want to get even with the bastard who fucked up my favourite flying machine.'

It was time for a little flattery, Tom thought. He leaned closer to Ivanov. 'Ivan Petrovich, you just happen to be one of the few people in the world who can bring us all out of this alive. With your KGB connections and . . .' He gestured through the window. '. . . your new associates, you can organise secure transport to Irkutsk where the film is and a safe house when we get there, plus local transport and body-guards.'

'Have you any idea what that'll cost? This is a clandestine military operation you want laying on at zero notice.'

'The value of the icon will more than cover it,' Tom promised. 'You can keep the lot, but I want you to pay for the damage to Vlad's helicopter – as my share. Agreed?'

Ivanov grunted, 'What do we do, once we've got the film?'

'Develop it and beam the pictures to all the news agencies direct from Irkutsk. Once the world has seen them, we don't have to worry about Viktor Nosarenko. He won't be President. He'll be in prison, I'll be safe and you'll be rich.'

Ivanov had already come to the same conclusion. 'There's one other person we have to involve,' he said. 'I want the icon authenticated by Arkady Sergeyevich, the moment we have it.'

'Can't that wait?' said Tom.

'No,' said Ivanov flatly. 'Over the next few days I'm going to be borrowing something like a million dollars at a rate of interest you wouldn't believe. I need to reassure my bankers as soon as possible that their money's safe.'

'I get the impression,' said Karen, 'that you three men are treating me like an embarrassing package. For various rea-sons, I can't be despatched somewhere else, so I must be taken along for the ride. Well, it just happens that I have a brain too – and there's one thing you've all overlooked. We can't be one hundred per cent certain that the film is still there. Even if it is, it may be damaged by damp or God knows what. Then what do we do?'

'Pray,' suggested Volkov.

'I wasn't joking,' she snapped.

'Neither was I.'

.5.

They chased the setting sun westwards to Irkutsk – the only passengers on a Tupolev jumbo chartered by Ivanov from Transaero, the luxury long-haul Russian airline. It came complete with cabin crew and inflight meals for 250 people, and was escorted all the way by relays of two Mig-29s.

As the endless landscape of eastern Siberia scrolled past below, Karen stretched out across the centre rows of seats and fell asleep, not to wake up until the plane was landing. Tom took the opportunity to closet himself firstly with Ivanov and then with Volkov, planning the recovery of the film and the icon without disclosing to either of them exactly where the *byvshi dom* was. Volkov seemed to have no need for sleep and spent his time when not talking with Tom on the flight deck consuming endless beers and swapping God-was-I-scared-that-time fliers' stories with the senior pilot, who had also started his flying career in Afghanistan.

At dusk, they were on final approach and in radio contact with Irkutsk tower, slipping lower and lower across the vastness of Lake Baikal. The last pair of Mig-29s stayed with them all the way down, circling above the airport, which had been closed to other traffic until the Tupolev was on the deck and the passengers disembarked. As Ivanov said, the 3,500-kilometre flight had cost an arm and a leg – but they were there and safe, which was all that counted.

Once on the ground, the arrangements Ivanov had made swung smoothly into action, with a team of ex-KGB close protection minders escorting him into the airport buildings while Tom and Karen were shepherded into a stretched Mercedes. With another vehicle ahead and a third behind, they swept along the centre of the highway, the front-seat passengers waving other traffic imperiously out of the way in a style that only heads of state and royalty could afford in the West.

The safe house which had been made ready for them was a large and elegant wooden mansion known as *Vasiliévsky Dvorétz* – the Vasilievsky Palace. Built for one of the nobles exiled to Siberia after the revolution of December 1825, together with his family and wealth, it bore a weathered plaque on the street side commemorating the fact that the young and wily Josef Vissarionovich Djugashvili, aka Koba, aka Melikyants, better known as 'Uncle Joe' Stalin, had eaten a picnic in the garden during his exile to Irkutsk in 1916. There was no mention on the plaque that his fellow Bolsheviks and companions on that occasion had included Lev Kamenev, whom he would later execute, and Yakov Sverdlov, who gave the order to murder the royal family and then died of influenza, thus cheating Stalin's paranoia of one victim.

The floors of the Vasilievsky Palace creaked but otherwise the building was in pristine condition, having been meticulously restored as a Decembrist museum just before the collapse of the Soviet Union. The reception rooms on the ground floor had been completely refurbished with period furniture. Backstairs and upstairs every modern luxury was available: bars well stocked with Western booze, a gym and sauna, *en suite* bathrooms with Jacuzzi spas. The new owner was not in evidence, but clothing in the wardrobes and drawers, together with food and unwashed dishes in the kitchen, indicated a recent evacuation.

The houses on either side had also been taken over by Ivanov's people. There were enough thickset men in suits patrolling the floodlit gardens and the street to make up the crowd for a heavyweight championship boxing match. In the dusky sky, the flashing beacon of a militia helicopter described circles overhead, its crew in constant radio contact with the men on the ground.

Tom had vetoed plans to use the militia machine as transport. Only Volkov, he insisted, was going to fly him anywhere during the next few days. So the red-haired giant had been left at the airport with an escort to check out the local possibilities of helicopters for hire.

In the house, Karen and Tom were treated as virtual prisoners, not allowed to go outside for any reason. Tom picked up a telephone to ascertain how Volkov was doing at the airport and found that both telephone lines into the house had been cut for the duration of their stay.

Karen had needed the long sleep on the plane, but was now wishing that someone had woken her up for meals. She was ravenous. Tom followed her into the kitchen, opened beers for them both and sat at the breakfast bar, watching her make an omelette with hands that trembled and were covered in cuts. It seemed the right moment to apologise: 'If I'd had any idea that Viktor would ever resurface in my life, I would never have dreamed of suggesting the Kamchatka volcanoes to you, believe me.'

'Yet you were going to use me to get the icon out of Russia?'

'I intended secreting it among the equipment and samples you'd be taking back to Canada,' he admitted. 'But there would have been no risk to you. If it had been discovered, I'd have had to confess that I did it and no one else was involved.'

Karen turned the omelette out of the pan onto a plate. She ate quickly and felt immediately hungry again.

'Tell me about this man, Nosarenko,' she said, to distract herself from thinking of food.

Tom had to admit that he knew hardly anything. 'He was apparently Ponsonby's star agent-in-place. As far as I'm concerned, he had the nerves of a mouse. If he had not panicked that night in Alma Ata, there would have been no need to kill his wife.'

'But why didn't he try to silence you immediately after the murder? Why wait until now?'

'I suppose because he took me for a Russian. Remember that we spent less than two hours together, under conditions of considerable stress. From his point of view, I was the ideal accomplice, unable ever to testify against him without forfeiting my own life.'

'But you could have blackmailed him, couldn't you?'

Tom shook his head. 'How could I have gone to the police without exposing myself as an agent of Western intelligence? I'd have been committing suicide, because they execute traitors here.'

'You could have denounced him anonymously. That's a Russian tradition, isn't it?'

'I thought about it, but Viktor was counting the money while I was busy photographing the documents. All my personal papers were in the case. For all I knew, he had taken the precaution of noting my name and address, whereas I knew nothing about him until now. I didn't even know that Viktor was his real name. If he hadn't become a public figure, I would never have been an embarrassment to him.'

'You said that you destroyed Ponsonby's material on the train to Novosibirsk, but I didn't understand why.'

'Until that night, espionage had been a game.'

'A game!' She raised her eyes to heaven. 'What is it with men . . . ?'

Tom held up both hands in surrender. 'Everything I did, I did for kicks. It may sound incredible to you, but I never thought about the consequences of my actions until that night. The fact that Viktor was prepared to kill brought me to my senses. I understood that handing over to Ponsonby material which had cost half a millon dollars and one human life might just change the balance of power. Every time I closed my eyes I saw a mushroom cloud blossoming over Moscow, turning Rada and Svetlana into carbonised husks. It wasn't a rational decision. I just felt a stronger bond of loyalty to my wife and child than to Ponsonby and Big Ben.'

Her hunger unsated, Karen started beating some more eggs with her back to him. 'If I had to choose,' she said, 'I hope I'd protect two people I loved, rather than some abstract concept of patriotism.'

Tom put his arms around her waist. She turned, using the bowl in her hands as an excuse to push him away. There was a hardness in his eyes when he was talking with Ivanov and the others, but for a moment they were as gentle as when she had first met him, thirteen years before.

'You're such a contradiction,' she said, turning away and pouring the beaten eggs into the pan. 'You spy for kicks without any conscience. You put your girlfriend's liberty at risk and then do the same to a wife and child. Then you throw it all away on the spur of the moment and keep silent for years when you could have bought your freedom by talking.'

Some of the steel that prison had put there came back into Tom's eyes. 'I was right to keep my mouth shut. If MI6 had known that I can prove President Nosarenko is a murderer, I have a strong feeling that Ponsonby would have arrived at Longfield prison with something worse than eye drops to put in my coffee.'

'How d'you work that out?'

'If you were sitting in Number Ten, who would you rather do a favour for: President Nosarenko, head of state of a nuclear-rich republic inhabited by fifty million people – or Tom Fielding, failed academic, failed parent, failed spy? I don't blame anyone, that's just the way it has to be.'

There was a commotion in the floodlit garden. Two of the long black Mercedes saloons had just driven in through the massive wooden gates, which were being shouldered shut again behind them. They crunched over rose beds and lawn to park a few metres away from the French windows at which Karen and Tom were standing.

Through a cordon of wide-shouldered men in double-breasted suits, Ivanov was pushing his way into the house, carrying a large brown-paper parcel. Behind him, a silver-haired old man was climbing laboriously out of one of the cars, helped by a very well-dressed woman.

'Who are they?' Karen asked.

'The elderly gent is Arkady Sergeyevich Sibirsky, probably the greatest iconographer in Russia.'

Sliding the omelette deftly onto her plate, Karen caught the intent expression on Tom's face out of the corner of her eye. 'And that stunningly beautiful girl with him is your wife?'

'Ex-wife,' Tom corrected her.

When Ivanov had insisted on Sibirsky coming to authenticate the icon, Tom had suggested that Rada should accompany her father, in order to look after him. The subterfuge had avoided the necessity of alarming her with the real reason why he wanted her to be where he could keep an eye on her, until Nosarenko had been neutralised.

Sibirsky looked a lot frailer than when Tom had last seen him. They embraced Russian-style with a kiss on both cheeks. Rada looked as though it hurt her to see Tom again. She stretched out a hand, to keep him at a distance.

'Hallo, Tom,' she said coldly.

'Hallo, Rada.'

She avoided looking at him and asked, 'Who's this?' indicating Karen.

'A Canadian friend. Let me introduce Karen McKenzie.'

The two women eyed each other for a moment. Then Karen stepped forward with a smile, wanting to meet this person who had known Tom so well.

'I've heard a lot about you,' she said.

'Oh, that sort of friend . . .' Rada turned away and swept out of the room in the wake of Ivanov and her father.

'Now that,' Karen said when they had gone, 'is what the folks back home would call a very frigid welcome. Is she always like that with strangers?' She sat down to eat her omelette, which was now cold, and pushed it away after a couple of mouthfuls.

Tom tried to justify Rada's behaviour. 'I think she was upset at seeing me. Just before we landed, I accused Ivanov of betraying me by selling me back to the British. He said it wasn't his idea.'

'Because London asked for you in the first place?'

'Apparently not.' The three once-familiar voices coming from the next room were dragging Tom into the past. 'If I believe Ivanov, he just made the arrangements. He said that the *idea* of selling me back to London came from Rada. So I suppose she must be feeling embarrassed.'

.6.

After being woken up and driven from their homes in black Mercedes by silent men, the bleary-eyed and apprehensive proprietors of the two best photographic stores in downtown Irkutsk were all too eager to please when they learned that the reason for the midnight knock on their doors was nothing more sinister than Tom's urgent need of some specialised developing and enlarging equipment and chemicals.

He set up all the equipment in the wine cellar below the Vasilievsky Palace. It made an ideal darkroom, with complete blackout, electric sockets and hot and cold running water. To save time next day, he mixed the fixer solution and stop bath and left everything else ready, then climbed up the three flights of stairs to his room.

His wristwatch said 2 a.m. Sleep was out of reach. He did not want to lie awake worrying about the possibility which Karen had voiced – that the film might be useless after all this time, or simply not there any more – so he began analysing the noises of the night.

Overhead a militia helicopter was droning in circles, playing its searchlight on the ground. There was a creak of floorboards; no one was walking on them, it was just the old house breathing. But there was another noise that caught his attention: a faint but rhythmic grunting and thudding as though someone were making love at the far end of the house.

Tom padded across the creaking floor to the open window and looked out. The floodlights were still bathing the house on all sides. One of the bodyguards looked up, saw the face at the window and spoke into a walkie-talkie. Tom turned his head from one side to the other, trying to locate the source of the sound. A thud and a grunt. Another thud and another grunt. Somebody was being beaten up in the garden.

He pulled on his trousers and took a silk dressing gown from the wardrobe. Downstairs one of the local musclemen tried to bar his way out of the front door, where two others were systematically beating a shirtsleeved stranger. One held his arms from behind while the other hit him repeatedly in the solar plexus.

'What's going on?' Tom asked.

'An intruder,' grunted the doorman. 'We caught him sneaking in through the shrubbery, so we're finding out who sent him.'

The two thugs paused for a moment, disturbed by Tom's presence. Their victim took advantage of the respite to look up. Despite the bloodied face, torn shirt and messed-up hair, Tom recognised Ponsonby.

He pushed past the doorman and shouted, 'That's enough. I know this man. Let him go.'

'Our orders . . .'

'Fuck your orders. I'm taking responsibility for this.'

Ponsonby followed him indoors and along the corridor into the kitchen. Badly winded, he slumped onto one of the tall stools by the breakfast bar, tore off his ripped shirt and used it as a face-cloth to dab cold water from the sink over his face and chest.

Tom took off his dressing gown and threw it on top of the breakfast bar. 'You can put this on.'

Ponsonby filled a plastic bowl with cold water and dipped his face into it repeatedly. 'You don't seem exactly pleased to see me,' he said, coming up for air.

'I'm amazed you've got the nerve to come here. How did you know where to find me?'

'You told me yourself that you were coming to Irkutsk.'

'But how did you get here?'

'I managed to get away from Viktor's people because they thought I was sicker than I really was. Then I did the innocent thing. I went to the British Consul, and told him my tale of woe: that I was a businessman who'd been mugged. He lent me money for my fare home and issued me with a temporary travel document.'

'What about your escape from the Hotel Alyaska?'

'Escape? Well, I suppose you could call it that. At the time I was conscious but unable to do a thing for myself. Two hoodlums looking remarkably like the mob you have here broke into the room, nobbled my minder, dressed me in some clothes they had brought with them and took me for a ride.'

Seeing the sceptical look in Tom's eye, Ponsonby added, 'What the hell could I do? I had no passport, I was groggy as hell, I could hardly stand up and I couldn't see straight enough to piss without doing it all over my feet.'

'That's not the way Ivanov's man told it.'

Ponsonby seemed to be recovering rapidly from his beating. He took his time replying, in between the cold water treatment. 'He'd had a few drinks after everyone left. Perhaps that's why he was stupid enough to open the door to Viktor's men. If he admitted to his boss what actually happened, he'd be floating in the harbour tomorrow. So what was his version? That I leaped out of bed like Rambo and karate-chopped him to the floor?'

'Something like that.'

Ponsonby raised an eyebrow. 'It's very flattering, but you saw the condition I was in, Tom. Did I look like I could floor a muscle-bound hunk of bodyguard?'

'And how did you find this house?'

Ponsonby laughed. 'If I may say so, dear boy, it's the most obvious place in the whole city. You can see the helicopter's searchlight and the floodlights for miles. And you've got more bodyguards outside than Yeltsin can afford.'

'So why are you here?'

Ponsonby looked puzzled. 'I thought we had a deal.'

'It didn't include killing Karen.'

'She's dead?'

'Two men kidnapped her on Mount Tolbachik and tried to throw her into the crater.'

Ponsonby gave a low whistle. 'Tried?'

'She got away from them.'

'A tough lady . . . And you think I was responsible for this?'

'Nobody else knew where she was, so it had to be you who tipped off Viktor's people where to find her.'

'You could be right,' Ponsonby admitted. 'When that pneumatic blonde whore drugged me, I don't know what I told her. I don't even know who her accomplices were. I think they were two men who came into the room and nicked all my clobber, but I can't even be sure of that. I was hallucinating badly. You can't blame me for what I may have said if they put the right questions to me.'

'You weren't hallucinating before you picked up the blonde,' Tom accused him. 'What were you doing during the two hours you were out of the hotel?'

'If you want to know, I was humping the most gorgeous Chinese girl I have ever fucked in my life.'

'What was her name?'

'She called herself Lei-Mee, but that could be a joke.'

'And what about the blonde hustler? I suppose you hired her just to mix your drinks?'

Ponsonby poured the bloodstained water away and dabbed his face dry with a tea cloth. 'Dolores was strictly a second feature, Tom. The Chink wanted $100 a time. When I'm really wound up, I need to get my end away more than once before I can sleep. But I wasn't going to spend $500 even on the best dish of *poontang* I've tasted in years. So I fucked the eyeballs out of her and came back to the hotel for an all-night workout with Dolores.'

'. . . which still left you plenty of time for your second phone conversation with Viktor whilst you were out of the hotel.'

'When was the first supposed to have been? I haven't spoken to Viktor in years.'

'You made a call from a lobby phone to Kiev, in which you agreed to deliver me to Viktor for one million dollars,' Tom said.

'You believe that,' drawled Ponsonby, slipping on the dressing gown, 'and you'll be hanging up a stocking on Christmas Eve next. I made a deal with you for a million dollars, which I have every intention of collecting. You think I'd throw that away on the strength of a promise from Viktor of all people? As I figure it, once you're out of the way, I'll be the next one on his hit list. So I have, as they say, a vested interest in your survival.'

'I heard a recording of the conversation, Clive.'

Ponsonby laughed softly. In the silk dressing gown and with his wet hair slicked back, all he needed was a piano and a long cigarette holder to do an impression of Noël Coward.

'Tom, I don't want to sound condescending, but you're in the land where the arts of doctoring tapes and fudging photographs were carried to their greatest heights ever – by the same firm that employed your pal Ivanov. Still, I admit I'm impressed that his people could turn out a fake phone conversation within a few hours. How long did it last?'

'Not long,' Tom admitted.

Ponsonby was helping himself to food from the fridge. 'If I had to give a history lecture, I'd ask your advice, dear boy. Now this is my game. You may not like me much, but I'm good at it. So use me.'

'What's that supposed to mean?'

'I understand why you felt it necessary to call in Ivanov when I was *hors de combat*, but remember he's the guy who stabbed you in the back and sold you back to us in '91. You can't trust his type. He's probably planning to grab the icon for himself and then hand you over to Viktor anyway. Had you thought about that possibility? I know Ivanov. I know how his devious Slav mind works. I may be a shit, but I am an English one. The devil you know and all that . . .'

The dawn was already lightening the cloudless sky. Tom watched Ponsonby eating and wondered whose side he really was on.

Was Ivanov playing straight? It was a fair question. Had the idea of selling Tom back to London really been Rada's? He only had Ivan Petrovich's word for it, although her behaviour since arriving in Irkutsk was certainly odd. Ivanov said she was worried about her father's health, but Tom wondered whether it was guilt that was making her so withdrawn and hostile.

Whatever the reason, he had already come to the conclusion that the only two people he could trust were Karen and Volkov. On the other hand, Ponsonby might have his uses as a watchdog, to bark at the first sign that Ivanov was planning a double-cross.

.7.

The breakfast conference in the kitchen of the Vasilievsky Palace was a continuation of the running battle on the flight from Petropavlovsk. To begin with, Ivanov had insisted that Tom should mark on a map the location of the hiding place and leave the recovery operation entirely in his hands. At last he conceded that Tom be allowed to recover the icon and film himself, but under escort by a convoy of cars, stuffed to bursting point with local mafia heavies.

'Crazy idea,' sneered Ponsonby. 'The security you've laid on here in Irkutsk is so obvious that all I had to do was home in on the lights and the bodyguards in order to find Tom. Viktor Nosarenko has electronic access to at least three surveillance satellites. He's probably looking at a picture of the roof over our heads right now. As long as we're here, he won't do anything because dropping a bomb on Irkutsk would be overkill. But, if we all set out in a convoy, he's only got to wait until it's in some relatively uninhabited area to blow us all away. Take it from me: the lower the profile, the better for a job like this. Minimum numbers. Quick in, quicker out.'

'Low-profile security is a bourgeois delusion, like democracy,' Ivanov retorted. 'Let me tell you guys something. If the Committee had been in charge of security in Dallas, Kennedy wouldn't have had his brains blown out in front of the book depository. Nor would we have let that madman get near enough to shoot Reagan. The difference between our way of doing things and yours is: ours works.'

'Well, I'm not leaving here in a convoy with fifty hoodlums,' said Tom. He had no intention of guiding a posse of mafia men to the *byvshi dom*. Never mind what Nosarenko might do, it would be all too easy for Ivanov to arrange an accident on the return journey, which would leave him in possession of both film and icon – and Tom, plus any inconvenient witnesses, consigned to an unmarked grave in the forest.

Ponsonby had helped himself to clothes from one of the wardrobes upstairs. Black was the colour of the day, from shoes to the collar of his polo neck sweater. Ivanov looked as though he had not slept for a week; his suit was crumpled, he had lost his tie and forgotten to shave. As the two men kept their distance, hackles raised like dogs circling round each other in mutual distrust, they put Tom in mind of a sleek black Doberman in its prime horning in on the territory of a scruffy out-of-condition mongrel.

The argument ended when Volkov clattered in and landed in the rose garden behind the Vasilievsky Palace. The helicopter he had hired for the day from a fellow *afgánetz*, with whom he had been drinking all night at the airport, was to Western eyes a strange beast.

The Kamov 32 was the civilian version of the multi-role military Ka-27, best known in the West as a submarine killer. Designed primarily to be carried aboard and flown off ships where space was limited, it had an elongated cabin stuck directly onto a truncated tail boom which ended in twin stubby tailplanes, making an overall length 20 feet less than Volkov's Mi-8. The two sets of rotors had a radius of only 52 feet and revolved in opposite directions, which obviated the need for a tail rotor and delivered all the power where it was most useful – for lift and forward movement – leaving steering to be done by the rudders. Even without extra fuel tanks the Ka-32 had a range of 500 miles and a surprising turn of speed for a wide-bodied machine.

At the controls, in the left-hand seat of the Kamov – which was unusual for a helicopter – Volkov waved good morning through the sliding cabin door and shut down the two 2,225-horsepower turboshaft engines which were making conversation in the house impossible.

Tom disengaged himself from Ivanov, still arguing about whether Ponsonby might be armed. Upstairs he knocked on Karen's door. Getting no reply, he went in to find the room in darkness and Karen fast asleep.

He shook her shoulder to wake her up. 'Come on. It's time to go.'

'I don't know . . . what's the matter . . . with me.' Karen was having trouble getting the words out. 'I can't keep my eyes open.'

Tom switched on the bedside light. Her face was grey and her eyelids heavy. It was impossible for him to tell whether her condition was a reaction to the trauma on the mountain or whether she had been drugged.

There was a carafe of water on the marble-topped night table and a glass that had been used. He poured some water into the glass, sniffed it and drank some. It tasted normal enough. He pulled Karen into a sitting position and dampened a towel in the *en suite* bathroom, wiping her face with it.

'It's no good,' she said drowsily. 'I can't get up. You'll have to leave me here.'

Tom slapped her face hard and shook her. 'You're coming with me, you hear?'

'What's up?'

He turned on hearing someone come out of the next bedroom. Rada was standing in the doorway.

'Karen's ill,' he said.

'I'm not surprised, after what she's been through. So leave her in bed.'

'I need her with me.'

'Take me,' Rada offered. 'I'm ready to leave.' She was wearing an outfit that would have looked good worn for *après-ski* drinks on the chic terraces below the slopes at St Moritz: a white angora sweater and white ski pants tucked into white calf-length leather boots. Despite the low level of light in the room, she had on a pair of sunglasses.

Tom did not want to discuss his dual reason for wanting Karen with him: she was a pair of hands and eyes he could trust, but also he wanted her where he could keep an eye on her.

'Help me get her dressed,' he called.

There was no reply. Rada had gone, so he pulled the bedclothes off Karen. She had slept in her bra and pants. Somehow he bullied and cajoled her limp limbs into the sweater, jeans and anorak she had been wearing the previous day, then put on her trainers for her and fastened the Velcro tabs. With her arm around his shoulders, he supported her down the stairs and made her drink a cup of hot black coffee in the kitchen where Volkov was finishing his fifth doughnut. Seeing Karen's condition, he gave Tom an odd look but said nothing.

In the morning room Ivanov was still refusing to give Ponsonby a firearm.

'Do it,' shouted Tom. His fuse was getting shorter by the minute. 'Give him a gun or I don't go.'

With bad grace, Ivanov relieved one of the bodyguards of his Czech-made BRNO 83. 'Better you have it,' he said to Tom. 'I don't believe Ponsonby's story one bit.'

'What would I do with a gun?' It was a rhetorical

question. 'I've never fired one in my life, Ivan Petrovich. Give it to him.'

Ponsonby slid out the magazine, ejected all fifteen of the 7.64mm bullets, reloaded them and chambered a round before thumbing the fire selector to safe and slipping the weapon into his waistband. Obviously relieved to be armed, he pulled the sweater down over the bulge of the gun and gave a smile of victory which Ivanov ignored.

Volkov was shouting through the open French windows that he had been unable to procure a hoist for lifting the slab. 'The nearest thing I could get was a pair of car jacks. You wanna take a look?'

Tom climbed into the helicopter, picking his way across the coils of rope, cables and assorted tackle left over from its last job, which had been hoisting lengths of pipeline into position in a swamp. The three bodyguards who had flown with Volkov from the airport were standing nearby, arguing about the Kamov's speed and carrying capacity.

Volkov drew Tom close so that they could not hear. In his large palm was a small plastic box of about the same size and appearance as the gadgets people use for hiding a spare set of keys underneath their cars.

'What is it?' Tom asked.

'A bug.'

'Picking up our voices now?'

Volkov shook his head. 'It's the kind rich people hide somewhere in their expensive cars, so that they can be tracked by satellite, if stolen.'

'Was it there when you hired this flying junk-heap?'

Volkov shook his head. 'I'm one hundred per cent sure it wasn't. And since I flew directly here from the airport, that means that someone in this whorehouse you're staying in has stuck this thing on us so that we can be tracked all the way to where we're going.'

There was no point in asking Ivanov about the bug: it could have been placed there on his orders. Both Rada and

Ponsonby had been near the helicopter at various times. She could have brought the bug in her handbag; he had been searched by the guards when they caught him, but he could have secreted it somewhere in the garden before he was apprehended.

There were too many possibilities to check out in a hurry, so Tom ordered Volkov to put the bug back where he had found it and then briefed him rapidly on a change of plan before storming back into the house cursing him as an incompetent oaf. The noise of the helicopter lifting off covered his insults.

'What's up?' Ivanov shouted.

'I told Volkov to bring sheer legs and a hoist. Instead, he brings two wind-up car jacks.'

'Perhaps he couldn't find a hoist,' suggested Ivanov.

'He spent the night drinking with some ex-Army pal at the airport,' snapped Tom. 'He didn't even look for a hoist, so I've sent him back to get one.'

'You should have sent some of my men with him.'

'Damn!' said Tom. 'I was so angry with the great drunken lout, I forgot.'

It was nearly 11 a.m. when Volkov returned. He kept the Ka-32 light on the wheeled undercarriage while Tom helped Karen in, followed by Ponsonby assisting Sibirsky and carrying the nineteenth-century copy of the Virgin of Kazan, still wrapped in its brown paper. Tom had argued that Sibirsky could do his job far more comfortably back at the Vasilievksy Palace, but Ivanov had insisted that he wanted Volkov to break radio silence and let him hear Sibirsky's authentication, the moment he was certain that Tom's icon was the genuine one.

Since Ivanov had given way on so many other points, Tom felt he had to accept Sibirsky's presence. He sat in the right-hand seat, a map on his knee and wearing a headset so that he alone could talk with Ivanov – the cargo-kicker's headset in the rear cabin was missing. Ponsonby, Sibirsky and Karen – who still looked very pale – were seated on the pull-down canvas seats in the cargo space.

As the Kamov gained height over the suburbs, the militia helicopter which had been circling over the Vasilievsky Palace abandoned station and started following them. Volkov keyed the radio on the local police frequency and asked what they were up to.

'Following you,' was the curt reply.

Volkov nudged Tom to look in the rear-view mirror. 'Watch this,' he grinned.

In the mirror, Tom saw two other helicopters closing in on the militia machine, flying across its nose so close that the militia pilot had no choice but to turn away. Again and again they buzzed him, forcing him lower and lower until the Ka-32 was out of sight.

'*Afgántsy*,' explained Volkov. 'The only good thing about our Vietnam war was that it gave the survivors a nationwide network of pals we can rely on all the way. Now we're going to pay a call on Crispy Critter.'

'Who?'

'The guy who's lending you his car. He's one of us.'

Volkov landed on the outskirts of the city in the small tree-surrounded garden of a shabby *dacha*. In the West, the word has become synonymous with the luxury villas of the Soviet élite, but *dachi* come in all sizes depending on the owner's pocket or status. This one was an economy version: a self-build two-room cabin with a felt and plywood roof and outside chemical toilet.

Standing under the small porch was a one-armed vet with a badly burned face. It was impossible to read any expression on the stretched and shiny skin where his nose, cheeks and eyebrows should have been. Only the two unblinking blue eyes were human. He tossed a casual salute to Volkov while the others were climbing out of the Kamov, and handed Tom the keys of an ancient Fiat Polski estate, parked beside the *dacha*.

'I didn't see you. I didn't hear you,' said the vet. The sound came out of a hole like a bullet wound, cut into the base of his neck. The tracheotomy had left him with a voice like a computer-generated rasp. 'If you're caught, I'll say you stole it.'

He went back into the cabin, slammed the door and turned the television on, with the sound at maximum volume.

Tom put Karen in the front seat of the car while Ponsonby and Sibirsky sat in the rear. The cold air rushing through the badly fitting cargo door of the helicopter had brought some colour to Karen's cheeks. To occupy her mind, Tom gave her the maps and asked her to navigate until they were back on the right road. According to the dashboard clock, which was the only accessory on Crispy Critter's car that still worked, the bug had cost two hours in delays.

.8.

Tom backed the Fiat Polski into the overgrown stable yard. There was knee-high grass everywhere. Rooted in the layer of dust, dirt and débris that covered the cobbles, it had been bleached by the summer sun and dried to tinder by the winds, themselves parched by their long journey over the wastes of Central Asia. The door of the tack room was warped shut and hanging crookedly on one hinge. He had to barge it open with his shoulder, dislodging a shower of dirt and cobwebs and startling one of Miss Addison's cats. Now half-wild, it shot between his legs with a screech, heading for the open air.

The tack room was as derelict as the rest of the stables. Slates had blown off the roof or been stolen. Rainwater had rotted roof timbers, allowing whole sections to crash to the ground. Someone had removed Miss Addison's pathetic remnants of furniture; even the old stove was gone. Only her treasured books remained: a mouldering pile of naturally recycling wood pulp in one corner.

Tom felt a surge of elation on seeing that the slab on

which the stove had stood was still in position. Ever since Karen had voiced the possibility that the film might no longer exist, he had envisaged the stable block demolished, a new house built on the same spot, the well capped with concrete. With Ponsonby's help he set up the sheer legs and attached the hoist. Within minutes the stone was swinging slightly in mid-air.

Karen took one look down the well and recoiled. 'My God! You wouldn't catch me going down there.'

'It's not as deep as it looks.'

'I'll come down with you,' Ponsonby offered.

'No,' said Tom. 'I want you up here.'

Once inside the ice well itself, he shone his torch round the walls and floor. Nothing had been disturbed since his last visit. He pocketed the plastic envelope containing the film, lifted the oilskin-wrapped icon from where it lay on Admiral Kolchak's travelling chest of drawers, grasped it under one arm and climbed back up the ladder.

Ponsonby took it from him and passed it to Sibirsky. 'Where's the film?' he asked.

'Inside the package, with the icon,' lied Tom.

'Then let's go.'

Even under pressure, Tom was still a historian in his soul. 'There's a rope in the back of the car,' he said. 'Go and get it.'

'What the hell for? We've got what we came for.'

'Admiral Kolchak's military chest is down there, packed with his diaries and maps. I want to take it all with us.'

Sibirsky had hardly spoken a word all morning. His frailty overridden by the call of scholarship, he sided with Tom. 'It would be vandalism to leave it in a place like this, Mr Ponsonby. Kolchak's personal papers will solve a thousand questions for students of the Civil War.'

Swearing under his breath, Ponsonby went out to the car to fetch the rope. Tom clambered back down the ladder. In the ice well he separated the two halves of the chest and carried the top half to the edge of the shaft, after taking out the pouch of jewellery and the revolver. When the rope came snaking down he tied it to the two brass handles and called to Ponsonby to start hauling away. The unwieldy box bumped its way upwards, hitting the rungs of the ladder at each heave. By holding onto the bottom rung and leaning out, Tom could see Karen's face above it. She was kneeling by the lip of the well and peering over the edge. Behind her, the veins stood out on Ponsonby's forehead as he pulled on the rope.

'It seems to be stuck,' he shouted. 'Lean out and tell me what's wrong.'

Tom leaned farther out. 'It looks free to me,' he called back.

He heard Karen's scream of warning and swung back out of the way just as the chest fell. Missing his head, it caught him on the right shoulder with an audible crack and fell past to land with an enormous splash in the water, far below. The pain almost made him let go of the ladder, but somehow he pulled himself back into the ice well and slumped to the floor, gasping for breath.

Up in the tack room, Ponsonby grabbed a handful of Karen's hair and pulled her upright. She felt the muzzle of his automatic pressed against the back of her neck. 'Say one word, sweetheart, and I'll blow your fucking head off,' he hissed.

She nodded to show she understood, and let him drag her back to the lip of the well.

'Tom?' he called, leaning over. 'Are you all right?'

'I don't know.' The voice from below was faint. 'I think I've broken my shoulder. I can't move my right arm.'

'Show me where you are,' Ponsonby called. 'Shine the torch.'

No, Karen prayed. Don't do it, Tom!

Her head pulled back savagely by Ponsonby's free hand, she caught sight of a flash of light down the well.

Looking up, Tom saw her face with Ponsonby's close behind. 'What's going on up there?' he shouted.

The first muzzle flash left him blind. The bullet hit a rung of the ladder only inches from his face and ricocheted away to bury itself in the soft bricks. The second round would have traversed his skull, throat and lungs to end somewhere in one of his legs if instinct had not made him shrink back into the shelter of the ice well.

The torch had dropped to the bottom of the well, leaving him in total darkness. Temporarily deaf as well as unsighted, he groped his way to where he had left Kolchak's revolver, unwrapped it and wondered whether it would still be usable or whether the grease with which the mechanism had been packed for so long would have become so hard that it would jam solid.

In the stable yard, Sibirsky was sitting in the back of the car, underneath the raised tailgate, totally absorbed in examining the icon. There were tears in his eyes as his fingers felt the texture of the paint and the gold leaf and the patina of the wooden frame. Satisfied that he held in his hands the true Virgin of Kazan, he put on the special high-powered spectacles which he had brought with him – they were like a double watchmaker's eyepiece – and began to examine the details of the icon in close-up. He heard the shots, muffled by the well, without recognising them for what they were. At that moment, for which he had waited so many years, a thunderstorm would not have disturbed him.

The gun pressed against her right ear, Ponsonby dragged Karen to where he could see out through the door. Finding the old man absorbed in his study of the icon, he decided that there was no need to waste a bullet on Karen when a shove would end her life just as surely, so he forced her back towards the well, intending to push her in. At the last moment, his attention was distracted by a movement overhead as one of the cats ran along an exposed beam.

Pushed askew, Karen fell half-in and half-out of the well.

Catching in desperation at a rung of the ladder, she managed to get one foot onto another rung, and clung there, wide-eyed and panting for breath. Above her the black-clad figure of death pointed the automatic directly between her eyes. She saw Ponsonby's finger whiten on the trigger as he took up the first pressure. Her mouth opened wider to beg for mercy but no words came out, only the raucous sound of her breathing.

The terror in her eyes, her open mouth and the swell of her breasts resting on the rim of the well fitted almost exactly one of Ponsonby's favourite fantasies, tempting him to keep Karen alive while getting rid of Tom and Sibirsky. Then he would force her back into the well and make her perform fellatio on him at gunpoint while she clung precariously to the top of the ladder. At the moment of orgasm, he would shoot her very neatly through one eye. Her mouth full of his semen, Karen would lose her grip on the ladder and he would watch her discarded body fall into the blackness below . . .

He blinked the pleasurable thoughts away and snarled, 'Climb down the ladder.'

Still deaf, Tom felt the vibration of feet on the rungs, conducted through the ironwork to his hand. He fought down the pain in his shoulder and cautiously leaned forward to thrust his head out into the main shaft. Looking up, his blurred vision made out a figure silhouetted against the circle of light at the top of the well. Assuming it was Ponsonby, coming down to finish him off, he lifted Kolchak's revolver in his left hand, took aim and pressed the trigger.

Nothing happened.

Unfamiliar with firearms, he had forgotten to cock the hammer of the Colt .45. He thumbed it back and took aim for the second time. A split-second before he was going to fire, he caught a glimpse of Ponsonby's face at the top, peering downwards, and realised that the person on the ladder whom he had so nearly shot, was Karen. He changed aim, trying to miss her and shoot Ponsonby, but it was impossible to take the risk.

And then the moment of opportunity was gone as Ponsonby stepped back from the well, satisfied that Karen was too far down to take advantage of him discarding the gun for the time it took to pick up a piece of fallen roof timber and use it to batter one of the sheer legs repeatedly until the hoist toppled over. It crashed to the ground, dropping the slab over the mouth of the well slightly crooked and leaving a narrow slit on one side where one of the sheer legs was jammed between it and the floor. Satisfied that it was far too small for Tom or Karen even to get a hand through, he threw away the wood, retrieved the BRNO and walked outside.

Sibirsky looked up. Through the close-up glasses, the man approaching him was an indistinct blur.

'It's the right one, then?' Ponsonby asked.

Sibirsky nodded. Words were beyond him at that moment.

'Vstavái!'

Ponsonby had to repeat the order: 'Stand up!'

Sibirsky got slowly to his feet, clutching the Virgin tightly in his arms.

'Now put the icon in the car,' Ponsonby ordered.

When Sibirsky did not comply, he stepped forward to pistol-whip the old man's face, knocking off the glasses and drawing blood to reinforce his command, then stepped back.

Despite the violence and the weapon being pointed at him, Sibirsky still did not part with the icon. Instead of putting it down, he staggered towards Ponsonby, the Virgin held in front of him as a shield. In his mind was the image of Dimitri Donskoi challenging the Mongols with the Virgin of the Don held aloft in one hand, a sword in the other.

Ponsonby took two steps backwards and deliberately aimed at Sibirsky's left knee. The bullet pierced one corner of the icon and shattered the kneecap. As Sibirsky fell to the ground with a scream of agony, the icon crashed into the long grass beside him.

Ponsonby walked close and shouted, 'Where's the film?'

'*Ya ne znáyu,*' Sibirsky gasped. '*Ya ne vídyel fílma!*'

His whole body spasmed as Ponsonby fired again, this time shattering the right kneecap.

'Where's the fucking film?' Ponsonby shouted.

Ignoring the moaning old man on the ground, he rummaged through the discarded wrapping material in the back of the Fiat. Suddenly understanding that the film was still in Tom's hands, immured beyond his reach beneath the fallen slab, he vented his fury by deliberately shooting Sibirsky in the chest on the safe side, away from the heart. Mercifully, the bullet severed the wires leading from the pacemaker to the electrodes implanted in the old man's heart. As his mouth opened in the rictus of death, Ponsonby kicked him again and again in the head until all the rage had left him.

He tossed the Virgin of Kazan into the back of the Fiat on top of the nineteenth-century copy, slammed the tailgate and drove cautiously out of the yard, avoiding the lumps of masonry hidden in the long grass.

Karen was holding onto the top rung of the ladder, her face jammed against the underside of the stone slab. Through the slit she could see the doorway and part of the stable yard beyond. Unable to look away or close her eyes, she had watched the torture and murder of Sibirsky without even blinking, letting the ghastly images imprint themselves on her brain. When the car had gone, she stayed immobile, staring at the bloodied body lying in the grass.

'Karen!'

She heard the shouting from a long way off: a voice she did not know calling a stranger's name.

'Karen!' Tom shouted again. 'Are you all right?'

Time had stopped. Whether it was the same shout or another one, did not matter. Nothing mattered. She felt the vibrations of Tom climbing up the ladder and then his head pushed against her legs. It was the only way he could attract her attention without letting go of the ladder.

'Go away,' she said dully. 'Leave me alone.'

He felt faint from the pain and the effort of climbing up one-handed. 'Come down the ladder, please,' he begged. 'I need your help.'

'Oh God!' she screamed. '*You* need *my* help? What about me? Who's going to help me?'

'Climb down, please.'

'No, no, no, no!' She was crying now, hands gripping the top rung of the ladder, her shoulders heaving impotently against the dead weight of the slab that – she was sure – was sinking lower and lower, second by second thrusting her into her grave.

'I don't want to die,' she screamed at him. 'Not here! I've spent my life looking for fire and light and I'm frightened, Tom. Don't you realise that madman has left us here to die in the darkness?'

'We're not going to die.' Despite the pain, Tom heaved himself level with her. 'Volkov is on his way here. He'll get us out, you'll see.'

'He'll never find us.'

'He will.' It was hard to find the energy to hold on – never mind argue – but Tom knew that if he didn't keep Karen talking she could drift off into shock, and that was a complication he didn't need. 'I gave him the co-ordinates of this place. He'll be here soon, come what may.'

She gave no sign of understanding, so he added, 'Tell me what happened. Tell me what you saw.'

'He . . . killed . . . Sibirsky.'

'He shot him?'

'You want to know how he did it?' Karen's voice was choked up, but she wasn't screaming. 'You want to hear what happened, I'll tell you.'

Putting the unspeakable into words for him reduced the horror she had just witnessed to the manageable level of television coverage of an atrocity: a busload of children blown apart by a suicide bomber in Jerusalem, a roomful of raped women in Bosnia, an arm sticking from the rubble of a collapsed building after an earthquake in Japan . . .

Listening to Karen's account, Tom wondered at the coincidences in Sibirsky's death. Arkady Sergeyevich had dreamed for most of his life of finding the Virgin of Kazan, only to die within minutes of setting eyes on the icon – in exactly the same place and in almost the same way as Kolchak had died.

What were the words of the curse which the admiral had placed with his dying breath on Commissar Sergei Sibirsky? '. . . and on your children and your children's children.'

Was the manner of Arkady Sergeyevich's death just coincidence? Or was it more than that?

'. . . and then he got into the car and drove away,' Karen finished.

'He took the icon with him?'

'What do you think?'

Awkwardly, Tom gave her a brief hug. 'You've been amazing,' he said. 'But I really do need help. I'm injured. Can you face climbing down there to attend to my shoulder?'

Karen took a look sideways and down. Tom's face was a pale blur. Below it was a bottomless pit of darkness. She flinched, fighting the vertigo and her fear of darkness, then fixed her eyes again on the daylit slit beneath the flagstone. As her eyes focused on the body outside she saw a cloud of large black flies buzzing around it already.

Some things were worse than darkness.

'Okay,' she said, feeling calmer after her outburst. 'You go down. I'll follow.'

.9.

Karen tore a rough square from one of Kolchak's night-shirts and folded it to make a triangular bandage.

'My guess is, you've broken your collar-bone.' She knotted the makeshift sling at the back of Tom's neck. 'Painful but not serious. There's no sign of damage to the arm bones or ribs, so far as I can tell in the dark.'

'Thank you, doctor.' Tom swallowed the last of Kolchak's brandy from the silver hip flask they had found in one of the drawers. With the arm supported by the sling and the alcohol going to his head, he felt a little better.

'Don't scoff,' she said. 'You'd be amazed how many injuries I've dealt with over the years. Marooned on a volcano hundreds of miles from civilisation, you have to be self-sufficient. Anyway, whatever's wrong with the shoulder, you could be a lot worse off.'

'Like dead.' Tom winced as she adjusted the sling. 'If you hadn't shouted that warning, I'd be floating at the bottom of the well right now.'

'So I did something right.' Karen stood with one foot on the ladder, looking up at the gleam of light above. She would have liked to climb up to it, just to breathe clean air and get away from the stifling blackness, but Tom needed her with him. 'I keep thinking it was all my fault. I was up there with Ponsonby. Maybe I could have grabbed his gun, if I'd thought fast enough.'

'It's a good job you didn't. He's very fit and totally ruthless. He'd have killed you on the spot.'

'You foresaw all this,' Karen accused Tom. 'You could have warned me.'

'I didn't foresee a damned thing.'

'Then why tell Volkov where we were going to be?'

'Because I never intended driving back to Irkutsk. On the ground, we'd have been too vulnerable to Ivanov, to Nosarenko, to any band of teenage muggers if it comes to that. I arranged for Volkov to pick us up and fly us back to the *Vasiliévsky Dvorétz* because it seemed the safest way of getting there in one piece.'

'Suppose something's happened to him, Tom?'

'Don't think about it. Volkov's a survivor. He'll be here.'

Karen tore her eyes from the tiny sliver of light at the top of the shaft and sat down beside Tom. Immediately she felt the darkness pressing in from all sides. 'My worst fear,' she confided. 'Being locked up in darkness. Sounds stupid, doesn't it?'

'Talk to me,' said Tom. 'You'll be doing me a favour too. It'll take my mind off the pain.'

'What about?'

'Any subject under the sun, except darkness and injured shoulders.'

She took his good hand in both of hers. The question surfaced spontaneously: 'What did you feel, seeing Rada again? Or is that none of my business?'

There was no simple answer, Tom thought. 'Confused, maybe.'

'Do you still love her?'

'That's a real woman's question.'

'I'm a real woman, so indulge me.'

'I don't know.'

'You're avoiding the question.'

'Let's say I've got too many things on my mind to be certain what I do feel.'

'Do you hate her?'

'No.'

'She's very beautiful.'

'I used to think she would put on weight, like most Russian women, but she hasn't.'

'Size twelve dresses, I asked her.'

'I didn't know she'd deigned to talk to you.'

'She invited herself into my room last night after you had gone into town to buy the chemicals. She sat down and asked me the kind of questions I'd have liked to ask her.'

'Such as?'

'How we broke up that time in St Petersburg and whether we had a relationship again now.'

'She didn't offer to read the Tarot for you?'

'What's that mean?'

'Nothing,' he said. 'So what did you tell her?'

'The truth. At first it was hard to talk to her. That woman is so damned beautiful she made me feel like a horse's arse.'

'You said "at first".'

'It took me a while to realise that I had met for the first time in my life that feminine stereotype, the beautiful woman who is insecure. Once we got talking, I began to understand her a little bit. She told me that she's always felt people treated her like a prize racehorse or a statue, because of her face and figure. The only time she felt confident in herself as a person was when you both worked together at the university. Oh, and when the kid was born, of course.'

'Real girl-talk.' Tom was wondering whether Rada's

midnight gesture of friendship had been just an excuse to get into Karen's room. 'It was very unlike her to be chatty with a stranger.'

'It's funny you should say that. I had the feeling that she wasn't so much talking to me as to you through me.'

'How do you mean?'

'It was as though she was trying to explain herself. She said that when she found out you were a spy and had only married her as cover, all the self-confidence she had built up deserted her and she reverted to her old behaviour patterns.'

'How did she find out about me?'

'Oh, that was weird. Some fat little guy with a pot belly and a beard . . .'

'Brodsky!'

'She didn't know his name. He came up to her in a store one day and showed her photographs of you with some men and a whole lot of money beside a suitcase on a table. He told her the whole story.'

'And what did she do, after Brodsky had spilled the beans?'

'She started picking up men, hoping that you would find out and get jealous. There was some American lover . . .'

'The fat cat in the fast-food business, I remember.'

'Maybe. Anyway, she moved in with him for a while but he was kinky, so she moved out and went back to live with her father.'

'I wondered.'

'She told me she's never loved any other man but you.'

'I don't think you can believe everything that Rada says,' Tom sighed. 'If she loved me so bloody much, why did she come up with the idea of selling me back to the British?'

'We didn't get around to talking about that.'

'So what else did you talk about?'

'One thing I didn't have the nerve to ask her . . . Rada's travelling wardrobe cost more than my clothing budget for a whole year. Where does she get all the money from?'

'That,' said Tom, 'is one of the questions you learned not to ask in the good ol' USSR. Arkady Sergeyevich was always rich by Soviet standards. He was an occasional bagman for the KGB.'

'You're kidding!'

'He probably just delivered covert funds to trade unionists and politicians, agents of influence – that sort of thing. Being a respected academic, he could move around relatively freely in the West. Whatever his function was, he used the customs privileges that came with working for the KGB to smuggle icons out to the West and sell them. Ivanov was involved in the illicit traffic, shepherding him through the airport each time behind the shield of his badge.'

He stood up, straining his ears. Entombed so far below ground level, it was hard to be certain what was the sound that had alerted him. 'Listen! I'm sure I heard something. Hopefully, it's Volkov. But it might be Ponsonby, come back for the film. So take the gun and climb up the ladder.'

'Me?'

'It has to be you,' he said urgently. 'With only one usable hand, how can I possibly hold onto the ladder and fire a gun as well? If it's Ponsonby, you may be able to shoot the bastard through that crack. He doesn't know we have a weapon, so you'll have the advantage of surprise.'

'What would that achieve?'

'At best, if you kill him, it could be a way of attracting attention, in case something's happened to Volkov. Eventually someone'll see the car parked out there and they'll come looking. Even if you miss, it should scare the bastard into leaving us alone.'

'I never handled a firearm in my life,' Karen said doubtfully.

'Neither did I,' Tom urged. 'But, given the chance, I'd kill Ponsonby. Can you do it?'

Karen weighed the Colt in her hand. It was heavy, the barrel far longer than she had thought. 'If you'd asked me seventy-two hours ago, I'd have said I couldn't shoot a living person under any circumstances.'

'And now?'

Recalling the cold-blooded way in which Ponsonby had tortured and killed Sibirsky, she said, 'I could kill that man.'

'Good.'

'How can it be good, Tom? What's happening to me?'

'Forget the philosophy,' he said. 'The only thing to remember is that you have to cock the hammer before you squeeze the trigger.'

In the subdued lighting of the war room beneath the presidential palace in Kiev, Viktor Nosarenko sat alone watching the repeater screens relaying a small selection of the information available in the Crimean Pentagon, buried deep in the hills above the port of Sebastopol.

Deprived of his HUMINT source aboard the militia helicopter which the *afgántsy* had prevented from following Tom out of Irkutsk, he had spent more than two hours watching the blip made by the bug aboard Volkov's helicopter as it moved across the screen in straight lines – first south, then west and north and now east, heading back towards Irkutsk along the line of the Trans-Siberian railway. Superimposed on a map of the terrain below the satellite, there was no obvious purpose in the box pattern. Nosarenko decided that the flight was a decoy.

He turned his attention to the next screen, which showed an aerial view of the city of Irkutsk, and pressed the control to zoom in electronically on the area where the dot which was the militia helicopter still buzzed back and forth. Cars were parked all over the garden. Only a few comings and goings of individuals had been noted. Nosarenko's assumption was that Tom Fielding must still be in the Vasilievsky Palace.

'Fielding . . .' Nosarenko breathed the name. It was inconceivable, he thought, that such an otherwise insignificant man should be in a position to bring to naught all the plans he had for his country.

On his whistle-stop tour of international banks the previous week, he had collected billions of dollars in no-interest loans. Everyone wanted to be friends with the man who controlled nearly two thousand ICBMs, temporarily unusable though they were. In the White House President Clinton had been eager to agree to his demands. Sitting on a CIA report which hazarded a guess that ten per cent of the rockets might be salvageable, what sane US President would have done otherwise, with less than a year to go before the next presidential elections?

Lack of money was no longer an obstacle to Nosarenko's plans; the programme of industrial and agricultural restructuring, for which the international loans to Ukraine were intended, would conceal a rearmament campaign that would take advantage of the missiles and the material in their warheads in many different ways. Nosarenko had no intention of going to war unless forced to, but in his view a nation which had been enslaved by Russians, Turks and Poles – to mention just the immediate neighbours who had overrun the country in the last two centuries – had every right to defend itself aggressively.

And luckily, for the first time in 500 years since Kiev was the capital of all Russia, Ukraine had a man to match the moment: Nosarenko saw himself as the greatest *hetman* of all time – the messianic leader who would claim for his country its rightful place as the world's third largest nuclear power, in a league that placed Britain and France way below the leaders and just above countries like Israel and India.

And all this grandiose scheming was now in jeopardy because of one man! If Tom Fielding could somehow prove that the President of Ukraine was guilty of murdering his wife, Viktor Nosarenko risked losing both his dreams and his liberty . . .

The fault is mine, Nosarenko thought. If I had had the

nerve to slam the door of the cage with Fielding inside, there would have been no witness.

It was tempting to destroy the Vasilievsky Palace with the weapons on board the militia helicopter, and sort out the political problems afterwards. The risk was less than in selling all the ex-Red Army tanks and guns to the Serbs, after all. But Nosarenko was curious; he wanted to know what was so important in Irkutsk that Tom Fielding should travel three-quarters of the way round the world to get there, when he had only hours to live.

Something was happening on the screen. The aerial view of Irkutsk blurred and the image rolled, due to the satellite camera executing a whip pan which ended 50 kilometres to the west. As the picture stabilised, the camera zoomed in on a long goods train hauling coal from the faraway Donbas eastwards to the steel mills of Irkutsk. A light flashed on one of the telephones in front of Nosarenko.

He picked it up and barked, 'Yes?'

'We've lost the target helicopter, Mr President.'

'What do you mean, lost him?' Nosarenko shouted. 'I can still see the blip on the map.'

There was an embarrassed pause at the other end of the line. 'It seems, Mr President, that the transmitter is no longer in the helicopter piloted by this man Volkov. It's actually on board one of the waggons of that train you're seeing on-screen.'

'*Yob tvoyú mat!*' Nosarenko swore. 'Well, search for the bloody helicopter. It can't have gone far.'

'We're doing our best, Mr President.'

Nosarenko watched as the satellite image went to wide-angle and then zoomed in on various moving objects which revealed themselves as trucks, a herd of horses, a flock of migrating birds. On the map screen the blip moved slowly along the railway track back to Irkutsk.

Nosarenko slammed the phone down. He could feel an asthma attack building. His pills and inhaler were upstairs in the presidential suite. He stood up and glared at the screens, then made for his personal lift. Thank God, he thought as it whisked him through 150 metres of solid concrete and rock . . . Thank God I have an agent in the enemy camp. And if that too fails, I still have my final trump to play.

.10.

Getting rid of the bug creatively had caused even Volkov a few sweaty moments. It had meant overflying the coal train at exactly the same speed with only centimetres of vertical separation between the Kamov's undercarriage and the topmost lumps of coal. He was uncertain how big a shock the bug could tolerate. Praying that it was robust enough to continue working, he kissed it goodbye, thrust his hand out of the sliding cabin window and let go. Caught in the downdraught of the powerful rotors, it spun sideways and bounced twice before lodging between two large lumps of coal.

Volkov banked and veered right, heading southwards towards the *byvshi dom*. Not knowing how long it would take his satellite watchers to work out that the bug was travelling far slower than it had been, he wasted no time in gaining altitude but sped across country to the co-ordinates Tom had given him.

In the semi-dusk the ruins looked exactly as described, except that there was no trace of the Fiat Polski parked outside. Volkov flew low over the buildings and saw the swathe of crushed grass leading into the stable yard and another swathe leading away. Had Tom changed his mind about waiting to be picked up? he wondered.

He was about to follow the tracks when a hunch made him fly a second pass lower, skimming the ridge of the stable block. The down-draught, parting the long grass, revealed Sibirsky's corpse lying on the ground. Volkov executed a tight turn and flared to a landing in the old stable yard, a few metres from the body.

Wishing that he had a weapon, he shut down the turbines and kept both hands firmly on the controls until his ears had adjusted to the silence. After a couple of minutes, he stepped down to examine the corpse and straightened up with an eerie feeling of being watched. He picked up a piece of roof timber as a better-than-nothing weapon before walking warily through the door of the tack room.

Karen had neither seen nor heard the helicopter arrive. She reached the top of the ladder as Volkov walked through the doorway. Catching sight of the figure silhouetted against the daylight outside with a piece of wood in its hand, she thought for a moment that Ponsonby had returned.

Unaware that Admiral Kolchak's paranoia had motivated him to have the Colt hair-triggered, she pulled back the hammer until it clicked on the cam, ready to fire when the slightest pressure was applied to the trigger. She poked the barrel through the gap below the slab and sighted along it.

Then relief flooded through her as she recognised the huge build and red hair. 'Volkov! Oh, God, am I glad to see you!'

Unable to place where her voice had come from, he turned towards her just as the Colt's hammer slipped on the filed-down cam. The powerful main spring inside the hand-grip unbent, slamming the hammer forward to hit the firing pin, which travelled the few millimetres necessary to explode the detonator on the brass cartridge that had been waiting seven and a half decades to be fired. The expanding gases from the

28-grain black powder charge sped the 230-grain bullet on its way.

The explosion blackened Karen's face and the recoil nearly threw her off the ladder. The Colt leaped out of her hand and fell with a loud, echoing splash into the water at the bottom of the well where Admiral Kolchak's other possessions were floating.

Volkov hurled himself to the floor as the bullet shattered the last remaining pane in the door beside him, then lizard-crawled to the crack surprisingly fast for such a large man. Smoke from the black powder was still curling out of it. He coughed and waved it away with his hand, then peered through the gap below the slab, to see Karen's eyes staring back.

'Oh God, I'm sorry,' she said.

Volkov stood up and brushed dirt off himself. 'If this is glad-to-see-you, what the fuck do you do when you don't like someone?'

He tried using muscle power to lift the slab without success. The sheer legs were useless. One was bent and trapped beneath the slab. Every piece of timber he could find broke under the load. Finally he found a length of chain in the cargo space of the Kamov and passed one end to Karen, who fed it under the slab and up the other side.

'I'm going to use the sky hook,' he warned her. 'Stay well away from below in case I drop the thing.'

With the loose end of the chain looped over one shoulder, he scrambled laboriously up fallen roof timbers and onto the rotten floor of the first storey. There he spread the weight of his bulk on several floorboards at a time by crawling on all fours with the chain gripped between his teeth until he was able to heave himself up to the level of the roof. Making a loop in the end of the chain, he hooked it over nails projecting from beams on both sides of a large hole in the roof which was vertically above the well.

'So far, so good,' he shouted down the shaft.

There was no point in explaining to Tom and Karen the odds against success. The civilian version of the Kamov was designed to transport loads of up to five metric tonnes slung on its cargo hook, so the weight of the slab was no problem. What was exercising Volkov's brain was how to grab the chain with the hook while in a hover, single-handed. It was the sort of challenge to his skills that he would have relished, with more time to spare. At the same time, the fuel gauge made him do some fast mental arithmetic; getting back to Irkutsk would be touch-and-go.

He lifted off nearly vertically, eased the Kamov sideways until he estimated that the hook was directly above the hole in the roof and handed over to the automatic pilot. For its anti-submarine role, the inboard computer was designed to provide a hands-off approach and hover, maintaining constant rotor thrust and adjusting flaps and rudders to compensate for changes in wind direction and velocity.

Volkov felt the sweat start on his forehead as he eased his bulk out of the pilot's seat and clambered back across all the junk in the cargo hold. With the remote control for the winch in his hand, he slid open the door and lay down on the floor with his head over the edge. A safety margin of ten metres' vertical separation between the ridge of the roof and the undercarriage had seemed to him the minimum that was prudent when in the pilot's seat. From that height, the chain seemed a long way down.

He pressed the green button on the remote control and watched the hook descend, swinging slightly on its hawser. The stiff breeze kept lifting the Kamov as much as a couple of metres. Each time it settled back to the previous height but crept forward a few centimetres. Volkov shook his shaggy head to get rid of the perspiration dripping off his eyebrows. The hook reached the level of the chain but was too far to one side. How to make it swing, was the next problem to resolve.

He scrambled to his feet, took a deep breath and jumped

as high as he could. As his 130 kilos crashed back on the deck, the Kamov lurched, the rotors picked up revs and for a moment he thought he had taken one liberty too many. Then the auto-pilot stabilised the helicopter and left the hook swinging below so wildly that there was a danger of it catching in the roof timbers.

Lying down on the floor again, he nudged the swinging hook up and down with the remote buttons and caught the chain on his third attempt. Very gently he squeezed the red button and winched the hook in, centimetre by centimetre, until the chain fell free of the supporting beams and hung from the hook alone.

The next trick was to take up the slack so that the chain could not slide off the hook or tangle up in the projecting timbers. Taking up too much slack risked giving the auto-pilot a nervous breakdown, if it should sense the extra load of the stone itself.

When he was satisfied, Volkov stood up and found himself shaking from head to foot. Moving very slowly, he climbed back into the pilot's seat and switched back to manual with a mutter of thanks to the late Comrade Nikolai Kamov for being one of those rare people who seem to think of everything.

With both hands fully occupied, it was necessary to have the remote control clamped between his legs. Squeezing the red button between his knees, Volkov prayed that he was still vertically above the hole in the roof. If the Kamov had wandered even a metre or so off station, there was a risk of the chain catching on solid masonry so that pressing the red button would winch the helicopter out of the sky instead of hauling the slab up.

He poured on thrust to take the weight as the stone came free and squeezed the remote control again. The chain tautened and the slab swung free, rising to smash its way through what remained of the roof as it came clear.

Volkov gained height and flew a hundred metres clear of

the buildings, intending to jettison the spinning slab as soon as it was safe to do so, but the hook release was stuck. He had to land by paying out cable, depositing the stone first and then hovering gently forward to clear it before setting the Kamov down.

When Karen reached him, he was slumped over the controls, shaking his head and muttering, 'You're too old for these games, Vladimir. It's time you grew up.'

He looked from her to Tom, who was white-faced with pain and the strain of climbing the vertical ladder one-handed.

'That makes two things I'll never do again in my life, Tomski,' Volkov said.

.11.

'You can't do anything simply, can you?' Volkov grumbled.

Tom had stopped him hacksawing through the cable of the jammed sky hook, which complicated the lift-off. The spinning disc of the rotors was effectively stable, with the body of the helicopter swinging beneath it. Once the slab left the ground, hanging on ten metres of cable, a pendulum effect built up which would have tempted an inexperienced pilot to reduce throttle as it swung forward and then increase throttle to counteract the effect of the slab swinging backwards again.

Doing that increased the swing each time, with potentially disastrous results. Winching the slab in closer to the body of the Kamov too fast would reduce the length of swing but increase its frequency, which was simply an alternative way to die.

His huge hands light on the controls, Volkov coaxed and nursed the slab until it hung on less than a metre of cable. Meanwhile Tom had been working out on the map roughly how far Ponsonby could have travelled. It helped that there was only one direction to go: north, south and west of the *byvshi dom* lay only empty country. There was little light left by the time they were airborne and mobile, so he vectored Volkov cross-country, aiming to intersect Ponsonby's probable route and hoping to God that he had guessed right.

The clapped-out Fiat Polski was making poor time. Coming out of a stretch of forest Ponsonby saw the helicopter overflying the road, three or four miles ahead. He switched off the car's lights and hauled it off the packed dirt road to bump across a ploughed field in an attempt to regain the cover of the trees before he was spotted.

Only Volkov's eagle eyes could have caught the brief flash of sidelights at such a distance. He dragged the Kamov round and piled on throttle, dropping lower and lower as he flew nap-of-the-earth in the hope that they had not been seen.

In the cargo space, Karen braced herself between two metal stanchions for support. In addition to keeping her balance, she was using one foot to stop Sibirsky's body, shrouded in some plastic fertiliser sacks, from rolling out of the open door as the Kamov banked first right and then left to avoid clumps of high trees. She was thinking that time seemed to have stretched. Her ordeal on Mount Tolbachik had happened only seventy-two hours previously, yet a lifetime had passed since then. Through the open door she saw the ground rushing past very close below. Patches of evening mist alternated with branches of low birch trees that shattered with a noise like gunfire as they were snapped off by the undercarriage.

Tom was lying in the doorway, his feet wedged under some heavy junk and his useless right arm poking out into space while he clutched the remote control for the sky hook in his left hand. With greenery ripping past his face and twigs and branches shattering against the undercarriage wheels, it was tempting to scream into the headset mic, 'Pull up! Gain height!' He hoped that once again Volkov knew what he was doing.

And then they were into the forest, the narrow span of the twin rotors permitting Volkov to slot his craft lower and lower between the trees on either side. Tom saw the roof of the Fiat appear in his limited field of view. Before he could shout a warning, it was gone. But Volkov had seen it too. He stood the Kamov on its side in a tight climbing circle, reducing speed and returning to exactly the right spot as neatly as a yachtsman in a calm sea executing a man-overboard routine.

Tom was aware that there was no point in simply stopping a man who was armed and prepared to kill. The slab was their only weapon against Ponsonby and he might have only one chance of using it. Directly overhead the Fiat, he pressed the green button as deliberately as if it were a trigger – which in a sense it was.

The slab dropped, spinning erratically on the end of the hawser. It crashed onto the roof of the car, crumpling it. Ponsonby swerved wildly and narrowly missed hitting several trees. Somehow he regained control and hauled the Fiat Polski back onto the road.

'Get your finger out, Tomski!' Volkov roared over the headset. 'I can't risk another hundred metres, the trees are closing in.'

The shattering noise from the branches being slashed from the trees on either side by the rotor tips lent force to the command.

Tom pressed red and hoisted the slab a couple of metres before stabbing the green button. The slab lurched forward and down, then swung back – straight through the windscreen of the car below. There was a momentary glimpse of Ponsonby's face, frozen in a scream of disbelief or rage as the safety glass shattered into a thousand fragments that blew away in the down-draught like snow-flakes in a blizzard.

When the slab swung forward out of the way, the man at the wheel had a shapeless red blob instead of a head. The car slammed into a tree, bounced off and rolled over several times before coming to rest wheels uppermost in the middle of the road.

Tom felt no emotion on seeing Ponsonby's inert body lying where it had been flung out of the car when the driver's door burst open. He stepped over it and searched the wreck, finding only one icon. From the labels pasted on the back, he knew it to be the copy. The genuine one was lying on a pile of leaf-mould beside the road, its gilded haloes gleaming in the last light of day. Tom placed it on top of the other and wrapped them both in the brown paper that had blown out of the car.

After the noise of flying along with his head out of the Kamov's door only a few metres above the ground, the silence in the forest was eerie. Volkov had landed in a clearing not far away, from where the sound of a hacksaw was clearly audible. The car was groaning as it settled into the soft ground and the exhaust was ticking as it cooled. There was a smell of oil on hot metal.

Tom wished he had not spent so much of his life looking at the past and more in trying to predict the future.

He unwrapped the icons again; it was awkward, using only one hand. To his eyes in that light both the Virgins of Kazan looked identical except that the gilding on the original was possibly slightly duller than on the copy. He did what had to be done, wrapped them both up again carefully and collected Ponsonby's gun from the dead man's jacket pocket before walking back towards the clearing where Volkov's swearing was now louder than the noise of the hacksaw.

Halfway there he met Karen, who took the icons from him.

'Was it awful?' she asked, not understanding why he had wanted to go alone.

Tom looked at her blankly. She repeated the question. Only then did he realise that he had just killed a man.

Rada was numb with shock as she watched her father's body being lifted out of the Kamov by a couple of the local heavies. As the rotors of the Kamov slowed and the whine of the twin turbines died away, she clung to Ivanov for support, her back to the body being laid out on the dining room table.

'Did you get the film?' Ivanov asked Tom quietly.

Tom nodded. 'I'll develop it straight away and print it.'

Rada turned to him. Her clenched hands and the strain on her face made it obvious that she was fighting for control of herself. 'I want you to say a prayer,' she said in a strangled voice.

'I'm not a priest.'

'You're a priest's son. You must know a prayer you could say.'

'I don't know any Russian prayers,' Tom excused himself.

'Does it matter,' she screamed, 'whether you talk to God in Russian or English or Hebrew? Do you think he needs a dictionary?'

Tom lowered his eyes to Sibirsky's body. The face was grey and looked peaceful with the eyes closed. The neatly clasped hands concealed the chest wound and someone had placed a folded blanket over the blood-soaked trouser legs.

The images were of standing in the rain – it always seemed to have rained when he was at a funeral. There was the coffin being lowered and his father in surplice and cassock intoning the ritual words.

'Say something,' Karen nudged him. 'Anything.'

'Oh Lord,' he began, 'behold thy servant Arkady Sergeyevich Sibirsky . . .'

Rada stayed on her knees for a moment after he had finished, then stood up, took off her dark glasses, kissed her father on the lips and replaced the glasses.

She seemed much calmer, in control of herself as she turned to Tom. 'Is it okay if I help in the darkroom? I used to be good at it, remember?'

'You take it easy,' he said. He would have liked to embrace and comfort her, but Sibirsky's death was his fault; it would have been easier if Rada had screamed abuse at him or even attacked him. 'Ivan Petrovich can call a doctor,' he suggested. 'He'll get you some sedatives.'

She shook her head. 'I'd rather have something to do, something to occupy my mind and hands.'

Half an hour later she was standing in the red glow of the safe lights beside Tom, as the first print was enlarged from the roll of film. He looked over her shoulder as she moved the paper in the developing solution. There was no mistaking Nosarenko's hard-lit features: the piggy eyes and thick black hair swept back from the wide forehead. Presumably the good quality of the picture was due to the low temperature at which the film had been kept.

Beside him, Rada shuddered. 'How can he just stand there when that poor woman is being torn to pieces?'

'You shouldn't be here,' Tom said. 'You're upsetting yourself for nothing. I can finish this off on my own.'

He was troubled by Rada's fascination with the horrifying pictures that gradually took shape, one after another, on the blank paper in the developing bath. Several times he tried to get rid of her, but each time she insisted on staying to help, and left the cellar only when Tom began drying the prints with a hair dryer, taken from one of the bedrooms.

A few minutes later he laid out the hot and slightly curled-up prints on the breakfast bar in the kitchen for Ivanov and Karen to see.

'Nosarenko was right to try to wipe you out,' was Ivanov's verdict. 'These pictures are the end of his political career.'

He put through calls on his mobile phone to the Irkutsk stringers of several Russian and Western news agencies.

Without going into details, he invited them to come to the house with their portable satellite uplinks, promising a big story for the evening news shows in Europe and the breakfast shows on American television.

They were waiting for the newsmen to arrive when Karen saw Rada leave the house at the same moment that Tom returned from the bathroom and noticed that the prints were missing. He ran down to the cellar, where the film was no longer on the line on which he had hung it above the sink. When he came upstairs Ivanov was shouting at the body-guards in the garden, who replied sullenly that they had no orders to restrict Rada's movements. She had last been seen getting into a taxi at the end of the road, which had driven off, heading downtown.

'What do we do now?' Karen asked Tom. She was surprised how calmly he was taking the latest development.

'It's not a disaster.' He took the other half of the film from his trouser pocket. 'I tore the film in two before we started printing. The question is, why did she take the other half and the prints – and where has she gone with them?'

Karen was staring out of the French windows at Ivanov who was still haranguing the guards. She turned suddenly to Tom. 'You said you let Viktor count the money in the suit-case while you copied the documents and that all your papers were there for him to see.'

'And?'

'That kind of man must have noted your name, address, everything . . .'

'Svetlana!' Tom shouted. There was only one possible explanation for Rada's behaviour.

He picked up a house telephone. The line was still dead, so he rushed into the garden and grabbed Ivanov. 'I must talk to Svetlana, this minute. Let me use your phone.'

'I'll do it.'

The number in Sibirsky's apartment rang for one minute, then another.

'Redial it,' Tom snapped. 'Maybe it's a wrong number.'

'Sibirsky's housekeeper is old. It takes her an age to get to the phone.'

Ivanov's patience was rewarded when a quavering voice at the other end asked, 'Who's that?'

'This is Ivan Petrovich.' He spoke slowly and clearly. 'I want to talk to Svetlana Tomasovna.'

'She's gone away.'

'Gone away where?' he asked.

'I don't know.' The old woman sounded confused. 'You'll have to ask Ivan Petrovich. He sent some men to collect her.'

'I am Ivan Petrovich. I didn't send any men.'

*

Karen had lit some candles in the dining room and turned off the electric lights, converting it into an impromptu chapel of rest. In the kitchen, Tom was pacing backwards and forwards impatiently. Sibirsky's wallet lay open on the breakfast bar with several photographs of Svetlana beside it. In one, Rada and her father were sitting on an excursion boat on the Moskva River. The nine-year-old child between them was almost the double of Tom's sister Megs at the same age. Tom picked the photograph up and stared at the face beneath the blonde curls, wondering whether his daughter was still alive.

Ivanov read his thoughts. It was not the first time he had been involved in a hostage situation. 'Svetlana is Nosarenko's only bargaining counter,' he said. 'He's going to take very good care of her, so don't worry about that.'

Tom's eyes shifted to the second set of prints from the film of that night in Alma Ata. The thought of his daughter, in the hands of the man standing outside the wolves' cage, was intolerable.

He slammed his fist against the wall and groaned through gritted teeth, 'I should have realised that a man like Nosarenko would prepare everything before making his first move.'

There was a commotion in the garden. Through the French windows, Tom saw two pick-up trucks with satellite dishes parked outside and a couple of reporters being man-handled by the guards.

Ivanov's phone bleeped. He grunted a couple of words and started scribbling a number on a piece of paper. His associates in Petropavlovsk had just traced the number called by Ponsonby from the Hotel Alyaska. Tom grabbed the phone from him, punched in the number and was put on hold, to spend the next five minutes listening to a recording of the Ukrainian national anthem.

'Mr Fielding?' said the voice he remembered.

'That's me,' Tom said.

'Can you identify yourself?'

'We last met at the railway station in Alma Ata. You were wearing a grey suit, no tie, and driving a black Moskvich. You had trouble finding reverse gear . . .'

'That's enough. You have something I want, Mr Fielding. Before we discuss terms, there is someone you should talk to.'

There was a series of clicks and beeps in the earpiece.

'Daddy?' Tom heard.

He shut his eyes to hear Svetlana's voice better. 'It's been a long time since I was able to talk to you, darling,' he said, fighting to keep his voice steady. 'Are you all right?'

'I want to go home, Daddy.'

'I know,' he said. 'But are you okay?'

'I want to go home to Mummy. Can you fix it?'

'Yes,' he said. 'Don't you worry. I'll have you home very, very soon.'

'Mr Fielding . . .' Nosarenko's voice was back on the line. 'In case you might think of playing for time, I suggest you check the parking lot at the airport and then call me back.'

'Hold on,' said Tom, but the line was dead.

One of the guards spotted the taxi which Rada had taken

into town. The trunk was not even locked. It sprang open and revealed to Tom's eyes the figure lying curled up on its right side. Rada's face was paler than the white angora sweater she was wearing. It was the face of a marble statue: perfect but dead, its beauty marred only by the grotesque wide green gaffer tape that sealed her mouth. The back of the sweater was soaked in blood that had been pumped out of her wrist arteries. They had been slashed with surgical precision just above where her hands were bound together with several layers of the same green tape. More green tape bound her ankles together.

'We should call an ambulance,' Volkov said.

There was a roaring in Tom's ears. 'Too late,' one of the guards muttered. Nobody moved. Tom was rooted to the spot, speechless with guilt and grief. *This is all my fault* . . .

He bent down and lifted Rada's head gently with his good hand. The heaviness did not surprise him; marble should be heavy. The blood in which she was lying looked so incongruous. How could a statue bleed so much?

Someone was shouting, 'Get her into one of the cars!'

It was his own voice. He was certain he could feel a faint pulse under Rada's chin. 'Hurry! We can't wait for an ambulance.'

Volkov helped lift her into one of the stretched limousines, which set off for the hospital with screeching tyres and an illicit police siren blaring. In the back, Tom crouched on the floor beside Rada with Volkov's strong arm steadying him. Both men had placed their jackets over the cold body. The beige carpet was sticky with her blood and there was blood all over Tom's hands and shirt-front. He tore the tape off Rada's mouth, intending to give the kiss of life.

Her eyelids flickered open and her eyes focused on his face, so close to hers. 'Tom?' she whispered.

He held her close, wanting to warm her cold body with his. 'It's going to be okay,' he promised. 'I just talked to Svetlana.'

In answer to the mute plea in Rada's eyes, he added, 'She's safe. Everything's going to be okay.'

Her lips were moving. He put his ear closer to them.

'*Mne zhal*,' she whispered: I'm sorry.

.12.

There were tears running down Ivanov's face when Rada's body was laid beside that of her father on the dining room table at the *Vasiliévsky Dvorétz*. Despite the hospital staff's protestations, he had insisted on bringing her back to the Vasilievsky Palace, clad only in the simple green gown with which the trauma room staff had replaced her bloodstained clothing.

'From now on, you let me handle the negotiations,' he said to Tom. 'Arkady Sergeyevich and Rada were like family to me. I'm every bit as much involved now as you are.'

'I want my daughter,' Tom argued. 'I want Svetlana back safe. I don't care what I have to give in return.'

'You're both too upset to think rationally,' Karen said gently. 'I think Volkov should do the talking.'

'It's nothing to do with him,' Tom shouted.

'That's why.' She held his good arm to make him listen to her. 'Nosarenko must be mad. If you get into an argument or start threatening him, he could kill Svetlana. So let Volkov do the talking, okay?'

'I'm neither a psychologist nor a policeman,' Volkov protested.

'You don't have to be,' Karen told him. 'We'll agree what has to be done before we call Nosarenko. You're just the spokesman, okay?'

'I'm not going to negotiate.' Tom had already made up his mind. 'If he wants me to walk into his parlour and hand over the other prints, I will. The only important thing is to obtain Svetlana's release.'

'It won't work like that,' Karen argued. 'Once Nosarenko has both you and the evidence, why should he release her? Somehow we have to work out a simultaneous handover in a neutral situation. You give him the film and prints. He gives you Svetlana, alive and unharmed.'

It was Volkov who pointed out, some time after midnight, that Nosarenko might think the material which Rada had given to her killers was complete, and order Svetlana's death anyway. The big American made Tom and Ivanov leave the room while he dialled the call.

'I will only talk to Fielding,' said Nosarenko. In his hand he held the film. On the desk in front of him, the prints were spread out like a hand of cards.

'You'll talk to me,' said Volkov calmly. 'I'm looking at a picture of you right now.'

'Put Fielding on the line or I ring off immediately.'

'The photograph is one of several that show you outside a cage full of animals I recognise as Siberian grey wolves . . .' Volkov kept talking over the interruptions:

'. . . and if you check the piece of film you already have, you'll find that it's been torn in half. Fielding still has the other half. Waiting outside the house where I'm speaking from are correspondents from major news agencies, ready to beam these pictures round the world. Now d'you want to talk to me, Mr President?'

'What is your name?' Nosarenko asked. He was trying to

connect the voice with the people in the Vasilievsky Palace described by Rada before she was killed.

'My name doesn't matter. I'm just a mouthpiece.'

Not Ivanov because he has a Moscow accent . . . Not Fielding either . . . 'You must be the helicopter pilot, Volkov.'

'Must I?'

The haggling went on for half an hour, with Volkov refusing to give way on the all-important issue of simultaneous handover. 'If we don't get the girl, you don't get the film,' he said repeatedly.

'You could regret your obstinacy,' Nosarenko threatened.

'That's true. But so could you. If this isn't all resolved within the next twelve hours, we'll assume the girl is dead and go public with the material we have.'

'Very well,' said Nosarenko. He made it sound as though he was capitulating. 'I'll agree to a simultaneous handover. I get the film. You get the girl. The question is where . . . I insist it must be done on Ukrainian soil.'

Volkov's name did not mean *wolf* for nothing. He proposed alternative sites on the Ukrainian borders with Poland, Roumania, Moldavia, Hungary and Slovakia. Nosarenko vetoed each site on the grounds that (a) he insisted on conducting the handover in person and (b) he could not afford to be seen at such a public place.

'There is one RV inside Ukraine's borders to which we'll agree,' Volkov offered, to break the deadlock. 'Aleksandria.'

He knew the giant helicopter base like the back of his hand. It was where he had done his initial flying training and several familiarisation courses, and lay just over an hour's flying time by helicopter from the Russian border.

'Very well.' Nosarenko smiled to himself. 'Give me two hours' notice and I'll meet you there tomorrow morning.'

'With the girl?'

'With the girl,' Nosarenko agreed. 'But the handover must be done by Fielding himself. On that condition I insist absolutely.'

'He'll be there,' Volkov promised. '*Do svedánya.*'

'*Do závtra.*' Nosarenko put down the phone, well pleased. They had walked right into his trap.

Ivanov was sitting in vigil by candlelight at the head of the table on which the two bodies lay.

'If I hadn't come back into your lives,' said Tom, 'none of this would have happened.'

Ivanov looked up. 'Who can say? In any case, it was due to you that Arkady Sergeyevich didn't lose Rada one way or another, more than a decade ago.'

He stood up and embraced Tom. 'I haven't been exactly friendly since you turned up in Petropavlovsk, have I?'

'I don't blame you.'

'Life has made me a different man from the one you knew in Moscow, Feldink. Our whole society changed overnight. Given the choice of being submerged by a *tsunami* of social upheaval or surfing the wave of violence, I chose the latter.'

'I understand.'

Ivanov released Tom. 'Also, I have to admit that it's hard to forgive you for fooling me all those years. You were one of the most successful Western sleepers, you know. Most of them gave themselves away, sooner or later.'

'When did you find out?'

'Only from London's eagerness to deal when I offered to sell you back.'

'Your side made the first move. Why? Was it really Rada's idea?'

A sad smile warmed Ivanov's face for a moment. 'She wanted to give you back before you drank yourself to death, which was a very real possibility at the time. I think she hoped that, once back in the West, you'd be able to pull yourself together and kick the bottle. As far as I was concerned, you could have stayed in the gutter, but when I put out some feelers and London was positive, I thought I might as well make a profit on the deal. So I set it up.'

Tom shook his head to clear it. Try as he would, he could think only of one thing: getting Svetlana back.

'I know how you're feeling.' Ivanov squeezed his arm. 'Rada was the daughter I never had, so I feel Svetlana is my flesh and blood. I'm with you all the way.'

A door opened. Volkov stood there with Karen behind him. The haggling with Nosarenko seemed to have shrunk him. He looked tired and too small for his clothes, as though he had spent the day in a Turkish bath and lost ten kilos.

'I've done the best I can, Tomski,' he said.

The flight from Kursk, the nearest major town on Russian soil, had taken an hour and a half. Since crossing into Ukrainian airspace, the Mi-8 hired at Kursk airport had been accompanied by two black-painted Mi-24 attack helicopters bearing Ukrainian identification. Beneath a leaden sky they droned in formation across the endless unhedged wheatfields of collective farms, heading south-east.

'Those bastards could blow us out of the sky at any moment,' grumbled Volkov at the controls.

'Not on the way in,' Tom reassured him. 'Nosarenko won't risk destroying us until he's certain we're carrying the film.'

'And when he's got the film, d'you think he's going to let you go, Tomski?'

'I don't care about me. The important thing is that you get Svetlana back to Ivanov. He'll take care of her if I don't make it.'

As Aleksandria Field came in sight they saw, parked in rows on hard-standing and the grass between, several thousand helicopters ranging from old and battered piston engined Mi-4s to the latest Mi-28s. Three-quarters of the Ukrainian air force was grounded from lack of money for fuel or to pay the pilots' salaries.

Circling at a hundred metres above the ground, Volkov argued for five minutes with the air traffic controllers, refusing to land at his allotted ramp on the far side of the field, which was cordoned off by security troops. Only after threatening to fly straight back to Russia was he eventually given permission to land near the maintenance bays, where a hundred or so mechanics were gathered by the machines they had been working on, and staring upwards at the lone craft above the control tower.

Nosarenko's bullet-proofed black Cadillac sped through them with the Ukrainian flag whipping on the bonnet and the horn blaring. As the mechanics scattered out of the way, he was already opening the rear door. In a few minutes, he promised himself, it will all be over . . .

Instead of touching down, Volkov held the Mi-8 in a hover ten metres above the oil-stained concrete, waiting for the Cadillac to stop. Looking down, Tom saw an obese, black-haired man get out and look up. The torso had put on a lot of weight, but the face was unmistakably Nosarenko's. A blonde-haired girl of about Svetlana's age tried to follow him out of the car until an arm pulled her roughly back inside. The door closed.

Because of the steep angle it was impossible for Tom to be certain that the girl was Svetlana. He threw out of the window one of the prints which spun away in the down-draught. Nosarenko ran after it, picked it out of a puddle and examined it closely. He had been right to be cautious. This was a different shot. He gestured to Volkov that it was safe to land, indicating a spot midway between the Cadillac and the nearest hangar.

As soon as the helicopter was on the ground, Nosarenko walked towards it, his thick black hair lashed by the down-draught. Tom slid the door open awkwardly, one-handed. On the roofs of two nearby hangars he could see the supine forms of Spetsnaz snipers covering the area. The black metallic barrel of an assault rifle poked out of the front passenger window of Nosarenko's car but it was not possible to see through the dark glass of the other windows.

'Mr Fielding,' shouted Nosarenko over the whine of the turbines. 'Come with me.' He gestured to the car.

Tom stood in the doorway. 'You bring my daughter here,' he shouted back. 'Then I'll give you the rest of the film and the other prints.'

Nosarenko's narrowed eyes took in the sling on Tom's right arm and the fact that Volkov had stayed at the controls. He took two paces closer, to minimise the risk of anyone hearing what he was shouting. 'I've changed the rules, Mr Fielding. First you give yourself and the material up. You'll be well treated. Then the girl will be released. You have my word.'

Tom stepped down from the cabin. There were only five paces between them now.

If it has to be that way, he thought, I'll agree. 'I want to see her first,' he shouted back. 'Have her get out of the car, so I can be sure.'

'It's not possible, Mr Fielding. You have to trust me.'

At that moment, Tom knew that the girl in the car was not Svetlana. 'You bastard!' he shouted. 'Where is she? Where's my daughter?'

He forgot about the marksmen all around and strode forward, his left hand reaching inside the sling for Ponsonby's gun and jamming it against Nosarenko's right eye. By now he was too close for any of the snipers to risk firing.

'Try anything,' he growled, moving in even closer so that no daylight showed between their bodies, 'and I'll blow your fucking head off!'

In a parody of a tango duo, he duck-walked Nosarenko left-foot, right-foot back to the open door of the helicopter.

'Now get in,' he shouted.

'And if I don't?'

'I'll shoot you anyway.'

With no free hand to steady himself, Tom almost fell when stepping up into the cabin. Then, as Volkov increased power and pulled in the collective, lifting to a hover four metres above the ground, he did fall, landing in a tangle with Nosarenko on the floor. Pain from the broken collar-bone almost made him black out. Nosarenko made a grab at the gun. In retaliation Tom loosed a shot that went between the other man's legs high enough to have him worried but causing only a slight flesh wound.

Tom heaved himself upright, leaving Nosarenko on the floor, looking with mingled relief and horror at the blood on his hand. Through the open door Tom saw a sniper on top of a hangar roof taking aim through a telescopic sight. First one jeep, then a dozen with heavy-calibre machine guns mounted on the back, converged from all sides on ground zero directly beneath the helicopter. There was a series of noises *tick-tick-tick* as holes appeared in the side panels of the helicopter and an oath from Volkov as the Plexiglas panels of the front cabin disintegrated in a shower of plastic.

'On your feet!' Tom shouted.

He loosed another shot which just missed Nosarenko's knee and had the desired effect. Once he was on his feet, Tom forced him to the open doorway and stood close behind, with the automatic pressed against the head of state's left ear so that it was clearly visible to the men in the approaching vehicles. Nosarenko was making frantic gestures for them to get back. One by one, they skidded to a halt and the ragged firing stopped. Volkov increased throttle. Slowly the Mi-8 gained height and forward motion.

'Move it!' Tom shouted over his shoulder. He had no free hand to put on a headset.

'I can't, Tomski.'

Tom glanced at Volkov's right hand on the cyclic control between his legs. It was a mass of raw meat. Only willpower was holding the bloodied fingers around the stick.

'You'll have to take over in the left-hand seat,' Volkov shouted. 'I'll tell you what to do.'

'I can't leave Nosarenko loose.'

'So tie the bastard up.' Volkov's face was screwed up with pain.

'How can I, with one hand?'

'Then throw the fucker out!'

Tom looked down. They were a hundred metres above the ground now and the concrete hard-standing was carpeted with a blur of vehicle roofs and upturned faces.

'No!' Nosarenko dropped to his knees in supplication. 'You don't realise what you're doing. There are bigger issues at stake than a few lives, you know . . .'

'Get a move on,' Volkov called desperately. 'I'm losing sensation.'

At the last moment, Tom saw the SAM battery on the edge of the field clearly tracking them. Nosarenko's presence on board was the sole consideration inhibiting the men below from blasting Volkov's craft out of the sky.

'Move away from the door,' he shouted.

A smile of triumph flitted across Nosarenko's face. It was all Tom needed. 'Sit in the rear row of seats,' he ordered.

With his hands held out to the sides, Nosarenko walked unsteadily between the seats and sat down at the rear of the cabin. There was a moment of incredulity when he looked up to see Tom, white-faced, aiming the BRNO at the middle of his forehead. *A man like that – an intellectual – will not have the nerve to fire in cold blood . . .*

'Kill me,' he said coolly, 'and you will never see your daughter alive again.'

Without any emotion, Tom worked through the options. There was no way he could tie up or otherwise immobilise Nosarenko. But if he did not help Volkov within the next minute or so, the helicopter would crash and kill them all. So he would have to kill the man in front of him. What happened after that was another issue.

He steadied the automatic by resting his forearm on the seat in front of Nosarenko. The recoil surprised him with its force. The entry wound was clean, like a third eye in the middle of Nosarenko's forehead. It was not even bleeding. But the bullet's tip had been filed flat. After penetrating the frontal bone, it had splayed out, removing most of the brain tissue and the back of the skull. The cushion of the seat was a mess of blood, scalp, brain and bones on which the empty mask of a face lay tilted awkwardly to one side.

Tom vomited and threw the gun away. He staggered forwards retching and clambered into the left-hand seat. There was a gale blowing through the shattered cabin windows and Volkov's face was a pale shade of grey.

Tom pulled the headset over his ears and heard the calm voice in his ears. 'Lesson Number One. Do only what I tell you, Tomski. Got that?'

'Affirmative.'

'I'll handle the pedals and my left hand is taking care of the collective. Luckily for both of us, that's the difficult bit.' Volkov grinned at Tom to cover the grimace of pain. 'Now put your good hand over the cyclic. That's the stick between your legs. Very gently get hold of it. You've got it.'

'I've got it, Vlad.'

Volkov bit back a groan as he uncurled his torn hand from the stick. 'Now listen. This is what you have to do . . .'

.13.

Ivanov's apartment occupied the entire top floor of a tower-block near to the garden ring road in the south-west of Moscow. It was a fortress with armoured glass windows and floors and ceilings reinforced with sheet steel, immune to anything smaller than an anti-tank rocket. The staircases had been bricked up; a private lift from the basement car park was the only way of getting in or out. The roof was covered in two-meter-high coils of razor wire as a deterrent to helicopter-borne intruders.

The largest bathroom had been converted to serve as an emergency operating theatre. There Volkov's hand was finally attended to by a surgeon and two nurses who had been brought in for the purpose. The wound was less serious than it looked. Told that physiotherapy would help him regain full use of the hand in three or four weeks, he joked with the nurses that he would spend the rest of the time sleeping. After being stitched up he sat on the toilet, looking pale and drawn, and watched while Tom's shoulder was strapped up, the injury confirmed as a broken collar-bone. The burn blister on Karen's leg had turned septic, so she was the third patient to be attended to.

As the medical team were packing their equipment prior to leaving, Ivanov burst into the room wearing a clean suit and shirt but with his eyes still red-rimmed from lack of sleep. He ordered the surgeon and nurses out before announcing, 'I've found out where she is!'

'Where?' Tom asked.

'With the Ukes. When the old KGB was reduced to the new slimline FSB, a couple of hundred sacked Ukrainian officers based in Moscow set themselves up in a pretty heavy protection racket. Seems they did this job for Nosarenko on a freelance basis. He must have reckoned that, by hiring them, he could disclaim responsibility if anything went wrong and thus avoid causing an international incident.'

'So where is Svetlana?' Karen asked.

'Still in Moscow. The Ukes refused to take her to Kiev until they got paid. Since they never received a kopeck from Nosarenko, she's still here.'

Tom looked out of the huge picture window. Somewhere in the sprawl of buildings that vanished in the murk was his daughter. He stood up and shrugged on a borrowed jacket, cape-style. 'Take me to her.'

'It's not as easy as that.' Ivanov forced him back into his chair. 'I've found out who is holding her, but I don't know where. And there's a complication. The Ukes think Arkady Sibirsky's grand-daughter is worth a ransom.'

'How much?'

'Normally they'd ask for a quarter million, maybe a half million dollars,' Ivanov grimaced. 'But somebody must have overheard something in Petropavlovsk or Irkutsk. They know about the icon. That's their price.'

Tom sat down, stunned. Karen put her arm around his shoulders. 'So what do we do?' she asked Ivanov.

'There isn't any choice,' he said soberly. 'Kidnap victims in Moscow get killed if the ransom is delayed too long.'

'They could kill a little girl – just like that?' she wondered aloud.

Ivanov nodded. 'It's logical. Our inefficient and over-worked criminal police give a high priority to kidnap cases while the victim is still alive. They'll tap phones, lean on informers, send in SWAT teams . . . But once the victim's dead, the case becomes just another homicide file on someone's desk, so the heat's off.'

'The icon belongs to you now,' Tom interrupted. 'What are you going to do?'

'Give it to them.' Ivanov checked both his watches. 'It's midday. At three p.m. I have a meeting with a guy I used to know when we both worked for the Committee, name of Marko Dubanovich. He's got a kid of his own – a boy at Garov school in England.'

'It's pronounced Harrow,' said Tom.

'Yeah? Well, Marko's as straight as a Ukrainian can be. So I don't anticipate any last-minute problems.'

'I want to be there.'

'Sorry, Feldink. Strictly no outsiders. You think these guys want to be identified? But you can relax. Dubanovich won't go back on the deal at this stage.'

Tom heard the lift motor whine and was off the bed in a flash and out into the hallway. As the metal doors slid apart he saw Ivanov holding Svetlana by the hand. Two of the minders were standing behind them.

Svetlana was wearing the blouse and skirt in which she had been taken from Sibirsky's apartment, plus a borrowed sweater two sizes too large. She looked bewildered. Her face was pale and she had been crying.

Tom glanced at Ivanov. 'You told her?'

They had agreed a story about a runaway truck knocking down Rada and Sibirsky in the street.

Ivanov nodded and let go of Svetlana's hand. Her eyes travelled round the people standing in the wide hallway. 'I want to go home,' she said.

'You're going home with Daddy.' Ivanov pushed her gently forward. 'You'll all stay here with me for a few days, getting to know each other again – and then he's taking you home with him.'

Svetlana's eyes settled on Tom. His throat was too dry to talk. He was afraid that she was going to turn away from him and back to Ivanov. Excusing her in advance, he told himself that her memories of him must be faint after all the years he had been away. Had Rada ever shown her the photographs of himself that he had sent with each birthday card?

He knelt down and waited, reliving the dream in which she pointed at him and said to another man, 'That's not my daddy. You are.'

And then Svetlana ran to him. Tom moved his injured shoulder away and reached for her with his good arm, feeling her whole body quivering as she threw her arms around his neck and started crying. He stood up with her clinging to him, and let Ivanov guide them both into a bedroom and shut the door, leaving them alone.

Half an hour later, Karen took in a mug of hot chocolate and a glass of Coke. She put them down without speaking. As she closed the door, Svetlana was saying, 'Mummy said you'd come back to see me one day. I wish she was here.'

'So do I,' said Tom. 'So do I.'

On a joint shopping trip to the new, glitzy, face-lifted GUM, full of Western brand-names and the *novyrichi* purchasing French perfume for their overdressed wives and Japanese cameras or hi-fi equipment for themselves, Svetlana had insisted they all buy the same clothes to go away in: red anoraks, jeans and matching trainers. They had put them on then and there, left the old clothes behind in the changing rooms and driven to McDonald's for a hamburger lunch – Svetlana's choice.

Getting out of Ivanov's stretched Mercedes at Sheremetyevo airport, Tom felt relieved to be leaving Moscow. The two weeks cooped-up in the high-security apartment, with only occasional escorted outings to the shops or a park, had been too much like prison life.

The conversation at the airport was the usual stilted keep-in-touch and take-care as Ivanov led the way directly to the security desk. Two of his men who had checked in the baggage were waiting there with the boarding passes and passports. Placing them in an inside pocket, Tom felt the bulge of Kolchak's leather pouch. He had been going to give the jewels to Ivanov to defray the costs of the mission, until overhearing him boast in an unguarded moment of the deal he had pulled with the Ukrainians, to split the eventual proceeds of the icon fifty-fifty.

With his back to Ivanov, he palmed a large diamond and dropped it into Volkov's breast pocket. 'That's to pay for the damage to your beloved helicopter, Vlad,' he murmured.

Volkov's face broke into a grin. 'How didya know I was going to send you the bill, Tomski?'

Taking a suitcase from one of the minders, Ivanov handed it to Tom. 'Inside is Arkady Sergeyevich's copy of the icon,' he growled.

'Svetlana's going-away present?'

'It must be worth a few thousand dollars.'

Tom grinned. It was partly a spontaneous grin of friendship – to use Ivanov's phrase, he and Volkov were closer to Tom than his own flesh and blood, after what they had been through together – but it was also a grin of triumph. He had asked for the repro icon once and very casually, as a present for Svetlana, and not dared to ask again in case Ivanov became suspicious.

'You're a good guy, Charlie Brown,' he said, putting down the suitcase to hug Ivanov. It hurt his shoulder but made him feel good. Along the glass-walled corridors leading to the departure gate, Svetlana walked ahead, holding Karen's hand. Neither they nor Tom looked back to see Ivanov handing Volkov an envelope containing high-denomination dollar bills.

'That should more than cover the damage to your machine,' he was saying. 'Just remember you owe me a favour, Volkov.'

'Any time you want a flier, you know where to find me.' Mad Vlad had a feeling that the favour would be called in and lead to some interesting moments. He had rubbed shoulders with the Ivanovs of the new Russia many times and knew how to handle them. What amazed him was that a Westerner like Tom had been able to do the same and get away with it.

He refused a lift back into town. After the others had left, he stood alone at the bar on the observation deck, glass in hand. Watching the planes taking off and landing through the sound-insulant double glazing, he could feel and smell each one; no two aircraft were ever alike to him. He paid especial interest to the Helsinki-bound Transaero Tupolev 127 on board which were Tom, Karen and Svetlana.

Ivanov had lent them a luxury villa he owned on a lake outside the Finnish capital, for as long as they wanted to stay. Tom had not decided where they would go next or how he would sort out the complications of being on the run with false papers. It might be simpler to stay Colin Pearson than to unravel all the problems of becoming Tom Fielding again, but he had not made up his mind about that yet. When the seat belt sign went off, he took the suitcase from the overhead locker and flipped the lid open.

'Grandad's picture,' Svetlana said.

Tom turned it over. The labels attesting that the icon was a nineteenth-century copy were beginning to come loose. He had rewet them with saliva after peeling them off the other icon beside Ponsonby's wrecked car, and the glue had not properly restuck. There was a bullet hole in one corner of the Virgin's robe surrounded by a stain where some of Sibirsky's blood had dried on it.

Beside him, Karen and Svetlana were drawing consequences people, each adding a part of the body before folding the paper and swapping them over.

Gazing at the Virgin and the ugly man-child on her lap, Tom thought, I don't believe in religious images and curses. I don't even believe in religion; it all comes down to mumbojumbo, ritual and hypocrisy in the end. And yet, the cynical atheist Commissar Sibirsky must have had reason to fear Kolchak's curse. Why otherwise would a professional iconoclast ask his son in that last hour of freedom to return the Virgin of Kazan to its rightful place? Since then, three generations of the Sibirsky family had died violently. The next in line was Svetlana. If there was even one chance in a million that a dying man's undying hatred could reach out through some worm-hole in space and time to harm her, was the risk worth taking – even for $25 million?

'We're getting off the plane at St Petersburg,' he announced.

'Why?' both Karen and Svetlana asked in unison.

'It doesn't matter why.'

'Now you listen to me, Tom Fielding.' Karen switched to English so that Svetlana could not understand. 'We have one rule from now on – if there is a from-now-on between us – and that is that you damn well tell me what's going on before you ask me to do anything in future. D'you hear?'

'I'm sorry,' Tom apologised. 'But you're going to think me crazy if I spell this one out.'

'Try me.'

She listened without comment, all the while drawing grinning faces and bulging, over-muscled arms and knobbly knees and clown boots with the toes poking out and passing the papers to and fro with Svetlana.

'You do think I'm mad,' Tom said at the end.

'I don't know what to say.' Karen finished drawing a preposterous pair of bare feet, covered in hair. 'But that icon has cost so many lives, one way and another. If the choice was mine, Tom . . . I think I'd get rid of it.'

They took a cab from St Petersburg's Pulkovo Two airport direct to the Kazan cathedral, a massively exact eighteenth-century copy of St Peter's in Rome. In a side chapel a wedding service was in progress, filling the air with incense and the unmistakable sound of Gregorian chant.

Svetlana knelt in a pew, crossed herself and started saying a prayer. Tom caught the names of Rada and Arkady Sergeyevich. He felt Karen nudge him and whisper, 'She'd feel real good if you knelt down beside her.'

It was years since Tom had knelt in a pew. At Longfield he had vowed never to do so again.

'Go on,' Karen urged. 'Do it for her.'

When the service was finished, Tom stayed on his knees. Sheltered by the pew in front, he opened the suitcase and took out the Virgin of Kazan. 'Svetlochka,' he said quietly, 'Grandad wanted his picture to hang in this church. This is where it came from and where it belongs. Now that the old priest has finished marrying that couple, will you give him the icon?'

She took the Virgin warily, her eyes travelling from his face to Karen's.

'It's okay,' he reassured her. 'Doing this will help Grandad more than a thousand prayers.'

Svetlana walked up the aisle towards the wedding group, holding the icon in both hands. Her casual travelling clothes contrasted with the frilly dresses of the girls in the wedding party who were standing round the archbishop, asking for his blessing. To attract the patriarch's attention, she lifted the Virgin of Kazan as high as she could and held it there. One of the incense-swinging acolytes murmured something to an attendant priest, who beckoned her to approach.

'This picture belongs to your church,' Tom and Karen heard her say in a very clear voice. 'My grandad wanted you to have it back, so here it is.'

It was the longest speech she had made since her mother's death.

The archbishop kissed the icon, turned it over, read the attestations on the back and handed it to the priest beside him. He lifted his hand in the Orthodox blessing and made the sign of the cross above Svetlana's head. 'In the name of the Virgin of Kazan,' he intoned, 'may you have a long and happy life, my child.'

It pained Karen to see how withdrawn and unhappy Svetlana looked in comparison with the other children – as though she had forgotten how to smile and might never learn again.

'She's going to need an awful lot of loving, Tom,' she murmured, 'after what she's been through.'

'I know,' he said. 'Will you help?'

'Maybe it would be better if the two of you spent some time together alone.'

'I'm not very good at loving.' Tom brought his head near to Karen's. 'It's taken me a long time to realise that. I think we both need you.'

Instead of replying, she lifted her hands to his face and felt the lines of his brow and nose and mouth, searching his eyes with hers.

The wedding party were on the steps outside, posing for photographs. Svetlana was halfway back down the aisle when a sudden shower forced them all back inside the cathedral in a flurry of laughter. The groom kissed the bride, whose veil was bejewelled with raindrops, while the wide-eyed girl in the red anorak took it all in. The scene reminded Svetlana just a little of her favourite photograph, which had been taken on the Lenin Hills on the day when Tom and Rada were married.

A fat old *babushka* who had been watching the wedding

ceremony turned to her headscarfed friend who was lighting a candle beneath the icon of the Virgin, restored to its place in the side chapel.

'*Smotrí.*' The old woman pointed at the couple in red anoraks embracing on their knees, with the nine-year-old girl watching them. '*Oní óba plakáyut.*' They're both crying.

Tom reached out for Svetlana with his good arm and pulled her close. '*Eto tólko dozhd,*' he told the old women. 'It's just the rain.'

THE EAGLE AND THE SNAKE

Douglas Boyd

Branded on the soul of every Foreign Legionnaire is an unbreakable code of loyalty – to the Legion and to each other. But then Raoul Duvalier betrayed that code . . .

Already crippled, tortured and starved by the Viet Minh, he is court-martialled by the Legion, disgraced, and repatriated to France with no job and no prospects. Except the prospect of revenge . . .

For twenty years he has known of, and not betrayed, the whereabouts of the Foreign Legion's gold. Now, recruiting a private army from the Legion itself, he sets out to claim it for himself. But this time, one of his men has betrayed *him*.

Imprisoned in his own dungeon, Raoul reviews the lives of recruits, relatives and lovers – two decades of action and adventure from Algeria to Idaho, Belfast to Vientiane, the Dordogne to Dien Bien Phu – as he tries to identify the traitor. A traitor on whose unmasking depends not just his gold but his life, and other lives barely yet begun . . .

FICTION
0 7515 0012 7

THE HONOUR AND THE GLORY

Douglas Boyd

Basic training in the Foreign Legion is brutally tough. Its aim is to forge bonds of loyalty that stand the test of modern combat and last a lifetime.

Fifteen years after he took off his white képi for the last time, Peter Bergman is a No Release prisoner in a Gulag camp that officially no longer exists. The man he blames for putting him there is his old Legion comrade, Jack Roscoe. For such treachery, Bergman swears bloody revenge, if he ever gets free.

In St Petersburg during the autumn of 1992, Roscoe learns that Bergman is still alive and decides to rescue him. The plan is brilliant but the chance of success is small.

Roscoe's only ally is the beautiful woman over whom he and Bergman fell out. She warns that the price of failure is death. That doesn't stop Jack Roscoe. To him, something far more important is at stake: a man's honour – without which life is not worth living.

FICTION
0 7515 1340 7

THE TRUTH AND THE LIES

Douglas Boyd

A mysterious debt of honour saves TV news reporter Jon King from almost certain death at the hands of an Islamic terrorist group – a debt owed to his father, a captain in the French Foreign Legion named Koenig.

Raised as an orphan, Jon never knew his true parents. Now, he is determined to discover the truth about Koenig, even if it means embarking on the most lethal news story of his career.

With little help from the Legion and its code of anonymity, all Jon can find out is that Koenig could have been a political assassin, killed in an attempt on de Gaulle's life in 1962. But his instinct for truth tells him that it may not only be his source who is lying.

When a man who knew Koenig is brutally tortured and killed, it seems the murderous game in which Jon's father was a player years before is still being played, and now, trapped in the cross-fire of a civil war in Algeria, Jon is face-to-face with an impossible deadline and the toughest decision he has ever had to make. Whichever way he decides, someone close to him will die . . .

FICTION
0 7515 1677 5